VOLUME 5 OF THE D

"... ours is no Cinderella story, and I'd never be mistaken for Prince Charming.

Everyone who knows the dark king understands only one fits the shoes that walk beside him, because only one walks on thin ice and broken glass without falling through to her death."

— Klive King

Also by Lynessa Layne

The Don't Close Your Eyes Series

Killer Kiss – a novelette

Don't Close Your Eyes

Complicated Moonlight

Mad Love

Dangerous Games

Hostile Takeover

Target Acquired

Point Blank

Short Stories

The Getaway

Winter in Roatan

Whispers Through the Trees

The Crow's Nest

Magazine Articles

The Villains of Romantic Suspense

This is a work of fiction. Names, characters, establishments, places, businesses, social sites, institutions, organizations, locales, events, and incidents are either products of the author's imagination or used in a fictitious manner for entertainment purposes only. Any resemblance to actual persons, living or dead, or actual events is purely coincidental.

Copyright © 2022 Lynessa Layne

Adapted from original manuscript copyright © 2014 Lynessa James

Fast Layne Independent Publishing - All rights reserved.

No part of this publication may be reproduced, distributed, or transmitted in any form or by any means, including photocopying, recording or other electronic or mechanical methods without prior written permission of the publisher, except in the case of brief quotations embodied in critical reviews and certain other noncommercial uses permitted by copyright law. For permission requests, write to the publisher, addressed at authorlynessalayne@lynessalayne.com

ISBN 978-1-956848-12-0

Cover created by Lynessa Layne. Image courtesy of Shutterstock. All rights reserved.

Lynessa Layne does not own the rights to any music titles mentioned. All musical references are for entertainment purposes only. Reader assumes all responsibility for legally obtaining content.

Optional playlist Spotify

For Serenity,
An unexpected best friend under my nose all along. I'm so glad God threw us together through our kids. Never lose your contagious, nourishing humility or the love that drives your spirit to appreciate every single human you meet no matter what their station or status. If the world had more people like you, we may have chaos, but we'd also achieve peace. ;)

Cast of Characters

•**Klive Henley King** – anti-villain./hero also known as Complicated Moonlight and Kinsley's pirate. Enforcer of crime syndicate, Nightshade, leading double life

•**Henley** – Klive's alter ego for pulling hit jobs and undercover stings

•**Kinsley Fallon Hayes** – Protagonist. Bartender, college student, renowned sprinter known as Micro Machine

• **Andy and Clairice Hayes** – Kinsley's parents

•**Ben** – Andy Hayes' co-worker, Klive's friend

•**Jase Michael Taylor** – Navy SEAL, Navy SEAL, lead singer of Rock-N-Awe, lifeguard, Kinsley's longtime crush

•**Tyndall Taylor** – Jase's little sister, Kinsley's best friend

• **Mike and Bianca Taylor** – Jase and Tyndall's parents

•**Rustin Keane** – Jase's childhood best friend, combat veteran, cop

•**Nightshade** – crime syndicate

• **Joey** – Klive's personal security detail, private investigator

• **Eric** – Klive's Nightshade lieutenant

• **Christophe** – Klive's private investigator, Joey's employer

•**Marcus** – Kinsley's manager, Nightshade member

•**Gustav & Jarrell** – bouncers at the bar Kinsley works at, Nightshade members

- **Bayleigh & Garrett** – Kinsley's co-workers

- **Constance Marie** – Kinsley's friend, Jase's co-lead for the band Rock-N-Awe

- **Antoine (Sweetness)** – Constance's cousin, Gustav's brother, Kinsley's hairstylist, military spec-ops, has worked with Jase

- **Inferno** – biker gang crime syndicate comprised of dishonest firefighters. Rivals of Nightshade.

- **Ray Castille** – Inferno's disgraced leader, Fire Marshal

- **Pat Connor** – Inferno biker

- **Sara Scott** – Kinsley's co-worker, Patrick Scott's widow

- **Adrian Miller** – Kinsley's art professor

- **Ian Walton** – Kinsley's personal trainer and track coach

- **Eliza, Lindsay, Julie** – Kinsley's track relay team

- **(Looney) Lucy** – Kinsley's track manager and biggest fan

- **Brayden** – who Kinsley dubs Frat Toy, has huge crush on her

- **Shay** – Kinsley's alternate/replacement on the track team

- **Nolan and Devon** – Jase's buddies from high school

- **Matt** – lifeguard who works with Jase

- **Angela Ansley** – Kinsley's high school nemesis

- **Detective William Bartlet** – worked Sara Scott's murder, saddled with training Rustin

- **Sheriff Ansley** – William Bartlet's boss, Angela Ansley's father

Character Point of View

♂ = Klive King

♀ = Kinsley Hayes

VOLUME 5 OF THE DON'T CLOSE YOUR EYES SERIES

HOSTILE TAKEOVER

Lynessa Layne

USA TODAY BESTSELLING AUTHOR

1 | ♀

PING.

Ping. Ping. Ping.

"Ugh. Shut up, not yet!"

Ping. Ping.

Curses assaulted my phone and whomever dared disturb my slumber when I was getting to the sexy part of my dream. I patted the night table, expecting to feel my lamp and phone plugged into the charger. My lamp wasn't the small paper lantern, but a hot pink base with a fuzzy shade.

The phone wasn't on the night table. A few more pings sounded while I searched. *Under the pillow? How did that get there?*

I blinked hard to clear the fog from my eyes.

"Good grief! For the love of all things holy what could be so bloody important at this hour?! What hour is it anyway?" I twisted in my sheets. The red digital clock on my old desk read five till two pm. "Damn. No wonder everyone is blowing up the phone."

The phone vibrated in my hands. *No thanks.*

I left the phone on the night table before ambling through the upstairs hallway to my old bathroom. After draining the main vane, I discovered the red writing of my dark passenger.

"Come on! You're such a bitch with the best timing. Get the misery out all at once?"

I looked around the bathroom for feminine tools. Good thing Mom kept her less than dignifying girly products in here, so Daddy didn't have to see or else I'd be penguin walking up the stairs to my apartment. Too bad all undignified products were in here. There were some things I didn't want to know about my parents. Add these new scars to the ones Jase left last night.

Guess now that I'd started my period, I didn't need to worry about having created life with a dick who didn't seem to want me in his. What a mess.

Relief and sorrow joined the new cramps in my day.

My spare toothbrush sat in the cup on the vanity. I brushed hard—like scrubbing my teeth may scrub the recent discoveries from my mind. After splashing cold water on my puffy face, I curled back into bed to read the small font on my phone.

"Let's see. A million calls from Jase the Jerk, a few from Rustin, hmm ... Carmen, *five* from Tyndall? And ..." I cackled. "The Asshole Dick?"

My tongue traced inside my cheek. Klive programmed his number into my phone.

Did I want to listen to my voicemail?

No! I deleted my inbox without listening for fear I'd crumble into another debilitating bout of tears. Not to mention, I had a feeling I'd become a stupid idiot obsessing over anything Jase said. I could hope he'd apologized, but if he hadn't, I couldn't handle another vindictive word from him right now.

If Klive left me a voicemail, I may be tempted to replay his pretty accent the way I'd worn his stupid coat for two years of longing for the stranger in Daddy's building. The pirate who'd calmed the chaos. Without a doubt, Klive's voice was sure to be a crutch. I smirked.

Unless he'd called to tell me to get my shit together or to tell me he'd told me so about little boys. Klive was only five and a half-ish years older than Jase. Did that time frame really make all the difference between a boy and a man? *Ugh! Enough pondering men, dammit!*

Against Klive's wisdom, I rebelled by calling my father like a solid rock amid waves of unpredictable emotion threatening to yank me under the surface.

"Kinsley Fallon, your voice is a sight for sore eyes," Daddy joked. I chuckled. "How are you, honey?" Uh oh. His casual tinged with worry.

"I'm good, Daddy. Took a day of rest for once. You'd be proud of me. I played football with Jase and his buddies yesterday. Totally stomped that quarterback and his trash talk. Had a little issue here and there with chauvinists, but once they saw you'd taught me well, they supported me. Even used Mom's forced cheerleading to fly me over the other team into the end zone. Was E. P. I. C. Epic. The only thing that would've made it better is if you'd have been there. Mike would've probably put you on the opposite team, though, out of challenge."

"Someone's a chatterbox today. Bianca got video of your stunt. Your mom is thinking of posting it to your social media to project positivity, but then she's worried that it will further add to speculation about you and a certain gentleman ...."

Yikes! I'd forgotten Klive had caught me and fallen with me on top of him. "Psh. That? All for the love of the game. Nothing to worry about."

"Right. Like Friday night at the Ren Faire. I recall a football being involved in that as well."

I pursed my lips as I realized what a bad idea this had been.

"Daddy, let's save this for the porch swing when you get back from vacay? In the meantime, how's life in the mountains? Feel at home with Sasquatch? Smell like him yet?"

Daddy laughed. "Our cabin has electric and plumbing, thank you very much, young lady."

As he filled me in, I tiptoed downstairs into their kitchen and muted my phone for the seconds I needed to start the microwave with nothing inside. Un-mute. Daddy still chattered about going to some park where you could be in and look out on several states at once. Some cave they'd seen. How good a hiker mom was when she wore tennis shoes.

"You mean Mom owns a pair of tennis shoes?" I snickered.

"She tried getting away with those little, short heels, but I told her to save those for after we were finished with the day's hiking."

My nose crinkled. "Spare me the details, Dad. For real. I'm about to eat breakfast."

The microwave beeped on cue. I face-palmed when I realized my mistake.

"Breakfast? Kins, do I need to put your mother on the phone? You haven't been eating enough as it is. Ever since these men came into—"

"Hey honey," Mom's voice came over Daddy's stolen phone. "Explain."

I rolled my eyes and silenced the automatic sigh.

"I'm not starving myself over lovesickness the way Daddy is apparently afraid of, thank you. I slept in." Thankfully, Mom got bored with my football lingo after I explained how I'd overexerted myself after having gone for too long without practice or athletics of any kind. They wouldn't know about my self-defense sessions with Jase and Rustin.

"You hear this, Andy? You've made a mountain out of a mole hill," she called to him. In a quieter tone she muttered about how she'd have to endure more hiking because of my bad behavior. "He's graying at the temples now."

"You can thank me later for turning Daddy into a silver fox, then," I sang like a smart ass, unable to help smiling as her expression unfolded in my mind. I cleared my throat when a sudden pang of longing for her hit me. "I miss y'all. You and him. Not only him. In case you needed to know. Don't make a big deal of it. Love you. Bye."

I tapped the red button on my phone's touch screen before she had a chance to get gooey. At least she'd probably hike with a better attitude now. Rummaging through their overstocked pantry like a hungry mouse, I laughed like an evil villain when unwrapping the first of four packages of Pop-tarts.

I lined a cookie sheet rather than using the toaster, then used the time they cooked in the oven for texting the worried masses. Tyndall demanded proof of life. I recorded a small video message of my love and opened the oven door to show her how I was choosing to cope with the weather she'd predicted.

"Will call when I'm ready to talk, girl. Please," I begged, "all I'm asking is for the same courtesy you asked of me concerning ... you know. Love you, girl. No tiff with your brother will ever change that. I promise." I made kissy lips before I sent the message.

Without her knowing, Mom lent me the silkiest satiny wonderful pajamas and unfettered access to her media room stocked with troves of chick-flicks promising what we all wished love was.

I ate Pop-tarts and popcorn, daydreamed about Jase showing up at my stoop with a bouquet of more burnt orange calla lilies and white roses and a sweet card begging me to never leave. We'd tumble inside the threshold with him sweeping me from my feet while pouring sweet confessions of long-suffering lust and pained emotion over me. Then, he'd lavish my body with every apology he sucked at saying with his mouth and put that mouth to action over words in the ways I couldn't help missing when longing for a way to cope.

I could make his life miserable like Andie in *How to Lose a Guy in Ten Days*.

Ha! I should do some of this to Klive to test his devotion!

"Damn I suck at this chick-flick distraction thing! I haven't eaten a single bonbon either! What's wrong with me? I wanna be like all the normal girls ...." Tears fell onto my cheeks while I saw how awful even Kate Hudson looked when she grieved a man on her mind. "Never mind. I don't want to be like normal girls. Normal girls cry. I'm so tired of crying." I chewed my lip. "And talking to myself like a loser."

From there, I went deeper into looking for relief by turning off the movies, turning on their speakers, and blaring *Bad at Love*, singing with Halsey at the top of my lungs while I played with my mom's makeup. I removed all attempts to tame the puffy. In the reflection of their bathroom mirror, I saw her clock's digits and cursed.

"Duh, it's Monday." Damn I was out of my normal habits. I called Marcus, hoped I wasn't on the schedule for something or other I'd done wrong as always.

"Little Red, where are you?" Marcus demanded. "Of course, you're on schedule. I updated online. You were supposed to be in by four. It's five-thirty! If Taylor can still see his schedule when he's out there in the sticks, I know you don't have internet issues."

"I'm sorry. My allergies are killing me, Marcus. I can't even wear makeup or be cute because my eyes are crazy puffy, running, red, it's awful. Hear my sniffling? Patrons will think I'm sick or contagious."

"Kinsley, you rarely wore makeup before King and Taylor came into the picture. Jase's on the schedule too. I don't care if you're not cute and if he loves you like I know he does, he won't care either. Be in by six. The bar is so short-handed after what happened, I need all hands on deck to deal with these ambulance chasers. Got people in here gossiping and looking around like they're gonna see her body or evidence missed by police. I'm about ready to throw punches."

My eyes flared. "Alrighty. I'll be there, but you know my temper. Hope I don't accidentally punch someone tonight." Meaning Taylor! I hated that I'd have to be around Jase so soon.

When I went to my apartment for my uniform, I found my laundry folded and put away. "Mom, you shouldn't have," I said quietly as I opened the fridge to see brand new coffee creamer replaced on the stop shelf.

My bed was made, carpet vacuumed, counters neat and tidy. The uniforms were divided into shorts and shirts, which meant I was hiding absolutely nothing from my mother anymore. I removed a slinky shirt and pair of shorts while imagining her clucking her tongue with disapproval when putting them away. My arms stretched the skin-tight material as I forced my head through the shirt.

Should I cut Jase some slack since PMS played a big role in our recent tension? Probably not. Should change his contact in my phone to *Colossal Dick.*

In the mirror, I buttoned the shorts then traced the embroidered name over my left breast. Did this embroidery get Sara killed? Who killed her? Klive didn't kill her. Everything inside me said Ray did this, not Klive. I gripped my knees when a fresh wave of grief struck tears in very raw eyes.

"Get your shit together, Kins," I whispered to my reflection in the same full-length mirror where a confident reflection had stared at me from only weeks ago. "You can do all things through ...." My chin trembled. I couldn't finish the scripture right now. I wrapped my hair into an ugly bun, added waterproof mascara to my ugly eyes.

Every single part of what used to be my routine into the bar now weighed with bricks of knowing and slowed my drive over the gravel past the dumpster area, my steps over the rocks she'd died on and the back door she'd pulled open so many times like I did now.

Clock in. Greet others. Make till. Fill orders. Patrons. No crying. Smile!

"Come on, Kins, baby. Talk to me, please!" Jase pleaded with me on a short break. In a way, I looked through him, too, as hollow as his words in this context. I shook my head and took an order away from him. Rustin reasoned for my hearing his friend out until I fired the meanest glare of all.

"There's nothing he can say, Rustin. Excuses are like assholes. Everyone has one and they all stink. Know what else stinks? Bullshit. I'm done with both."

"Okay then." He silenced, hands held in surrender, turned on his bootheel and shoved Jase with an order to let me be.

Marcus tilted his head from where he watched. He cursed and said he'd known this was going to happen.

"Did you know anything else was going to happen?" I barked at him by accident.

Marcus cursed again, crossed his meaty arms, defensive and dismissive at once. Whatever. I wasn't going to entertain Jase's excuses or let him sweet talk away the truth in the words he'd said to me. Being around him again refreshed my memory for things I tried to smooth over when I'd been in my girly idiocy earlier.

I avoided the band throughout the evening by asking a noticeably quiet Bayleigh to serve their drinks and all the front tables. Back section for me, thanks. On a brief free moment, she grabbed my forearm when I reached for the broom without a real mess to sweep.

"Kins, I know everyone's trying to readjust to being here after everything, but last time I saw you, Jase kept you glued to his side. Now he's singing all these awful songs." She threw a hand toward him.

I snorted, bitter. Rather than the sweet Theory of a Deadman cover from last night with *All or Nothing* the band had practiced, he currently crooned an acoustic solo of *Maybe We're Not Meant to Be.*

"What happened?" she asked. "He looks like shit. The band doesn't seem pleased."

I glared at Jase while he sang. He held my eyes as he sang the chorus about coming to his senses about our destiny. Prick.

"I broke up with him last night," I told her.

"Like *broke up* broke up, or we *had a tough moment and I'm pissed* type thing?"

"He went scorched earth stupid with his mouth in a drunken moment, so I scorched his back. Broke up broke up. *Finito*."

Adam, the sweet regular who'd asked me about Bayleigh during my workout yesterday morning on the beach, sat down at his Monday night barstool, took one look at me and saw I wasn't myself.

"Couldn't help overhearing. May I buy you one of your pickle martini things you make?"

Bayleigh intercepted his payment. "She shouldn't drink when she's this rough." As I turned to argue with her, I paused, softening at the way she blushed when facing him. "What can I get for you?" she asked, then blushed deeper.

Holy crap! Bayleigh never blushed!

Adam blushed too, something shy and sweet aimed at her. "I'll take a beer, but can I buy you something, too?"

She smiled and nodded. When he had her distracted, I poured myself four of my own fingers' worth of vodka, tossed the liquor down my throat and followed with a beer I bought for myself. Marcus, I know, saw me, but didn't argue if I might be nicer when buzzed. I hadn't missed the bottle he kept in his office.

Bayleigh giggled and leaned on the bar with her chin in her hand toward Adam like they shared secrets. Hopefully, she'd walk straight when they were done with their next date. I smiled to myself, though envious and longing to travel back into time when I didn't know the mean side of Jase.

Adam laughed at whatever Bayleigh said. "I think we should go inland and see how we fare inside a restaurant?" He glanced at the stage. "With better mood music."

"Yeah, he's shitty tonight. Also been drinking like a fish," she said. "The restaurant would be amazing. You thinking the bathroom?"

Adam laughed louder. "Girl, I was thinking we eat at a restaurant."

"So was I," she said and winked.

I silently wished him luck taming her down. He didn't look at her like someone ready to eat the way she'd invited. He liked her humor but liked *her* overall. Meanwhile, the guy who'd claimed to love me butchered all things love for the whole bar to hear his newfound hatred of me. His eyes aimed for me to clear any confusion as to who the target of his hate was.

"Asshole," I muttered and downed another shot. Marcus's eyes climbed my back. I wanted to gulp another to piss him off but grabbed a towel to wipe the bar instead.

"I'll pay for that one and the double you downed only moments ago." Klive sat at a stool across from me. "Coke, cherries, grenadine on the rocks, please, love."

"Aw, no beer? Gonna make me drink alone?" I pouted playfully. He passed a sad smile with his credit card. "Thank you for the shots," I told him. In the mirror behind the register, I scoped him evaluating Jase's misery while I waited for the computer to catch up to my demands.

A light blue thermal hugged his shoulders and arms, hung off his pectorals. After work Klive, that's who this was. As in, *I've tossed the three-piece shark skin for something more comfortable, but no way I'm sacrificing the sculpted hair or intoxicating cologne, especially when you're in need of a scent fix, my sweet.*

The receipt printed as I smiled to myself with his accent in my head.

"An asshole, huh?" he mused, watched Jase. Even that vulgar word sounded sophisticated from his lips.

"In the flesh," I said, scooped ice, added a handful of cherries and poured his cola.

"I thought that was my name," he said and shined a little smile on me. His hand wrapped the drink I set on the bar for him. "Thank you, love. What's this?" he asked when I handed him the pen and receipt. "No tab?"

"Klive, there are other bars. What are you doing here? Come to look at the crime scene like these other nosy patrons?" I gestured discreetly at myself then Jase. Klive looked around the bar now noticing the gossip around us while we grieved the loss of Sara.

"Do not equate me with these bottom feeders. I may be known in some circles for my role in Nightshade, but even I have better decorum than these. At least they'll be gone by next week. They're getting a bonus two-for-one deal tonight, though, seeing the two of you this way."

Klive looked at me as he dismissed them altogether.

"Kinsley, if it helps, the man was an absolute wreck last night. He's sick without you," he told me with true sympathy. "Not that I've any interest in pushing you back into his arms. Quite the contrary." His drink tilted to his lips. I watched his Adam's apple bob a couple times, played my thumb nail in one of the grooves of the chunky wood so I didn't stare. He ran a finger across the groove, bumping my thumb to retain my attention. "When I look at you now, see your heart in pain, somehow I do not feel quite so selfish."

I raised my eyebrows like a skeptic, casting my eyes toward Jase to see if he watched me with Klive. "Oh, come on." I groaned as he strummed the beginning of *Broken* like all he'd have to do is sing some sweet lament and I'd fall over myself in forgiveness. Groupies might respond to that, but not I said the fly. Loved the irony in the mean Seether songs they'd practiced last night now turning to sappy Seether once Klive arrived on the scene.

Bayleigh drifted over to greet Klive but paused when she noticed the same thing about Jase I had.

"Good job," she told Klive, bitter resentment in her tone. "You got him to extend what he defines as an olive branch. Gimme a break. Does he think you're so shallow?" Bayleigh asked me, shook her head.

My eyes met hers. "Bayleigh, I know I told Marcus I'd stay and help late, but I can't do this for another five minutes, let alone another five hours!" I gave Klive a sad smile now. "Sorry, Klive. If you're staying, Bayleigh can take care of you for the rest of the evening." Stupid tears of humiliation rushed down my cheeks faster than I could swipe them away. Okay, the fact that Bayleigh didn't make a single flirty remark about taking care of Klive spoke of her sudden seriousness snapping at me when I reached for my things beneath the bar.

"Absolutely not. Kinsley, you've chased no food or beer with four vodka shots in the span of less than half an hour. You're not driving! Either you stick this out or suck it up and ask that off-duty officer for a ride home." She crossed her arms over her chest, not even trying to grab Klive's attention with her boobs like she normally might.

"He's not an officer. He's a deputy," I corrected. "I'd rather walk home than ask for any rides from anyone at that table over there, especially the best friend of the ex who so brutally trashed me. You think he'll drive me to my place without interrogating me like he did last week as if I were the one who committed last night's offenses? No way. He's not getting any information to feed to his bestie, especially when I've been drinking. Besides, I'm fine."

"Everyone says that before driving drunk. You are anything but fine."

I huffed at her determined authority cracking a whip on my misplaced anger. Rather than cry some more at her being mean to me when she was never mean to me, I rushed to the restroom to expel this round in the privacy of a stall. Again, I told my shitty reflection to get herself together. Micro Machine wasn't known for buckling under pressure or crying over anything. She handled everything that came her way with a knowing that this too would pass.

How long till this passed?

How long till that damn song was over???

When I came out, Klive leaned against the wall waiting for me.

"If you need a ride, I can take you home." His hand should've unfolded with a carrot on his palm to a hungry but wild horse. "She's right. We both know you can't handle your alcohol *and* you're not faking this time." He grinned. I glared. "Bad timing?" he teased then winced when I didn't smile. "Sorry."

I sighed, shook my head. "Klive, the guys would flip out if I accepted a ride from you."

"All the more reason to accept in this current mood, am I right?" He again enticed, little smirk playing over his lips, temptation dancing in his eyes.

"As tempting as that sounds, you told me yourself if you have an opportunity to kidnap me, you will. Thanks, no thanks. I don't get into the car with strangers, especially professed kidnappers. I don't care what kind of candy you're offering." I smiled at my own humor. Okay, that had to be the vodka.

Klive chuckled. "The way I remember; you enjoyed the last candy I gave you when you took a ride from this stranger."

"Klive King." I pointed my finger at him.

"Kinsley Hayes, what if I promise to behave?"

I chortled. "You mean behave the way you did yesterday at the party? Give me a damn break."

His lethal charm deployed; guy you ask directions from commenced: "I promise, if you allow me to take you home, I will be good."

Though he was legit sincere, his words slithered over the branch of the tree of the knowledge of good and evil. I had no doubts if I stepped into Klive's world, I'd come to know both, cursed forever by what I may learn. His fist came up before me, opened and keys dangled from his middle finger.

What a delicious apple. He didn't look too bad himself ....

I heard Jase begin Hinder's *Better Than Me*. My feet carried my body toward the siren's plea, to the end of the hallway. Jase's eyes closed while he sang pained lyrics into the mic. The band must've extended some kindness because they played their previously vacant instruments around him. When tears fell over my face again, I didn't swipe them away as I faced Klive. I made my eyes as pleading and sweet as I could.

"If I trust you, am I going to regret it? I already have too many wounds to lick. I don't want any more."

He studied my eyes, the tears on my face. "No regrets." He leaned against the wall, keys twirling around his finger. I turned toward the stage.

Klive came close behind me. I swallowed at what that action always did to me. No idea why the sensation drove me crazy. Maybe the true essence of his presence even when I couldn't see him? His head dipped so he looked over my shoulder beside my face, cheek-to-cheek. "If you stay, he will have you back in his arms by closing. Look at him. His misery played before the entire bar, guilt-tripping you into forgiveness. You'll be so weak when he's done with his set, he'll suck you right back in ...."

"No, he won't!" I snapped.

HOSTILE TAKEOVER

"Oh, my sweet, you think all these broken-hearted songs won't soften you toward him, especially when you're under the influence?"

Inside, I growled at the very picture he painted. I didn't want him to be right. Jase would charm me back with lyrics over actions or words of kindness and meaning from his heart rather than those of musicians he covered. I couldn't allow that.

Klive pulled back when I spun to face him, finger in his face. "Let's go. Do not make me regret this."

The pain of Jase's plea to *Never Leave* already tethered my heart to an anchor he decided to sink or weigh when he wanted. I didn't want to make up with Jase yet. I wanted him to suffer for how he'd hurt me. Vindictive, I know, but whatever.

Klive went out front as I walked through the back exit. He drove around in his pretty white Tesla. I opened the passenger door praying these surveillance cameras weren't recording, like Sara, the last moments I was ever seen alive again.

2 | ♀

Klive made his way to the highway.

"You know where my apartment is. This is *not* the way," I said with an edge in my tone.

"Relax, love. I'm not hurting or kidnapping you. Remember you've afforded me plenty of opportunities you know nothing about." He glanced over his shoulder to merge. "Then, there are the obvious ones you do know of."

"Right." I sighed and crossed my arms over my chest.

He headed into an expensive part of town through entertainment districts with swanky condominiums and apartments costing more per month than I make in three. Though I expected him to pick the most pretentious building to drive beyond the gates of, he kept driving toward the suburbs. The houses here were even more expensive. He bypassed a manned guard station to a private lane where large iron gates parted for him to enter the prestigious community. Tropical esplanades divided the directions of the roads and old gas lamps lit the pavement lining the maze of mansions we weaved through. I expected Klive to pull into the driveway of a cold, modern monstrosity with sparse decor and chairs one couldn't figure out how to sit on, like my father's co-worker, Ben's, house.

Klive hit a button before we turned into a driveway of cobblestones surrounded by thick palms as a privacy barrier. Two large, solid wood gates opened from a break in a high stucco wall with gas lamps lighting their tops. He drove inside and the gates closed behind us. Interesting. Guarded community and guarded home. I found myself leaning forward seeking whatever lurked beyond this paradise-styled fortress as his driveway curved like Jase's through palms, only rather than wild and untamed, this felt like the cobblestones should've been yellow like the brick road in the Wizard of Oz. When the lush curtain of landscaping and accent lights parted, a large two-story Spanish style stucco home stole my breath. I no longer focused on my irritation at being taken somewhere I'd not chosen to go but was now enamored in how the large lot opened wide for a circle drive with a fountain in the center and a portico over two heavy wooden carved doors mimicking the large gates we'd driven through. Several small wrought-iron balconies dotted the various levels as if this home were split-leveled, all branching from a cylindrical tower like a lighthouse of stacked stone with long windows lining what had to be a staircase inside. I looked at the top of that pretty element to see a widow's walk or observation deck.

Amazing!

Man, I tried not to wear my awe on my face or be as nosy as I was feeling, but I wanted to push through those doors and explore like a kid in his pretty castle.

While Klive's home was modest by comparison to the mansions we'd passed in the community around us, this was far larger than the home my parents owned, and our house was rather large for a family of three. All this for one man?

Klive stole my view of the front of his home when he pressed another button and drove inside a four-car garage on the side of the house. He shut off the car while the door closed behind us, leaving us to dark silence. He opened his door and lit everything up again. I followed as he unlocked the round-top door that led into the house from the garage, hitting a code for his alarm while holding the passage open for me. He nudged me beyond the threshold. I stepped inside with his hand urging the base of my spine. The space was so dark, I had no idea what to expect or where I was going.

Klive broke the silence. "Since I didn't technically take you home," he whispered at my ear, "do I still have to behave?" Hot breath sent warm thrills over my body. *Bloody hell. I shouldn't have taken that double shot.*

"Yes, sir, you do. I am nursing a broken heart. What worse time could you pick to make advances?"

"Church."

I gasped. He chuckled.

"What? Don't you agree? Church would be a dreadful place to be on the pull. So very inappropriate."

I snickered in thought of him doing such a thing in my own church. He'd be roasted toast.

"Yes," I agreed, "church would be worse."

Klive's hand on my back continued urging me along until lights flickered on.

"Wow," I whispered. Before us sprawled a kitchen with double islands of white quartz and white cabinetry. Color pops came in the copper pots and pans hanging from a ceiling rack, copper range hood, copper pot-filler above the stove, oil-rubbed bronze appliances and hardware, a rust-colored brick oven carved into one wall. Damn! I didn't need to be into architecture to know when someone had the kitchen my mother had always dreamed of. Hell, Mom had a photo of that vent hood under a magnet on our fridge at home!

My palms came to rest on the white quartz. So spotless. *The better to see germs with, my sweet.*

"This is beautiful, Klive."

"Thank you." He took one of my palms and walked me down into the recessed living area beyond the kitchen. "If you'd like we can sit and watch the telly?"

"The telly?" I asked with a small grin, though the word got lost in my love when I sat and sank into one of his plush couches. "This is so comfortable, I could lie down and binge crap TV for hours." He chuckled at my admission. I'd expected to see the round, lighthouse-looking spire from here, but no dice. Too bad. I didn't want to blatantly ask for a tour to appease my nosy mind.

"Do you have someone decorate for you? Or did you do this yourself?" I asked as I noted the drapery, wood flooring, designer tiling, the soothing colors in his choice of accents, knickknacks hinting at a larger personality without giving too much away. Tyndall would be pushing for more of this man if she saw his home. The finishes and coloring all came together to create something soothing and pleasing to the senses even as I wasn't sure which added what. Klive similarly puzzled me in how he created the same conglomeration to my own senses. Ha. He'd told me he had an old soul. This home reflected his odd dichotomy. Old and new somehow making something beautifully alluring and mysterious.

"Both," he answered. "I pick what I like, then have someone else put everything together. You like?"

I nodded. "You have great taste."

"I know," he said without a hint of humility. He cast a wry smile at my eye roll. "Come. We can binge crap TV another time. I have something to show you."

He gently plied me from his couch and guided me down a hallway diagonal from the kitchen where a personal library with those fancy tufted chairs and a sofa sat in the presence of a desk. Leather-bound books like the ones in my lawyer's office lined the shelves behind the desk. A stained-glass lamp cast a cozy glow over the space. While Klive asked if I liked reading, I ran my fingers over the soft velvet of a chair thinking of his pirate coat. On a shelf decorated with more eclectic odds and ends, a ship in a bottle caught my eye. I moved in close to look at the details, squinting.

"Is this the *José Gasparilla*?" I asked.

"Indeed. I made that myself. You can ask me how I put it in the bottle another time. This isn't what I wanted to show you." Klive urged me close to his side then turned a stone bookend.

"Sir, you need to hush," I said, a little breathless with awe, as the shelf did the cliche turn like a revolving door. However, I remained rooted to the spot I stood, stupefied. Inside wasn't a secret spy room, but a short, wide hallway with carved wooden double doors at the end.

"Come now." Klive took my hand and led us through the opening. The bookcase behind us closed and left us in darkness.

Danger! Danger!

"Klive!" I gripped his hand harder. "I'm afraid of the dark and claustrophobic." Or was my proverbial tie too tight at whatever lurked beyond these doors? Would he show me secrets I couldn't handle?

Klive's lips brushed ever so softly against my temple and that one tiny touch in the dark nearly caused my knees to give. I wasn't sure how to rationalize the way the fear somehow amplified his allure for me, but I heard my breathing between us.

"Shh … it's okay, Kins."

"Is it?" I gulped.

Klive's lips whispered against my skin again before he spoke into the quiet space. "The darkest thing in here is my soul and you've braved that darkness from day one. What is this hollow blackness with no hands to touch you?" he asked as his free hand skimmed my bicep with the back of his fingernails. "What danger is there from darkness when the light inside you has the power to snuff it out at your will? If anything, the darkness fears you."

I sensed him shift in front of me. My forehead found his chest, but Klive's fingers tucked beneath my chin. He tilted my face up. Surely, we would kill each other with the warring darkness and light coming together to create so many gray areas when our mouths met. He was right. What power was darkness when I held in my hands the very thing he claimed was darkest? If I love—

NO!

I pried myself from his delicious mouth, in more fear of my thoughts than the darkness around us now. Klive chuckled like he knew.

He tugged me toward those double doors, and he released my hand to push them open where dim mood lighting illuminated a dream. Yep. That's what this had to be. One of my lucid sleepwalking episodes where I might end up pressed against my locked front door or tripping over the backs of one of my couches when at last I met with a rude awakening. Hold on to the dream while you can!

My lackadaisical gaze spilled over the beautiful lair before me. A solid wall at least ten feet tall of the same stacked stone from the tower outside surrounded an elevated glass fireplace. Carved niches with soft, built-in accent lighting cast a cozy glow in various places along the stone. Just beautiful, stunning even.

"I don't even know what to say about the splendor of your hidey-hole, er, hidey man cave … gah, I don't even know … who thinks of something so cool?"

"I designed this home myself," he said with another small chuckle. "And I refer to this area as my master suite."

"You're so good at what you do," I gushed more to myself. Rather than make another immodest confirmation, Klive quietly thanked me and seemed more interested in my perusal of his personality on display. Maybe if he were this curious about my thoughts on his environment, he wouldn't be disappointed in my desire to know too much about the rest of the house? "Is there an observation deck on the roof at the top of your castle's tower, sir?" I grinned at him.

His brows lifted in pleasant surprise. "There is. The stairwell leads to the other levels but also leads to a rooftop deck overlooking the water. Perhaps, I will show it to you soon."

I swallowed the urge to beg him to show me now in favor of taking these morsels he chose to give me. Klive was such an enigma, I needed to pace myself with the bits he allowed me to know as we went. Who needed photographs or that first date type interview when you had walls like these speaking with such a lovely voice?

A little nervous, I tiptoed like a snooping child further into the bedroom.

"Bloody hell," I whispered in wonder as the main attraction adjacent to the stone fireplace came into view and stole my ability to think straight. Klive's bed! The enormous canopy bed was positively palatial! "Who knew this existed outside Disney princess movies?"

Without thinking, I ran and jumped onto the bench at the foot of his bed frame. I propelled so my back landed on all the feather pillows and goose down comforter. Butterflies soared as I bounced once, then sank down into the softest bliss. The canopy above me was lined on the underside with the same thick taffeta fabric tied back like curtains at each large, hand-carved post. I sighed and closed my eyes wanting to nestle like a lazy cat tucking in for a long nap. Oh, to untie the curtains and close Klive inside this dreamy cloud with me and nothing between us but his cologne! *Hush, Kinsley brain!*

Klive's shoulder leaned against the wall with his hands in his pockets as he laughed. Oh gosh! Face-palm!

I sat up and leaned forward on my hands with my knees bent behind me. My shoulders shrugged with apology as embarrassment lit my cheeks. Well, what should've been embarrassment, anyway.

This heat was from vodka and wayward thoughts. The liquor kept me from being embarrassed about anything.

"Okay, a teensy part of me is so very sorry. I may be a tad tipsy ...." I cast my sweetest smile with a playful batting of my lashes.

Klive pushed off the wall and stalked slowly toward me, hands in his pockets, gaze holding mine with unwavering intensity. More butterflies fluttered through my belly while warmth spread through my limbs. He'd looked at me, walked toward me the same way, when we'd been on the balcony in St. Augustine. He'd been holding frozen custard cones. He'd kissed me so deeply the current should've burst the bulbs in our vicinity and now, seeing his slow stalk toward me, I prayed for a deeper kiss with his body pinning me to his pillows, maybe for the restless hours he'd described at Delia's.

My mouth dried while my heart hammered against my rib cage when he stood at the end of the bed.

Please, please, please!

His shoulder leaned against one of the thick wooden posts. Was that smirk from him reading my mind? Or from my jumping on his bed?

Who cares?

I fell back into the cushiony softness, my hair spilling around me while I reached into the mass of pillows and thew one at him. He caught the burnt orange, satin marshmallow and raised his eyebrows in playful warning.

Ooh la la!

"Klive, you know this bed is ridiculous, right?"

He shrugged with a smile that matched mine. "Would you like to see the lavatory? If you like my bed, I know you'll love it." Lavatory. What a proper term. I'd have to tell Tyndall to nix the water closet label and use lavatory instead, heehee.

His hand extended. I nodded and took his fingers.

"Never thought, if I got you into my bed, I'd ever pull you out of it," he muttered to himself.

My feet met the carpet while I studied him. Klive's eyes warned me to traverse our undeniable chemistry with caution. Fortunately, he deployed the best distraction when we entered the master bathroom or should that be *the master's* bathroom because this was ah-maz-ing! The huge stone wall from the bedroom was a wall for the bathroom too. The glass fireplace was double-sided and elevated because this side sat beside his jacuzzi bathtub complete with an infinite edge like the swimming pools!

"Damn," I whispered.

"Had a feeling you'd love the tub," he said. "Look. You can fill this basin to the max and the water spills over the side, re-circulates while re-heating. You never get cold and may completely submerge. I hate that annoying draining when the water levels get too high, you know?"

"Do I?" I kinda looked at Klive in awe because this was such a ... *human* observation. "I hate that, too. The draining, I mean. And getting cold. I *love* the tub. It must be so relaxing, especially after conditioning when your muscles are sore."

He cleared his throat and nodded. "Sore muscles. Maybe bruises after a good battle. Perhaps wounds that need soaking." He winked at me, but I understood he was alluding to the nature of his own business and not only my fight with Angela. Not wanting to imagine what his Nightshade side caused, I studied the two separate vanities at either side of the bathtub. I saw his crowded with product, mainly for hair and skin. I looked for a cologne bottle for any hints, but Klive hit a light switch and I was pulled back to the stone wall, noticing now this side had accent niches of lighting but also other small shelves with false candles he controlled with the flick of wrist as well. He tapped another control and the fireplace ignited. Klive turned the dial on a dimmer and the niche accents went low. The two of us glowed beneath the embers of dancing flames.

Oh, boy. If I'd thought that bed was dangerous, the dark alcove, the library, along with the man who owned the castle, this was no less than seduction. If I looked at Klive, I'd cave into pure temptation. I cast my attention to the pretty flecks glowing golden in the granite vanity tops, roving over the second vanity in a way I didn't want to look and see that someone else may exist in his life, and over the glass enclosure he called a shower. This one rivaled the size of Jase's in how three people could comfortably fit inside if they wanted. I hoped that never happened!

Klive tugged my hand like he didn't want my mind going to bad places. He turned a knob on a door. We entered and he flipped another light switch. A low curse tumbled through my numbing lips. Was this a closet or a small boutique?! Shoes galore lined a row of ten shelves. Women's shoes! My head turned his way with trepidation and some dread of my worst fears realized.

"Klive King, is your wife about to come home and beat my ass? I may have screwed up with two men, but I am not into that kind of thing and will not be any home-wrecker!" I snapped my fingers.

Klive chuckled and pulled me deeper into the closet. "Believe me, love, I am well aware of the fact that you prefer to be the only one in a man's life." He set a pair of snakeskin heels in my hands. My mouth parched again as I recalled these shoes the day Constance and I had been trying on heels. These were the pumps he'd confessed to buying for *me*!

"Yours," he echoed that last observation. "I've told you before, I am not married, nor involved with anyone. I do not get involved, Ms. Hayes. It's simple. I saw these things, thought of you, so I bought them for you," he stated in that way he has, as casual as asking whether or not you wanted white or wheat for your sandwich. "If you want them, that is." Klive studied my face. I couldn't mask my incredulous shock.

"Klive! Don't you think that's insanely inappropriate? It was one thing when you said I was on your mind, and you wanted to do something nice. This is too much, especially when I'm involved with someone else."

Then a dawning understanding hit me.

"Oh, wait! *This* is set up perfectly for when you kidnap me, right? How damn convenient."

Klive was undaunted by my anger and attitude. He pointed a finger at me.

"Uh, uh. You are not involved with anyone anymore, remember?" He tilted his head, considering me. "I suppose you're correct in your perception of my kidnapping you, though I truly never thought of it that way. I liked these things and liked them more when I pictured you in them. No kidnapping and that's the truth."

I arched my eyebrow, but didn't want to fight right now, so I walked over to the dresses. So many dresses! Pretty dresses I wouldn't even know where to wear some of them. I thumbed through the color-coded fabrics, even some evening gowns in dry-cleaning bags. In fact, a great many garments were inside dry-cleaning bags, but if they'd not needed cleaning from being worn before, why the dry-cleaner?

Duh! Germaphobe, Kins!

I looked at a built-in dresser, curious what may be inside. Behind drawer number one, panties galore! Oh, goodie! I thumbed through and produced a lacy pair dangling from my fingertip. "I guess we know what Mr. King's favorite style of panty is." He agreed, mouth etched in that wry grin, heat hitting his irises as would be natural. I swallowed and replaced them, shut that drawer and kept traveling. Next stop only the most beautiful bras I'd never buy more than one of at a time. Hmm ... when I looked at the size, I arched a disapproving brow at him asking with my eyes how he'd know such an intimate thing.

"I have my ways." He nodded that I keep exploring. "I was in your apartment, was I not? Did you really think me gentlemanly enough not to look around or take a souvenir?"

Was that a dare to find exactly which souvenirs he'd taken? Bold SOB! I moved to the next drawer.

Whoa! I whistled and lifted lingerie I didn't even know how to put on! If I'd been sober, I was sure I'd be magenta from head to toe, but I looked this man in the eyes when I said, "You, sir, are a very dirty man ...." I couldn't help smiling as I twisted the material trying to figure a way into the costume. Meh. I tossed that one in the drawer to look at more. These were not only from fine shops. Some were from those raunchy sex shops. Klive's tastes were all over the place! I was heating up just thinking of him thinking of me this way!

"Indeed. A treasure trove of all the ways you've inspired me in weak moments," he said, his voice lower. "If I buy what I imagine, it makes the pain more bearable and worth the wait, like it's possible even if it's not imminent satiation. Now, maybe you see why I have been so frustrated."

I gulped while my stomach flip-flopped. Next drawer, now, please!

There, like the snuggling during afterglow, rested the plain, innocent cotton nightgowns I loved wearing to bed the most. Hmm, these drawers were arranged almost like the order of his mind. Panties, bra, lingerie then comfy cozy. These looked so soft and inviting. I imagined how amazing a soak in the tub beside the fireplace might be before changing into one of these and climbing into his bed. How not to envy Klive of his luxuries was the question.

Klive walked over and rifled through the comfy drawer until coming upon a short, aqua, baby-doll style gown. "Here. You look so sweet, and this color is amazing with your hair and skin." He tucked the cotton into my hands then pulled the top drawer open again. A matching pair of aqua boy shorts rested on top of the gown he'd given me. Unable to resist, I rubbed my cheek against the set.

"Don't you think these are so snuggly?" I smiled up at him. "I love them and what you said about my skin and hair," I admitted. "Thank you, Klive."

For a moment in time, I saw the oddest look cross his face that forced a flashback of our night at Delia's when I'd needed help in the restroom. Klive had kissed me then as if helpless after promising to love me forever.

As though needing to escape my scrutiny, he went back into the master bathroom while calling over his shoulder that I continue looking around. I heard the bathtub turn on, smelled chamomile and vanilla. Yup. Someone had been in my bathroom and done too much homework. Freaking creepy, seductive stalker.

I scanned the shoes with indulgent eyes, sighing when I spotted a pair I'd circled in one of Constance's magazines. Six-inch craziness, wrap around ankle strap, sexy, edgy, and right now, mine all mine. No way he could've known about that magazine. So, did we have the same taste in some things?

I pulled them from the shelf as I shucked the work shoes from my feet, but I fell when trying to peel the socks away with my toes. On the floor I laid and laughed as I gazed at the closet around me like a dream. All these colors and choices were like a beautiful, fuzzy hypnosis after so much turmoil and sorrow. Was I really here now? Did I really have a man like Klive King pining for my affections? Could I love him, the real him, the way I'd loved him before I'd known the truth about who he was? Tyndall's words assaulted me. I was unattached right now ... *oh, alcohol brain, you are just as crazy as Klive and Tyndall ....*

To make this better, Lana del Rey's *Million Dollar Man* started from a sound system I couldn't trace. I must've fallen asleep with my phone playing music again. What a perfect song for Klive's role in dreams he'd starred in for far longer than I cared to admit. Like every other time, now my mind set the tone before I allowed him to ravage me at the end of the dream.

So, if this was a dream, I was free to follow my hormones, right? Who cares what Jase said? If I let Klive fall in love with me, I would still be helping him. I couldn't help wondering how much was alcohol and how much was just my natural reaction to Klive's heady seduction, and our chemistry birthed the night he'd walked into my life from that lift, as he called the elevator.

3 | ♀

Klive was like an eighty's hair-band rock ballad: bad boy showing a sweet side. Who in their right mind could resist that? Since I wasn't in my right mind under the influence, should I really expect to resist?

He walked back inside the closet boutique. His lips perked into a crooked smile.

"Whatever are you doing on the floor, love?"

I sighed. "Dreaming, right, Klive? You are a dream. Your house. This closet of Kinsley. Your bed, that bathtub with the fireplace, the library and a tower just for Rapunzel to look down from and dream of better things, but why dream when all the best things are inside?" I sat up and leaned forward on my hands, looking up at him. My hair spilled over my shoulders, my long bangs shifting over my right eye. I ran my hand through my hair to push the red tufts back. Klive's eyes filled with storm clouds. Oh, my! Had I just triggered something?

Klive asked if I normally dreamed of him. In *French*! Ooh la la! Yes, this was the best dream!

"Oh, Klive, what you do to me when you speak French with your pretty accent," I confessed.

Lana del Rey's beautiful voice crooned about a dangerous man she was unable to resist, about not knowing how she couldn't be drawn to him. Woman, I feel ya, especially when this million-dollar man dipped to his knees before crawling across the carpet of the closet to me. His hand tucked behind my ear. My eyes lingered on his, helpless as she sang about how easy he was to be liked and loved, ready for him to take her. Yes, please! The most dangerous words inviting him with my eyes to do what she commanded. He obediently leaned forward, and I met him halfway. As soon as our lips touched, my hormones spilled into his like colliding waterfalls. I rushed to my knees and grabbed his head to press him harder to me. He rose to his knees, too, and tugged me hard against him, hands gripping my waist, such desperation in his soft, pliable lips so feverishly coaxing mine with his warm tongue and weak groans driving me to the point of madness for more!

My whole body heated with pure desire for him. Alcohol or no, I couldn't deny I wanted him. Though everything should've shifted and changed, weakened once I'd learned who he was, somehow his forbidden life made this harder to walk away from.

Suddenly, Klive ripped away and jumped to his feet to run into the bathroom. I heard the water stop running. My bottom sat back on my feet as I daydreamed about the mouth that was just on mine.

Klive returned and urged to my feet. He took the nightgown and panties from me, placing them on a shelf beside him. To my shock, Mr. Manners-Make-Me-Wait-Forever gripped the bottom of my top and lifted the shirt over my head.

"I made you a promise and I never break my word," he said at my evident shock. Any response died in my dry throat at that look, those words. I felt like a pauper with her nose pressed to the glass of a bakery, longing every day for the most sinful looking cake, desperate for a taste, but always too poor to afford one. Now, I'd been invited into the bakery for the whole cake and wasn't sure how to finally take a bite. Klive reached behind me, pinning me to his chest. My bra came loose, and my breasts rose and fell with how I couldn't breathe enough air as he stood back to blatantly look at me. I resisted the powerful urge to cover myself, so nervous that I'd not be what Klive hoped for. *"Je pense que je suis l'un rêver...."* Klive told me *he is the one dreaming.* "Magnifique."

"Really?" I couldn't help feeling shy, my hands wringing so I wouldn't cover myself.

"I just told you I never break my word, Kinsley. You are beautiful." His voice seemed as low and dark as the lust clouding his eyes. I sucked my teeth when Klive's fingers whispered over my birthmark, his index tracing the shape before running along the fading lines of the bruised shoe print. "When you asked me if you were ugly at the club after your fight, I never got to answer." He retraced the footprint. Goosebumps broke over my flesh. "I was going to say I'd never seen a prettier little vampire, so bloodthirsty and brutal at once."

I grinned, and though he did, too, his expression darkened as he tested the most sensitive flesh of my nipple.

"Klive," I whimpered.

"If this is what happens with my fingers, I wonder what would happen if I kissed you there." His arm wrapped my waist as my knees gave under the weight of such words. I gripped his shoulders as I tried to get my legs to cooperate, but Klive tested my lips with his, only this time when my body pressed to his, I groaned at the feel of his shirt against my bare flesh, the way his fingers dug hard into my back, how rough and ragged our breaths were as we lost ourselves to the inevitable. I wanted the cake! The frosting was delicious so far but what did the whole bite taste like? While his hands kneaded my back in ways I could use more of without any lust at some point, dude had skills, I reached for the button on my shorts. Klive fumbled for the button on his pants, too, but from nowhere, my dark passenger's villainous laughter ruined everything.

Internal record skip! This was no dream! This was a nightmare! I cried just that in French as I threw my hands like a block between us.

"*Pas un rêve! Ceci est un cauchemar! Je suis sur ma période, fiche il!*" I cursed. Tears rushed to my eyes as Klive groaned then whined as his head fell back. He cursed in French and agreed this was a nightmare.

"How bad is it?" he asked. "Can you still take a bath?"

"Take a bath? You ran me a bath?" I asked, just understanding why the water had been running with the sweet oils I loved. Yes, a nightmare indeed. He nodded in answer to my question while I looked at him in despair. "Really, Klive? That's so sweet and now this nightmare grows because you're seriously asking me about my flow. Oh, *me tuer maintenant!*"

Klive's mouth fell into a crooked smile. "No, I think I'd rather keep you than kill you, my sweet. Thanks for permission, though." He snickered. I slapped his arm and gave a rueful smile, trying so hard to calm my frazzled hormones and emotions.

"If you must know, my flow is not so much a crime scene as much as a persistent wound, so yes, I could probably still take a bath. There's no way I can stay though. I have to get back to my place and the comforts of feminine products and chocolate before this beauty turns into the beast." I cast an animated cringe.

Klive laughed. "What if I were to put you in the bath while sacrificing my masculinity to buy you some? Would you stay?" The hope in his face was irresistibly adorable. Didn't help that tonight he was so gorgeous with his hair lacking product and all messed up from my hands, the way that thermal hugged his pectorals and biceps, gray eyes pleading with me to stay .... I needed to get out of here, but he was so tempting.

"I dunno, Klive." My fingers ran beneath the hem of his shirt along the unbuttoned waistband of his slacks. "You are a very bad man, and I am such a good girl, I probably shouldn't be spending the night with you ...." Though I pursed my lips, my eyes couldn't help the naughty smile when toying with my tiger. What can I say? These stupid words just flowed on their own.

Klive exhaled while his chin rose, eyes cast down like I was a subject who'd dared defy the authority of a ruler. He stepped out of the closet and the music changed to a cover of Duran Duran's *Undone*.

Woo! Now, *that* song was like fighting dirty. He walked back in; his air having expanded in that autocratic way he has. In charge. I was going to tease him about deploying such a weapon, but I couldn't speak as I watched him divest himself of the shirt I'd toyed with. I swallowed hard when he took three commanding strides across the closet and jerked my naked torso against his. We simultaneously cursed at the sensation. His hand went into my hair to tug my head back before his mouth tasted the column of my throat. Damn! I gasped his name while his breaths panted between kisses to areas that felt they'd never been touched before. In fact, my whole body trembled in his arms like no one had ever held me, pleased me, teased me because no one had ever caused the surges through my skin the way Klive's current shot straight to my toes and every nerve. If he plugged himself into me, would we light the darkest corners of everything we hid from one another; somehow free ourselves from everything holding us back? Factor the song calling both our crap as we faced the truth of who each of us may be when coming together, who the loyalty really belonged to, who owned the real love ... a dark reality to face, something maybe both of us resented the other for that only drove us harder in the way we gripped one another's skin, sipped the sounds of weakness we drew from the other while siphoning the control, getting off on the raw sensuality of the undeniable ....

By the time Klive's lips climbed over my jaw, then planted to my very weak mouth, I drizzled into his touch. Never could I recall feeling more fallible as if under a spell until his fingers splayed around my throat and tightened a mere fraction. Thrills and chills met like fire and ice and sent me into an overstrung state of arousal and suspense like the type he'd sent through me when he'd grabbed me in the elevator before studying my lips like he might kiss me.

Klive broke our kiss to stand at his full height while looking down at me with dark domination. One of his fingers found my pulse as he bent to nip my lips once more before speaking.

"Do you know that if I wanted to kill you, this is how I imagined you," he whispered at my ear. "Weak with lust in my arms. My hand around your throat while you scream my name as I push myself forcefully inside you ...."

Ho. Lee. Shit. My eyes closed.

His words and heavy breathing ratcheted my own. Twisted heat shot straight to my core. How was I so incredibly turned on and afraid at once? Was this what Tyndall meant with Austin? No way in hell he was this heady because no way in hell he was anything like Klive's legit danger.

God, forgive me for wanting Klive so badly!

His words should've disturbed me, but right now they didn't, and I knew not only the alcohol was to blame, but the cold hard truth that I'd been a goner for this man from the moment the elevator opened.

"I spend my life in blood, Kinsley. I do not care if you are bleeding. I *will* have you tonight."

Oh! The sweet side of the bad boy blew to smithereens! The more primal his desire to have me, his words unchecked, the real Nightshade Klive King revealing himself to me, unveiling a weakness for me, the more powerful I felt. Like the Syndicate Barbie Jase had joked of.

Klive's hand gripped my shorts. The metal button flew into the wall as he popped them open in unchecked lust. Oh! Boddice-ripping romance had nothing on this raw reality! Klive tugged them down past my hips. Ugh! Just like at Delia's, why, oh, why did this have to be the circumstance? Maybe he meant what he said, and blood wasn't an issue .... No!

My hands shot to his chest. "Klive, stop! You may be okay with blood, but I am not."

"What's that?" he asked against my throat as he stole my argument with his tongue on my flesh again.

"Ooh ... Klive ..." I swallowed. "Klive, Klive, please," I begged. He grunted like he could care less. Again, I pleaded his name, but moaned when he hummed. "Klive, you don't want me like this. You want me when I can fully enjoy everything that you are while I let you take me mercilessly ... we've waited for each other for so long ... doesn't matter if I was with anyone else, I've always been waiting for you ... like this ...."

He groaned before growling and nipping my throat with his teeth. I hissed and panted harder, afraid, aroused at him not wanting to care much about my wants in this moment. How long I'd been dreaming of him losing his manners with me, losing all control and shoving me up against a wall to let loose with the beast we both knew he pinned back around me, *for* me. How I wanted him to tear my clothes away and take me with no mercy! I *wanted* this rough man with his powerful hands saying dirty things in my ear with his elegant accent as he came undone like the song playing.

I gulped hard, thinking of anything realistic enough to keep from having to admit I didn't want him pulling my panties down and seeing a liner inside them or having to pause this amazing passion to pull a nasty plug from my body. I almost shuddered and hastily recalled his own plea to me from Delia's when I'd wanted him to sleep with me. He'd asked me to be strong for him and that was the ultimate challenge to honor because I couldn't stand the idea of dishonoring him in some way. We shared this; I knew.

"Please, Klive, I need you to be stronger than me right now! I am half drunk, take me sober, please!"

Even as I said them, knew they'd work, I felt lame because while Klive himself gave me an intoxicating buzz, his touch was so jarring in sensation-overload I think I'd have sobered under any influence. No way he'd not see through the bullshit excuse.

He sighed while his lips traced my collarbone, the same one that had been dislocated, as if he could belatedly kiss something better. His hand left my hair while the other abandoned the hold on my throat. Like a final effort to make me confess my lie, Klive's hands went to my breasts instead. I arched and sucked a deep breath, my eyes crying out to his for mercy and more at once.

"Are you sure?" he asked, squeezed, brushed his thumbs so I squirmed with desire. "I would love to take you any way I can, blood be damned," he said like another indication that I didn't need to pretend. Klive had a way about him that knew the weak spots, the places of shame or pain, the areas of anyone he might exploit. Never would he make a lie easy to tell. The decision to accept an explanation was his.

He walked me back slowly, holding my breasts, pushing against me until I pressed against the wall as if he'd read my desires. His face dipped close to mine. I looked up into his eyes, at his lips, back to his pretty irises. Bambi eyes deployed as I felt real fear, though for the wrong reasons. I didn't want to have sex on my period. No matter what he said, I thought menstruation was gross, and I hadn't waited this long, gone through this much torment *for* him, *because* of him, *with* him, to hand myself over during the worst time of the month. Nope. I shoved the conviction through my eyes. When we had a first time, anything less than epic wouldn't do. I refused to accept anything else. Klive's gaze took on a dark sort of smile as if we spoke the same language.

"You're so sexy when you plead with me. Are you trying to provoke me, love?"

Hot damn! Could I? Best to find out another time.

Against my body's longing, I managed a "No."

"Are you afraid of me?" he asked with a tone silkier than the burnt orange pillowcases I wanted him pressing me to. The only thing I was afraid of was my acute attraction to every single side of Klive when I shouldn't be. A fraction of myself was afraid of him. The other parts didn't care how scary he was. One part was *very* into how intimidating he was now.

"Do you want me to be?" I tossed the words like bait with a shaky voice.

"Hmm ... good question. I can't decide. You are so beautiful already, to mix your fear into it, well, I don't know that I can behave. I'm already struggling with your begging my name. You see, Kinsley, you try to reason with me, but at this juncture, I don't have a bloody reason to listen."

His hand went back to my throat. The other traveled slowly down my side, tickling but torturing too much sensation from my skin.

"You see, all I can think of is your hot, wet, tight —"

I clapped a hand over his mouth. "Klive King," I said his name like channeling Syndicate Barbie. "If you think I haven't thought about Lord Rion's sword in the time since the Ren party or even our night at Delia's, I'd be lying. I get it. My mind is ready, but my body isn't in the condition I want to be in when we have a first time. I will let you make out with me, clearly let you go to second base," I teased, drawing a little chuckle from him. "Don't give yourself away or take me as I am now just because we are too selfish in the moment to refuse what we want so desperately. We've waited so long …."

"Blast! Must you live to use all my words against me? However do you remember them so well?"

"Your words matter to me, too," I admitted. "You asked me to be strong for you, then. I'm asking you to be strong for both of us, now, as a courtesy to your pride." I smirked.

Klive's chin rose, eyes cast down over my face as if he suspected I was lying. If only. I allowed conviction and the depth of my vulnerability for him to show on my face for a fleeting moment. I was so tired of pretending that I hadn't found the one whom my soul desired!

"Oh, Klive, I just want to remember everything and what if you take me now and half is a blur by tomorrow?"

"That's right, those shots. I forget what a lightweight you truly are." Klive's eyes took on the familiar softness I now knew was only for me. Oh, bless him, surrendering his weapons. Rustin's pretending to hit a baseball for me to send my point home popped into my head. *Hit this home.*

"Yeah." I chewed my lip and drew an arc in the carpet with my toe, looking up at Klive with wide, innocent eyes. "I never thanked you for helping me in Pensacola, both in my sorrow over the dreaded ex and carrying me to my room, cleaning me up. Really, I was grateful you were there, and I am tonight just the same." I searched his face.

"Careful, you're treading close to labeling me a convenient rebound."

"Oh, Klive, no!" I cried, horrified. "You're not the rebound, you're the one — shit! I meant —"

"There's that self-esteem again."

"Oh, hell no! You don't get to imply that my feelings —"

Klive's hand cupped my mouth while his eyes urged me to calm down. As I caved, he finally gave a reluctant smile. His hand left my mouth to draw my bangs away from my eyes where his fingers traced my cheekbone. Hitting that home hadn't worked so well for me when staring at the umpire calling all the shots. Though my awful confession appeared to be doing a great job warming that cold heart of his, the sad thing was, this was truly me, not some act to pull Klive into screwing up. How did Klive draw the truth so easily? Seemed I was destined to screw up with him since I knew that fondness replacing his hard steel made me fuzzy. Alcohol buzz had nothing on whatever this thing between us was. No way I'd dare define this emotion after the crap I'd just blurted about him being the one.

As if Klive mirrored my insides, his shoulders sagged in defeat as he sighed.

"You win this round, my sweet. Would you like anything from the closet before I take you home?"

4 | ♀

His sorrow pulled at my heart, but I gave him the huge smile my father loved. The same smile I knew Jase usually melted under.

Ugh. I pushed that A-hole out of my head as Klive backed away from me. I felt oddly chilled without Klive's body heat now.

"Really?" I gushed, hoping my excitement would cheer him.

"Yes." He walked to the drawers and opened the bras to produce an aqua t-shirt bra that looked as pretty and comfortable as the nightie and undies he'd gifted me. He walked back to me and ran the straps up my arms, leaning against me to fasten the clasp at my back. "Let's put these away before I lose my resolve," he teased. He stood back but grabbed my breasts and kneaded them once more through the soft bra. I cursed while he said, "Goodbye, lovelies, until next time, I shall miss you both." He squeezed, then bent to nuzzle them like a naughty boy.

"Klive! Behave, sir!" I laughed and lifted his head. He rested his forehead against mine, studying my eyes.

"I am trying very hard to behave." He strode out of the closet to kill the music before coming back to me. "Here, you can take these home with you, too." He handed me the nightgown and undies, then went to the dresses. He chose a sophisticated cream pencil dress, cap-sleeved, nice lines, slit in the back, open V between the breasts. Elegantly revealing, not trashy. Demure and sexy. I took the hanger before he went to the shoes to pick a pair of nude platform pumps.

Okay, Klive had put together a very grown-up ensemble for me. So grown-up, my mother would've knocked me out of the way to steal the dress and some of the closet. Her feet were bigger than mine, so she'd have to envy the shoe selection, though. I was busy imagining what she'd say if she saw me in such refined threads when I saw him move toward a safe disguised as another chest of drawers. The whole panel opened. Klive entered a code then reached inside.

Oh, shit! He rifled through jewelry boxes! Hell, he'd bought me things needing a safe? I swallowed hard while my breathing labored in legit panic.

Klive looked up and smiled. "Relax, love."

Ha! Yeah right! This was more than one-night-stand material. Jewelry meant intimacy just the way Coach Walton and my mother had warned me about. Every lie I'd ever told myself about Klive's superficial interest in me shattered as he held before me a pearl tennis bracelet. Should I ask him if he'd bought me the beautiful necklace for Valentine's? But, if he hadn't, he may grow concerned enough to pop this happy bubble with the bad one while I'd worked so hard to draw the sweet one out. I studied the bracelet, shivering a little inside.

"Wow, Klive, it's beautiful. Are they synthetic?" I touched the cold clustered orbs.

Klive scoffed like I'd insulted him. I pursed my lips and pulled my hand away.

"I can't accept this. It's too much. All of this is too much. I can't accept any of this." Chilly sobriety clawed at my happiness.

Klive dipped his head and stuck his bottom lip out. Ah, hell. I couldn't help cupping his head in all his adorable idiocy. He laughed at me.

"Kinsley, as much as I am enjoying this, I'm not a puppy. You're petting me." He stood back up and grinned like a sneaky brat before he said, "If you don't take it, I'm going to have to give it to Angela.

Do you think she'll like it? I should see if the dress may fit her, too, since you don't want any of this." He grabbed for the hanger, but I snatched the dress from his reach. "What, love? Do you not want her to have it?" he asked with the cutest mock confusion. "I think she'll at least love the bracelet. I mean, what woman wouldn't?"

"Klive! You just told me you weren't involved with anyone! Are you, or have you ever been seeing Angela?" That didn't make proper sense, but who cared right now?

"Why? Would that bother you, love?" Klive smirked while visions of her massaging his sword filtered through my memory, stealing all fuzzy warmth from my body.

My eyes narrowed at him. "Anyone I know seeing her would bother me." True story. I was still hella disgusted that Rustin slept with her before he'd touched me. Klive was freezing me out now at the mere thought of him sharing his body with that ho ....

"Oh, but you don't want to *know* me yet, so it won't bother you if I give these to her instead?" Klive taunted while my anger expanded. I knew I should resist his bait, but right now the only thing I resisted was landing my palm against his face all over again like the night she'd touched him at the club before our fight. I hated the way he'd smiled back at her over his shoulder. Mine!

"Do you know her? Because at the Ren Faire you made it seem we were on the same wavelength concerning her. Is that why you are so disgusted by her? Something go awry in the bedroom?"

"Meh, once or twice. She's mediocre at best, but she likes pretty things." His play cut off at the stupid tears clouding my eyes. *My* pirate. *My* creepy stalker. *My* drug lord, crime boss, hitman. *Mine!* Twisted junk for sure.

Klive lifted my wrist to clasp the bracelet around my skin. My hands were far too rough to wear something so dainty and elegant. Klive sought my gaze while his lips planted to the back of my hand.

"Kinsley, do us both a favor. Accept what I give when I give it," he said with suddenly serious sincerity. I realized he wasn't only speaking on shallow terms of the outside appearance like clothing and accessories, but his sweet side. "Will you do that for me?"

"Yes, sir," I whispered, a little teary feeling for different reasons; deep, soul-searching Biblical reasons.

"Now, that's what I like to hear." He teased the heaviness of our emotional impossibility off my heart a tad. That weight would return heavier than ever before when real sobriety hit, that much I knew. This night, there was no coming back, no sex necessary. The words he'd just spoken could never be unheard with the conviction in his eyes never again unseen or felt.

"Love, do you know the difference between synthetic pearls and real?"

I shook my head.

He tilted my wrist. "If you look closely, no two pearls are the same. See the imperfections?" I nodded at the misshapen pearls I now saw weren't so round. "Real pearls aren't perfect. They're flawed, cold to the touch but warm when worn. They're gritty in your mouth, but satin to the fingers. To drill into them takes a real effort on both sides. Synthetics are cheap, almost hollow in weight, plastic, easy to drill straight through, recreated in a snap while real ones take years for an oyster to create. Do you understand what I am saying to you?" But he didn't give me a chance to respond as his eyes conveyed that I'd better listen. "Many may be fooled into believing the fakes are real, but those who pay closer attention know how to spot impostors and seek imperfection because it's real. I'd rather wait for years to have something real than hasten for a cheap synthetic any day. Such is my personality."

Oh. My. Gosh. My throat filled like a bowling ball dropped into my windpipe.

"Kinsley, she may have warned you about shattering slippers because she'd love nothing more than to force her big feet into shoes that she believes are glass, but ours is no Cinderella story, and I'd never be mistaken for Prince Charming. Everyone who knows the dark King understands only one fits the shoes that walk beside him, because only one walks on thin ice and broken glass without falling through to her death."

Klive cupped my biceps while I seemed rooted to the carpet as the first true fear of Klive raced through my veins. Klive was no synthetic either. He was so real, so imperfect, gritty yet smooth, difficult to drill into, heavy with his reality ... was I strong enough to wear glass slippers, traverse thin ice and carry what he was without falling through? I sent another impossible prayer to God even as I was such a hot mess of a sinner. Klive planted the softest kiss to my forehead, his lips lingering for a meaningful moment. His lips left my skin before his chin rested against my temple.

"Kinsley, she'd never be able to wear that bracelet. On you it is a decoration. On her it would draw the eye as the only overpowering truth in the mix of lies. So much truth shines through in you, you overpower the bracelet. My world is made of lies with a cast of lying people. You may have things you hide, but you shine as the one genuine thing I'm drawn to."

Shit! "You shouldn't say such things," I said, my heart aching worse than any other part of my body now.

Rather than our normal quips when we tell one another we shouldn't do something, he said, "I know."

I felt his jaw muscle jump while I wanted to leap back into my apartment, hide away and cry for the liar I was in Klive's life after such words. What to say when I was speechless? When sorrow stole what was so wonderful and lust-inducing only minutes ago? How did we bounce from emotion-to-emotion like skipping from stone-to-stone between small streams of lava in our lives? How could I keep doing this?

Klive broke the tension I sensed him battling as well. He released my biceps and kissed the back of the hand he lifted to his lips, then placed my palm to his chest over his heart. Sonuvabitch!

"Please accept it, Kinsley. I saw it and thought only of you. Before you, I'd have bought it anyway because it was so beautiful, but with you in my life, it now has a worthy arm to compliment." His thumb stroked my hand. "I will say this now and never again because I should never have to reiterate, nor will I: *never* have I been involved with Angela. *Never* would I. She has made several attempts, like she did at the festival, but she's too high or dense to take a kind hint rather than a rude threat. The festival was the most brazen attempt she's ever made. She broke the last straw of patience I'd exercised for her. You've no idea the pleasure I derived from seeing you beat her ass. Because I didn't want you badly enough already."

I couldn't help myself. My free hand wound behind Klive's neck to urge his lips to mine so I wouldn't accidentally say *I love you.*

Klive smiled against my lips after pulling them with his a few sensual times. "If I'd have known all I had to was talk shit about your nemesis to earn a kiss, I'd have confessed my irritation sooner. Hell, if I spill more confessions, perhaps you'll stay the night." His lip popped in a pout. I chuckled and pulled that lip between my teeth.

"Sir, you need to behave."

"Your wish is my command. Just tell me which behavior you'd like most and I'll hit that list."

"Klive King, I'm gonna hit *you* if you don't stop." I grinned and pulled my hand from his heart to point at him.

He growled, quirked his brows, irises heated. "Tell me more and why I should stop when you deliver such threats." He laughed at the look I threatened him with. "All right, I concede. One more thing to appease Her Majesty while I'm being generous." He shut the safe and reached above to a cabinet too high for me to ever open without standing on a stool.

"Oh, Klive!" I cupped my awed mouth when he pulled the copper vase with the metal roses he'd bought at the festival.

"All of these were for you when I bought them."

"But you said they were for the women willing to please you in my place," I almost whispered. "You rarely say things you don't mean." Which hurt like a bitch, and now I realized why those words had stung so bad.

"Part of me meant what I said and liked the idea. I couldn't resist punishing you for bad behavior when you rejected me. Seeing as how we are now on friendlier terms, I'm revealing my cards." He offered the vase. "As I told you the day after the festival, I didn't touch another, nor did I allow another to touch me. Seems my vindictive pride is no match for your sweet sorrow, and my birthday didn't go off with the bang I'd longed for if only to end the torment you put me through. Neither did tonight for that matter." He winked at me when he drew a smitten grin.

"Klive, you didn't sleep with Natalie?" I sighed with girly bliss.

"Must you love my pain and suffering so much, my sweet?"

"Must you make me love your suffering because you're so willing to?" I placed my empty hand on his shoulder, stood on my tiptoes and kissed his cheek. "Klive!" I gasped when I saw deeper in the cabinet at this new angle. The brown suede top hat I'd thrown at him before driving away two years ago. He noticed me noticing the item and tsked with a small shake of his head.

"You don't get that back. You gave it to me fair and square."

I shook my head this time. "Klive, is that how you found me?"

"What do you mean?" he asked.

"Pass it over."

He shook his head like he was afraid I'd seriously keep the memento. Ha! We had a commonality. He loved my hat the way

I loved his coat! Girly sigh! Though I almost giggled at the idea of him wearing my hat around the house the way I wore his coat, I waved him to trust me. His sigh was not the fuzzy one mine was. He grabbed the hat and plunked the steampunk accessory into my hand like a petulant teen relinquishing a phone when in trouble. Klive's annoyance tugged the corners of my lips while I traced the inner elastic seam that helped the article stay on my head. Klive tilted his head as he watched me wiggle my finger until I produced a small slip of paper.

"Klive King, are you telling me you've never inspected this?" I asked when his lips parted as he read the handwriting.

"Kinsley Hayes," he said my name while reading, then met my eyes. "You shouldn't put your phone number out there for people to find." But the reprimand wasn't in his tone.

"If this wasn't how you found me, I'll interrogate you another time. Since you revealed your cards to me, I'm reciprocating. This paper, sir, is why I tossed my hat at you."

Klive's lips parted further as he seemed at a loss for words. The radiant smile that could turn any woman into a willing servant for him cast my way, boyish and bright, younger, disarming.

"You *wanted* me to find you? To call you?" he asked.

"To know me?" I offered with a small twitch of my eyebrow. I nodded.

"Now, it's you who shouldn't say such things if you don't want me to throw you into my bed and get to know you to the fullest." His eyes filled with so many emotions. I almost told him not to tempt me to say more so he'd do just that, but I wisely kept my mouth shut for once. He cursed under his breath though he also appeared short of oxygen. Was there a better feeling?

"For the sake of both of us, grab your effects. Get your shirt back on," he said with a wistful sort of wanton. He gingerly took the hat from my hands and tucked the article back behind the cabinet doors. "I'll be in the kitchen. Turn the Shisha Dog in the alcove to re-open the passage to the library. It will close on its own." He pressed a chaste kiss to my forehead and left me alone to redress while he walked out of his bathroom. I stood in the doorway of the Closet of Kinsley and watched the fire dancing in the fireplace, but jumped when I saw him walk past, my metal roses clanking in their vase.

Duh! Double-sided, Kins.

5 | ♀

When I turned the little stone artifact Klive called a Shisha Dog, I marveled at how the hidden passage opened like an adventure movie. I looked over my shoulder at the opulent, yet cozy room, like an explorer forced to leave the discovered tomb of a pharaoh to prevent curses from adhering to me and everyone in my life. I chewed my lip in thought of my parents, if they had any idea of who this man was ....

   I stepped through and watched the passage close behind me like leaving the portal of another world and coming back into the ugly reality of the problems Klive and I faced when passion wasn't our distraction. Especially since I heard him in the kitchen speaking on the phone to someone. I entered as quietly as possible so as not to disturb his business. To my dismay, the phone was on speaker, lying on the white surface as Klive rifled through the contents of his refrigerator. He took note of me and waved me toward the eat-in bar across from him. A conversation in the background like dispatch static paused the speech between him and whoever he was talking to. Klive handed me a couple of cookies, then leaned across the solid surface for a kiss he drew from my now tight lips.

   Why wasn't he hiding this from me?! What if I heard damning information? Did Jase want this type of stuff from me too?

   "Copy to dispatch. Fire extinguished. No signs of arson found."

My body tensed. I knew Klive felt the shift. Hell, he knew he'd caused this!

"You there?" Ray Castille's voice asked. Klive's eyes had this odd glint as they narrowed on my face while he was somewhere else in his mind.

"I am. Where is he?" Klive asked.

"If I knew, I damn sure wouldn't be calling you. He's in the wind."

Another voice in the background cursed about Ray calling Klive, how they should've waited or thought of anything else.

"Where's the product?" Klive asked, his gaze growing darker. He took my hand with the bracelet and turned my palm to trace the callouses like a coping mechanism. I could use one of those myself.

"He dumped it. One of the guys found it at the rendezvous point, but my guess is because he wasn't there, the buyer was spooked. Hell, for all I know, the cops could have him. Ansley's been pulling some weird shit and that's the real reason I'm bringing you in on this."

Yay! Sheriff Ansley in this mix of misery. Ugh. This just got better and better.

Klive's hand closed over mine. "I'm not cashing in favors with Ansley over something that isn't Nightshade's business. Especially after the disrespect I've endured because my girl doesn't want me spilling your blood for some reason." My mouth dropped. "Maybe she wants to do it herself." Klive tipped my mouth closed. "Who can know? Either way, I don't buy it."

"Come on, King. Can you just send one of your guys in to retrieve the product? I know y'all have your ways. We lose this, the Cubans might get involved."

Klive scoffed and rolled his eyes. "The Cubans are kosher with Nightshade. If Nightshade retrieves the product, we keep it *and* you back the fuck off my girl without me pulling another weapon, otherwise I'll call the Cubans myself."

Ray cursed. "Fine. Deal."

"Ray, this isn't a game. I'm serious. Kinsley's kept me from painting your brains in my crosshairs. I'm not keen on taking orders for too long when my finger is itching to pull this trigger."

When I gasped, Klive cupped my mouth and shook his head.

"Ray, I know you've been working with Juan Perez. You and I don't do work together while you work with him. He's been cut off and shunned. Is this his product your guys are pushing? That why you're afraid of the Cubans getting involved?"

I pried his fingers away to silently mouth, *I shouldn't be here!* with real fear in my eyes. Klive released my hand to walk around the bar to stand at my back. His arms wrapped around my body; his cheek planted against mine as we looked down at his lit phone. Ray stuttered through an explanation about this Juan guy. Klive's face lifted from mine while one of his arms tightened and his other hand came over my mouth. "Shh," he breathed at my ear.

My soul jumped ship when Klive shouted, "I don't *fucking care* what either of your excuses are! He's got a bounty on his head and I'm eager to add one on yours! You've the audacity to disrespect me, my girl, Nightshade, then call upon us to get you out of the bind you're in?! The police are breathing down your neck in some sting they've concocted to take you and Juan down together. Who do you think put them on your scent, asshole? You don't fuck with me or mine and live to tell the tale! I hope your little grunt in the background can hear my warning because if any of them so much as looks her way with anything other than reverence ever again, I'll take them all down without getting my hands dirty and notify the Cubans to claim your ground."

"*You set us up?!* King, *please*, call them off! I promise! The bullshit escalated into some stupid revenge plot, but what Juan wanted to do is beyond Inferno's scope! I wouldn't have let him have her! Shit, tell me how I fix this! I'll do anything!"

"I don't *believe* you!" Klive boomed while his thumbs brushed my bicep and cheek to somehow soothe me, but nothing could. Ray speaking of not allowing this guy, Juan, to have me, saying that whatever Juan was up to was beyond the horrid tales every local knew to steer clear of Inferno for. *Dear God! Was that why the crowd looked the way they did the night Patrick Scott and Pat Connor harassed me? Had Klive arranged for them to be in the bar?!*

"Name your price, King. I'll throw my job, house, Inferno up as collateral."

Whoever was with Ray cursed.

"What's it gonna take, King? This is my last chance. We go way back. I've never asked for a favor of this magnitude. I'm surrounded. Aside from the Cubans sniffin' blood in the air, the cops think I killed Patrick's wife. I was bangin' her, but I'd never kill such a good lay. I'd have sold her or loaned her out if I'd tired of her, but never killed her. You know it makes no sense to kill a source of income."

"Ha!" Klive laughed without humor while I trembled and twisted in his grasp to place my face to his chest. His arms came around my back and his fingers lightly scratched up and down. His warm breath slapped my temple. "I see what you're doing, trying to convince me to keep you alive like I need you for any value. I'd rather take the man to your right."

Ray gasped.

Klive grinned against my cheek once more. "Oh, yes. Eyes everywhere. Don't you love laser technology? Can paint a target without them ever seeing the beam or a dot."

My eyes bugged at how great Klive was at bluffing.

Ray cried out, along with his partner, that Klive not pull a trigger. Ray began asking what else Klive could want.

Klive's lips drew very close to my ear in a faint whisper. "Do you want me to kill him, love?" A hard tremor raced my body. I couldn't answer, so I shook my head. "Would *you* like to kill him?" he asked.

Again, I shook my head, unable to really figure out how to feel my limbs. "No violence?" Klive whispered. At first, I shook my head, but hurried and nodded. Klive's chuckle reverberated through my hair. "Do something for me?" Klive turned me in his arms and produced a steno pad and pen. He scrawled *Pads* or *Tampons?*

What the eff? What did Klive want me to do?

To Ray he said, "I'll accept your offer of collateral, including your bike, Inferno, the bars, the whole lot on the condition of proof in your word. If I think of anything further, I'll expect that demand to be met without hesitation, are we clear?"

"Deal. What do you want me to do?" Ray asked the same question. I swallowed as that bowling ball of earlier sweetness now expanded to a beach ball of dread in my throat.

Klive forced the pen in my palm and gestured I circle one. I hurried to circle tampons then write the level. Klive left my back to open a bread box. He produced a .40 caliber pistol and checked the clip right over the phone. Ray and his friend both remained silent, their breathing the only sound from their side.

"Eric, do me a favor, keep the target until I say. Have Sanders call in an anonymous tip to the police about the package Ray's man bailed on. Gives Ansley a small pacifier. If Ray fails to keep his word, fire on my signal. You know where to watch from."

But Eric wasn't on any phone line, at least not yet. *Was this part of seeing behind the curtain as Jase had stated?* Fascinating and terrifying.

"Ray, listen up and listen well. I'll say this once. Screw this up, I'm done." Ray agreed. "Come up the mangroves to my dock no less than fifteen minutes from now."

"I can do that."

"Ah, but I have something I want you to do first. Both of you." The men stayed silent for Klive's directions. "Since you've both behaved like bloody pussies and put the whole of Inferno on the line to save your own asses, stop on your way and buy a multipack of tampons. Not regular. Not super. I want a variety."

My tongue lined my cheek at Klive's British double entendre, especially in this tense capacity. I almost burst out laughing for relief from such an awful reality check.

"I don't know if we can get the boat in the slip fast enough if we have to stop first."

"Fifteen minutes starts now. If you're late, I'll make you shove them up each other's asses before I shoot you both and feed you to the sharks." Klive snickered silently across at me as he loved their panic.

"Yes, sir! Yes, sir!" both men said.

Klive ended the call, then relaxed like a stage actor who'd finished his lines.

"There. Situation resolved. I know it's not the original offer I gave of going myself, masculinity on the line and that lot, but it has to count for something, right?"

"Yeah." I managed a small smile for him, then bit my lip, looked down at his white counter and drew invisible shapes between the small speckles of silver ingrained in the solid surface. Though he'd lightened up, I was still afraid at this side of him. Klive was so very unpredictable. One minute sweet, even romantic, then domineering, arousal disappearing into a cold fiend, like a stranger. A mean, calculating man who now gave directions to Eric and a guy named Sanders.

Was Jase's cruelty toward me as bad as I'd thought if this were the side he got to see and watched me grow too close to in front of him without my giving him a choice? Ugh. What should I do?

Not befriend the bad guy, Kinsley. That would be colossal stupidity on your part, love, I thought with Klive's accent.

Klive ended the call and put his phone in his pocket. He rifled through the refrigerator once more, producing leftovers he offered

to me. I politely refused. For some strange reason I had no appetite
....

"Kinsley, I have to take care of this, then I'll see you home, all right? This won't take long."

To my surprise, Klive walked around the bar to scoop me into his arms, carrying me back toward the library while I held the stuff he'd gifted me. I could've walked, but why bother with words or protests when he'd just been so scary? When he paused before the passage, the stone Shisha dog turned under my grip. I noted the appearance in this one was a tad different, though they were made of the same stone.

He carried me through the double doors I'd left wide open to his bedroom and laid me on the plush bed. From his nightstand, he took a remote and pushed a button that made a large projection screen drop from the ceiling. When he turned off the lights, I felt I was in a movie theater with the best seating ever. The fireplace still flickered, and anxiety collided with exhaustion at once.

"Here's the remote." He gave me a sweet kiss, though his look was still serious. "I know I made you nervous. I know Ray makes you nervous for good reason. I want you to stay in here. He doesn't need to know you're here. I'd hate to have to kill him for looking at you the way he did last time."

"What are you going to do?"

"It's simple, Kinsley. My job. Tonight, that doesn't entail killing unless he oversteps the boundaries I've defined. We've a few matters I need to iron out. Please, don't fret your head about this. It won't take long, then they'll be gone, and I'll take you back."

"Klive, that night at the Ren fest when you said Ray had been punished, is this what you meant?" I knew I shouldn't pry in order to maintain plausible deniability but couldn't help my curiosity. "Did you really set him and his guys up with Ansley?"

"Indeed, my sweet. And I may have called the Cubans to scare the shit out of him just for you." He winked like a cat who'd just murdered and disemboweled a squirrel as a show of loyalty for my doorstep. I had a hard time accepting his version of a gift. The bracelet and clothing were far more preferable. Klive studied my face while I nodded the only thanks I might muster. He crawled on top of me, forcing me to lie back on his sumptuous covers as he loomed over me. I blinked hard to dispel how hot this image was even if I was on edge. His mouth descended to warm my cold blood with his hot lips. How naive I am.

Klive's lips nudged mine apart. I almost lost control as the need to feel anything but tension engulfed me to the point of moaning moments later. His body rested heavy enough to press hard against the perfect distraction from the awful truths he forced me to face before he pushed off the bed too soon.

"Relax, love. Please. Watch something and put this out of your mind."

Ha! As if!

I swallowed as I watched Klive vanish behind the double doors he closed tight. *If I crept through the doors, would I be able to hear anything with my ear near the shelf passage thing? Was I as green as I felt?*

Had Klive really come to kill me at some point or was it all a bluff like I'd witnessed in the kitchen? Had he had conversations like the one with Ray while contemplating how to take me out?

In the here and now, I couldn't think straight enough to recall all Klive's words to me when the only ones hammering my temples now were about him coming for me, that I'd be a willing participant, that I'd hold tight. Well, here I was, willingly beneath him in his plush bed, ready to be beneath him for far longer than we'd had before he'd left. He'd said he'd be creative, well, how creative was this? To stay with the guys at all times. Lookie, lookie, as soon as I stepped away from Jase ....

If Tyndall hadn't been in the room at Pensacola or with me at the faire, would Klive had tried something then?

I gulped several deep breaths while reasoning with myself. Even I was putting too much of myself out there for Klive to exploit, I was still doing my part for Jase. Tyndall's voice chimed through my thoughts, urging me to grow a conscience in someone so capable of evil. *Was that possible?* Even my education seemed out of reach in my current brain fog. Reformation was always a good idea in theory, but if reformation worked, we wouldn't have places like the Ohio State Reformatory filled with demons and disastrous attempts to fix problems that only grew.

He did confess to me making him want to be a better man ... then again, he was deceptive, complex. Maybe some borderline personality disorder or Bi-polar?

I crept up to the double doors and pressed my ear to the wood. The only sound I heard was the low hum of air conditioning. I pursed my lips while easing the knob open and crept toward the passage. *Would they be in the library? What if they were and Klive decided to come back into his room? Crap.* I swallowed as I heard voices. *This was a very bad idea! I didn't want to be used as a witness! Abort!*

I eased behind the double doors and pulled them closed as quietly as possible then dashed to the bed. *Where was the remote?* I patted the blankets and hurried to speak "Too Cute" into the remote. The kitten episodes were my favorite after watching scary movies. Since this felt like a scary movie, I needed sweet kittens to calm my racing heart.

The remote stayed in my palm like a stress ball while I nestled into Klive's pillows. I closed my eyes, taking measured breaths and silently counting. *Cologne. Aftershave. Shampoo. Detergent. Clean, fresh, soothing. Klive.*

After a few minutes, I opened my eyes on the stories of the little litters and wondered what Klive was doing. I wished I had a kitten right now. When I got home, I planned to grab my mom's cat, Sphinx, and force him to sleep with me against his will.

My body jolted when Klive strolled through his double doors and smiled the way a king might toward the concubine he'd chosen from his harem to please him for the night. At this point, that might be easier. Rather than toss me an innuendo, I caught two boxes of tampons and laughed in surprise.

"All done, my sweet. No violence. Tough to resist, but it was for you."

Wow. Would he have done things differently had I not requested he behave? Tyndall!

Klive snagged the tampons and tossed them to the other side of the bed. "Come here, love."

I crawled across the comforter, sitting on my knees before him. He wrapped his arms around my waist and rested his head on my chest above my heart. *Um. Was he* hugging *me?* After a beat, I wrapped my arms around his head, cradling him, forcing myself to release all the tension coiled between my shoulders.

"I'm proud of you," I offered.

"Proud of me? Whatever for?" he asked with his chin to my chest, brows creased.

"No violence." I smiled. "Thank you."

He chuckled then tossed me across the bed, making me squeal. *Wow! Affectionate and playful Klive in one setting?* He jumped onto the bed and tugged me back to him once he'd settled into the spot I'd kept warm for him.

"What are you watching, love?"

I told him, admitted why and he folded his arm beneath his head.

"Interesting. I should watch this, too. Might make me a nicer person." He smiled up at me where I sat leaning against the pillows beside him. The companion pillows. I couldn't help committing this to memory, the way his face lit while he looked at me the way a normal couple studies each other. He evaluated me on his pillows like he'd dreamed of me the way I had him. The radiance in his expression was almost breathtaking. *If I stared too long, would I be cursed like staring at Medusa? If I got lost in this man, would I turn to stone, or would he soften? Who would win?*

I swallowed and forced myself to watch the kittens playing with one another. Klive took my hand to urge me down beside him. I cuddled into the crook of his left arm he wrapped around me. *Woo! I thought his kisses knocked the breath outta me! This was far more intimate than I should care to be but couldn't help enjoying.* I laid my face against his still bare chest, listening to his breathing and heart beating, relishing the strength in the arm around me, his fingers trailing my arm ever so lightly.

"Kins, you're safe, all right?" he spoke against my hair. "I'd never allow Ray to get near you. You're no longer in danger with me. You never really were. I'm not going to do anything to put you in danger, either quite the contrary."

My breath hitched at the sincerity and emotion behind his tone. If Jase were telling the truth, wouldn't this count as mission accomplished where my being on Klive's hit list was concerned? Not only that, but Klive would *protect* me against everyone, including Ray—hallelujah!

I mustered the courage to tilt my head enough to see his eyes. "Thank you, Klive." He just looked down at me, his hand absently playing in my hair, caressing and curling small strands around his fingers like he might be memorizing me, too.

"Anything you want, love." He grinned, lightening us both from the heaviness that was this chemistry. "Are you certain you wouldn't like to stay ...?" He smoothed the hair from my forehead. Dammit. His expression was the sweet, fuzzy one I buckled under. I sighed and pushed up from his chest though I wanted to sleep there all night. *What would happen if I took him up on that invitation? He wanted me to stay even though sex was off the table? Gosh, I was easy to win.* Seems Jase weakened my once strong defenses. So much for playing hard to get anymore, especially with how Klive studied my face for clues. *Here, sir, have all the ice cream you want! You want the whole damn truck, go right on ahead and take it. I mean, we both know you wanted to drive anyway.*

Couldn't even blame alcohol on this.

"I can't, Klive. Not in good conscience. Besides, I have class tomorrow."

He nodded while that jaw muscle flinched in his cheek, disappointment stealing all the radiance like dousing a fire.

I sighed. "Hey, don't look at me like that," I almost pleaded. Our dynamic had shifted so much in a few hours, and I was so weak with want for the same things he wanted at the same time.

Klive tickled my ribs, making me laugh out of nowhere, then he rolled off his bed. He walked to a door I assumed was his closet. He went inside and came out wearing another nicely casual shirt, then extended his hand. When I took his fingers, he pulled me to my knees on the mattress in front of him.

"Your purse." He placed the leather in my hands. "Tools." A tampon box went inside while I giggled. "These stay here just in case." He waved the other box and went into his bathroom. I heard a cabinet close before he came back to stand before me. "Ready?"

Hell, no, I most certainly am not.

I nodded. "Klive, thank you." I climbed off the bed to wrap my arms around his waist, head resting against his chest again, hugging him to me this time. "I love the bracelet, the dress, the shoes, the nightgown, the roses ..." I tipped my head back, added the doe eyes like a weapon. "This ..." I squeezed him a fraction. Even if I knew what I was doing, I was genuine. "Thank you for thinking of me both then and now. For not wanting anyone else even after I was so mean so many times ...." I cast my eyes away for an insecure moment, Jase's words haunting my heart. A whore in heat — a category with the women he'd meaninglessly screwed. I hated that my soul sought nourishment and found such in a man who was everything bad, but professing to finding me worth sacrificing birthday sex, all sex for *two whole years*, even though we were no way close to being together at the time.

Klive's hand skimmed my hair as if he sensed my ache. His fingers hooked my chin, and this time when I looked at him with the same big eyes, there was no adding the vulnerability by choice. His cheeks puffed as he pulled his hand to run his fingers through his always perfect hair before scrubbing his mouth as he searched my face. His other arm wrapped tighter around me.

"Woman, you are going to be the death of me," he said like a resolution rather than an endearment. "I should've killed you when I had the chance. Now I will regret it every time you look at me that way." He grinned down at me. I warmed instantly and sagged against him.

"Should I take that as a compliment, or ...?" I cringed like a fool to make him smile, which he did.

"Indeed. That's the first time Klive King has ever given a woman such credit or influence. If I were you, I'd be flattered," he said with a smug smirk. I rolled my eyes, though my lips split on a full smile. Klive shook his head again and pulled away to grab my stuff before taking my hand. We made our way out of the room, through the kitchen. I inhaled deeply wanting to remember the scent of vanilla, sandalwood, cedar, cologne and soap — Klive.

He reached over the bar for his keys, hit the lights and once again, we were in the darkness. I could no longer see.

"Maybe I should put you across the kitchen counter, take you right here, right now," he growled at my ear, sending electric thrills through my skin. I heard my stuff being laid on a counter before he tugged me back against his chest and walked me forward until I pressed against his counter. He bent us both over so I laid on top of the solid surface, him on top of me. "What do you think, love? Sound fun?" Klive's naughty hand traveled over my bottom, and he squeezed while I jumped in surprise at how bold he was after remaining chaste toward me for so long.

"Klive, let's go," I breathed, desperate to fight my longing for him.

"Where? Right here, or back in the bedroom?" he asked with a smile in his voice.

"Your car."

"Oh, I dunno if I want you ruining my new leather," he teased.

"Klive! Come on!" I looked at the clock on the oven. Ten-fifteen. "If I get back now, I won't have to explain to the guys where I was or who I was with. They won't be done with their gig until eleven. Please?"

"Hmm ... you make an excellent point. I don't want you in trouble until there's a real reason. You win. *This* time." He lifted me from the countertop and guided me back down the dark hallway to the garage.

6 | ♀

On the way back to the bar, Klive decided I may have the best shot at pretending I'd never left at all and just worked in the back with the bar-back and dishwasher. I praised his creativity, but considering I'd disappeared as soon as Klive had, too, that was likely wishful thinking. Then again, who cared considering I was no one's girlfriend?

Klive stopped at the by the back employee entrance. I opened the car door but looked at Klive one last time.

"Thanks for cheering me up, Klive. You made a very bad night a good one."

He leaned across the seats, stole my fingers, then planted his lips to the back of my hand. "Glad to help, my sweet."

I almost shuddered from his touch like instant tingles to my skin. Klive cast a victory smile when I accidentally sighed like a fool.

"Now, that's what I like to hear," he told me.

I rolled my eyes. "Uh, huh. Don't let that go to your head."

"Already has. I'm ruined and you've only yourself to blame, beautiful. Sweet dreams."

When he drove away, I did shudder to get the jolts out of my skin. I texted Bayleigh to please bring my keys so I could put my things in the car without the guys seeing me. That and to get myself under control before I needed to pretend I hadn't just had the most incredible crazy intense experience. She met me at the back door and pressed for every crumb I'd feed her.

"Can I tell you another time? I'm just trying to get myself together while making it seem like I still don't have it all together, if that makes sense?" I opened my car as I filled her in on my plan.

"I get it, girl. Happy to help."

We walked inside to the room with the cooler, sink and stainless-steel counter where the bar-back chopped fresh fruit. He told Bayleigh he was almost done with her orange slices.

"Thanks, babes. Mind if we send you to the front to put them in the bins and sweep the floor while Kins chops the rest of the fruit and washes some dishes?"

He looked over his shoulder, his knife pausing.

"I'll give you half my tips if you pretend I've been back here helping you the whole time," I threw in. His eyes traveled between us before he dried his hands on a towel he had over his shoulder. He shook on my offer and vamoosed with the orange slices. Bayleigh tugged me to the sink, then looked down at where she gripped my wrist.

"Holy shit, Kins, did TDH give *this* to you, too?" I nodded and gnawed my lower lip. "Damn, he's not one to wait for the blood to dry on someone's wounds, is he?" Oh boy. That was quite the phrase where Klive was concerned. "I'm not complaining. Jase was a dick. It's beautiful, but you need to take it off before anyone sees this and spreads word to him because you and I both know drunk guys don't rationalize anything."

Oh, thank the Lord for her. I hadn't even thought of this.

"He's drunk?" I asked.

"Yeah. That's putting it mildly." She helped me take the pearls off and slipped them into her apron pocket before dousing the front of my waist with water. I tossed a towel over my shoulder after we wiped our hands dry.

"Kins, I need five limes and a refill on cherries, maraschino and stemmed. Good luck. Stay strong and stay back here if you can. Make a pot of coffee, please?"

Damn! We only pulled coffee for emergencies!

"Whoa, Bayleigh. He's seriously that bad?"

"Yes. Marcus is ready to have him hauled out, but he's afraid of Jase driving drunk, so Rustin is singing lead while Mel drums, but Dan is foregoing his bass to babysit, so it's more like an acoustic session or something."

"Wow. I don't think I've ever seen Jase do this to his band before. Coffee, limes and cherries coming up. Want me to deliver his coffee?" I almost cringed. Her nose crinkled like we smelled something awful as she nodded.

"I'm sorry, babes."

"I'm sorry I left y'all in a bind earlier. Not to mention dating someone from work. Never again."

She snorted and nodded, then left me alone. I went into the cooler for the fruit but paused inside to cool my nerves and the heat I still felt in my cheeks from Klive's hot touch.

"You can do this, Kins. Man-up," I whispered to myself. The cartons of fruit in hand, I made quick work of cleaning and cutting the produce, though for the first time in my life, I wished the coffee pot took longer because when I came up behind the bar to refill the fruit bins, I glanced at the stage area. Jase was tucked into the booth he'd tucked me into when I'd gotten drunk by mistake. His hair hung with his head. He weaved in a daze as he stared at the table. Ugh. Beside him, a dyed redhead ran her fingers up and down his left arm, nails strumming along his dragon tattoo. That one. I hated her. Then again, I couldn't be upset about this considering I'd almost had sex with the enemy.

Go time. I released a nervous breath and plastered a realistic expression of bitterness on my face. Rustin's sober survey stared right through me as I carried my tray of coffee and their drinks toward the stage. To make matters worse, Rustin announced a short break. Did he intend on lecturing the two of us in that time-out booth? Rustin said something to the redhead. She nodded and left before I got to their table. Damn right, bitch.

Really, Kins? Effin' hypocrite. I shook my head at my thoughts and Rustin must've thought I was shaking my head at him because he took the tray out of my hand. Jase snatched my fingers exactly the way Klive had only fifteen minutes ago, but for the first time ever, the butterflies inside me were too sleepy to flutter at Jase's touch. He hugged me so hard, my back popped, which was a nice bonus, but I couldn't breathe for too many reasons.

"Jase, you need to let go of me *now*," I told him like the growl before a bite. This wasn't the best idea. Klive should've taken me home instead.

"Kins, baby, please hear me out."

My finger automatically shot to his lips. "Don't call me that. If it was bad before, it's ten times worse now."

He put his finger beneath my chin and forced me to look into those honey eyes as if he were a deaf man with a death wish.

"Jase Taylor, you're a fool to do this here and now."

"I'm a fool for more than that, sweet Kins."

My arms crossed beneath my chest like a petulant child. I loathed my threatening tears seeing the similar sheen in his bloodshot eyes, not to mention the alcohol fumes burning my nose. I tried looking away, but he begged me not to.

"Baby, I'm so mad about you. Please forgive my pathetic ego and wounded pride for so eagerly destroying your honor and good name?" His words were so beautiful, so Jane Austen, as though when he was unfiltered, this was how he thought. I'd have liked the words far more without the slurring. He went on. "I'm bad at love, you know, like that song?" Ugh. Come on. Was he spying on me? "I don't know what the hell I'm doing. I've never been in a relationship where I loved the person. Like, I've never loved someone else. I've never known what it's like to care if I push someone away or how to keep someone. I'm new at this and at our first fight, instead of easing your mind, I insulted you. I cut your heart when I was the one who used to mend it. I'm such an asshole. I'll spend the rest of my miserable days making it up to you. Just please forgive me and say that you won't cut me out of your life?"

"Hey, whoa, whoa, calm down, Jase. Shh, shh." I placed my fingers over his lips without wanting to slap him this time. My eyes darted around us to see how many eavesdropped on his shrill pleading. The only eyes I found staring hard were the redhead's. He calmed. I stewed.

"I'll lower my voice," he said quietly. "Please, please, Kins, don't cut me out of your picture."

I almost chortled at the image of me going through my things and cutting Jase's head out of photos of us the way his sister, Tyndall, loved to do before burning the remains. I only had a few photos of Jase with me in them and they were more like family memories. The only recent photo was the one of us on the beach that he'd texted me.

I gnawed my lower lip while his head weaved as he searched my face from beneath his hanging hair. I was sober. He was not. Best we do not have this conversation when he wouldn't remember much. Then again, maybe if I confessed now, he may not give me such a hard time when he did sober?

With a sigh, I caved and said, "Jase, stop apologizing. I'm not innocent and you shouldn't be begging me for forgiveness when Klive whisked me away to his castle for the past few hours." I waited for the surprise to register, jealousy or anger, something like last night's verbal death match, but none came. In fact, his eyes stayed so still and focused I wanted to scratch my hair and side-eye Rustin to see if I was imagining things. Jase wasn't clouded the way most drunks stared. How did this make any sense?

"I know." Jase's honey irises searched mine. "I pushed you into his arms. His bed, too?" he dared, eyes darting to my chest.

Ugh. Didn't matter if Klive and I wanted to sleep together, I hated Jase's presumption that I was so easy, and what a slap in my face that tonight, I'd almost been. Thank God for mother nature's curse keeping my morals in place when I wasn't thinking straight! Though my tongue traced inside my cheek for a sec, I didn't want to make the scene or provoke the mean side of Jase again. Best to opt for pretend peace.

"No," I said, "Not his bed, well, I mean I jumped on it because it was so ridiculously plush. I had no choice, but I didn't sleep with him." I smiled as best I could to sell my playful bit.

He laughed, then pulled me against his chest to squeeze me. I hugged him back, desperate for us to go back to normal, or some sort of version of how we once were.

"Thank God," he whispered. He pulled back, assessing my face. "Kins, you really jumped on his bed? Did you mess it all up?"

I cackled and slapped his chest. "I messed it up, yes, but not enough to get under his skin." I glanced away and chewed my cheek.

"Hey, baby, right here. What is it?"

His warm hand cupped my cheek so I couldn't hide from him.

"Jase, he was sweet. He gave me things, and, well, I took them."

"Like what? Jewelry or something?"

"A beautiful bracelet, a dress, shoes, an open invitation." I wanted to be honest because I wanted to wear the bracelet, and I didn't want him asking me not to later.

"Yet here you are in my arms, not in his bed as we speak. You were able to resist. Amazing, Kins. I'm very impressed. That guy is an operator." He squinted and looked up like he was thinking, stupid smile across his face. "Much like myself, no female could stand against powers like these."

"Ah, so I see." I glanced down the way at the redhead. When I looked back at Jase, a guilty blush stole across his cheeks for the first time in my reflection of him. I didn't like this look or nagging alarm bells. This was nothing like the bashful blush around my father when planning life. This held a heavy burden.

A quietly observing Rustin decided to jump in. "Hey, in his defense I told him he needed to get laid by someone that wasn't all Kinsleyesque, but he kept pointing out things in each one of them that you had, you know, like breasts and legs." He winked at me while I fought a grin. Rustin made air quotes and replayed their conversations. "'What about her, Jase?' 'Kinsley's boobs are better.' 'What about that one, Jase?' 'Kinsley's legs are in way better shape.' 'Jase, you want another drink?' 'Kinsley serves me drinks.'"

Hmm ... was I imagining things, or was Rustin's rascally demeanor peppered with overcompensation?

My mouth dried like I'd eaten too much salt, but I forced a smile to keep ice on both mine and Jase's hot tempers. If what happened last night ever happened at the bar, Marcus would fire us on the spot.

"Is this true, Jase? Was Rustin urging you to sleep with other women?" I poked Rustin's chest. *"Si oui, essayait-il de vous obtenir aussi lui permettre de dormir avec eux en même temps, juste comme avec me?"* In other words, *was he also trying to get Jase to share them like me?*

"'Rustin, want some French fries?' 'Kinsley speaks French.'" Jase jabbed Rustin's ribs.

Rustin side-eyed his bestie, then lifted his lips in a smirk very reminiscent of Mr. King. "Does this mean I can still kiss your ass?"

"I swear, you are one dumb cow-poke, Hickleberry."

"I prefer Oracle. You see, I know you're gonna tell me to kiss your ass at some point. I'm predicting the future and seeking clarification on this vision of mine."

My arms crossed under my breasts; lips pursed. *Do not smile. Do not smile.* Rustin read me too well. Bastard.

"I also see a future of forgiveness," he said with little nod. I chuffed and shook my head. "Ah, c'mon. Isn't forgiveness the cornerstone of your faith? Here I am giving you a way to practice outside the holy walls and you're turning down the opportunity?"

He winced when I punched his bicep. "The tray is there with your drinks and his coffee. I have work to do."

"Jesus knows!" he called after me. I scooped empty bottle necks between my fingers, three in each hand from a nearby table. Before leaving them for the bar, I faced both men staring at me.

"How about this? I'll consider forgiveness only if I can keep my pretty gifts."

Jase's ankles crossed as he leaned back against the stage. "Baby, I'm not your boyfriend. You can keep whatever you want." Oh hell ... no need for an oracle to predict impending doom after such a dismissive tone and body language.

"Jase ..." What to say? Not like I was eager to run back into his arms, but if he'd just spouted all those pretty words, why was he now shoving me away?

"Kins, you broke up with me for a reason. You needed your space, then I pissed you off, and you took more space than I liked. Fact is, you shouldn't have to worry if I am going to be mad at you if you kissed someone, accepted gifts or anything else. Golden rule applies."

My eyes bugged then squinted. Hot ire burned my cheeks. Yes, he'd had more to drink than was good for someone who didn't want his balls kicked.

"If you want Klive, go be with Klive."

"Jase," Rustin said, "Know when to stop talking." I nodded with this advice.

Jase grimaced at Rustin and shrugged. "What? I am not hers, she's not mine. She shouldn't be asking permission for shit." My cheeks stung like he'd slapped me across the face. Sure, alcohol could be blamed for his dramatic mood shifts, but I'd rather not make excuses for a grown-ass adult who'd claimed a desire to marry me a few short weeks ago. What bullshit!

"All meaningless," I muttered when I crossed behind the bar. The bottles slammed into the trash can. Bayleigh rushed over and put her hands on my cheeks.

"No, don't listen to him. He's drunker than I've ever seen him, remember?"

"Bay, we both know some shitty alcoholics who come in here spouting hard truths no one wants to hear. Don't lie for him."

Was Jase in the habit of proclaiming love to get laid the way he did to me?

Bayleigh swallowed. At least her palms were cold from lifting brews off ice.

"I should call Moonlight and tell him I'll be over in fifteen minutes."

She shook her head. "You don't want to do that."

"Why, Bayleigh? I thought you wanted me to pick him." I sniffled while she brushed away the tears leaking down my face.

"Kins," she whispered, glanced around us to be sure no one eavesdropped. "Moonlight isn't a booty-call or a rebound. He's too important to use."

"I know." My voice cracked. I sucked breath trying to stave off sobs in public. "Thank you." She was right about Klive, but I wasn't seeking sex from Klive as much as longing for his authority to check these emotions, his still gray gaze calming the churning tide inside me.

Bayleigh released my face, squeezed my shoulders then hustled refilling orders. I used a cocktail napkin to clean my face in the mirror behind the liquor bottles. Rustin appeared in the reflection. Bayleigh offered him another drink, but he politely refused.

I spun on my heel and gripped the chunky wood bar. "Rustin, look me straight in the eyes and tell me the truth. Did Jase sleep with anyone since last night?" No answer. Betrayal sliced the last thread on my patience. "I'm clocking out, Bay. I refilled the fruit bins, made coffee. I'm done. I need to leave now." Not a soul argued with me. A minute later, I shoved through the back employee door and gulped fresh air. Rustin's leather jacket crinkled when his arms encircled me. "Who did he sleep with? When? Where? Why?"

"Kinsley, he didn't mean to." Rustin's voice vibrated through my ear at his chest. "He was drunk. Carmen's pulling surveillance tonight. She followed but had to stay out of the community. When she reported, he found out you'd gone to Klive's house." He stroked my hair and continued. "I was only joking with you about trying to get him laid, that's the awful irony. A girl pulled him into the bathroom, took advantage of him. I walked in and stopped him. He cried. Real tears. I haven't seen him cry since my father's funeral. He's a wreck. I don't think he could tell you what she looked like."

Oh, I knew what she looked like! *The effing redhead! She must've been watching and waiting for my reaction, that bitch!*

"I've had to sing most of the set. Marcus isn't paying him because his performance has been so shitty. Do you know how relieved he is that you didn't sleep with Klive? How relieved *I* am?"

"Rustin, I'd know because that's how relieved I'd feel right now if you said that everything you just told me wasn't true!" I sobbed.

"Stop it." He grabbed my shoulders and held me at arm's length. "Let's be real for a second. You didn't sleep with Klive out of moral obligation, but because you're on the rag. I know it. Don't be like this! Forgive him. Get over it." He dropped his grip and grabbed his waist like a cop, his eyes locked onto a suspect he was ready to draw a confession from. "How close were you, Kinsley? Would you have stayed the night? The week? I was honest with you! Return the favor! Now! Did he give you that stuff before or after he almost slept with you? Did you promise him a raincheck? Huh?"

Whoa! Rustin was angry with me, and he should be.

"Extend the same courtesy you asked of me. Be honest. You are so into him," he finished with too much personal emotion mixed into his previous professionalism.

"All right! Fine! Yes, I am attracted to him!" I threw a hand his way then rubbed the back of my neck thinking of Klive doing the same. I sighed and looked Rustin in the eyes. "Yes, I might have slept with him if it weren't for my period! He still wanted to! I couldn't do it. Yes, I gave him a raincheck! He already had the stuff at his house mixed with things in my size; these were things he gave me to take home! I am a despicable person, yes! Are you satisfied?" I fisted my hands on my hips, though my head hung dejectedly.

"I'm not satisfied, Kinsley. I'm *sorry*." In that moment, Rustin dropped all facades, his shoulders relaxing, hands cupping the back of his head as he glanced at the sky before his pleading eyes landed on my face again. My insides quaked seeing that depth of emotion, an evident longing that he wasn't tethered to his foolish friend. In the open here and now, I read clearly in his eyes that he wished to take me away from all of this with him somewhere alone. The same look I give Klive.

God, help him if he cared for me the way I did for Klive. What an effed-up mess!

Rustin sighed, weary and exhausted from a strain he kept to himself. "Kinsley, no one knows him the way I do. *Please*, forgive him. I know it might be hard, but he's afraid of you. You are everything to him. He's afraid of losing you on your terms, so he's trying to make it on his terms for self-loathing material. Would you do me a solid and refuse him the satisfaction?"

I couldn't agree more with his summation. My emotions met the backburner when seeing Jase's bullshit in dawning light.

"All right, Rustin." I nodded. "Let the juke box finish the set while you take him home. Marcus will understand. I'll drive to Jase's in the morning and fix this."

"I appreciate that … and … well, yeah …" He nodded at a loss for words when he'd already evidently said more than he should've. Rustin cast one, final longing gaze over his shoulder before his back disappeared behind the slamming door. I bent and gripped my knees, gulped more air while choking down Rustin's personal revelation. Jase may have treated me like one of his gauche groupies tonight, but Rustin stared at me like his one-night-stands were over.

Oh, Klive, get a grip on my mess so I don't destroy these men and myself in the process!

7 | ♀

When I got back to my house, the clock read almost one. I trudged up the stairs, dragging the weight of Jase's rapid descent into someone's panties along with my reciprocal near miss with Klive. Though Rustin called my shit and made me own up, I puzzled over Jase's justification. I hadn't trashed Jase to hell and back, he'd trashed me. At Klive's, my alcohol consumption revealed truths I didn't want to confess to Klive or myself. Did that mean Jase, in all his drunkenness, was eager to sleep with someone else?

Ugh. Remind me why I wanted a relationship with anyone?

The doorknob twisted under my hand. *Unlocked! Shit, shit, shit!*

All anger toward Jase fled my mind as I flew back down to my car, looking up at my balcony as I yanked the driver's door open.

Twirling keys around his finger, Klive leaned over the railing.

"Sonuvabitch!" I slammed my car door and fisted my hands on my hips. "What the hell?" I yelled up at him.

"Shh …." His finger tapped his lips. "The neighbors will hear you," he said with a smile.

"Maybe I want them to!" I shouted.

"Come now, love, don't be angry. Join me up here and have a chat. Where's your bracelet?"

Oops! The bracelet was still with Bayleigh. I'd have to text her ASAP.

I trudged upstairs and motioned for him to go back inside while I followed.

"Should I even bother with the lock? I mean the only monster I'm trying to keep out is inside. For convenience, I should just leave the door wide open, huh? Easier that way. Like rolling out the welcome mat."

Klive cleared his throat, barely concealing amusement, and straightened his face. "You left your purse in my car. Forgive me, but don't you females have a hard time living without them?" He dangled my house key off his finger.

Nice. I jerked my keys and purse out of his hands.

"You couldn't have brought it to the bar?"

"I was under the impression you were done working when I took you earlier. I didn't know you were going to stay. I've only been here for about thirty minutes."

I arched an eyebrow. "*Only* thirty minutes?" I slammed the door closed.

"What's the matter? Bad night?"

I threw my hands up and nodded. "Is it showing?"

He shrugged. "That or PMS. No idea which. Perhaps a bit of both?" That same stupid smirk checking his real smile lit his lips. "I've always wondered, why *pre*menstrual syndrome is somehow the explanation for the same symptoms *during* menstruation? Is it supposed to be a private understanding that we are all expected to navigate? Asking for a friend since I don't have relationships and the lot." He watched my tongue trace the inside of my cheek. "Need some chocolate?" He winked, so I shoved him hard at the same time kicking a leg under his feet. Though surprised, he went down like someone practiced in the art. Rather than trying to catch himself, he reminded me of a kid preparing to do a somersault from their back before he peered up at me from the carpet.

"You've got a lot of nerve. You know I love him, right?" I'd been enamored in Klive enough to sleep with him earlier but were I to sleep with him now that the buzz was gone, I knew I'd hate myself — not only for inflicting pain on Jase like what I felt now, but because I couldn't just jump into bed with Klive after everything we'd been through.

I watched his jaw muscle flinch. "I love him, Klive. You still want someone who loves someone else?" I stood over him. He didn't try to get up, he just looked up at me and I hated that I loved Klive, too.

"You're *hurt*?" Klive's smug amusement vanished while realization dawned. "Whatever must've happened in the short span since I left you?" His brows knit as he snagged my hand and pulled me down. I sat on his belly with one leg at each of his sides. Far too intimate given the context, but I didn't care.

My face fell into my palms, and I sobbed, unable to keep from breaking in his presence. Klive sat up and urged my head to his shoulder, then wrapped his arms around me. I wrapped my arms around his neck and nestled close to his skin to breathe his cologne. I gravitated to his distinctive scent like a pouty baby to a tasty pacifier.

"Klive, I can't sleep with you. This hurts too bad!" My voice broke as tears fell to his collar. "Jase slept with someone ... he had sex with her ... in the bathroom at the bar! Tonight! Sure, it's not the same as going home to sleep together the way we almost did, but I didn't set out to your place with the intention of sleeping with you! Damn, that's *my* workplace! A bathroom I clean! He was so drunk, but that's no excuse! My heart hurts so bad! I hate love and relationships. I hate sex and what people do with it, for it, without it—"

"Hey, shh, shh, shh ... let's not get too carried away, love."

"How am I supposed to be after he—" I gasped for air without finishing. "I can't breathe, Klive. I can't get enough air! How could he claim the L-word? Act like he's loved me, for like, forever, then turn on me so viciously at our first fight?! Call me a whore so easily, tear me down, then do everything he projected onto me? I don't want love if this is what it means. You're smart to never love anyone, Klive. What a fool I am."

"Shh, Kins, you shouldn't say such things." Klive tightened his arms around me and rubbed my hair while he let me cry. I went on and on about Jase, about what a horrible person I was for almost sleeping with Klive, about how right Jase was about my slutty behavior. No matter how annoying I was, he stayed put and let me hurt while he held me till I was down to hiccupping whimpers at his neck.

"Alright, enough," he said when I fell silent. "You've spoken your piece. I will hear no more on this matter." His chin turned and nudged me away from his neck. I sniffled and stared at him, surprised by his firm tone. "*No more* talk of you being a trashy whore or being unworthy of love because you chose to wait. No more comparing yourself to others who came before you. None of it, am I understood?" The look in his eyes was so ... *severe*. His eyebrow arched.

I cringed. "Yes, sir," I whispered in intimidation. He sighed and stroked my hair, his lips brushing my own with a soothing kiss as though we were fully operational in that capacity. He kissed me until I reciprocated.

"There's my girl. My girl is not a whore. She is not a slut. She is beautiful," he told me with a kiss. "Courageous." Another kiss. "Spirited." Kiss. "Doesn't run from pain. She's stronger than any foolish man behaving like a bloody boy tells her. *You* are smarter than allowing another to define your person. I will hear nothing else. If I see these things, love them, he'd be a daft wanker not to love the same," he said against my lips while I melted into a smile.

"Did you go into full Brit mode for me?"

"I've no bloody idea what you mean." His smile presented while he coaxed my lips a couple more times. I relaxed and studied him as he pulled away. "Now, onto the other matter. Were you officially his girlfriend when *his* slutty incident occurred? Was he exclusively yours?" I shook my head as I began to protest my case, but he put his hand up to stop me. "Kinsley, you need to be fair. You cannot keep doing this. You do not get to sleep with multiple people because you cannot make your mind up, or simply made a randy mistake, and not expect to offer him the same freedoms. Both of them. Make no mistake, Rustin is in as deep as Taylor which isn't right. You either commit to someone, or you don't, period."

"But —" Every time I opened my mouth to argue, he hushed me.

"Do I appear the sort to trifle with your fickle emotions? Or did you need a replay of the night on the lift?"

I grinned, reluctantly. "I'd love if you got your knife and let me point at the boy who hurt me."

Klive chuckled and shook his head. "You have my knife."

I bit my lip, guilty.

"I do not want it back. Nor the coat in case you were worried I'd ask. I left the knife with you if you needed to castrate who I now know was Nathan. It's good you chose to spare him so his wife might have a shot at more children. You need to keep the knife away from Taylor's appendages, as well. If you promise, I'll let you keep it."

I giggled and nodded.

"Very well, love. You have a decision to make. You may go to him, or Rustin, and commit, or you can date and be open to the idea that they get to date as well."

"Klive, Rustin really was a mistake. I wish you wouldn't lump him into this as if I love him."

Klive ignored my words. "It doesn't have to be painful to see either with other women. You can make a game of it, kind of like foreplay," he suggested. I creased my brow in confusion. "Oh, love, are you truly such a novice?" He sighed when I bit my lip and blushed. "Here is what you are going to do. You listening?" he asked me with an authoritative raise of his eyebrows that I was coming to love about him.

I nodded.

"You will go to his house as you stated. You will inform him you would like to date other people, including Rustin, and that they both have the liberty to do the same. Even if you do not feel for Rustin as he does you, this releases him and conveys how you feel without causing harm to an ego. With these basics aside, you will inform them of your date Thursday night with Klive, and should they care to join they are welcome to bring dates. Trust me, you are so irresistible, anyone they bring will not compare."

True fear filled my eyes with a silent plea to not be in such a vulnerable position. He shook his head and held my chin in his fingers.

"You are not a coward. Let them pine for you properly. Have the courage to leave yourself open and available to each of them while maintaining the flexibility to protect your heart. Let them show you how much they truly want you. It is the ultimate test. If one of them moves on, it wasn't meant to be anyway," he reasoned. He was right, but that was my fear. After tonight, the idea of Jase increasing his brutality by blatantly not wanting me seemed a killer more lethal than the one holding me in his arms.

Klive swiped at my remaining tears before kissing my puffy eyes and cheeks just to be sweet. Again, gestures that didn't make sense with a killer. Then again, none of our liaisons really did.

"Up you go." His hands cupped beneath my arms, and he lifted me like a child, then pushed off the floor and walked out the door. I stood in the living room, confused. By the time I followed, he was jogging up the stairs with my stuff in his hands.

Aw, he'd gone to my car for me.

I stepped aside to let him back in and closed the door. Klive strode directly to my room like he went there every day.

"Nice, Klive. Way to make yourself at home in my place, especially considering you've never been invited," I said in sarcasm. He smiled over his shoulder. I trailed him into my room where he laid my stuff on the bed.

"I do love what you have done with the place," he told me like a smart-ass.

I chuckled with a disapproving shake of my head.

"After you, love." He gestured to my bathroom.

I scoffed. "Klive, despite our earlier interlude, I am not going in there with you." Now I was sober and able to keep my wits around him.

"Kins, where is your mind, love? I was simply suggesting you take a shower to cleanse yourself of this dreadful night. Whatever is wrong with that?"

I snorted. "Klive, just the fact that you are playing at innocence tells me that I need to be very afraid." I raised my eyebrows and smiled at him. "Besides, you did say, 'after you', meaning you plan on coming in there with me. Not happening, bud."

"Aw, why not? I will behave." He stuck that petulant lip out. "I bet I could soothe your aching heart or distract you from the pain."

I laughed and walked over to him to push that lip back in place. "I'll confess that you have both soothed and distracted me, no nudity necessary. Besides, you told me you would behave if I let you take me home, too. You also ask me how you can behave damn near every time we are together, indicative of your *inability* to properly behave. Shall I continue, sir?"

"Aw, but I was a good boy tonight." Damn, he was on fire! "To be fair, I did take you home. To *my* home. Still honest."

I sighed, undeniably caught up in this man's blatant charm, and shook my head with a grin.

"Honestly, Klive, do women really fall for all this?" I looked up at him, his pretty lips, the angles of his chin, his dark lashes. "Is this how you get women into that plush bed of yours, or do they normally come willingly, and I am just presenting a challenge as you told me?"

"Well, I don't share my plush bed, or room, with anyone, *ever*, so no. Yes, women come willingly as you saw at the faire, but I send them away unless I am too randy to resist, which I was that night, though I sent them away anyway in your honor, love. If they fall for 'all this', I've never known because you're the only one I've wanted to know in every sense which is why you present a very real challenge, both for my bed and my mental state."

"Klive King, what will I do with you and all your fluctuations?" I looked up at him, unable to resist adoring his every confession. Tyndall was right, and I didn't know how not to be excited about having a hold on this man. "Congratulations, sir, you've rendered me a tad speechless, and I love every word."

"I'd love giving them as good girl treats, but you afford me so few opportunities I have to pass them to you when I have a spare moment."

I cupped this man's face and rose to my tippy toes to taste his yummy lips. Klive's arms wrapped around my waist. I inhaled when his head tilted to increase the angle. My palms pressed us apart to prevent me from pushing him to my comforter for the make-out session I craved.

"I need you to leave so I can take a shower and try to get some sleep, sir. I have class super early," I gushed. "By super early, I mean at ten." I cracked out my super bright smile. He smiled brightly, too. *Whoa! Keep it together, woman!*

"Oh, yes, I can leave now. My work here is done. Seeing that smile again has made this all worth the mascara stains on my collar, love." He chuckled and dodged my punch to his bicep. "Your nightgown is on the bed. *Les rêves doux mon amour.*" He bent to kiss my cheek, then decided to kiss my mouth. My blood heated at his open lips prodding mine apart. Our tongues tangled. We had heavy chemistry, and I had a sneaking suspicion our need to keep kissing wasn't due to our sexual restraint or my sorrow over Jase's betrayal.

I kissed him for just a second longer than I should have and broke our kiss. We both took deep breaths and cleared our throats.

"Don't forget our date Thursday night, love."

"How can I forget a date I had no idea existed?"

"You know now. No using work as an excuse because I know you can take off. I'll pick you up at seven. Wear what I gave you, including the bracelet." Yeesh, he'd noticed and chosen not to give me a hard time.

"You've gotten far too used to bossing others around. Perhaps you should try asking."

He hummed his consideration. "Don't forget to invite your precious boy toys if you want to, otherwise I look forward to having you all to myself. It was great fun earlier." He lifted my hand and kissed the back before making me follow him to my door to lock up after he left.

"Why lock it?" I narrowed my eyes.

"Are you truly arguing?" he asked me incredulously.

"Someone needs to argue with your trifling ass to keep it humble." I arched an eyebrow as I crossed my arms. I watched his lips twitch with his effort to conceal his amusement before he cleared his throat to keep his authority going. My turn to hide my humor. We both rolled our eyes with stupid smiles before he continued.

"I am the most dangerous person you should come across in your place, but just in case, lock it. Good night, love," he said as a resolution rather than a sentiment. Then, he turned to me once more and caught my chin. "Kinsley, my sweet, I would love the pleasure of your company Thursday night, will you please do me the honor of being my date?" he asked, turning up that quiet charm with an expectant gaze. *Oh, hell yes!* My megawatt beam presented without pause. I nodded, flattered to have his affection.

"I'd love to, sir. Was that so bad?"

"Ask me no questions ..." he trailed playfully, then gave the gorgeous smile I loved, though he appeared flattered by my acceptance. His gaze shifted into a wistful longing as though no longer caring about my knowing my effect on him. "Good night, good night. Parting is such sweet sorrow ..." My breath hitched at his quoting *Romeo and Juliet*.

He blinked hard as though I'd broken his trance. Klive brushed a finger down my cheek, and those eyes narrowed slightly. His smile shifted into the rarely seen sexy-ass smolder belying desire like a needle popping the romantic balloon. I snapped the hearts from my eyes and rolled them.

"Thank you. Now lock the door behind me."

"Back to bossy so soon?"

He nodded as he walked outside. I closed the door behind him. "I am waiting, love, lock it!" he said through the hollow steel. I smiled to myself as I locked the deadbolts and pulled the chain. "Thank you!" he called.

"You're welcome, sir! See you Thursday night!" I called back.

"Looking forward to it, now go think of me in the shower, and try to behave yourself!"

"Klive! Shocking! I should say the same thing to you!" I yelled, unable to keep the splitting grin off my face. So long, sweet romance, hello randy Klive!

"What a gaffe!" he said with a wicked chuckle. I snickered to myself as I heard him whistling while he took the stairs and left. I pulled my curtain and looked out to the street, watching him open his car door. He looked up at me, so I waved, smiling like a teen at her ultimate crush. He kissed two fingers, held them out, and got inside. I let the curtain fall, and I sighed.

"That I shall say good night till it be morrow ..." I trailed softly in completion to that quote, mocking his pretty accent.

Oh, sweet, sexy, romantic version of Klive, what you do to me!

8 | ♀

I CURSED AND JOLTED upright in a bit of shock while my alarm intruded on my lusty dreams. Seven AM. Not as early as my norm, but earlier than I wanted to wake up during a depressive phase. I hit snooze, then forced myself out of bed. I turned on my rock ballads and listened while I dressed and tried clearing my head of the most recent scary-ass dream of Klive. Wait, was I dreaming of Klive or Henley? Seems like I'd said Henley. Yikes. Two men were enough drama for one woman without adding another to the mix, but I did wonder if asking Klive about Henley would ruin the peace we'd made or send us into another fight we were so fond of.

I pulled on some red skinny jeans, black flats and a white peasant shirt. Brushed my hair and teeth, pulled my hair into a high ponytail adding a pretty bow at the base. Simple makeup to sweeten up Jase. His sins were his own. I couldn't ignore Klive's conviction on how Jase and I weren't a couple when he'd screwed up. I knew enough men who came into the bar looking to drown their most recent breakup with a new fling without feelings attached. Not that I enjoyed watching the ritual or the women who willingly took part in them because I found them worth more than they clearly found themselves, but now I had to see Jase in the same light.

I could do this. If not for us, for Tyndall.

I juggled my books, laptop, purse and phone, heading out the door with a Pop-tart in my mouth. When I locked the door with my hip and arm bracing my effects, I turned toward the stairs and screamed, my Pop-tart taking the dive Jase protected me from as he caught me.

"Whoa, Kins!" Jase braced my books and laptop while helping me recapture my balance and nerves.

"Jase! You scared the shit out of me! I didn't even know you were there!"

"I'm sorry. I thought you heard me and figured you were coming outside to keep me from knocking."

"No. I was gonna come to your place before school," I told him, surprised. "Didn't Rustin tell you?"

"Hell, if he did, my memory is wiped clean of the last eighteen hours, I was so wasted. Head's killing me now, but I had to see you the moment I sobered."

I eyed him, contemplating the definition of sober considering I almost tasted the liquor oozing from his pores. He looked at our feet under my scrutiny.

"Come on, Jase. Let's go inside."

I unlocked the door for him, then put my things in my car for later and set my alarm on my phone so I wouldn't skip another class and see Miller's frowny face aimed my way. When I walked back into my apartment, Jase sat on the couch, his arms resting on his knees, hands clasped together and frankly, he looked like shit warmed over. Remarkable for such a handsome man. Anytime Jase was tired, he looked sexy tired as if he was rocking the look on purpose.

Not today. He looked up at me so solemnly, my heart clenched. He licked his lips, trying to find words. I relocked the front door before walking over to him. I sat on the coffee table, pulled his hands apart, cupped his face and looked him the eyes. Like I did at the bar for our regular barflies, I stifled my nausea at their beer-drenched stench and saw to the pain instead of judgement.

Jase's eyes flickered to a plea. He scooted to the edge of the couch and wrapped his arms around me.

"What good are words when I suck ass at talking to you, baby?"

"I believe that's the first intelligent question you've asked me." The corner of my lips twitched to show I was teasing. He appeared afraid I wasn't. "I'm not much better at communicating with you, Jase, and for that I am sorry." He tried to speak, but I placed my fingers over his lips. "For now, maybe don't argue with me. Can you that? Just be quiet?"

He made duck lips and fearful eyes I couldn't help giggling at.

"All right. Lay it on me. I'd tell you to do your worst, but I fear you're probably better than me in the tongue-lashing department."

"I believe Rustin told you last night, know when to stop talking," I warned and fought my emotional upheaval at the last time Rustin told him that in front of me. Jase nodded, sensing the shift inside me, wisely keeping his mouth closed and cupping his hands between his knees again.

I reiterated everything Klive told me, along with the fact that I would no longer tolerate any of his insults, drunk or not. I may have been naughty as of late, but at heart I was not the girl he tried to claim I was.

Jase took everything well enough, but I saw his discomfort in my dating Klive beyond his ordering me to do so. He cleared his throat and apologized for being so mean to me on Sunday night.

"Have you ever watched something you want start slipping from your fingers and you wonder if you caught it because it came to you or if you stole it from nature and put it in a cage for your own pleasure?"

"Damn, Jase, that's a little too deep for so early in the morning."

"Rustin reasoned with me and while I only remember a few bits and pieces, what I do remember was something like that, how I was guilty of trapping a butterfly or some shit. Kins, I really don't want you to feel that way, baby. And ... yeah, this is too deep for so early. Just know I'm willing to leave the cage open." His lips tipped up, but he also squinted a bit like he might get hit. "I think as much as I've dreamed of you for the last ten years, I'd hate to chase you off because you felt too much pressure. If anyone can understand not committing until you're ready, it's definitely me."

This time when he blushed, there was genuine shyness and a little shame of a different sort coloring his face rather than the awful brick to the gut last night's blush had been. Finally, I addressed the elephant in the room. "Jase, was she at least good to you?" I sighed. "Did she take the edge off my sting or whatever?"

"Was it a *she*?" He chuckled when I cringed in panic. "I'm kidding. I only swing one way. I'm just saying, I was so wasted, for all I remember, Rustin could be lying to me. Hell, I don't remember drinking as much as I did. I'm half-drunk now and I shouldn't have any business driving, but sober by comparison. After all my bullshit, the memory of your face in pain haunting me, I couldn't wait till I was one hundred percent. I've been here for a while," he admitted.

"Marcus is so pissed at me. I drank half the bar and spoiled the whole show. The fan club website is already cursing my name and demanding their cover charge back, it was already bad enough that Constance wasn't there. I have a lot of ass-kissing to do, starting with yours, Kins."

I shook my head and told him no more, but he waved his hand like slapping my words to the ground.

"No, really. I'm pretty sure after you left, I let go of all that mushy shit and did women trashing songs before Rustin kicked my ass of the stage. I may have mentioned your name a couple of times ...."

He cringed and so did I, though I understood vindictive anger better than most. I told him about crying over him while Klive was with me. How Klive had come to his defense many times and put me in my place about my selfishness. "Klive also told me that us seeing other people with each other is like foreplay?" I quirked my brows and Jase gave a sexy growl like a playful fool.

"Mmm ... is that so?" he waggled his brows in return. His hands unclasped and planted on my thighs. "Where do I start?"

I cackled and cupped Jase's cheeks. Though I hated the flavor of too much alcohol, I granted him a kiss of peace. What can I say? I'm chronic in the avoidance department when battling too much emotion. If I were an electrician, half the lights in my place would be burned out. If I were a plumber, my sewage would be backed up.

In my effort to dispel the pain and make brief peace, his talented tongue talked me into a steamy make-out session without saying a word. However, when Player Taylor went for the bases he normally ran, I slapped his hands, changed the rules and basically treated him the way I'd treated Klive all along. Jase whined a few times before stomping his foot and holding my head instead. I laughed as I pulled us apart.

"Baby, I'm gonna have to piss you off more often if this is how we make up."

"Ha! Funny," I said without humor as I straightened my hair and clothing back to normal. I shot him a look to indicate my adjustments proved how hard he'd tried to misbehave. His lips pursed.

My alarm on my phone went off as a perfect excuse to cut this short before anything further happened.

"How bad does a guy gotta screw up to get some makeup sex?"

He winced but laughed when I punched his pressure point in his thigh.

"Baby, how about this, you fake all your orgasms, and I won't make you wear a wire."

"Jase Michael Taylor! Quit thinking with the wrong head." The idea of him trying to get over his haunted thoughts gave me hope that he would think on my level; that or realize this shit hurt and I hadn't even gone as far as he had.

If I didn't get out of here, I was gonna swing the opposite direction and screw up any semblance of peace with my jealousy. After I pecked his cheek goodbye, I drove to school mulling his parting words: "You can punish me by getting this out of your system so that we can be together forever." He'd kissed my neck. "You can punish me by making that killer a slave to you so he will falter in his operations, and I can arrest him and his contacts for good."

I'd swallowed while looking at his irises glowing golden in the morning sun. How many times he'd warmed my skin to the point of flushing with every grin my way and now I felt chilled even with the intense humidity gluing my ponytail to my neck.

"Thank you, Kins," Jase had said, "I know that me and Rustin have selfish motives for this whole thing, but all-in-all, you're really helping us out and I'm sorry I was such an asshole about your help. You're so much closer to him than we have ever gotten before. I owe you big. I'd never put you in this situation if I thought Klive was interested in hurting you. You know that right?" He'd cupped my cheek. All I could do was nod with a tight smile. Fortunately, my phone had chimed with a text from my father wishing me a blessed day and telling me how much he wished I were there to help drag my mom up the mountain trails.

In front of the fine arts building, I now busied texting him back while I walked through the door.

"Miss Hayes."

I ripped my phone down at the sound of Mr. Miller's voice. Every nerve stole my voice like my guilty girl talk with Tyndall scribbled across my forehead for him to read.

"You okay there?" he asked, an eyebrow arching like I was odd. My cheeks puffed with air before I let the nervous breath go. Did

I still have a voice? Why couldn't I freakin' talk? I nodded. He did, too.

"Well, you're a great listener today. I assume this means you're coming to class?"

I nodded and gave an awkward wave before turning to follow him to his room. Art snob, Assholio Anthony, chatted with someone else in the spot I usually sat in, so I had no choice but to take the front row. Thankfully, Miller's lecture over fine art was easy on the eyes and ears.

When I exited the room at the end of class, Miller wrapped around the door frame with my name in his mouth like I was in trouble. I swallowed and walked back in as the rest of the class filed out of the room. Assholio Anthony made duck lips at me like he'd requested my torment. I rolled my eyes at him and looked at Miller while he watched the others leave the room. When a smart-ass closed the door to *give us some privacy*, Miller slapped the door to keep it open while his tone changed so fast, the student left red-faced with the door wide open.

Damn. My mouth dried as I dreaded whatever he was going to say.

"Should I be worried about you?" he asked. "Even if you don't need this class to graduate, you signed up for this, not me. You need to show up to get the grade, Miss Hayes. Skipping will lower your GPA. I understand if you have Senioritis and are ready to graduate, but stay strong in the final stretch, young lady. Rumor has it, you're gonna wear ropes at graduation. I don't want to be the evil asshole who makes you lose one of those because I was honest in my grading, you understand?"

"Yes, sir." I wanted to cry all over again now. When I got to the door, Miller piped up again.

"For the record, Kinsley, I couldn't say this to you last week with your friend in tow, but anyone who can kick ass to the levels you did in the video Walton showed me, as well as on the track, should go out kicking ass. He's gonna put you back on soon. You're dismissed."

I grinned. "Thank you. My father has been tempting me to join them on vacation next week, so if I'm not here, please send me the link online?"

"We'll see."

I shook my head but left with a smile on my face to head to the Science department where I typed rigorous notes in two more lectures in preparation for finals. As Miller predicted, I received a text from Walton ordering me to the track for practice.

Oh, sweet heaven walking back into the stale stench of sweat, body odor and dirty socks! My track duffel should've had a sheen of dust by now, I thought, as I zipped my street clothing inside and trekked out to the track in my shorts and tank top. My relay team rushed to throw their arms around me. I couldn't remember the last time I was so happy for affection. My arms wrapped Julie, Eliza and Lindsay tight. Eliza and Lindsay left me at Walton's instruction, but Julie ignored him for a few to grab my face and study my eyes.

"The hot singer?"

I pursed my lips in a tight smile and nodded.

"The better to rebound with Klive." She flared her eyes so big I couldn't help laughing.

Walton waved her toward the hurdles. "You okay, kid?"

"I am."

"You gonna be able to practice with your injuries? I'm not saying you're going to meets yet, but I'd rather keep you in condition in case."

"I can run. I need the practice to get used to playing through the pain. Do your worst if it makes you feel better."

He shook his head and made me warm up before forcing me to do hurdles, which did hurt my ribs to a degree, but in a way once I was done, basic sprinting didn't hurt as bad as the hurdling, so, I could see what he was doing. When I got home, however, I was longing to drive to Klive's house just for his amazing bathtub. I ran my own and submerged in Epsom salt. Too bad there wasn't something like this that eased the pain of an aching heart. I couldn't help longing more for Klive than his stupid bathtub because Klive was what numbed the pain the most.

My toes drew little whirlpools in the water as I thought of Thursday night and wondered where Klive would take me in such a refined dress as the one he'd told me to wear. If I wore something different, would I throw his plans? I smirked to myself, but knew I'd wear the dress just because I couldn't help loving the mystery. Wearing brand new heels on a first date? Now, that was the true challenge and could cause him to have to carry me up the stairs to my apartment at the end of the night should my feet hurt to badly. Hmm ... surely Klive wasn't that cunning in the planning?

I dried my hair, put on a little makeup and sat in my robe doing homework until I needed to get ready for work. Normally I wouldn't be working a Tuesday, but the same issues that forced me in yesterday applied today. Hopefully after this week, the rubberneckers would be past looking for signs of a crime and leave the bar to the regulars again.

A knock at my door made me drop my computer mouse to the floor. "Shit," I whispered and scrambled for the little device. "I mean shoot. Gotta work on that mouth, girl, if you're gonna look refined. Gotta fit the part," I told myself quietly before opening the door to a man my age holding a damask box with a single red rose on top. My smile split automatically.

"Kinsley Hayes?" he asked with a rosaceous blush I pretended not to notice. I nodded and he smiled. "My boss sent me to deliver this to you."

Boss? This guy looked too clean-cut and professional to be some drug-running thug.

"Klive?" I tested, though I knew that box from the other gifts he'd given me.

"Yes, Miss."

I couldn't help noticing his curiosity for me as he extended the box my way, though he tried to hide his glances at my face. He wished me well and left. I locked my door and set the box on my island beside the laptop. The bow on top was real ribbon I untied to pull the lid from the gift. So traditional. I loved presents and wrapping paper, so this was wonderful. I came to a note on top of folded tissue paper that again smelled of his wonderful cologne. As if I could resist bending to inhale so deep! I opened the note to see his elegant handwriting.

For my sweet Ms. Hayes.

Figured you could use this. I personally sacrificed my pride and masculinity to make this happen. Hope it gets me places ;). Can't get you out of my bloody mind. Looking forward to Thursday.

X – Klive

9 | ♀

MY FIST FLEW INTO the air with a cheer. "Eff yes! He signed his name! His name! Can't get me out of his bloody mind! Whoop whoop!"

He personally went to get this stuff, eh? Let's see what he sacrificed himself for. When I unfolded the tissue, I burst out laughing. Inside were a set of super soft sweats, a box of Midol, a box of panty liners and deluxe box of designer chocolates. Okay, could this man be any more adorable right now? Imagining Klive buying panty liners at the drug store fell into perspective when he humiliated Ray and his cohort last night. Klive was willing to be humiliated for me. I sighed like a pathetic girl until I came to an etched glass egg.

"What in the world is this for?" I asked and had to catch the egg before the glass shattered on the floor as my phone chimed. "Damn, Kins, jumpy much?" I muttered to myself as I opened my texts.

You received my package. Do you like?

I laughed since Klive's title on my phone was still *The Asshole Dick*. I might change that. I texted him back.

Yes, sir, I like very much. Thank you. What is the egg for?

AD: *Cramps. You heat it in warm water, then put it inside yourself and it brings relief. You can also use it when you're not on your period for strength training. =D I know how you like exercise ...*

My jaw dropped. "You've got to be kidding!" I bit my lip through the scandalized grin overtaking my shock and awe, not to mention the hot blush in my cheeks. Dirty Klive was a whole new side I'd barely met. Thank goodness for the hidden world of texting because I was so not brave right now.

Me: *You, sir, are a dirty man! =D*

AD: *You have no idea, my sweet ... there's that smile. My work here is done. See you Thursday, love.*

Me: *See you Thursday 'Asshole Dick'. Should we change that?*

AD: *Whaaat? I haven't earned a new title yet? Bloody madness. You are quite the angry ginger, Lynessa.*

I giggled.

AD: *Are you smiling, my sweet?*

Me: *Are you, my overcompensating naughty Pirate Rion? Curious, do you use that name when undercover at Gasparilla too?*

AD: *Me smiling? Only in the dirtiest fashions as I recall your glow in the dark blush at me proving just how honest LORD Rion was about his long sword, love.*

I felt the glow in the dark blush intensify at this side of Klive and the unforgettable moment at Jase's house I could never unsee.

AD: *I'm betting you're blushing right now, though I'd love nothing more than to see the vicious predator lurking beneath that sweet veneer at my dirty speech. Affirmative on Gasparilla moniker. I'll see you on Thursday my little predatory perverted novice. Oh, the things I could teach you ...*

Me: *Klive King! You ask how you are to behave, well, sir, lemme tell you that you're behaving very badly, I am not blushing, and LORD Rion needs to learn some manners about not flashing his private parts in public to sweet, unsuspecting females that lack said predatory perversion ...*

I squealed when my damned phone rang with his sexy pirate picture flashing onto the screen! Eek! He knew I was holding my phone! I had no choice but to answer! I exhaled, shook my shoulders loose, plastered a smile to my face, hoping like hell my voice wouldn't betray my nervousness.

"Hello?" I quickly opened my laptop, tapping keys as if typing and distracted.

"Really, love?" *Ooh la la! Klive's voice on the phone for the first time ever! Could I be any stupider?* "You think I don't know that you're hot under the collar and flustered?" Oh, shit. Seductive Klive on top of this? I held the receiver away from my face so he couldn't hear me gather my breath.

When I put the phone back to my ear, I cleared my throat and said, "Klive, I'm terribly busy doing research. Did you need something or were you calling to dole some more sexual harassment, sir?" Yay! Charming flirty voice won over the nervous shaky one! When he chuckled, a huge smile spread across my teeth. I heard him begin typing too.

"Are you typing my name repeatedly, a sentence perhaps?" Klive practically purred. "Like a naughty student caught texting when she was supposed to be doing schoolwork? That's what I'm doing because I was caught texting at work. My lines say that I cannot wait to train this sweet novice in my wicked ways this weekend when she spends the whole thing lying blissfully nude between my satin sheets begging for more, more, more ...."

Oh. Shit. Double shit! I'd whispered the curse aloud! I chortled.

"Mine doesn't say that at all. Mine says, subject appears to be suffering delusions and shows masochistic tendencies. He quotes Shakespeare while his heart bleeds from repeated rejection. Yet he seeks more pain knowing all the while the result will be the same in the end with my shooting him down. Creature of habit. Aren't you dizzy from running in circles?"

Klive laughed to himself. I could see that steamy smolder in my mind when he gave the sexiest growl. "Speaking of shooting one down ... My little novice is addicted to my danger, for she asks for such at our every meeting, don't you, my sweet?"

I snorted and rolled my eyes.

"Don't roll your eyes. You know I've hit the bullseye."

I gasped and looked around myself.

"Relax. I can't see you. I know you, Kinsley. You hold my rapt attention anytime you're around. Is that something you're unaccustomed to? The men you're used to are too busy longing for your body to give attention to your eyes, but they are my favorite of the exotic mixture of features you are, love. Your body is better than I've dreamed, however, you captivated my heart with one glance of your eyes."

A sigh tumbled from my open mouth as I closed my eyes. "Klive." I didn't know what to say. I recognized those last words as a sentiment from King Solomon to his bride. My heart filled with the same agonizing longing I'd felt since he'd pulled me against him in the elevator.

"Cat got my pretty Lynessa's tongue once more?" he asked. "I'll snag it back when next I see you. Have a good night at work, love. I must run, but I've so enjoyed hearing your voice to get me through the rest of my dreadfully slow week. Why is it that time drags when you aren't around, yet goes by so fast when we are together?" He sighed like he felt the same longing I suffered.

My sweet everything fizzled into jealousy at the sound of another woman in the background calling his name. Ugh, Kinsley you moron! The man is being incredibly romantic, and you focus on a voice in the background? Stupid!

"You have company, Klive?"

"I assure you it's not the type you may be thinking. Even if it were, you'd be the only one in my thoughts all the while." I heard him muffle the phone. "Ingrid, please tell Paul I'm finishing an important phone call and I'll be right there." His voice came back at full volume. "Kinsley, my sweet, will you please cease distracting me with your eyes like doves and your breasts like sachets of myrrh or some lot."

I held the phone away as I burst out laughing.

"No, I got that wrong. Her breasts were like David's towers or something, right? Am I warmer, love?"

"Klive!" I laughed through his name.

"There's your pretty laugh. I'll see you on Thursday and you may turn over the correct scripture, so I won't butcher anymore biblical erotica. Deal?"

Again, I giggled. "Deal. Have a good night at work."

My head tilted back as I breathed his name like a prayer after we hung up. A text pinged while my heart raced with new excitement.

AD: *As a lily among brambles, so is my love among the young women.*

"Damn," I said while reading Song of Solomon 2:2 from his text. "As an apple tree among the trees of the forest, so is my beloved among the young men." Rather than texting the following verse back to him, I decided to get ready for work and dig into the chocolate. I popped a piece in my mouth as I carried the sweats to my room for later. When I looked at my reflection in the long mirror, I gave her a sad smile and said, "... refresh me with apples, for I am sick with love."

10 | ♀

THE NIGHT AT WORK dragged slower than normal. A few karaoke regulars lit the stage with their same ol' songs, same off-key fun they always had, but asked me a few questions about the crime out by the dumpster.

"We came in around the back like you do, and I was shocked to see how clean it was. Like nothing ever even happened," one guy said.

"I heard there was no blood so why would you see anything different?" a girl observed, then sipped from her tiny stir straw.

"Well, I heard from ..."

I let their gossip fade to the background while Jase's words about Klive battled the soft fuzzy conversation I'd had with Klive today. Klive was a bad man. Purple Nightshade petals had scattered over Sara's corpse. I didn't buy Nightshade's involvement for a second. At that moment, I realized the closer I got to Klive, the closer I may come to knowing what really happened to Sara. Ray insisted he didn't kill her, someone was in the wind, he wanted Klive to find the guy. What did that say about Klive's power over Ray's when Ray could waltz in here, claim a violation and shut us down at his whim?

Jase wanted damning information on Klive for his own reasons, very legit strong reasons like not going back to prison, but I had my own questions. A lot of questions. From the moment the elevator opened on Klive, I'd had the instinct he was dangerous, but I'd had enough Psych courses to know those who seemed the best could hide the worst.

"Hey, Little Red, thanks for working a Tuesday again," Marcus said. He shoved his cell phone in his pocket. He looked tired. I told him. He nodded. "Baby girl, you have no idea."

"Does it have anything to do with Nightshade?" I asked for the first time since the day of Patrick Scott's funeral.

He shook his head. "We don't talk about that here. Besides I'm not Nightshade, I'm just a patron of their services. They keep shit straight."

My eyebrows rose, but so did his finger.

"For once, Kins, can you cut me some slack? I'm having a rough couple of weeks. Like I said, thank you for coming in. I'll try to make sure you don't have to work anymore Tuesdays for a while."

"I'll mind my own for a while. You saw I need Thursday off, though, I hope?"

"Yeah. Taylor took that day off too. I figured you two may be mending fences."

My brows creased. Marcus cursed under his breath. "Baby girl, don't ask me nuthin'. I'm out of the drama. In fact, I'm writing in an employment clause stipulating no one dates co-workers. No one." He walked away like I'd added to his burdens. Great. Way to go, Kins.

On Wednesday I went to my classes and practice, did great on my times considering I hadn't run in a long while. The pain in my ribs and recently conditioned muscles helped tame the thoughts of dark-rimmed gray eyes and soft pliable lips with the smoothest accent bringing to life the scandal of Song of Solomon. Biblical erotica. I grinned to myself before hauling across the finish line. Walton scrubbed his chin like he evaluated my inside thoughts as much as my outward performance.

"Times?" I asked.

"I'm not telling you. Just know they're damn good, kid, but I don't want your head inflating to the point that you add those numbers to the thoughts that have you smiling. You're liable to float away from all responsibility. Clear?"

"As glass."

On my way home, I stopped for a touch-up wax and decided why not get the rest done, too? Well, I'll tell you why the hell not now that I was done. I got my underarms, legs and eyebrows done in addition to the French wax I usually punished my nether regions with and went home in more pain than yesterday's conditioning had put me through. This time I took a nice long oatmeal bath to soothe my aching skin.

I lounged in the super soft sweats Klive had given me and did as much of my schoolwork as I could cram to make up for any time I may be out if Daddy successfully talked me into visiting them in the mountains. When I wasn't typing, I was up humming to girly romantic music while admiring the dress and pearls Klive gave me. Bayleigh had told me she couldn't get the bracelet back to me fast enough. Too much stress. I tested the heels and wore them around the apartment to break them in a little until I changed into the cozy nightie and snuggled under my covers to say prayers.

Okay, okay, I admit I may have stared at Klive's note propped on my nightstand until I just wanted to smell him so bad that I fell asleep on the paper and woke with crinkled skin.

In the morning, I stole my mom's soothing eye gel and cold cream to try getting the creases out of my face. I'd slept in till ten thirty. Which, damn, that's great, right? I couldn't recall the last time I'd slept in so late without having cried myself to sleep or drank like a fish the night before.

"Thanks, Mom. I am too young to have crow's feet just yet and since this keeps you smooth still, I figured I'd ask if I could borrow it," I said over the phone.

"Well, I don't want you getting Botox yet, so I'll let you believe that's how your mother stays pretty," she teased on speaker. "Don't tell your father, though. He doesn't know. Sometimes it's best if they don't know how the magician performs her tricks. May I ask why you're suddenly caring about your skin?"

"Well, if you don't tell Daddy, I have a date later."

"With Jase?"

"Uh ..." Shit! I walked right into that! "Don't be mad?"

"The pirate?"

"What about a pirate?" Daddy's voice asked from the background.

Mom hurried, "No one said anything about a pirate, Andy. I asked her about a pie plate. She was attempting to cook. I told her best to buy one and not chance the house burning down."

"Ha!" Daddy chuckled. "If my baby wants a pie, I agree with her mother. Go buy a pie and wait till we come home before you bake your key lime. Wait." He paused. "Who are you baking a pie for?"

Great. "Well, I was gonna bake a pie and eat my misery over not running, but now I don't need to because Coach put me back on the track! Yeep! Isn't that great? He doesn't have a date for me on when I might compete again, but yay! I'm training and my times were really good yesterday!"

Daddy cheered for me at first, then paused. "Kins, you were gonna bake a pie today to eat your miseries when you were already put on the track yesterday?"

"Andy, honestly. Can the girl just do girl things without a reason?" my mom asked him. "Kins, if you want to bake the pie, I won't stop you, just be careful you have the right temperature and stick to the recipe I taught you, understand?"

Mom was giving me permission to go out with the pirate? I mean, not that I needed permission. Rephrase. Mom was giving me her blessing to go out with the pirate?

"I'll follow the recipe. Thank you, Mama. Love and miss you. Both of you."

"Will there be whipped cream and sprinkles on top?" she asked with the most pathetic lilt as if she wanted to see me all pretty. I almost laughed if she didn't sound so sad.

"Yes. Want me to send you pics when I finish?"

"You two are weird. It's just a pie," Daddy muttered. "I love you, Kins. These mountains are beautiful. If you want to hike instead of baking pies, one gets you closer your goals as a runner, the other takes you in the opposite direction. If you want to be logical —"

"Okay, Andy, go shower. You stink from the last hike you went on."

"I'll shower if you come with me," he teased. I groaned in disgust while he cracked up laughing. When his laughter faded from the room, Mom picked back up.

"What are you wearing? Where are you going? Are you ... uh ... gonna be safe?"

"Ugh, Mom! I don't want to talk about sex. I'm not the sort of girl to sleep with someone on a first date. Thanks. I'll be wearing a dress, heels, and don't know where we are going yet. Just know I will look like the lady you always wished I were. And, yes, I'll send you pictures."

"Are you going to wear the diamond and emerald necklace?"

I swallowed. "No. I'm wearing simple pearls." I didn't tell her Klive bought the pearls.

"Do you think he was the one who got you that piece? He's wealthy enough to afford it."

"No, Mom, I don't think it was him. Sorry if that makes things worse concerning the necklace. Believe me, I feel ya. Just try not to worry. I trust the pirate."

"You mean Klive King?"

"Yes. Klive King. The British bachelor you said I was using Jase to make jealous?" I said with a smug smile on my face. "Must all our conversations end with me getting smart? Will you please pray for me instead of giving me a hard time?"

"Only if you do the same for me, Kinsley Fallon. I won't ask you to text me tonight because I know kids your age stay up to all hours of the night, but will you please text me tomorrow so I can get the latest chapter in the saga of your life, sweetie?"

"Nice. I will. Love you."

"I love you, too, honey. Have an amazing time. Just a few things. Look through my cabinets in your old bathroom; you can borrow the feminine deodorant spray, so things stay fresh down under. Oh, and don't forget extra deodorant because that natural stuff you swear by wears off too fast when you're nervous. Do the loose French braid with the twisted knot at the base of your neck like I did for that one pageant. You looked so pretty with that one. To get rid of the crease and puffiness under your eyes, use the hemorrhoid cream instead of the stuff you borrowed from me, it's in the top drawer. Spritz your makeup with hair spray to keep from sweating. And if you're wearing white, honey, I know you, keep the sanitizer on standby so you can rub out any stains. Don't forget the table manners —"

"Jeez! I'm gonna get a complex. I didn't realize I reeked and sweat so much. Want me to add Vaseline to my teeth so I won't stop smiling, too?"

"If I thought you'd have a hard time smiling around him, I'd say yes, but I saw you behave like a fool at the festival."

"Funny, I remember you behaving like a fool there too. Mom, I'm not going to Prom or a pageant. I'm going on a date, but thanks for TMI on the deodorant spray for the lady bits and your input on my breast-cancer-free deodorant. Still have the double-sided tape so I can keep my boobs from popping out of my dress?" I asked like a smart-ass.

She chuckled. "If your date goes well, you may not want your cleavage glued to the dress."

I gasped as my jaw dropped. "Ugh! I'm going now. Love you." I hung up on her laughter before she could say anything else. After finding the things Mom told me to grab, even if I thought they were gross, I called Tyndall.

"Holy crow, Kinsley, I didn't realize you still knew my number," Tyndall teased, a happy giggle following.

"Are you busy?" I asked.

"Just got out of a designer's clash with the snob I've been paired with for my final presentation. Ugh, Kins, our styles are opposite and I'm pretty sure the prof did that on purpose. I'm sure it's to help teach us how to think outside our own boxes for what the client wants over what our visions are or something, but he's so in love with vintage fashion, he wears bell bottoms and I'm expecting him to throw lime green shag carpeting into our staging."

"Hmm, kinda of reminds me of Henley. The first time I met him, he was wearing like this ugly tweed jacket that made me itch just looking at it. Is your partner cute? Gay or straight? You're annoyed which is a really good sign." I grinned.

"Nope, we aren't talking about me. You're far too happy after my brother tore you to shreds, yes, he confessed, and, yes, I saw the writing on the wall, and, yes, I knew you'd shred him back. If you want to talk about it, I'm here, but I figured you didn't and that's why you didn't return my calls."

"Want to talk about something fun?" I asked, a little nervous and feeling the tingle of sweat my mom had talked of. How did she know that crap?

"Yeah, fun like another guy? You brought up Henley. Is it him?"

"No way. He's ... I don't know. He gossiped about Klive. You know I never trust anyone who gossips."

"You trust me," she reasoned.

"Should we call a YMH meeting for the remainder of this convo to stay between us?"

"Yes," she whispered. "No! Not the shag! I was half joking! Don't— hold on Kins. He's looking through AutoCAD."

Oh boy, this could be the beginning of something fun ....

"Okay, I'm back," she said. "I'm leaving the room. Okay, YMH meeting commencing. You did not hear this from me, do you understand?"

My stomach filled with dread. "Yeah. Pinky promise."

"Jase is crashing your date."

"What?!"

"It's not what you think. Klive called him and invited him and Rustin to come with their own dates if they wanted. He wanted you to feel comfortable, and, well, I'm trying to make sense of this. Like, is Klive babying you or afraid to be alone with you? I have no clue. Crazy, right?"

"I — I ... what the hell? Like, I don't know what to say."

"Agreed. When I asked Jase why he was taking Klive's invitation, he said he wanted to see how Klive handled you and how you handled Klive. Jase has that morbid curiosity for something awful he can't look away from, ya know? Like gory roadkill on the side of the road. Even though you want to cry, you can't help looking at the damage."

"How am I supposed to handle this? What would you do?" I asked. "Is he bringing a date or coming alone?"

"They're both bringing dates, but trust me, you'll be pleasantly surprised by who Jase is asking."

I snorted. "Are they bringing each other since they don't do anything without each other?" I couldn't help a bitter bite.

Tyndall chuckled. "No, but Rustin might like that." We both laughed. "Kins, just be you. If you want to get all girly and pretty, do it. You don't do fake, so don't fake. If you were excited about this, stay excited about it. Remember what I said at our YMH meeting in Pensacola? Any time together, use that to urge something good to the surface."

I confessed to some, not all, of what happened at Klive's house and the sweet stuff. She couldn't have squealed or clapped louder. She made me go into detail on Klive's house and the designs. I didn't tell her about Klive's secret passage room. Something told me if he wanted his room secret, then I'd better keep the secret for now. I did tell her how crazy the Closet of Kinsley was.

"Your period protected your purity, eh? Well, what little purity my brother and Rustin have left you. I love that Klive gave you a period survival kit. Who does that?" She sighed wistfully. "Aunt Flow, I mean the Crimson Tide, still in town?"

We busted out laughing in thought of Constance's label for her period.

"Nope. All gone."

"Mmm ... danger, danger, high voltage," she quoted an Electric Six song.

"Indeed. But I plan to behave. Klive is way too fun to torment to give in at the soonest opportunity."

"I have no idea how either of you have held out this long. I'm proud of you. Have you heard from Constance and Delia since they left?" she changed the subject.

I chewed my lip. "No. They've been way too quiet. I'm really trying not to start thinking of the movie, *Taken*, but if she doesn't call soon, we must get your brother on a mission. I don't know if they thought to get international service on their phones before they left the country. They might've just forgotten."

"When you get into your next brawl over Klive, will you ask Delia's father at the hospital, please?"

I cackled. "I did that over Jase."

"Bullshit. Jase has sluts all over him all the time at the bar and you've not pulled hair once. I know you. Anyway, it's almost time for you to go to practice and I'm about to lose the battle on the shag carpet if I don't get back to my project."

"You mean both of y'all's project? I dare you to keep the shag to the carpet alone."

"Duh. Way softer a surface than the wood floor."

"Tyndall Taylor, you little hussy!" I grinned through the word both our moms used.

"I dare you to do the same. Love you, Kins. Have an amazing time no matter what. Don't let Jase ruin anything and y'all try not to ruin each other anymore than Sunday night, please, please, *please*?"

I promised to give that my best shot, then disconnected our call. Why would Klive invite Jase and Rustin? I smirked to myself. Foreplay? Funny, wasn't the foreplay supposed to be between Jase and me? Klive, I realized, might get off on rubbing shit in Jase's face as much as Jase loved when I tormented Klive. Whatever. Tyndall was right, I wanted to have fun no matter what or who was there. The last time I was this concerned about my appearance, Mom was taping my bikini top to my boobs and hair-spraying my bottom before spritzing glitter spray over my skin to make my tan glow like a golden goddess.

Rather than go to practice, I called Walton to tell him I had an appointment I couldn't miss. "I'm sorry, Coach. I didn't know you were gonna allow me back so soon."

"You couldn't have told me yesterday?" he demanded.

"I didn't remember. My calendar just pinged the reminder."

"You're killing me, kid. You've got to get better at life before you graduate and go into the work force."

One eye bugged while the other squinted. "Actively working on it, Coach. Thanks."

I went to get a mani-pedi and tilted my head back while the man massaged my feet and calves. "Tight. Stress?" he asked. I nodded. He urged me to relax, but I couldn't remember the last time I relaxed without Delia's father sedating me and force-feeding me fluids. I couldn't get Coach Walton's comment out of my head.

You've got to get better at life.

I usually championed myself as being far more responsible than my peers in school, and I was. While they partied their scholarships away or blew off whole course credits, I was doing extra credit assignments, finishing before the half-semester mark, training harder and extra on the beach before training again at the track. I worked extra shifts at the bar when I was asked or just to be kind to another server who needed their spot filled. How was I bad at life when working so hard to be good at what was before me? If I was bad at life, as in real life, then what did that mean for my hard work at school and track? Was this all meaningless to the older adults around me?

"Kinsley Hayes? Is that you?" I heard a familiar voice and couldn't have said a faster prayer.

"Greta?" I opened my eyes to see a beloved adult voice of reason asking to be seated beside me. "Oh, my gosh, how have you been?" I asked about her daughter and husband.

She thanked her pedicurist and settled comfortably into the plush leather chair. She thumbed the massage remote while telling me all about how her daughter was making the honor roll and her husband surprised her on Valentine's with a trip they were about to take to Jamaica for their anniversary. "That's why I've got to get the paws and claws prettied up before we leave. I'm so excited. We haven't gone on vacation in about five years. Not since our daughter had cancer. Thank God for remission and normal boring life, Kinsley. You never know how lucky a thing boring life is."

"You still doing the art program at the Children's Cancer Center? I was thinking of volunteering at Moffitt, so I don't suck at life so bad. Who's babysitting while you're gone? I'm sorry if you needed me and I didn't pick up or something. Boring life sounds wonderful."

"Oh, honey, she's staying with my parents for the week, and they couldn't be happier. They missed out on a year of her life during the outbreak. Yeah, I'm still doing the art program. You should be my helper sometime. I'd love to have you. You're so good with kids. Funny, I was bragging on you not long ago, how I wished you'd gone into oncology because of your dedication and manner. Don't suppose you'd change your major?"

I giggled and waved her words away. "You're sweet and quite the opposite opinion of me as everyone else in my life right now, so your words are like medicine. Thank you. I think I've got Senioritis. But I'd love to be your helper some time. Text me when you get back from vacation. Coach Walton just allowed me back on the track for the first time." We chattered about the women's track coach being on maternity leave, about their plans in Jamaica, about a pre-med student helping her and how if I came in, I might be able to dispel the girl's opinion of me. "Ah, she heard the rumors around campus. Greek row never forgets."

"Yeah, but the best is when you change someone's mind just by being in the same room. One person at a time. I have it on good authority someone in my class thinks very highly of you. I believe his crush on you is contagious. I caught a fifteen-year-old with your track article. He was showing another boy your picture."

I cackled with flattered adoration. "This why I should come help? Am I someone's Make a Wish?"

Greta laughed but nodded with her head tilted. "Kinsley, while that boy and his friend are close to being out of the woods, I do believe you *are* someone's Make a Wish without an illness involved."

"That's so sweet," I said, softened and touched by such an idea. My pedicurist was finished and urging me to a table for my manicure. "I'm sorry, Greta. Please let me know how Jamaica goes. We should have lunch when you get back. I could use an adult friend I'm not related to."

"I will be in contact when I return," she promised. "Don't think one mistake makes the rest of your life. Life is a series of mistakes we learn from. No one gets it perfect. No one. You keep going. We'll do lunch and I'll get you into the art room to make wishes come true."

A bright smile replaced all the inner voices that had me frowning when I'd come in. When I left the salon, I admired my pretty red nails and toenails. They'd stand out nicely next to the dress. Did Klive like red? Every time he gifted me a present, except for the lavender bouquet, he'd included a red rose, so maybe red was his favorite color?

I rubbed my hands together when I got back inside my apartment with mine and Mom's tools in my arsenal. At last, the time had come to get ready for my date with the pretty pirate I'd fantasized about for two years.

11 | ♀

I took another unnecessary shower, exfoliated my skin with homemade sugar scrub, then rubbed myself down with essential oils to make my skin extra supple. Mom was right. I was nervous and had better opt for her toxic aluminum deodorant and feminine deodorant spray for down under. Was I asking for advances? Seemed I was packaging myself to be unwrapped when the better option would've been something like what I'd worn on Jase's date. Flip flops, Daisy Dukes, no makeup.

While I opened my accordion doors for the dryer, I squatted and glanced at the mirror in the hallway. I shook my head at the towel-turbaned, low-maintenance girl digging blindly for the undergarments I needed to prevent lines beneath that dress. I slammed the dryer shut and stood before that girl dangling lacy nude undies and an expensive bra from my finger.

"Ready to kiss the last remnants of normal life goodbye?" I arched my eyebrow at myself. "You know there's no going back from tonight. Call him with an excuse ...." My eyes closed as I blew a long breath. When I opened my eyes, I let my gaze go cold. "He may very well screw this up. You're holding to nothing but who you really are, your achievements, your grades, your future. You made this life. They're all guest stars in your show."

I shook my body loose and left my reflection. To help get over my nerves, I turned on my rock ballads and sang along with all those bad boys being sweetly torn to shreds by women. Was I wrong for hoping Klive was being sweetly torn up right now?

With a mouth full of bobby pins, I threaded my hair between my fingers into two loose French braids along the sides toward my neck, then brought the remaining hair together, twisting the long waves into a relaxed pretzel I pinned in place. After finger-combing a few strands free, I curled and combed them into soft spirals. Mom would be proud. Lips glued together with the hairspray she'd ordered over my hair and foundation, I then batted my lashes slowly against the mascara brush after applying sultry shadows geared to draw special attention to my eyes. Klive's compliment remained in my mind. I couldn't help praying he'd be as enamored as he'd claimed. When I finished, I took a selfie for Mom, asking her opinion.

Mom: *Soooo BEAUTIFUL!!!!! *Add a hint of highlighter under the arches and inner corners and they're perfect!*

Rather than chew my cheek over the critique, I did as she said. I sent her a corrected photo, then she begged to see my dress.

Me: *Mom, I'm not dressed yet. Didn't want makeup mishaps just in case.*

Mom: *Good girl! Hair is beautiful! Quit getting so good at this! You won't need me anymore!*

I sighed when she sent a group of crying emojis.

Me: *I need you. I love you. I'll send you a pic when I'm done.*

Finally, the moment I'd been waiting for. I stepped into the top of the proper dress and wiggled the material past my hips until the bottom clung to my thighs an inch above my knees. My arms gingerly found the cap sleeves. Only when I adjusted the material over my shoulders did I realize I couldn't zip the damn thing by myself without causing a stabbing pain through my recovering ribs.

"Come on! I thought I was past this!" I whined when I tried. I cursed a few more times, hating weakness and vowing to stretch against the pain no matter how bad the stab during my next training session with Walton. He'd frown on me, but whatever. Pride wasn't worth living with this self-inflicted defect. Welp. Mom would just have to wait for her selfie until I found a solution.

I stepped into the nude platform pumps Klive had issued for this date and strode around the apartment as best I could to get comfortable. When I passed by the sheer curtains, I hurried to tug the heavier curtains over them, wondering if Jase was watching tonight like the night he'd stopped by my place way too quickly. If he were coming tonight, would he spend his time getting ready rather than spying on me?

Ugh. Stomach acid churned my empty guts. I needed to soften up otherwise I was going to be so tense by the time Klive arrived, I may not need an excuse to get out of the date. In fact, the more I thought of Jase spying, the more I wanted this date with Klive to be great. This confusing back and forth was too much to navigate right now. I didn't want to think of surveillance or Nightshade! I wanted to think of Klive on Monday night in his room. In his bed with his arm up for me to snuggle beneath. The way his fingers played with my hair as he asked about the show I'd watched.

The music drifted into a softer playlist. As Mazzy Star sang *Fade Into You*, I thought of my dad and how he said this song played when my mom walked into their first solo, on-purpose, date. "I said I'm gonna marry that woman," Daddy always recounted. I smiled to myself. Fading into Klive's arms at the end of the night seemed a great way to conclude the evening. No sex. Just cuddling. I chortled to myself and rolled my eyes. *What a stupid little girl, love.*

By the time Klive knocked on the door, I'd added pearls to my ears, spritzed perfume and was securing the bracelet after dabbing on pale lipstick. A million butterflies unleashed with the *Wild Horses* The Sunday's crooned about. My cheeks puffed in the mirror while my eyes went wide. I cheesed like an idiot at my reflection. "You're officially a dumb girl. Congratulations."

I counted to ten as I slow-walked to my door, so I didn't seem too eager. Catalog model Klive deployed a devilish smile when I opened the door. The bud of a single, long-stemmed, red rose tapped his lips as his eyes roamed my body.

Hot damn! Get out while you can!

Psh! I was too close to leaning against him rather than pushing him away to consider canceling now. Rather than reciprocate the predatory smirk, I brandished a bright smile, genuinely excited to see him, and stood aside. He crossed the threshold smelling so damn good and looking even better. *Focus. Don't breathe so loud!* Klive looked like a feature in *Men's Health* on how to dress for success. A feature that might include sub-sections of different types of success and closing *every* sort of deal. If he were, I'd cut that page out to hang in my closet. I glanced away, smiling at my private thoughts while I shut the door.

As I took in how he'd sculpted his hair and the way his pin-striped shirt fit just enough to hint at a fine physique, I couldn't help noting how Jase's physique would've popped every button from the front and split the back, too. I shook my head as I couldn't help running my finger along Klive's chin to test the feel of his unshaven face.

"Another impulse, love?" He urged my hand to his mouth and kissed the back. Meanwhile, I warred with how I wanted that mouth back on mine so bad! Thankfully, Klive was more disciplined and looked down at his watch. "Whenever you're finished devouring me with your pretty eyes, we will leave."

I rolled my eyes and pulled my hand from his but was thrilled he thought my eyes were pretty. Dido's *Here With Me* started and I freaked at the intimacy. Klive laughed when I tried to bolt to my room to silence the player, but he snatched my wrist and urged me back to him. I stumbled in my heels, and he caught me like he had the night we met. I couldn't get enough air as I looked up at him leaning over me enough to keep me from falling. He shifted his grip on my wrist to threading his fingers in mine while his other hand splayed over my bare back. Sonuvabitch this was a lot! Too much! So were his eyes examining my appearance like an appraisal with a deep soundtrack.

As he lifted us both to standing straight, his fingers tip-toed up my back. I sucked my teeth and arched away from the tingles he caused, which made me arch against him. Before I could say a word or give him any shit, he raised our hands over my head and twirled me beneath his arm like we were dancing.

"Let's zip you up or else I may be tempted to strip you down," he said, low and promising, stealing the little breath I fought for. "I have reservations and confirmed we'd be there." While he grasped the zipper in one hand, he ran the rose bud along my spinal column in such agonizing slowness, I needed to reapply my lipstick and check my teeth from chewing my lip so bad. He wrapped his arm around my waist to my belly. His nose nuzzled the crook of my neck.

"Klive ...." My lips fell open.

"I love your hair this way." His lips brushed the back of my ear. Tingles fired through my nerves like I'd stuck my finger into a light socket. By the time he released me to kill the music and grab my effects, I had to grip the vanity counter in my bathroom.

"Shit, Kins," I whispered to my mirror. "Get yourself together! Man-up!" I nodded, shuddered, then pulled my shoulders back.

The rose rested on my kitchen island and Klive stood on my balcony while I turned off the lights and locked the door. I looked at him like locking up was pointless since he was right here, but he shot a look back that had my eyebrows creasing my forehead. I turned around and gasped. A black *Ferrari* parked in the circle drive!

"Whoa! That was *you*?" I recalled the night I'd lusted over this exact car. He'd parked in the VIP spot beside the bar. The same night Klive made me cry and said I was like everyone else. I swallowed. *Please don't let this night end with me crying!*

Klive's finger beneath my chin tipped my lips closed. "You didn't think your boyfriend was the only one with a pretty toy, did you?"

My mouth fell back open at him still calling Jase my boyfriend. I'd have given him a piece of my offended mind if I weren't so blown away that I was about to ride in that car, that Klive owned a Ferrari!

"Come now, love, if you stand and stare all night, you'll cause us to be late and force me to open her up on the highway to make up for lost time."

I gawked at the car like a dude stares at a bikini model. "That sounds like a motive to stare longer ...."

Klive whistled like I'd said something salacious. "She plays gridiron, fights like a man, dresses like a lady, dances like a whore, is breathtakingly beautiful and loves fast cars?" He sighed and made prayer hands as he looked at the stars. "Thank you, Lord, she is perfect." He cast a little grin and a wink at me.

"Ugh. A whore? That hurts a little." I grinned as I kicked off my heels to jog downstairs with them in my fingers. He followed and hit the locks for the car. Klive escorted me to the passenger side where he opened the door. "What kind of feminist am I if I allow you to open the door for me, sir?" I flirted as I tilted my head.

"The kind who allows me to open the door because she keeps my bollocks in her little fist. Or at least we can hope," Klive flirted in kind. I cackled and slapped his chest before sliding into the low seat so close to the ground. I slipped my shoes back on and swung my legs inside, catching Klive ogling the motion. After he closed the door, I wondered how he made getting in on his side seem so easy while being so tall. He looked over at me, boyishly excited out of nowhere, younger in an instant. *Yes, I could use more of this look on him!*

"Not a cheap whore. A very expensive escort. Will that do?" he asked as he started the car. The growl of the engine coming to life right behind my seat was a whole new rush. Wind whistled through my lips as I sucked air while lust shot through my body. When I registered what he'd just said to me, I gave a playful purr of my own. He licked his lips like he wondered whether punctuality was important.

He shifted gears and we were off. Several neighbors in the park gawked as we left the driveway. If my mom was worried about a necklace, I didn't even want to imagine what she'd say about this.

"Great," I said. "Now they'll probably call my parents to ask who we know with a car like this and why little Kins was with him. What happened to your low profile, sir? The Tesla would've been just fine."

"Understated is a far better description. Only people with something to hide keep low profiles," he explained with a tinge of arrogance. When he entered the highway, he smiled at me. "What can I say, Kinsley? I finally earned a date with you fair and square. No kidnapping necessary." I rolled my eyes but couldn't help snickering with him. "This is special. I couldn't leave my favorite car in the garage for this."

"How come I didn't see it the other night?" I asked.

"I have a separate garage on the back of the house I built exclusively for her. That's where she lives."

"Like another woman. Your car has her own guest house. Nothing pretentious about that."

"Exactly. Were it pretentious, I'd have placed the Ferrari guest house in the front for all to see. She's too special to share." He sent the words straight to my eyes with his.

I nodded and said nothing else. We hit an empty stretch of highway, so Klive pinned me back to my seat as he lit her up. Tingles shot through my stomach to the palms of my hands. I pumped my fist, unable to help myself.

"Hell yes! Klive, do you feel that? She's *amazing*!" I tilted my head with closed eyes, relishing every super-fast, exhilarating second, beaming bright like an idiot.

"Yes, *she* is ...." Klive trailed, mocking the scandalous car conversation he'd had at Jase's.

Oh, hell. I blushed as I opened my eyes to see his gaze raking over my body between glances at the road. *Knees together. Ankles crossed and tucked to the side. Manners!*

He slowed as we came upon the next group of vehicles with no way to weave through them. Thank God he didn't drive the Ferrari the way he'd driven the Ducati. And, holy crap Klive had some expensive toys!

Klive tapped his touch screen. My tongue traced my cheek when Dido came over the system singing *Here With Me* to rustle up those far too intimate sentiments I'd panicked under at my apartment. This man ... always making me face what embarrassed or discomforted me. Rather than fretting over the emotional implications of Klive beside me with such a deep song playing, I sang softly along and dared a look at him. Yup, same arrogant grin, if not tinged with something adorable, but overall that expression told me I was playing right into those greedy hands, and he'd enjoy every moment. Bayleigh once confessed to loving the game too much to be tamed by any one person. I shook my head at myself more than him because in the here and now, I couldn't help feeling played and loving the process. But wasn't that the whole point?

No matter what I told myself about Klive having shallow ambitions, I knew he was aiming for my heart over *gunning for my knickers* as he'd said when he'd taken me to the Fort Foster

Rendezvous. If he didn't want a relationship, why bother? He'd said he didn't have relationships or get involved, but he'd also confessed some deep longings for me in our brief history, too, that kinda contradicted everything he claimed to want or not want. Did he just want me to want him? I couldn't help thinking of Rustin and understanding if that were the case, even if I didn't agree with tormenting someone that way. Hell, if I didn't get out of my own head, I was going to go all girl-crazy over-thinking every little thing.

Like he sensed me navigating roadblocks in my mental mind map, Klive lowered the volume a tad.

"Just so you know, I'm not purely screwing with you. Let's say in addition to your lustrous eyes, I've noticed your love for all sorts of music. Quite an eclectic mix, much like your personality. Which mood will she be in? Soft, slow, sweet or hardcore rock goddess?" He chuckled when I did. "I may not be a singer, but if I were to dedicate a song, outside of *Big Girls Don't Cry*, that is ..." He paused to cluck his tongue while I scoffed and smiled too big to really be offended. *Confirmation of his shit-calling, whoop whoop!* "I think of you when I hear this."

Klive tapped the screen again. I clapped my hands and cackled when Klive's voice synchronized with Bon Jovi's shouting the beginning of *You Give Love a Bad Name*.

Whoa! Be still my effing heart! Not just playful Klive but *hella* playful Klive, pointing at me, accusing me with the lyrics as he belted the chorus, drummed his hands on the steering wheel, altogether going garage band on me the way Jase had, but this was so much better because this man would be the last one I'd have expected this exuberant stupidity from. He was calling my crap and admitting to the games we played with one another as if they were trivial moments rather than as heavy as they'd been.

The tension in my shoulders melted into the seat. I shifted slightly to watch him like a hypnotic fan girl for a lead singer she'd just discovered. Klive looked away from the road to touch my lips in time to the lyrics of the song then snagged my hand to display my nails like I'd choreographed my color choice to fit his music video. Thank goodness for darkness because heat filled my cheeks at the irony and how every legit word rang true for us. Too bad I'd not toyed with him all along. Acting would've been far easier than falling for the man making a fool of himself without looking foolish at all.

Klive pointed his fingers in the shape of the gun, shot kissy lips my way, then grabbed his heart like I'd wounded him rather than him wounding me. I couldn't help falling into a fit of giggles and wanting an encore, but he paused his play to exit the highway and look over his shoulder to be sure traffic yielded for his pretty car. If they didn't, I was sure he'd still get ahead of them. I admired the city lights bouncing off the dark windows of the high-rises as we cruised through town near the river walk. We stopped at a light, and he drummed the steering wheel more casually rather than rock star. Bummer. Silly Klive was so damn sexy.

The light turned green. Klive left the little Z next to us in the dust then turned the music down again.

"You know, sir, I could turn around and dedicate that song to you, too." I smiled without any guard or hesitance, so he'd see just how pleased I was with his performance. Maybe he'd let his playful side out more often? He raised his eyebrows. Though he didn't say anything, he did kiss the back of my wrist again while focusing on the traffic. I shifted my attention back to the buildings, searching for hints of where he was taking me. Would Jase be there like Tyndall said? My hands clasped in my lap. How did I feel guilty for kissing Jase again the night after he screwed up? The same night after Klive had thrown everything separating us to the side long enough to lay me down in his bed. I swallowed as dark places in my brain lit like the festoons atop one of the trendy roof-top restaurants.

Klive's car turned into the lot where valets in crisp uniforms opened doors for passengers. My head tilted as my mouth dropped open.

"Klive, are you freaking kidding me? This is too upscale."

"Hey, cut that out. He helped pick this place. You so easily underestimate him because he performs in lower establishments?"

Was my jaw on the floor yet?

"Personally, I'm nervous you'll see a side of Taylor you can't resist because of this."

Klive was indeed honest to a painful degree sometimes. This was one. I wasn't even sure how to look at him or what side of Jase to expect, nor why Klive would even freaking invite Jase if he knew there was a risk of my being attracted to another man. On top of that, I'd been painted a snob by an exquisitely dressed, exotic car driving millionaire. Talk about humbling. As miffed as I was, or nervous as he claimed to be, Klive didn't allow me to get out of hand. However irritating, I liked his frankness.

"I'm sorry, Klive. I'm not sure how to feel about you inviting Jase when I thought you wanted me all to yourself …." What I left out: *and I wanted you all to myself.* As we waited in the line of vehicles filing toward the valet, Klive ran the back of his fingers over my cheek like he read my mind.

"I never said I didn't want you all to myself. To have that, I extended this opportunity to him. To you both."

"Huh?" Head scratch.

Klive chuckled and glanced out the window before casting a fond smile at me. He grabbed my hands and separated their grip to run his fingers between mine.

"Kinsley, look at me, love." I did. "Let's have an enjoyable time, come what may." I nodded and rubbed my lips together before releasing a breath.

"Klive, I'm nervous, too. I've only been here a couple times on special occasions. It's too much. Not for him, but for me, especially on a Thursday night."

"You've never balked at the other places we've been in the same place at once. Why should this be any different?"

But this was different. He'd gone to lunch with my father, Ben and me. Sure, he'd reminded me that he'd given his shirt to me before a hundred people with cameras, but that was still speculation. This was the public display he'd hidden the day I'd left him at brunch.

Klive eased us to the front of the line. Two valets opened our doors as we held eye-contact for the last few moments before confirming swirling rumors.

12 | ♀

KLIVE CAME AROUND THE car, so I'd take his hand instead of the valet's. He'd pulled his suit jacket over his crisp shirt and tie. He'd buttoned the middle button and placed one hand in his pants pocket. As my fingers gripped his, I stood a lot taller than I remembered beside Klive in these heels. The unexpected difference startled me for a brief second. Klive took advantage of my surprise and planted a kiss to my parted lips. The affectionate display was a blink of an eye, but I smiled far too bright, surprised now for his lack of prudence compared to brunch that day. No secret rendezvous now.

"Your ticket, Mr. King," the valet said, obviously familiar with Klive, and perused us with open curiosity. I looked up at the roof. The sound of live music mixed with clapping. How exciting! This was happening! I was going up there with this man! Me! Okay, Kins, get your white trash shock and awe off your face, I told myself in the way the rude catering manager had accused me of at Delia's party. *God, please let their trip be going well. Please let them call soon. Please let them be safe ....*

"Thank you." Klive took the ticket, then gave him a dismissive smile. "We barely got out of the bloody car and already these men cannot take their eyes off you," he said under his breath near my ear as I bent to retrieve my clutch.

"How do you know they're not staring at you, sir?" I grinned at him, glad for his hand coming to the small of my back to keep me stable as he guided me around the back of the Ferrari. I couldn't help a lusty gaze at the pretty car as we left her to their care.

"Hmm, the idea never occurred to me, but I doubt mine are the legs they're ogling. Nice of you to say so."

I looked up and caught another valet ripping his eyes from me as he stared the way I had at the car. Wow! That had to be from the same shock I enjoyed at Klive's affection, not my appearance.

Klive fired a look at them and cleared his throat. Yikes! The valets hastened back to their jobs, intimidated. Klive cast a conspiratorial grin and wink as he dipped his head toward me. Tilt-a-whirl belly and brain activated. I managed to tame my butterflies to a casual giggle as we walked through doors that were opened graciously for us.

"Good evening, Mr. King," an efficient hostess said with a tablet in her hand while wearing an earpiece and tiny microphone. She escorted us through an impeccable lobby of the boutique hotel into an empty restaurant on the ground floor. "Your company is already seated upstairs at your favorite table. Appetizers? Champagne?" She leaned forward to call for the elevator.

I marveled that Klive had a favorite table, knew the menu by heart as he ordered appetizers and the type of champagne he preferred, then I focused on the opulence going to waste down here. The only thing bustling was the kitchen. Dishes, pots, and pans clanked and clamored with servers who bustled in and out with trays they must be carrying up on a hidden elevator. She saw me looking. "This area is open on the weekends or in case of inclement weather."

I nodded. The elevator opened. Klive's fingers walked up my spine. I swallowed. Elevators would never be normal for us. When we boarded, the hostess stood just before the doors while we stood behind her staring ahead at the same, but like our chemistry in my father's car where we didn't need to touch, longing filled the empty spaces in ways that made my pulse beat harder. Klive's hand cupped my left hip as he stood close at my right side. Shit. He had a sexy grip. In my mind, I saw the veins on the top of his hand, the olive tone of skin against the cream of my dress. Straight. Ahead. Klive's grip squeezed, and I heard the slightest hint of a deep, slow breath suck through his nose.

When the doors opened, only about ten seconds later, I sucked deep the smells of food and ozone after a good rain. Klive gestured I follow the hostess off the elevator the same way he'd gestured I get off the elevator before him two years ago. I'd been spitting mad at him then. Now I shot him a smart-ass grin and squared my shoulders, lifted my chin like a playful snob and sashayed after her, relishing the chuckle I'd earned from him.

"I thought your ass was fit in the leather. This is almost worse with the slit in the back of your dress," he said low enough for my ears only. My turn to chuckle. The hostess glanced over her shoulder at us. I saw her make eye contact with a passing server who I caught staring at me as she carried her tray. When I averted my eyes and pretended not to know exactly what that was like when Bayleigh and I gossiped about patrons with our eyes only, I caught multiple people at tables watching our trip to a table directly beside the wooden dance floor. I ignored them and couldn't help a broad smile when I saw Jase scoot his chair and stand with our arrival.

"Jase Taylor, don't you clean up nicely," I flirted and kissed his cheek. "You trying to one-up me with two dates over my one?"

"You could never be one-upped in my eyes, baby." Jase kissed my cheek back. "Carmen is my date. Bobbie is here with Rustin, but if there's a dance floor, he's gonna be on it."

"You two couldn't have picked better dates," I said, grateful that Jase chose to spare my feelings and competitive side with his partner rather than finding a blow-up doll sex partner for the night to rub in my face.

Carmen greeted me from where she sat beside Jase wearing a little black dress that on her was more like a weapon. On her other side, my bubbly friend and university cheerleader, Bobbie, clapped her hands like she was delighted beyond words to see me. I leaned in for small hugs to each woman, very happy to see them, too, then I took the seat Klive pulled for me. "Thank you, sir."

I sat and allowed Klive to help me scoot toward the white linen tablecloth. A waiter greeted Klive and poured champagne into each of our glasses, holding the bottle over his arm complete with the starched linen napkin and all.

"Thank you," I said when he'd filled mine.

"You're most welcome." He nodded.

I hummed in no less than bliss, not only at the flavor, but the warm ambiance of glowing festoons overhead, the best view of a live classic jazz band with real horns and instruments, and a duo of singers dressed like they'd walked right out of a bygone era. The woman in a figure-hugging wiggle dress, red lips, and pin curled hair crooned into a microphone she cupped in her gloved hands. The man singing beside her could've been a mobster smuggling bootlegged booze for Al Capone. I'd once been to a murder mystery dinner that felt a lot like this. I'd missed my pirate beyond words that night and now I looked over at Klive with a new appreciation for this reality. He was here! With me! Not a foreign longing of my memories! We were making one together right this second!

Klive caught me staring at him and sent an expression that urged me to relax and enjoy. I said a silent prayer of thanks and turned my attention back to the band. They covered an Ella Fitzgerald song when I spied Rustin in perfect form with an elegantly dressed old lady. Bobbie saw me looking and gave a cutesy shrug that made her curls bounce. Good grief, I prayed he wouldn't make a mess for me to deal with if this went sour.

I stole a private smile from Klive as he watched me studying everything with new eyes. The male singer carried the lyrics of Louis Armstrong, and I couldn't help realizing as I eyed Klive that I was staring at the modern-day outlaw. Was Klive the Al Capone in the scenario, or the enforcer for an unknown Capone figure the way Jase thought and Henley implied?

Klive held eye-contact without an awkward need to look away. In this suave capacity, he had a confidence that conveyed the stealth hired gun he claimed to be. Were there more like him in this place? If I didn't quit thinking of the criminal element, I'd ruin the calming intimacy of our surroundings. A wonder the restaurant managed an intimate vibe with at least fifty tables.

"So, King." Jase snatched our staring contest away. "I hear they actually have smoking jackets and a lounge with cigars. True or false?"

"Very true. Do you smoke cigars?" Klive asked him. I shriveled my nose and told them to chat amongst themselves while I swapped seats with Jase to sit next to Carmen and Bobbie.

Carmen grabbed my thigh under the table. "I thought you'd transformed from a caterpillar to a butterfly in the dress he'd bought you at the mall. Girl, you're a little chameleon. We should take a selfie to send Tyndall and Constance so they can be jealous I'm hanging with their bestie." Her phone rose. Bobbie and I leaned in at her sides with bright smiles on our faces. Carmen leaned close to my ear. "Should I caption this *mixing business with pleasure?*"

I cackled by accident and clapped a hand over my loud mouth. Carmen and Bobbie giggled.

"And just like that, she ruins all that sophisticated effort," Carmen teased. "Tyndall will be pleased to see you tying her brother in knots for how he did you on Sunday. You'd better not be too sweet to him after what I was told he said to you. Forgive too easily and men think they can get away with it again and again. You set those standards and keep them high. Keeps them in line."

Now she tells me? I could've used this common sense a few days ago. Duh, Kins! Would Jase now think I was going to roll over for his every screw-up? Ugh. Again, another thought train I didn't want to ride in this blissful place.

"It's a shame you aren't into Jase. Or single," I joked. She chuckled, then Bobbie raised her hand and told me to tag her instead.

"Just kidding," Bobbie said, eyes bright as she watched Rustin escort the elderly woman back to her table before winking at her like she was next on his dance card. Bobbie cringed at us and shook her head. "Hell, no. I can't dance like that. He's lost his mind."

"That I have." A very dapper Rustin bent to kiss my cheek, engulfing my senses in a heavenly cloud of Obsession cologne. "Can you dance to this?" he asked. "I know you were okay at the two-step ...."

I shook my head at this brat. "Tell you what," I said up to him as he stood tall again. "You ask Klive if he minds if his date dances with you, and if he says yes, I'll dance with you. My grandmother taught me you dance with the one you came with."

"Ooh, I believe that's one for you, Miss Hayes." He licked his fingertip and drew me a tally. Bobbie reiterated her fear of dancing and Rustin tried convincing her to trust him to lead her.

"Psh!" Bobbie sat back and looked him up and down. "I don't trust any man to lead."

"Tough crowd," Rustin joked, then went into telling light jokes to make her laugh and lean in closer to him.

My eyes smiled at Klive above the rim of my crystal glass as I sipped champagne. I almost spit when Carmen squeezed my thigh under the table again. Was I wearing my desire to dance with him too boldly on my sleeve? Or the fact that I had no problem trusting Klive to lead, well, unless he took me to truly scary places, that is.

When the waiter returned for our orders, I deferred the decision for my food and drinks to Klive, hoping he'd take my little indications as a sort of thanks for this night, for the silly side he'd shown me in the car, for even making such a deal about taking me out that he'd brought the Ferrari at all, that despite all our push-pull I trusted him the way my girlfriends did, though I could never define why. I knew Klive would gauge my intake to keep me from getting sick or making confessions of the drunk variety. Plus, he had all the knowledge on the snobby wine and champagne selections that little people like me didn't.

Okay, in fairness, my family aren't exactly paupers, and as a bartender I'm not completely uneducated. I never really pay attention to wine, but the alcohol I serve at the bar.

Klive stole my mind from my thoughts by engaging the rest of us in light conversation topics as if he wanted to know how we saw the world and our places in the vast expanse. Anytime I thought too little of myself, Klive scoffed, but Jase would warn him not to inflate my ego to a degree we couldn't fit in the same rooms together.

After a bit, I laughed and slapped Jase's belly. "You should take Carmen on the floor," I told him. "Rustin got Bobbie out there."

Klive took the cue I'd given Jase and stood. "Kinsley, love, will you join me on the dance floor?" He shrugged out of his blazer and hung the piece over the back of his chair. I took his hand and he led me to the shiny wood floor filling with other couples wanting an intimate moment together. My chest filled with a deep breath of his fragrance when he tucked me against him, his hand at the small of my back making my eyes close from the sensations swimming up my spine through the back of my neck. His other hand cupped mine between our chests. I smiled as he threaded his fingers in mine rather than maintaining perfect form. I wrapped my free hand around his shoulder and Klive's unshaven jaw rested against my temple as I followed his effortless lead. My eyes remained closed as I committed to memory the warmth of his skin, the softness in his firm torso. I had no way to make sense of how those two could be possible at once, nor how we so drastically swung from friend to foe and back again so fast.

The awareness that this peaceful bliss could end faster than beginning made my fingers curl harder around his shoulder. If I held tight enough, he couldn't slip away into the darkness of the real world until I let him.

Was Jase dancing with Carmen?

Did Rustin talk Bobbie into another round?

Would they give me a hard time when the night was up or if I accepted a dance from either one of them? Oh, why did everything need to be about work without play? I wanted to play and pull the playful side from my date for the rest of the night beneath these warm lights glowing above our heads as the siren on stage sang a beautiful French love song.

You'll have to open your eyes eventually.

"You're doing an amazing job tonight, love." Feeling Klive's voice through my skin, I smiled again. "That infamous temper is nicely in check. I'm impressed. Carmen is a friend of yours, correct?"

I finally opened my eyes to pull my face back and peer into his pretty eyes.

"She is, but she was Jase's friend first. She's happily engaged to another man and Jase is like a brother to her. She came on a favor," I admitted.

"Taylor's being gentle with your heart," he observed. "This I respect. And the other woman, Bobbie, right?"

I nodded. "She's a good friend of mine. She's also the real deal in all of this."

He nodded now and when he looked down at me, his eyes held a fondness I almost couldn't handle for the genuine kindness and softness I had a hard time accepting.

"Are you enjoying tonight?" I asked to cope with the emotional overload.

"I need a way stronger word than enjoyment to describe what tonight does to me. Odd, I seem to have lost my head and the dictionary in my brain. I'd sooner describe how exquisite you are tonight, how easy you are to talk to, how fun to learn your thoughts. I can focus on little else, but why would I want to?"

Heat spread through my cheeks as I glanced at our feet before braving his eyes again. "Wow, Klive, I should say the same about you. Or, perhaps the word, *ditto*, encompasses all."

Tingles fluttered through my fingers around his shoulder at the vibration of his laugh.

"Touché. Are you enjoying tonight, my sweet?"

"I'm having a wonderful time. This is so soothing and a great jumping-off point. Did you pick this calm place to keep me in check?"

Again, he laughed, and I beamed brighter when he nodded, a boyish grin lighting his face.

"That, and I just wanted an excuse to hold you for as long as you will let me."

Aw! I leaned against his shoulder because this was too much sweetness! I didn't want this night to end!

"May I kiss you, Kinsley?"

A silent whistle whispered through my lips before I looked up at him and shook my head.

"Not yet, Klive. I'll tell you when. I promise." I kissed the pad of my index finger and placed the tip to his soft lips. The adoring expression intensified when he kissed my fingertip. I placed his kiss to my lips, allowing the reciprocal sweetness to show through for him. Klive ate my sweetness with far more gusto than he'd had with his food. I decided to devour as many morsels of this romantic moment as I could get too. If Mr. Manners wasn't hiding his desire, why should I? Screw undercover, laying bullshit on thick. As we held each other's gazes, the songstress took center stage to sing a cover of Etta James' *Trust in Me* as her counterpart took a break to dance with a fan in the crowd.

The irony of the song singing about trust while being held in hands that not so long ago taunted me into believing he'd hold my own life over my head was surreal. Not that I extended Klive some unwavering forgiveness. I chose to see this as an olive branch or an act of mercy until our next inevitable argument. Did we only argue so much because we warred ourselves apart when we wanted to be together? If we were allowed to be together, would we fight as much?

Carmen and Jase returned to the table to watch the dance floor. I looked away from his haunted expression and caught Rustin planting a tender kiss to Bobbie's smile.

"Klive," I whispered, uncertain why this bothered me. My finger squeezed his.

"Shh, easy, love," Klive murmured against my ear, tucking me closer into the crook of his neck. My nose and lips brushed his Adam's apple. His hand around my waist caressed the small of my back while his lips brushed my temple with a kiss just as tender as Rustin's to Bobbie. There you had the problem. In this moment, seeing Rustin's ability to respect a woman, I found myself envious of something she possessed that I must not have since he'd disrespected me.

For the rest of the song, I released all that hurt my heart into Klive's arms holding me during an inner meltdown. Hopefully, I'd concealed my sorrow from those who'd made no secret of staring at us. As we swayed and turned about the floor, I realized envious glares speared my back like javelins flying from all sides of the restaurant and I understood how silly a fool any woman would be to be envious of another when I was in the arms of a man who'd before avoided public scrutiny.

"Jase wants to dance with you," Klive said "Would you like to?"

I nodded, though I wanted to remain for as long as he'd hold me. Then again, seeing Carmen's ultraviolet blush when Klive took her into his arms was worth the sacrifice. Wonder what she'd talk about.

"You all right, Kins?" Jase asked. He took the same form with me Klive had, but the vast differences in their bodies blew my mind. Jase was so much ... fuller, I guess?

I nodded, a little lost for words as I sought a way to explain.

"I'm okay. This not being so selfish thing is hard to get used to."

"Tell me about it."

Subject change! "Are you having fun with Carmen?"

"Actually, this is the first real time we've ever spent time together where we weren't all in on surveillance. I maintain a professional distance. Emotional attachments are collateral damage I don't want. I wish you didn't make me like her so much. She was on my nerves like she was on yours before. Now, you've made her too human." He winked down at me. I rolled my eyes, though I smirked.

"Well," I placed the hand I had on his shoulder to my chest. "She had *me* in Pensacola when she gave Queen Diva a run for her money. I don't think Constance is used to being put in her place. You haven't heard from her since she left, have you?"

Jase's brow furrowed. "You haven't?"

I shook my head then chewed my cheek, unable to help worrying worse than before.

"Don't freak. I'll make some calls and see if I can get them on the line. It's possible they were foolish enough not to bring international plugs for their chargers. No way Delia Duncan's father isn't in touch.

If you want, we could go up to the hospital and visit him without you needing stitches or a cleanse for once."

I punched his bicep and he laughed. "I was planning to take a personal day tomorrow. No guys, no killers, no women to envy. Just me and the spa treatments I never allow myself. I need it. My back would probably pop fifty times if you lifted me off the floor." Jase's arms wrapped my waist, but I threw a finger. "Sir, don't you dare in such a refined place. But, when we get to the parking lot, I don't care about manners."

Jase chuckled and laced his fingers together at the base of my spine. "I don't know who you'd be jealous of when you look so amazing, refined and grown-up, like a *real* adult. Crazy, huh?" He tickled my sides till I slapped his chest, then his arms went around me again. My hands held his shoulders like a middle schooler. "Kins, I'm not kidding. You easily belong in this place." He looked down at my body. "I know what place I want you to fit in right now, though."

I tsked his bad behavior and kissed his cheek as Klive came to trade on the next song. Klive offered a polite kiss to Carmen's cheek and passed her to Jase. Carmen gave me huge eyes. I knew mine reflected the sentiment considering Klive's aversion to physical touch. He'd clearly made her whole night. She couldn't wipe the stupidity out of her giddy grin even when she looked up at Jase and tried to present an indifferent facade. Jase shook his head at her. I snorted to myself, happy to be back in these arms, even if I'd enjoyed dancing with Jase. Klive's hand wrapping around my back once more fit like a cozy fleece blanket on a chilly night fraught with scary storms; warm, comfortable and somehow safe. He didn't speak, but he didn't have to. Several times we seemed to test our capacity for silent communication with our eyes, though I did feel a tad hypnotic like this may be a dream I'd wake from at any moment.

13 | ♀

"**May I?**" **a man asked** at the break before the next song. Oh, boy. This one took better care of his hair than Klive did. In my head, I heard, George Clooney's character from *O'Brother Where Art Thou* saying, "I'm a Dapper Dan man" as he took the place Klive vacated.

Hmm, interesting Klive had asked me earlier if I'd wanted to dance with Jase but didn't ask one way or the other with this guy. Were they friends? The Dapper Dan Man made polite conversation. His Southern drawl didn't grate on my nerves once, so only Angela Ansley's annoyed me. This man was a good leader as we weaved a path around and between other couples. I didn't see Klive at the table, though I saw Jase and Rustin sitting together watching the dance floor where both their dates danced with others. Poor Bobbie. So much for not dancing.

Did Klive vanish to the restroom? I tried to hide how I sought his head of dark hair as I so often did, but relief swept down my spine when he appeared at the bar beside another man. Klive turned and our eyes locked immediately. Hopefully, the red in my cheeks wasn't as bright as that of my nails since he'd caught me red-handed.

Klive didn't bother looking away to spare my embarrassment, though I glanced down for a beat. The man leading me around the floor remained in conversation while I wondered more about who was conversing with Klive. The man saw Klive's stare and turned, too, smoothing his hand over his shirt, a bright smile at Klive a moment later. Klive waved at me, but not in the shit-calling way, more in a way that made me smile with the same bright and shiny I found in Klive's array of gorgeous teeth as he cast the man the smile he so rarely revealed. How flattering! Klive wanted that man to know exactly who he was with.

How different this was from our brunch date. Rather than wanting to walk away the way I had that day, I wanted him to walk back toward me and exercise a greedy authority to keep me to himself and unavailable to the rest of the guests. My smile dimmed when Klive turned his back on the dance floor at the same time as his company did. The man tugged a small, folded paper from his pocket and when the mysterious origami unfolded in Klive's fingers, Klive glanced down, nodded, then tucked the paper into his own pocket.

Please, God, tell me he isn't working some sort of drug deal in a refined place like this, on an amazing night together, a night as special as he claimed ... please don't let Klive be lying to me or tricking me ... using me for some sort of cover.

Suddenly, I didn't want to dance anymore. I wanted to be away from everyone and everything, to hide from my observations and keep pretending our date was just that. A date.

As though he sensed my shift, Rustin walked toward us with bubbly Bobbie holding his hand like a couple with a plan.

"She wants to dance with you," Rustin told my partner, "But was too shy to ask on her own. This is me proving I do not mind if you don't?"

My partner said, "Not in the least." He fed her some flattery, thanked me for my company and the dance, said some shmoozy something that went in one ear and out the other. Rustin took his place and didn't say a word until we were away from their earshot.

"You do remember he leads a double life, right?" Rustin asked.

"Did you say that so I can't forget?"

"No, I'm saying what you're thinking may not be what you're thinking. If I can see what you're thinking, others may read the same."

"I'm not an open book, Rusty. You've had a backstage pass, so you can see. I doubt others see the same things. Can we just not do this?" I looked into his electric blue eyes.

"Would you rather me talk about how great your ass looks in this dress?"

I gasped, affronted. Rustin chuckled, did the stupid tally thing, then said, "Girl, you're far too uptight. Where's your sense-of-humor? You're lookin' like you did before you beat the shit outta Ansley. He's not chatting with anyone of the opposite sex and those who have approached him for dances, he's waved away like a true king. Damn snob. His trash has been my treasure all night. I've picked up the spirits of far lower-class ladies. Now, I'm thinkin' I'm missin' out."

I fought a smile and lost. "This may be your ticket to being someone's toy. You must aim older, though, Rusty. You know the younger ones haven't inherited yet. Where does Bobbie fit into this?"

Rustin laughed. "She's a lot of fun, but she's too natural in here. When we drove into the lot, she greeted the hostess by name, so you so see I may be aiming right after all."

My turn to laugh, though mine was more smart-ass. "Please don't screw this up, Rustin. She's one of the few good friends I've made and held onto during my college years. I don't want the awkward tension like with Constance. You really wrecked her."

"What's that? I can't hear you over this amazing song that guy onstage is starting."

"He hasn't started a song yet. We're just standing here swaying to elevator music." I turned my head as I rolled my eyes. My breath caught as Klive's gaze snatched mine once more from where he remained at the bar, blatantly watching now.

"Elevator music? Girl, you need to watch your mouth. If you listen, you can hear them turning the instrumental toward the beginning of *Feeling Good*."

I peered into Rustin's smiling eyes.

"Know what time it is?" Rustin asked as the song took shape. My brow arched as I waited. "Time to say I told you so and show you what you're missing, Mizz Hayes. Hope you can keep up."

"Oh, Rustin, dear, you have no idea who you're messing with. Bring it." I sent him a daring smile through my eyes as Rustin adjusted his form to competitive ballroom style posture. I swallowed, forcing my nervousness to the pit of my stomach. I didn't back down from a challenge, especially when this man was the one throwing the dare. The man onstage crooned the opening lyrics into his microphone.

Butterflies flew into my throat as Rustin dipped me slowly back until my neck relaxed and my hair brushed the floor. *God, please don't let me screw this up!* He eased me up out of the dip even slower, so I had to suffer the whole way up or else appear clumsy. Brat! At least the champagne dulled the pain in my ribs.

No matter how I wanted to give him crap, I was far too excited to play his game when he looked at me with such a glow of adventure in his eyes. His hand at my waist forced my body flush against his. As the beat changed, Rustin stepped confidently forward in such dominance I had no choice but to obey and match his intensity or else look subpar, which was his goal as he guided us professionally around the floor to the point of garnering spectators I had to ignore to remain focused on his sudden shifts. He pushed me away from him as he held my hand tight, twirling me into his grasp as he pulled me back to him, making me laugh and relish spotting once more to keep from getting dizzy. He allowed no time to recover as he twirled me twice beneath his arm, released me altogether, and ran his hands over my hips, up along the sides of my torso until he wrapped his arms around my back as he bent me low again, coming right along with me, experimenting with my flexibility. Rustin gave me no choice but to follow his lead because I had no idea where he would go at each turn. As he manipulated my body, performed small moves that produced clapping from onlookers, I couldn't help thinking of Constance, myself and the ways we were in lust with Rustin's hands in the dark.

Rustin knew how to apply pressure to certain points in the body that created sensuality and made the woman putty in his calloused, country hands. His hand currently ran up the back of my neck, the other holding the back of my thigh as I bent to his will all the way toward the floor again. When he raised me slowly up, my thigh remained in his hand, pressed to his side while his other kept cradling the back of my neck. How he forced me into a spin on one heel and walked me forward with his chest to my back was a dizzying guess I'd have to analyze later. Back and forth as we walked, he'd twist me to face him and away from him, walking us along all the while, a sexy control exercised in a demur place. By the time the song slowed, I worried sweat may bead down my forehead and ruin my makeup along with the dress.

Rustin spun me beneath his arm three fast times, laid me out so fast I nearly cried out in fear, then caught me just above the floor, pulled me back before him, then took a bow before all the new fans of his ability, leaving me with no choice but to pretend I wasn't reeling inside from his showing off and with the unwanted attention he'd drawn.

He leaned near my ear after kissing my hand. "Great job, bitch. I say you get five tallies for only losing your footing once."

I spoke through smiling teeth. "I didn't lose my footing once. I get one of your tallies for you trying to throw shade on my ability to keep up." I clapped my hands for him, gestured toward him to give credit where credit was due, then booked my buns toward the table for some much-needed water.

Bobbie burst with excitement about how she didn't know I could do anything but run. She wanted to know about my background because she'd been in jazz classes when she was little, etcetera, etcetera. Carmen studied my inner mess with the eyes of a detective who didn't miss even your ugly inner crime scenes. Jase beside her had the dumbest adorable, crooked grin, not bothering to hide his enamored awe of this hidden side I'd never shown. Rustin pimp-limped to the table with his collar flipped up, shining his nails on the lapel of his suit jacket.

"I'm heading to the ladies' room to dry my pits," I joked to dispel the girly crap.

Carmen and Bobbie offered to come, but I shook my head. In the restroom, a few ladies asked me about Klive and the guy I'd just danced with. I didn't know how to answer the women, but I did know I wasn't allowing them an inch with Klive, wherever he'd drifted off to during that stunt. Had I just been a great diversion for something he needed to do?

"I am with Mr. King, as his date, yes," I answered a woman reapplying lipstick in the mirror. I dabbed my forehead with the fancy cloth an attendant handed me while this woman's friend watched my face in the reflection. I looked in the mirror and said a silent praise for my mother's tips because my makeup was miraculously intact.

"Are you together?" her friend staring at me asked.

I let the door slam behind me rather than entertaining any further questions, pretending I hadn't heard.

"Oh!" I gasped before a warm hand smothered my squeal of surprise as my back slammed against someone's chest and I found myself in the darkness of a closet. If this wasn't familiar ... speaking of that murder mystery dinner last year. But this was no scripted event, and I had no damn clue who held to me. Alarm rose as I realized Ray could be holding me!

"Don't turn around. Don't scream. Don't trust him," Henley's voice said. Klive's cologne wrapped my panicked senses. Before I could struggle in the pitch blackness, a bright flash of light blinded me. I heard the click of a door. No more Henley or anyone else. I fumbled around, green spots clouding my vision as I pat things, knocking what sounded like stacks of cutlery on the floor until I found a wall I followed, finally wrapping my hand around a door handle. Smooth jazz mixed with sounds of pleasant laughter, glasses clinking, dishes clanking from a bussed table.

"Are you okay, madam?" a waiter asked on his way past.

I nodded. "May I have some water, please?"

"Certainly. You're at the table by the dance floor, correct?"

"That's right, yes."

"Your company was just asking about you."

"I got turned around is all. Nothing to worry about. I appreciate your concern." I hurried to replace my alarm with the calmest expression and posture as possible. Do I tell Klive about Henley? Should I tell Jase? I didn't want to ruin this night! What was Henley doing here and was he meaning for me not to trust Klive? Why was he wearing Klive's cologne?

Rustin intercepted my way through the maze of white tablecloths. "Hey, I was just playing with you. Did I make you dizzy? You seem off."

Game face. "Dammit, Rustin. Yeah, it's been a while since I've turned about a floor so fast, but I had a great time. Next time you won't get the best of me, though." I licked my finger and drew a tally for him. "One for you, bitch."

Rustin laughed with legit pleasure, and I knew then I'd just passed the ultimate lie detector. Well, not the ultimate. Klive stood when I neared the table. Rustin thankfully filled the space with his gloating victory over making me dizzier than Klive had. Klive and I chuckled together.

"Do you need to rest, love?"

"No, actually, if you wouldn't mind, I'd love to dance again to gain my bearings."

"Anything you want," Klive said with that suave charm I loved. He held his arm open. I wrapped my hand around his offering and walked onto the floor with him. Eyes followed us as if they expected an encore. I shook my head like Klive may have offered but that I wanted to take this one easy. Klive smirked as we assumed a far more relaxed posture than Rustin had forced earlier, though Klive had a different vibe now, like I'd held out and he now knew there was a lot more I was capable of.

The male onstage sang in what sounded like Italian, akin to a lullaby in how slow and beautiful the cadence of his voice carried over the floor and tables.

"Out of shape, are you?" Klive joked.

"Hey, I'm working on it. My ribs took quite the twisting, thank you very much." I smiled, praying he'd buy the act, though I wasn't sure I should act. If one of Klive's men was planning mutiny behind his back, he should know. Dammit, I hated Nightshade so much for stealing this night from me! If I told Klive now, Nightshade would steal this night from him, too! Then again, Nightshade may have already stolen him from me with that guy from the bar during my dancing with that Dapper Dan Man and Rustin. *Leave this alone!*

The more I tried, the more something familiar sparked between our bodies, our eyes doing the silent communication again. This time, however, he seemed like he was hiding something the way I was. If I was dating someone, didn't that mean I had a right to ask questions of my date, especially if said date may taint my reputation with his dealings?

Klive broke our silence. "I stand corrected."

My head cocked.

"You're not only great at dancing like a whore," he teased with a wicked grin. I giggled and shook my head. "Another tool in your arsenal against my bloody resolve. You're a beautiful high, my sweet."

I examined his pupils. Had he gone and taken something, shot something up or whatever drug addicts chose to do? Weren't dealers required to try their own products? Was that what that little paper held?

"Klive, are you on drugs right now?" I asked.

He laughed aloud and shook his head like I was crazy. "No. Never. I'm pure. Always coherent. It's vital I remain on my toes so your cop boyfriend cannot touch me."

I gaped at his open candor. "So, you admit you have things to hide?" I challenged.

He tsked softly and continued moving us across the floor like nothing contentious brewed in our conversation. I side-eyed our table. Rustin and Jase chatted with Carmen and Bobbie over some sort of dessert.

"Kinsley, we both know there are things about me others shall not. There are also things about me you're better off *not* knowing. Haven't we been over this?"

I cocked an eyebrow. He cocked his right back. Oh, now I wanted to try him. I pressed forward.

"You mean like knowing you kill people for a living, sir? That sweet, innocent Kinsley was on your list not so long ago?" I sang in false pleasantry with venom underlying my tone.

His grip tightened around my hand and his jaw muscle flinched. His eyes grew dark with warning. Like a stubborn fool, I kept on him.

"That why Henley had the audacity to pull me into a janitor's closet and warn me not to trust you? Am I still on your list? Answer me, Klive." I squeezed his hand right back.

His eyes narrowed a fraction. He licked his soft lips. I couldn't help watching before looking back at his stormy eyes, finding a flicker of heat lightning in those gray clouds.

"I do not kill anyone who doesn't deserve it. You were an exception in many ways. Honestly? I *wanted* to kill you without an order because you're a liability, a distraction, and clearly a problem for a very disobedient dissident who's now earned his way onto the list."

"No! You can't!"

Klive's lips flattened. "I can and will if I feel this merits a permanent solution. Do not mistake who I am or what I do. Mercy shown to criminals encourages further mutiny and crime, not less. It also dents my credibility. I am not a serial killer, nor an impulsive fool. I do not, have not, nor will I ever be gallivanting around killing *sweet Kinsleys*." His eyes flashed with anger. "Although, again, it seems I *should* have."

I gasped and gripped his shoulder tighter so I wouldn't slap him in public. "I dare you, Klive." I stomped my heel, standing up to this side of him, pissed off. His eyes surveyed the room before landing back on mine, his jaw muscle flinching again.

"Sweet words, love. Maybe I'll take you up on that," he practically growled. His mouth dipped toward my ear. "I need to fuck you first. Maybe kill you after I make you climax over and over, so you die happily, and I have a memory to keep."

Klive pulled away only far enough that our lips were an inch apart. His warm breath bathed my mouth as twisted heat pulsed through my body and the desire to kiss him overwhelmed my temper toward him. His palm at my back spread wide and he jerked me against him so I would know, *feel*, I wasn't the only screwed up one in this demented desire. My eyes sought his. His angry irises hot with passion like blue flames branded me with unfulfilled promises he created a silent deadline for. How long before he got those hands on me the way he'd said? How long till I could take no more and begged for what I should've been ashamed of wanting?

"Ahem." A throat cleared. We both looked at the source with the anger we had for each other. Jase cringed. "Is this a bad time? I have to work early at the beach and wanted to see if I could get one more dance with Kins before we have to leave?"

Klive's smug arrogance landed on me, as if I were lucky Jase had come to my rescue and couldn't handle his temper on my own. Psh! As if! Maybe I make Klive come to the point of begging me rather than me wanting to beg him! Put him in his place and make him submit! Be the real boss!

Carmen blushed when Klive took her to dance and accidentally pulled her too close. Jase cleared his throat again, so I'd look at him instead of casting Constance's voodoo curses against Klive in my head.

"Down girl. Tame it down. If it gets any hotter between you two, the sprinklers are gonna go off and ruin everyone's attire. I paid a lot for this damn monkey suit I'll never wear again."

I grumbled instead of laughing at his joke.

"He tell you anything interesting? Something must've pissed you off pretty bad."

"Nah." I shook my head. "Nothing we didn't already know. Same ol' shit I hate about all this. What can I say? We are talented at pushing each other's buttons. Or mashing them. Can we please drop the subject? I need you to lighten me up or take me to the bathroom for an unrefined moment."

He laughed at my vulgarity. "No can do, baby. Your dark passenger is visiting and I'm a law-abiding citizen who doesn't run red lights. I'll be waiting when you're done so you can take the anger out on me if you'd like. Rustin could help if it's really bad." His naughty grin was meant to ruffle my feathers, but I wasn't in the mood.

"Jase Taylor, you're supposed to be helping me, not making me angrier. Next time I get with you on the course, I'm beating your ass the way I did Rustin's. I don't care what y'all say. I took him down."

That memory did make me smile.

"Rustin will be pleased you enjoyed taking him down."

"Yeah, well, so long as you don't give him the impression that I enjoy going down with him, understood. I meant what I said. I'm not doing that ever again with you guys. I'm not polyamorous."

"Uh, huh." Jase pursed his lips and avoided my eyes on purpose. Bastard. "Look, I really do have to be at work early. Rustin and Bobbie rode with me and Carmen just in case Bobbie was too needy toward Rustin. He needed a buffer."

"Jase, sometimes I'd love not seeing behind the curtain of men's brains, please. Leave some hope for women, even if it's foolish and pointless."

"Klive's got his hands full tonight."

"There will be no tonight beyond this date. I'm letting him drive me home and I doubt he'll even get a kiss at the doorstep unless I offer an ass cheek."

"Glad to see I've helped," Jase joked. I rolled my eyes. "I'm serious. You just smiled even if you didn't want to. My work here is done."

His strong arms hugged me hard enough to pop the tension from my back. Jase led us off the floor toward ur table. Klive's voice said something to Carmen I couldn't quite ascertain, but I heard his tone was light and charming again. She blew a kiss at me for the favor she'd done. Time to put my weapons down and surrender for now. Jase thanked Klive for inviting them, Rustin seconding behind him. Bobbie rushed to pull Klive's cheek down to her lips. He grinned at me with a tone that said, *see, not all women hate me, just you, my sweet love.*

Klive signed the check and refused anyone's attempt to contribute toward the total or tip, then he grabbed my hand, wound his fingers between mine and we walked out of the restaurant with eyes following every move.

14 | ♀

When we reached the valet, Klive's arm snaked around my waist. "Were you serious about knowing how to drive a manual transmission?"

"Huh?" I asked as he handed the ticket to the man in the red uniform.

"It has the ability to drive in automatic as well, but paddle shifters are so fun."

"Klive, what are you saying?" I peered up at him like he'd lost his marbles.

"No obligation, mind you. But, if you'd like to drive, here's your chance."

I gasped and eyed him like he held the most sinful piece of chocolate cake I'd ever laid my eyes on.

"Klive, don't play like that."

"Who's playing?" He dipped his forehead toward mine, little glint in his eyes as the corner of his mouth perked. "But if I am, it's to win. Anything less is unacceptable."

I pursed my lips as I fought the insane urge to rip his head toward me and kiss the hell out of him. Who cared what others thought of me at this point? I'd already become a scandalous subject, what was one more thing? My heart hammered against my rib cage as the car pulled up to where we stood. Jase and Rustin cursed, jaws dropping like Klive had snapped their legs right out from under them. I giggled, beaming brighter than a Maglite in the dark, unable to tame my girly stupidity.

Jase walked around the car, wiping the corner of his mouth, tilting his head as he scoped the back like a woman's ass. "A 458 Italia ... you sonuvabitch ... she's super sexy, King."

Klive smirked at me while Jase drooled over the silky black beauty gleaming spiffy clean beneath the parking lot lights. "Yes, she is." He quirked his brows.

Bobbie openly complimented Klive on his pretty car. Carmen chewed her lip like she'd throw Klive on the hood and rip his suit off him if no one were around.

Rustin tapped his invisible watch and cleared his throat for Jase to get over his shit since the truck was parked behind the Ferrari.

Jase thanked the valet, tipped him, then looked at Klive. "Take good care of my girl tonight, asshole." He grinned at me though. "Next time I get to be King's date so I can ride in the Ferrari, understand?"

We all chuckled.

"Oh, Jase," I sang, "it gets better." I kissed his cheek, wished him sweet dreams and accepted the valet's hand when the driver's door to the Italia opened for me. Jase pulled his phone and snapped several pics of me sitting down in the driver's seat.

"Screw the races. Can we pose her with this car in that dress?" Jase muttered more to himself.

Rustin and Klive laughed. They said their goodnights while I adjusted the mirrors, seat, steering wheel to my liking, familiarizing myself with as much as possible so I didn't make a damn fool of myself or ruin Klive's generosity. I pulled the door closed and inhaled a long, steady breath, the insanity seeping in for how freaking cool this was! Music. The touch screen glowed ready for a command. A line slowly formed at the valet, but most of the groups seemed too interested in Klive's interest in me to care about the wait. I did care, however, and was tired of sharing my date and my business with strangers. Finding the window buttons, I rolled the window down and ordered Klive to get his fine ass inside the car before I jacked his toy and he walked home.

He laughed and sank into the passenger seat a second later. "Surely I could play the hitchhiker in this?"

"Sir, you can play whatever role you want right now. I'm so ready to go." I reached across and buckled his seatbelt before he had the chance. I was so thrumming with energy. As I eased us into drive, I allowed him to instruct me on her handling and sensitivities before I caught the hang of the exotic car's luxury. Jase's truck followed, his headlights in my back window for how low we rode. "Klive, music, now, sir! You're the navigator, you're supposed to be on top of this." I snapped my fingers. "Something totally heavy, please."

To my delight, Klive requested Little Smirk from his sound system. We stopped at the final red light before the highway entry ramp. As we idled, I peered over at him, unable to hide my ridiculous smile.

"I can't handle this anymore!" I gushed and pulled him by the back of the head to kiss the hell out of him until I saw the light glow green from the corner of my eye. I pushed his face away and burned rubber up the ramp. Pleasure and adrenaline raced through my veins and fingers at the seamless acceleration of the dream car in my hands. The highway was dead. My turn to fly the way Jase and Klive loved to.

This time I watched Jase's headlights fade as I pinned Klive and me back to our seats and yelled in triumph like I'd won a heat, the engine growling just behind us. The music blared and I went into the same competitive focused zone I have during a great workout. After a beat, I risked a glance at Klive and laughed. He'd turned in his seat, his head lying against the head rest, watching me, openly enthralled.

He didn't mind at all that I took advantage of this moment. He relished my enjoyment!

Klive produced his phone, lifted the device for a photo of me, then tapped his screen. The music changed. I swallowed the sudden dryness in my throat. Whitesnake. Slow An' Easy. Chills broke over my skin as the lyrics started. I bit my lip while I held both hands firmly on the wheel. Dirty, sexy music for a dirty sexy car and a dirty sexy guy beside me. Not a good place to be when trying to keep chastity intact, well, the chastity I was working to repair at least.

How would Klive know about this song? This was one of my guilty pleasures when I was alone, dirty dancing in my apartment while cleaning. Did he know? How? Maybe this was coincidence, and he liked the song, too? Either way, I sensed he'd not taken his eyes off me and stared harder if possible. I tried ignoring the chemistry brewing in the little space between us much like the day we'd had lunch with my father. Focusing on the way this amazing car felt didn't help the way I needed what I shouldn't have. This was like a drug for me!

I sang along with the song and eventually slowed to a cruise at about ninety miles per hour, not believing I'd been driving so fast by mistake! Yikes! How fast had I been going if this seemed slow? Jeez. I released a heavy breath, tension coiling between my shoulder blades, and slowed the car even more. The exit was about a mile away. If I were in Jase's car, I'd have asked for a lesson in doing donuts, but this was far too elegant a car for that. This must be how Jase feels when driving his Charger. I understood him a little better now.

As I slowed for the exit ramp and looked for anyone yielding, I noticed Klive's enthralled trance hadn't wavered, but intensified. I couldn't help the dirty sexy smile I gave him. I pushed loose strands of hair out of my face as we coasted toward the red light in the lonely intersection.

The moment I stopped, Klive quickly shifted the car into park and threw his seatbelt off, lunging across the space between us. In breathless seconds, he was all over me and I was moaning for more of the heady high as his hands roamed the way they had when we'd been in bed at Delia's. My fingernails dug into his hair to force his mouth harder against mine as if we could be any closer. Hot lust burned my insides, inflaming every desperate part of my body when he groaned my name between angle changes. Oh, what the sound of Klive's animalistic need for more did to me!

I cracked one eye open to check the light and saw distant headlights gleaming in the rear-view mirror. The green light turned red again. I shoved against Klive against my own will.

"Klive," I sighed against his mouth. "Someone's coming."

He mumbled a protest against my jaw, his hungry lips working their way down.

To my dismay, red and blue lights flashed behind us.

"Shit! Shit! Shit!" I forced Klive off me as I freaked! I was so damn screwed!

Since the car was already stopped and the intersection remained empty, I didn't move the car.

"Relax, love." Klive sat back against his seat and adjusted himself and his clothing, a hand swiping his hair. I smoothed my appearance before the cop arrived at the window. Too bad he wasn't a deputy I was familiar with. Klive quickly silenced the radio and I looked up into the face of the cop.

"Officer," I said by accident, thinking of how Rustin hated that. I cleared my throat, my cheeks red hot, and I cast my most innocent doe eyes.

His stoic lips twitched. There may be a chance!

His lips flattened again. Dammit.

"Ma'am. Do you know how fast you were going back there?"

Curses barraged my brain while I shook my head, praying I'd already slowed down when he'd tracked my speed.

"License, insurance and registration, please."

I dug through my tiny wallet while Klive passed the insurance and registration to me. The deputy took what I offered without looking.

"Kill the engine and step outside the vehicle." He lifted his flashlight to my license and backed away to give me room.

More mental curses. I peeked at Klive one more desperate time, but he was chill if not a little amused. Easy for him. He wasn't on thin ice with the Sheriff. Klive shooed me out of the car. I stood up out of the low bucket seat, realizing too late how high Klive had pushed my dress up my thighs. As I rushed to right this wrong, the cop's flashlight beam hit my legs. How effin' unprofessional!

"Have you been drinking tonight?" His light rose to my face. I squinted and turned away. He shined the light at the ground for me. Well, hell. This was a tricky one.

"Yes, but only a little, and I had a lot to eat, and it was a couple hours ago." Shit. Stop talking!

"I see, Ms. Hayes. I'm gonna need you to blow into the end of this device, please." He held a breathalyzer. Come on! No walking the line? ABC's? Nothing? Not that I was familiar with sobriety tests on a personal level, but I'd seen less for drunks leaving the bar for goodness' sakes.

My tongue traced inside my cheek. Man-up. Accept the consequences. I blew into the device.

He winced. "Point-oh-nine. I'm going to have to place you under arrest. You were going one-hundred-twenty-three miles per hour back there. That's fifty-three miles per hour over the speed limit and you're over the legal limit for alcohol consumption. Please, turn around, lean up against the back of the car and place your hands behind your head."

At first, I stared, awed at my gross violation of the law. Damn, that was a fast car! Then, when he walked behind me to urge me to comply, reality set in worse than after my fight with Angela. I was under arrest! For real! All my own fault! No more track! A record, possibly involving a suspended license! A paragraph in the local paper! Daddy would read that and weep!

My heels scratched the pavement through my reluctant shuffle toward the back of the Ferrari. As I bent over, the deputy took one of my hands before I could even cup the back of my head. Shit was never so real as this moment when the cold harsh metal of a handcuff cinched tight around my wrist. I heard and felt Klive's passenger door slam.

"Come now, Jerry, let her go. She's never been in trouble before."

"Klive?!" The deputy choked on his name. "I didn't know she was with you." His hand around my free wrist paused, bracing the dangling cuff near my skin. In this insane moment, I had the audacity to thank God for how clean this car was since my dress was cream. Thinking of anything else was better than this fate. "Man, I already listed the charges on the dash cam. I have no choice but to bring her in."

"No, allow me to call Ansley. He owes me several favors. I'll take care of this. You won't be in any trouble. Hell, I'll even throw a generous bonus in your locker. What do you say?" Klive leaned against the back of the car, hands in his pockets like this was a casual business transaction. I did my best to stay quiet and neutral, though Klive tilted his head as he perused my predicament. "I'll throw extra in for the cuffs. She looks very sexy in them, don't you agree?"

Holy shit! I swallowed. Klive walked close enough to nudge the cop out of his way and took his place behind me, cuffing my free wrist. He was hard against me as I lay bent over.

"Jerry, you may leave now. She's been apprehended. In my custody she will no longer pose a risk to other drivers."

Deputy Jerry chortled. "Right. I suppose you were pumping gas and this girl just stole your vehicle with you in it." I heard Klive chuckle. Jerry leaned into my eye line. "Ma'am, is this consensual?"

I rolled my eyes. "Yes, Deputy, unfortunately it is," I admitted, furious I had to take ownership of such slutty scandal. Clearly that's how bad I didn't want to be arrested.

The deputy clucked his tongue before grinning at Klive like he admired him. "Alrighty, King. Enjoy. I'll put in for more cuffs, but you'd better call Ansley ASAP because I don't want my ass on the line for yours, got it?"

Klive scoffed. "Jerry, you know me better than that. I'm good for it. It'll be in your locker in the morning. See you later."

The deputy's tires crackled over the pavement, his engine echoing beneath the empty overpass moments later. The only light left was from the traffic light flicking from yellow to red.

15 | ♀

"**Oh, my sweet Kinsley Hayes,** what am I going to do with you?" Klive asked, taunting and teasing. "You are in so much trouble and you look so good under a red light." He tilted his head to my right enough for me to see him give the sexiest smoldering grin. I clasped my fingers together and bit my lip because I wasn't sure how to handle the erotic aspect with the emotional overload of almost being arrested again. Holy crap I had to quit finding myself on the wrong edge of the law.

Klive twisted me to face him and lifted me to sit on the back of the car. His eyes held mine while his hands drifted from my waist over my hips, along my thighs, fingertips whispering against my knees. I swallowed when he wet his lips as he watched mine open wide when he splayed his fingers over my kneecaps and pulled my thighs apart.

I whispered his name, trying to fight the shocking impropriety of him stepping between my legs, his hands running up the insides of my thighs. Again, I tried to plead his name, but I wasn't sure what I warred with most; the fact that this was so bad or that I wanted his bad side. His thumbs squeezed, pausing their traveling just before hitting the motherland.

"Hmm ... do I take you now? On top of my car like the ultimate fantasy to get you out of my system? Out of my head so I might think straight for the first time in over two years?" Klive's thumbs dug slightly. His tone made me think of those thumbs pulling back the hammer on a pair of gray pistols as cold as his eyes could go when angry. Right now, those eyes could've lit the way in the dark they were so alight with naughty adventure.

This predator was a different animal than Jase. This one took no prisoners. He killed them instead. I believe these hands could send me to the darkest depths if they traveled any further, but I also gleaned a ruthlessness that said he got what he wanted when he wanted and right now, he wanted me wanton in his grasp, begging for more. Thank goodness I was so on edge I wasn't as ready to wilt as I'd been on Monday night in his bedroom.

Klive released one of my thighs to clutch the back of my neck beneath my hair, pulling my face closer to his.

"Kinsley, you drive me fucking crazy, love." His nose skimmed my throat, a deep inhalation of my perfume reminiscent of how I suck wind with his cologne. Why did Henley wear Klive's cologne? Because I liked the smell? Why didn't Klive make a big deal of what I told him about Henley? That had to be bad, right? Calm before the storm?

"You smell amazing," Klive mumbled against my sensitive skin. No way Klive loved my perfume the way I loved his fragrance. The weak groan said otherwise and sent a pleasing power surge through my heartbeat. His lips brushed my jaw and kissed toward my earlobe. I tilted my head, wishing for his lips on my mouth, but he didn't give me what I wanted. His rough stubble skimmed down my neck instead. The fingers around the back of my neck trailed to the back of my dress, making me arch against him.

"I'm so ready to unzip this dress. You'd be so sexy if I took this off you and left you in cuffs on my car." His lips parted over the skin he'd just scraped with his stubbled chin.

"Klive," I panted his name, trying to think straight through the fog of lust. "Not yet ... not here ... please ... please ... wait ...." I moaned when his lips nipped mine.

"Why not end my torture now while I have you at my *complete* mercy?" His tone lowered, darker. The cuffs bit into the flesh of my wrists when I struggled.

"I told you the other night," I said, trying to back up a few inches, failing.

His hot cheek met mine. "So? His voice stroked my ear.

"Klive! Please!"

"Hmm ... that's what I like to hear. For what are you begging? Would you like me to use my thumb for things I did at Delia's?" His thumb brushed the satin of my panties. I gasped and squirmed for less and more at the same time, trying to fight the image he painted of how he'd made me cry his name at her house before his kisses smothered my voice so we didn't wake anyone. We were alone here, for now, but that could change with a single set of headlights exiting the highway.

"Oh, Kins ... your hot, sweet breath against my ear, pleading, moaning my name ... how do I behave?"

"Please, behave, Klive. Please, just take me home now. I need you ... need you ... need you to be stronger again. You know I want you so much, but not here. I don't want to rush."

Please, let these trigger words work again!

"Klive, I need you to be strong for me!" I shoved the words from my weak lips before I added to my foolish regrets. The hell if I was gonna have a first time with Klive on the back of the car, rushing to keep from getting caught. Nope.

Suddenly, Klive jerked away like I'd kicked him in the stomach.

"Shit!" He ran his palm through the side of his hair, then tossed his hand at me. "I have to take you back to *my* house. Jerry has the bloody key!" His words slapped the lust out of my head. He lifted me from the car, but kissed me hard, his tongue stroking mine like he needed me to know how difficult this waiting game was becoming. I kissed him back, thinking of anything I could say or do to convince him to take me back to my place instead. His bed with him in the sheets played too tempting a movie in my mind for my liking.

Klive broke our connection to call Jerry. While he arranged for Jerry to be at his house in twenty minutes, he opened the passenger door for me. I backed toward the seat, feeling for the leather in a light-headed dizziness, my knees weak. Klive placed a hand to my back and bent over me as he guided me down to the seat.

"I'll be flying home and I don't want anyone stopping me for speeding, understand? Clear my path." He paused, nodded. "That's what I like to hear."

He closed me inside the car like he didn't want to see the awed expression on my face for how he pocketed police like lucky pennies in a parking lot. Was Rustin in Klive's control yet, too? On one hand, if Klive hadn't had the authority he did, I'd be in jail and facing DUI charges. On the other, if bad guys ran the show behind the scenes, were good people buying an illusion funded by their own taxes while wicked entities used good guy uniforms to indulge their naughty habits? Inferno established their reputation through various undercover busts over the years. They no longer bothered hiding in plain sight. But how much were the rest hiding and how deep were they beholden to crime bosses like Klive to keep their secrets?

I heard Klive bitching at someone on the phone at the back of the car. He now had this secret on me. This was scary. So was the sinister glare in his eyes when he sat in the driver's seat. Someone pissed him off bad. He didn't speak and I didn't dare break the thick silence. The only sound was his thumbs prancing rapidly over his phone as he texted like crazy. I watched his jaw muscle tense and untense about five times in a row. His phone hit the cup holder, then he leaned across to buckle my belt the way I had him earlier, only he didn't have the giddy joy I'd had.

He sat fixing his seat, steering wheel and mirrors, then held the center of the wheel and rested his other hand on my thigh. I didn't detect a sexual undercurrent. More like he gripped me like he wanted me to remain in his grasp, protective in a way.

I found a tiny flicker of voice. "Maybe you should still take me to my house."

"Kinsley, this vehicle is a vacation of sorts for me. I don't keep lock-picking tools in here. This is my reprieve. Now, love, think about it. Your neighbors' interests were already piqued when I picked you up. How would it look if you get out of my car wearing handcuffs, then a sheriff's deputy pulls into your driveway? Give me a little credit." He squeezed my thigh once more, then patted my knee. "My turn to blow off steam." He tapped his touch screen. The heavy chords of *Welcome to the Jungle* came through his speakers and he turned them up loud. "Hang on, love!" Klive's head tossed back on a laugh. "That's right, you can't."

My jaw clenched and hands clasped behind my back as Klive threw me against the door when he gunned the hell out of his engine and took the U-turn under the highway. I screamed when we came around the other side and slid across a couple of lanes for all the G-forces in the turn. He straightened the car and floored the pedal and clutch, shifting with the paddle in his hand, checking over his shoulder as we merged onto the highway. As Axle Rose sang, Klive found his cruising speed, which was faster than anything I'd done, and cast an evil smile at me. Fabulous. Nightshade Klive King was in the house and feeding off my fear like a demon eating enough energy needed for wicked games. I knew normal Klive was a sucker for me, but I wasn't sure if this compartmentalized side cared more for me or the job.

Speaking of fear, a car merged onto the highway coming right into our path. I squeezed my eyes shut, unsure how Klive would maneuver us around them without spinning out or sliding too hard to the point of throwing us into the concrete barrier between the directions. My body pinned harder against my hands when he didn't slow or hit the brakes at all, but sped up! I braved a look and saw in my right mirror that the headlights faded fast. Damn!

"Klive!" I shouted over the music, my anger joining his. "How damn fast are you going? That was some crazy scary bullshit and I want to live to see tomorrow, asshole!" I watched Klive chuckle, though I couldn't hear the sound over the engine and the music.

"You don't want to know!" he shouted. "Just sit back and trust me! Your boyfriend isn't the only one who can drive, baby!"

I rolled my eyes and chewed my lip, trying my best to sit back. My shoulders were starting to ache, and my wrists were cutting off circulation to my hands. Every time I bumped my fingers, pins and needles shot up my arms. Seeing my inability to move, Klive reached across and pulled my dress high up on my thighs. His hand rested at the top of my exposed skin. I wanted to bitch at him about only holding the wheel with one hand while going so fast but was too distracted by the cop we passed sitting on the side of the road. We passed the cruiser in a blur. No lights or sirens. Nothing.

"Imagine that!" I shouted. He could do whatever he wanted! He side-eyed me like a mind reader.

"Exactly!" he yelled over the change in tempo on the song. "That's how I roll! Don't you forget it, either!"

I narrowed my eyes at him. Was that a threat? Hell, I should feel threatened that cops were nothing to him. This town needed Jase; someone with real muscle to bring this cocky bastard and his ilk down. I shoved him out of my mind. I needed to be good, so I didn't accidentally blow Jase's cover. Also, I wasn't looking to give Klive a real reason to kill me.

Just breathe. In one ... two ... three ....

I watched Klive and the road, then Klive again. He sang along with a particular set of lyrics that had undertones of violence and death mixed with a sexually-laced current aimed at a woman. I'd never listen to this song the same way again and the heavy rock was one of my favorites for kicking ass on the obstacle course. This was the same man I'd seen get pissed at Ray on the phone. The one who'd felt me up at the Ren Faire and towed me on a rope. He was dark, not sweet. This guy had pent-up aggression and wanted his release.

He looked at me when Axle asked if someone knew where they were. Klive narrowed his eyes as he told me I was going to die with the lyrics.

Holy shit! Scary Klive in full force!

Think, Kins! Something must've set him off and might have to do with you. The way he grabbed your thigh like he needed to protect you. Think of the things he said on Monday about keeping you safe, not harming you. He wants you afraid, just like he wanted you afraid when he threw the rose at your feet. All bullshit. All pretend. He's pushing you away. Pay attention. Observe. Remove the personal from this.

Taking the personal out of this proved difficult with the pain in my hands and arms, not to mention everything else making me super pissed at him.

He removed his hand from my legs as he came to our exit, which was insane! One song. What was that, like five minutes? To get us to an exit that takes twenty minutes to get back to? Klive slowed considerably. When we were doing the speed limit, the car seemed to be crawling compared to how fast we'd been going. He merged onto the exit ramp, down shifting again while slowing us to a real crawl until stopping at the light before the intersection. Five Finger Death Punch flowed through the speakers. *Never Enough.* Another favorite, but the heavy fed his aggression. Then again, the more I listened to lyrics I usually blindly sang along to, the more I realized he may be venting through his music, especially because he sang along with every lyric from the start where he hadn't on the Guns-n-Roses. He glanced at me with drawn brows, kept singing. I licked my lips and pursed them tight to remain silent when I really wanted to pick his angry brain about what had set him off back there.

The light changed and my give-a-damn left, fear back in place as we took a road I'd never been on through so many curves he took way too fast through dense forest at either side. The car held to the ground very well, thank goodness, because Klive loved speed, could definitely drive and made Jase's stunt on the bridge pale in comparison.

In the distance, streetlights and esplanades came into view. His neighborhood! *Thank you, Lord!* Only a couple more miles and we'd be crawling again!

Just as I released some of the tension from my shoulders, Klive floored the pedal again and we fired forward on the final straight-of-way, nailing me back on my hands, pain, pins and needles stabbing my arms.

"Klive! What are you doing! The gate!" I shouted, pleaded, then screwed my eyes shut tight and prayed like crazy the way I had on the bridge. Suddenly, the seatbelt cinched me in place as Klive slammed the brakes and sent us into sideways slide! I screamed and kept my eyes closed until we came to a complete stop. The smell of smoking rubber came through the air vents. Klive turned the music down and I heard him laughing at me! WTF?!

"You crazy sonuvabitch asshole dick! You're so lucky I'm cuffed right now!" I spat while my blood boiled. Klive laughed harder and drove casually toward the gate like nothing had happened. The heavy iron moved for us, sensing what I guessed was the little barcode in the top of his windshield. No guard on this side. Interesting.

Klive threaded the car like a needle through the beautiful streets and manicured esplanades. His private gates opened for him, and he drove the car through the trees around the back of the house to a side I'd never seen before. From here, before he drove into a smaller garage, I glimpsed a boat tucked beneath a two-story deck.

The car turned off while the garage door finished closing behind us. The dark silence was the best solitude. *Thank you, God, for getting me back to solid still ground again.* I closed my eyes in prayer and kept them closed, listening to Klive exit the car and the garage as well a moment later. I didn't care. When he came back to unlock the cuffs, I was going to give him a piece of my mind and a sharp slap to the face, but right now, I was content with the sound of the car cooling, my breathing and the silent gratitude I said in my mind.

16 | ♀

After nodding off for however long, the door opened. Klive carefully removed me from the car, cautious not to bump my painfully numb, yet not numb, arms and shoulders. He closed the car door with his hip and chirped the alarm. I relaxed against his chest as he carried me through his house, beyond the passage, into his room where he laid me gingerly onto my belly in his bed. When he grasped my wrists, I winced. The cuffs came loose and Klive rubbed the blood back into my hands, forcing me to bear the pain of feeling coming back into my skin. He released me and rolled me over to my back. Klive stood with his legs pressed to my knees while looking down at me in that way he has with his eyes only, not angling his head.

The gray in his eyes was stormy, conflicted. The dark lashes cast shadows on his face, making his whole appearance seem mean. I noticed his tie was gone and his shirt was unbuttoned at the top. Both cuffs rolled up on his forearms and his watch had vanished. I spied a single red dot above one of the buttons, tiny, but there. He looked down to where I stared.

"Bollocks! This is one of my favorites! Certainly, the cleaner will get it out," he muttered to himself. As he began unbuttoning, I noticed one of his right knuckles had dried blood caked over the skin. I sat up and grabbed his hand for a closer look. My thumb nail dug against the spot and fresh blood flowed forth.

"Klive?" I tilted my chin up at him. "What happened?"

"Just business, love. Nothing to concern yourself about. It's handled," he finished cryptically, the pissy anger coming back into his face, jaw muscle flinching.

Fear filled my eyes as my breathing shallowed. He'd needed release. Had the person he straightened out, or killed, deserved the punishment, or had Klive taken to beating the hell out of someone because he was in a rage? Paralysis stole the feeling from all my limbs. If I wanted to run right now, I'd be out of luck, and I hated this weakness!

"Hey, don't look at me like that," he said. "I didn't kill anyone if that's what you're thinking. I had to set someone straight, that's all. Don't you think if it were that bad, there'd be more blood on my shirt?"

"Where's your blazer?" I challenged like a fool.

A slow smile lifted the corners of his lips. "You, my sweet, are a very smart girl." He pointed at me, impressed, then his face turned to stone with his tone. *"Right?"*

Okay, clearly someone didn't want to be fucked with.

My breathing picked up at his real threat, but I wasn't ready to give in so easily. I was so tired of bullies. I didn't date bullies and I didn't put up with them anymore!

Gripping my panic was like holding sand. Though some leaked through my fingers, I held enough to force my limbs to move through the fear. I pushed against him, but he didn't budge. Klive stood like a solid wall and wanted me to feel threatened.

"Klive King, if you do not move and let me stand up ...."

"What? What are you going to do, Kinsley?" He cocked his head to the side, peering down at me as if I were a creature he'd never seen before, challenging me to buck his authority.

I decided to lie back down and relax on the mattress, though I held his gaze. He shifted slightly and that was all I needed. I pulled my legs up and sent a kick straight to his balls, nailing him with both high-heeled feet. He doubled over and fell onto the bed. Rather than run from him, I rolled to my side and propped my chin in one hand. With my free hand, my nails skimmed up and down his back the way I'd pondered doing not so long ago. I almost laughed at the ability to finally do so under these circumstances. Up, then back down ....

"You okay, Klive?" I asked in a sweet tone. I'd face him and force him to face me. Whatever repercussions I suffered, I deserved. If I didn't test my limits, I'd never know them, or his.

Klive's hands went to either side of his head like he prepared to push off the bed. He remained there, face down on the comforter for a while. Probably trying to cool those hot jets.

"Whenever you're ready to quit planning my murder, let me know."

He rolled to his side and kept his left cheek pressed to the blanket as he sought my face with utter disgust all over his. "You're *not* a smart girl at all, are you?" he asked elegantly, pissed off.

I gasped. "Oh, so you're calling me *stupid* now?" I clutched his shoulder and kneed him in the balls again, this time throwing my anger and offense behind the force. Wow. That was my training kicking in, pure and simple. Jase would love the way Klive grabbed himself and rolled to his stomach.

Leaving him whining like a bitch into the blanket, I walked into the bathroom to run myself a bath. Remaining calm was the best option. With a bear, you play dead. With dogs, you never run. The animal may lose interest in hurting you and you may get out with your life.

The scents of chamomile and vanilla softened the air as I poured the bubble bath I'd so longed for on Monday night. In the Closet of Kinsley, I gathered fresh panties and a pale pink cotton nightie. I took a private moment to take care of my lady business, then sauntered out to turn off the water. When my bare feet padded across the carpet in the bedroom, Klive still laid on the bed, unmoving.

"Klive, get your ass off the bed and unzip this dress. Don't even think about coming onto me right now!" I snapped my fingers. "Thank you."

I sat on the bed beside him. He rolled to his side, looking at me again. My eyebrows shot up in authority.

"Klive, unzip it, *now*. I have a bath calling my name and I'm done waiting. If I have to pull this dress over my head, I will," I said through clenched teeth. In honesty, I was amazed at this new side of myself that didn't take shit anymore.

Klive didn't say a word. He sat up on his elbow and dragged the zipper down with the other hand. When his nails skimmed my skin, I turned on him in a flash.

"What did I say?" My finger pointed in his face.

His hand flew up in surrender. I got up from the bed, pulling the dress and undies off as I went. He had a punishing look at my naked backside, then I slammed the door to the bathroom, killing his view. I locked the door and pulled the tufted stool from beneath the vanity and turned the pretty seat sideways to wedge the length beneath the doorknob. My fingers worked the hair style from up-do to sloppy bun on top of my head, then I figured out the lights and the fireplace. When at last I sank into the full tub, the only light was the glow of flickering flames beside the water. Too bad I didn't know how to work Klive's hidden sound system. I could use some music to soothe the tension from the terrifying car ride and scary Klive.

My head tilted back against the porcelain as I counted breaths, my body slowly releasing the tension and pain in my shoulders. I chose to look past Nightshade Klive as some scary legend and see him for what he was: just a man who could be a tyrant when his temper raged. A man who would not intimidate me. If he wanted to kill me for my attitude, he best bring the shit, but I wasn't living under someone's thumb in fear any longer or ever again. Beating the hell out of Angela had opened me up to the freedom of standing up for myself. No turning back.

I jumped about ten minutes later when Klive's sound system came on with a song I'd never heard before at the same time as Klive bravely dipped into my reheating water. My chin twisted toward the door. The stool was still wedged in place. What the hell? I looked at him with angry confusion. He nestled into the other spot carved for a second person while a male sang about not needing a lover but liking keeping someone around.

Klive scooted up to put his hands behind my back and pulled me against him. My legs had to wrap around his waist, which was intimate as hell! Naked me with naked Klive! I could barely breathe, but I did my damnedest to ignore what I could. His hand held the back of my neck as his eyes searched mine with an intensity I'd never seen before. This wasn't lust. He seemed afraid and I hated the pain there, but damn if he'd just had his balls handed to him twice, he should be afraid. The fact that he pulled me close or touched me at all meant he was either very stupid or those balls were made of steel.

I turned my face from him, still angry, determined to be stronger than the ache in his expression.

"Kins, love, please forgive me. I'm sorry. I won't speak to you like that again." His forehead leaned against my temple for a few seconds, then he hooked my chin with his finger, forcing me to look at him, but I resisted and kept my face turned away. He sighed. In my periphery, he ran his wet hands over his face, his head tilting back. "Please, Kins, I *promise*. Please, don't turn away from me. I hate it."

Hmm ... a Klive promise? That wasn't a word he used often. When he gently urged my face toward him again, this time I braved another look into his eyes, finding them filled with sincere apology beyond words. He laid back against the porcelain, bringing me with him as he hugged my body close. Though he didn't try anything sexual, my heart practically pounded out of my chest and hammered his ribcage when he kissed me ever so softly, pausing between each peck of his pliable lips, nuzzling my nose with his. Eventually, I kissed him back. We didn't fully open our mouths, no tongue action, just parted lips seeking sips of affection that thawed my ice more and more with each sweet kiss he gave. This was far more intimate than raunchy making out or feeling each other up in bed. The effort to hold back coupled with the discipline of small gestures rather than caving to every repressed desire said so much about not only him toward me, but me toward him. Dammit, Klive. Jase going all in after I'd waited for years was easier to handle than this.

This man, I later learned was named Noah Gundersen, was singing about not letting someone down. Klive sent a playful pinch to my side, so I'd know to listen to what he didn't know to say with his own mouth. I laughed since that was a tickle spot, then took advantage of him holding my ribs as I lifted my arms over my head the way I'd done in ballet, stretching into beautiful form. My eyes closed as my smile broadened at the sensation I so rarely indulged in anymore, but I'd not had a man holding me in this way since my *pas de deux* partner in my final recital. I sensed Klive watching, or staring at my breasts, but I didn't care because what man had a rack in his face and didn't make a move? Meh, I guess a gay man.

I smiled brighter at my thoughts and let the music wash over me with whatever these new emotions I couldn't define might be. My arms folded over my head, but my chin remained angled up to the ceiling. I needed this peace, this joy, the amazing something happening between us that defied meaning.

He needed to know he could release, too, that he didn't have to be professional hitman, crime boss all the time.

When the song ended, I looked down at him with a relieved smile. Klive's every fear melted into the warm water, instrumental violins soothing the remaining trepidation away from those pretty eyes as classical music replaced any further lyrics. I sank back down on his torso and tucked my sore hands between our chests as I listened to the pretty music and Klive's heart beating. Klive's arms wrapped around me, and he caressed my back. When I felt the heavy weight of sleep threatening, I lifted my head. His damp hands cupped my cheeks and he kissed me softly again. I could use more goodnight kisses like these.

He whispered another apology and kissed me some more. I loved the pillowy feel of his lips pulling softly at mine. His hands went to my back, drawing small circles I arched against him from. His pretty lips grinned through kisses at finding another ticklish spot on me. No one ever touched me there, especially bare skin on skin. Was there a better feeling than being wrapped in a strong man's arms, sweetly kissed, without anything more than my company asked of me?

My girly psychological side wanted to ponder each significance and pick the moments apart for meaning, but for the first time in forever, this other side, the tamer, subdued not only him, but me as well. I was so tired of thinking and wondering all the bloody time.

Klive paused kissing me for a beat and cupped my cheeks, gazing at me with the oddest resolute look on his face. Hmm ... what could that be for? What resolution had he come to? Ha! And I'd just been content to stop wondering!

"You've no idea ..." he trailed in a tiny whisper. My brows dipped in question, but he pulled my mouth back to his, only this time he did kiss me fully. His arms wrapped tightly around me, his slick hands running over my back. His tongue was hot, urgent, but this kiss seemed more of longing than lust. Not saying he wasn't ready to go, I mean there was no hiding his arousal, but Klive seemed to be ignoring that part to satisfy a different urge altogether. For him, whatever depth he experienced, I released myself, my guard, my tensions, everything I tried denying about him, so he'd have a complete moment. I kissed him back the way he kissed me because though I couldn't understand the instinct, there was something inside that sex wouldn't soothe, that this nurtured. I ran my fingertips into his hair, pressing my mouth more firmly to his, changing angles while he leaned up to cradle my body fully against his.

"Kins, I—"

"Shh." I covered his mouth with mine like my hand would've so he wouldn't break this moment with words when his body and mouth said everything better than speech. He hummed and released himself to this thing between us, an unbridled insistence to meet my physical demand. My arms wrapped around his head while his wrapped as tight as possible around me to be as close together as possible without being inside me. I won't deny that I wanted my body joined completely with his and I knew he obviously wanted the same, but slowly we calmed the chaos back into a relaxing grip. When he seemed softer, I stopped kissing him and pushed myself out of his arms. Though his eyes begged me to stay, not to mention my own body screamed for the same, and ... I admit a lot of my heart, too ... I shook my head at him with a soothing smile.

My hands covered his eyes until his lashes closed against my palms. When I pulled them away, his eyes were closed, though he gave me a resigned sigh and sank deeper into the bubbles. I rushed to look away before seeing all of him through the spots that dissolved. Wrapping a towel around myself, I took my clothes back into the closet to change in there. I thought about pulling my hair down to tackle the tangles the crazy car ride had caused but left the sloppy bun on top of my head as I walked back across the bathroom tile, removing the stool, unlocking the door.

HOSTILE TAKEOVER

The beckoning bliss of Klive's plush bed hugged my body like a heavenly cloud as I tucked between the satin sheets and goose-down comforter. My head snug on his companion pillow, a pillow no one else but Klive had ever laid upon, I peered through the fireplace to find him watching me from the bubble bath. I smiled, kissed my finger, and showed the tip to him. He placed his finger to his lips like he'd received the kiss, then kissed his and held the finger up to me the same. Oh, sweet Klive. I placed his air kiss to my lips. Butterflies fluttered with my sigh of contented victory. I'd powered through another round in the ring with scary Klive and come out the winner. Progress! Victory! Hope!

I snuggled deeper into the pillow and fell asleep.

17 | ♂

I GOT OUT OF the car and locked Kinsley inside though the windows were still down. The side door on the small garage slammed behind me and I strode toward the back yard where Eric and Sanders along with four other Nightshade members held two men in their grasps.

"White room or water?" Eric asked me.

"White room. It's too late on a Thursday night for loud music." I led the way to the hidden back entrance to my house. "Is this what it looks like?" I asked Sanders and held the back door open.

"It's worse. One of them is still in the wind. We think Ray knows where he is."

"You know what?" I asked the group that huddled into the library, through the secret entrance opposite the one I used for my hidden bedroom. We walked through the hallway until we came to the open area. "I'm tired of Ray being a common denominator. In fact, I'm ready to erase his name from our vocabulary." I pointed. "I want that one cuffed to the rope on the ceiling. The other, I want chained to the wall about three feet away."

"Yes, boss." They went to work while I grabbed tiny clamps akin to jumper cables.

"Remove their shirts."

Eric saw where I was going with this and sneered at one of the men. I placed a taser in my pocket and watched the horrified man chained to the wall watching me open the alligator clamps. He sucked his teeth when the small metal teeth bit into each of his nipples. I pulled the three-foot length to the other man's chest and clamped his nipples to connect them.

"Every time one of you moves, you pull each other's nipples." I tased the one hanging from the rope and watched both bodies jerk with the current. They went limp when I pulled the electricity from their flesh. I punched the guy hanging from the rope. Blood sprayed from his nose right onto my blazer and the other man jolted forward as this man's body flew back with the force of the hit. They both cried out. The man on the wall began singing.

"Don't hit him again, please! I'll talk!"

Sanders handed me a washcloth to wipe my hand.

"Go on," I said. "I'd hate for one of your nipples to be ripped off because your friend refused to cooperate."

"Ray told us to watch her house. He needed to talk to you and word was you took the girl out on a date. He was trying to get a channel to you, not her. Ray's wanted on murder charges for Sara and some drug deal gone wrong. The woman running for his position wants to make an example of him. Pat Connor is helping her."

"I don't *believe* you!" I decked him right in his lying mouth. The man hanging on the rope jerked from the movement and cried my name.

"You're right! You're right! He's lying! I'll tell you! King, please! Don't kill me!"

Back and forth I went for an hour and forty-five minutes before I had all the bloody answers I needed and more blood on my blazer than I cared for. Eric, Sanders and my four other men took the snitches to the boat out back while I washed away the evidence from my floor, spritzing ammonia all over, then running a hose over the floor so the water drained in the center of the room. I washed my hands and went out to the car, exhausted and drained physically and mentally, guilt for her being cuffed for so long eating the last shreds of calm I had left. Ray was a bloody liar and I'd known all along!

I loathed the way Kinsley felt limp in my arms when she slept. I wanted her lively, reminding me she was fiery enough to handle the shit rolling down on me for loving her. What kind of man killed his own girl? Ray and Pat were the same species, a very common species to the underground. Unfeeling, inhumane. All their emotional characteristics erased with the cold-blooded tasks that came with climbing to the top. This foolish woman in my arms accusing me of galivanting around killing sweet Kinsley's all over the place like I'd ever harmed an innocent. I was nothing like those bastards! Nothing, dammit!

I placed her gently onto the bed spread and eased the cuffs from her wrists. Dark red lines tainted her pretty skin. She winced when I rubbed the feeling back into her flesh like I might rub the marks away. I nudged her to roll over so I might brave those angry eyes. She inspected me like she peered into my black soul for the things I'd done tonight and every night before her. I couldn't stand her conviction now on top of everything else. Nightshade ruined our first date and now Nightshade stole all kindness from my depleted reserves.

I laid in darkness disbelieving Kinsley stayed the night *and* I'd managed to keep my body parts to myself even after she'd breached the pillow perimeter I'd built between us. I was trying my damnedest to correct my mistake after I'd sorely misbehaved toward her. The asshole side of me was tricky to switch off when the job called me to be mean. I'd never needed to shift so fast without decompressing, nor had I had to answer to anyone in a long while.

I'd resolved to wake early, but this was quite possibly the hardest time I'd ever had forcing myself out of bed. I found myself lying between the sheets for a long while, certain my alarm wouldn't disturb Kinsley's slumber. I'd watched her sleep a few times before, however, last night ... hell, last night was a great effort to fall asleep at all. I kept dozing only to find myself jolting awake in hopes that she wasn't a dream I'd wake from.

Can this be real? Had she really slept in my bed on her own free will? Had I managed the enormous feat of holding Kinsley's nude form against my own, kissing her with everything I'd so carefully kept back, yet not made any advance to try and get inside of her?

As insane as I told myself this was, seemed I'd been gifted with this sort of compass that occasionally screamed at me to go in the right direction with her, even when I sorely misbehaved. Though a moron would have known better than to make any advances on her after the beating my poor bollocks had taken last night.

I'd never in my life had anyone brave or foolish enough to pull that shit on me; unless you count when my brothers and I were dicks to each other as kids. One thing was crystal clear after last night: Kinsley wouldn't take my shit. She wasn't to be bossed around, controlled, nor manipulated. If I wanted her, she'd accept nothing but the respect she knew I was capable of. As angry as I'd been, the lesson was deserved and painfully learned.

As I rested here with her, I knew I wouldn't have handled the men any differently, but for Kinsley, I'd have to lean hard on the compass for more nights like the good parts of last night. Dancing with her, watching her reverence of my car and the desire she'd not hidden for me when we'd buckled in, the feel of her body against mine. She had to be mine. I had to make her love me back somehow because I was completely in like, love and IN love with her. All three in one.

How would I explain this to my nephew, Christian, without my brother, Lachlan, eating my pride for breakfast? Though I'd told Christian love was for men who couldn't think for themselves, I also wondered if I'd been functioning on a selfish brain for too long?

Maybe I needed what Kinsley added to me to teach me new ways of navigating life as a whole human. For too long I'd become a shell I'd never known I was till she'd wrecked shop on my existence ... this was some cocked-up crow to eat. That's okay, Lachlan still had to raise Christian who was mini me. There were plenty of other things to teach the little genius that would annoy Lach. I grinned at my wicked new plans. Besides, there was no need to reinstruct Christian on love just yet. I'd do that when, and if, I was able to hold onto Kinsley. If she ended up staying with Jase, she'd prove my bitterness correct.

No!

I shoved that out of my head. Failure is not an option! I'd come this far. No looking back. Eye on the target.

I'd sat in the tub staring at her through the fireplace as she'd fallen asleep, and I had a new resolve. I wasn't only keeping my eye on the target; I was going for the big one.

Kinsley giggled in her sleep. Her long hair had come loose from the bun and now fanned in a tangled mess over my pillows. The color was nearly identical to the sheets, and I loved the sight. I also loved how she'd destroyed the barrier between us to curl against me, so I was forced to spoon her while we slept. She slept far better than I had. Blue balls hurt worse after a double beating. After her rubbing against me in her dreams like a cat in heat, I felt bruised and black. I'd never slept with a woman overnight before. Nor had I ever slept with someone else. Not even before Nightshade because I never wanted anyone to get the idea I was interested in more than a roll in the sheets. The only women who came to my residence were dates of others for dinner parties or get-togethers. My space was sacred, and no one had ever been inside my secret bedroom.

Kinsley was sacred ground, too, though. Combining the sacred space with the sacred person blended two of my favorite things into one amazing experience I wanted more of. What an amazing idea to rise every morning with a view like this and nights filled with holding her close because I was allowed to. I needed a cold shower to cure what holding her close was doing now.

"Klive, behave." Kinsley mumbled in her sleep. Ha! Was she a mind reader as well? I hoped not because none of the ideas I entertained in my head were fit for a rating. She laughed and mumbled my name once more. My bloody heart tumbled into my throat while the urge to feel like the happiest sap took me by surprise. She was dreaming of me, and I wasn't even at the helm! No lust, just happy Kinsley. Dreaming of me on her own!

"What did I say to you, my sweet? How do I behave?" I whispered near her ear. She smiled and snuggled closer. "How the hell will I leave you when you keep tempting me to stay in bed with you all day, love?"

There's a heavenly idea.

"Don't leave," she whined.

"I'm far too in love with you to leave you for longer than necessary. No worries."

"You love me, Klive?" Her face straightened like she knew how significant this was. Shit! Had she awakened? I didn't want her to know yet! "Klive loves me ..." she mumbled. Thank goodness. Definitely sleeping.

"More than anything else, Kinsley."

Her entire face brightened. She rolled over to face me and nestled into the crook of my neck. I swallowed hard as her warm breaths bathed the most sensitive skin. My heart pounded so loud I heard the beat in my ears. No hiding my desire since she pressed so close, though she didn't seem to notice in her sleep. Her face tilted back. I answered her lips with the kisses she sought. She hummed, then moaned my name. How in the hell did people newly in love ever care about things like morning breath and such? I didn't care so long as I was able to kiss this sweet mouth this morning.

I groaned in pain when she wrapped one of her legs around my waist and tugged me against her. I exercised every ounce of control to keep from grinding against her for relief.

"Klive?"

"Yes, love?"

"You love me!" She beamed with a silly giggle that had me stifling laughter. "Klive?"

"Yes, love?"

"When I wake up, will you be normal?"

"Huh?"

"Will you be the lawyer instead of a crime boss?" she asked in a childlike way. During the few clandestine night visits I'd indulged in, she often seemed childlike in her sleep, that is, when she wasn't busy trying to ravage me or wanting me to do so to her.

"A lawyer? Normal? Why a lawyer, Kinsley?" Had she investigated me? What else did she know or suspect?. If I kept my hold to her heart, I'd wake up early just to have these candid conversations with her. She was too honest in her sleep and sometimes that came in quite handy.

"You look like a lawyer. I wish you were on that side, that you weren't bad. I could be with you. Keep you without feeling guilty. You could be friends with my father, and I could introduce you to my mom."

I'll be damned if I didn't back away at the sting of tears in my eyes. Shit. I should leave. She wanted to introduce me to her mum, be close to her father. Guilt ate my insides deeper than ever before for how I'd allowed my life to go. The constant guilt was nothing compared to this sudden shame.

Enough! You're on your way out for her!

I blinked the sting away and cleared the emotion. "Kinsley, are you saying you want to keep me, love?"

Did I want her unfiltered honesty to such a vulnerable question?

"Duh!"

She suddenly cheered so loud I jumped. I cupped my mouth to stifle a laugh. She mumbled once more.

"Rustin ... need me like a book. I hate. Wish I wasn't easy. Will you eat ice cream without paying?"

Need her like a book? Ice cream? Odd statement and question. She kept going.

"Jase and Rustin take my ice cream! No one is gonna pay for it! I'm a bad person." Her face fell into sorrow so deep a tear fell from her eye. Damn, she was emotional. Was this lingering PMS talking? "Jesus is mad at me."

Blast! Not my favorite subject. Where to go from that?

"You aren't a bad person. From what I understand, all you have to do is ask for Jesus not to be mad and he won't be," I told her, though I had a hard time believing a killer like myself could just say, *'hey, Lord, I know I've sent many to you for judgement when I had no business making that decision in your place, but can we forgive and forget like none of this ever happened?'*

I rolled my eyes and sighed. I didn't want to think about this shit.

"I am!" she argued. "Jase and Rustin eat free."

I barely pieced together what she'd said. *Jase and Rustin eat free.* This was like a bloody riddle and here I was staying in bed far past my alarm trying to figure the shit out. If she weren't so bloody bothered, I'd have left her to her dreams and rantings. My compass told me to stay put. That this was important somehow.

Ice cream. Jase and Rustin eating for free. Will I eat without paying?

"Your ice cream?" I asked.

"Yes."

"You don't like them eating for free. Have you asked them to pay?" I reasoned.

She gasped as though I'd said something salacious! *Well, damn, you want them to pay or eat free? Which one?*

"I can't sell my truck to two men! That's illegal!" she told me as though I were daft. I smiled. This was mental. I rubbed my mouth for a moment in contemplation. A truck.

"Are you selling ice cream or a truck?" This was like playing a game with my nieces. I was about to scoot out of bed when she answered.

"My ice cream truck. Mama would be so mad if she found out they'd both eaten from it ...."

Ohhh ... that old analogy. Why did I suddenly feel so shitty? I hated how she hated herself on a level as though Jesus was angry with her or didn't love her anymore because of the guys.

"How much does your truck cost?" I asked to lighten childish Kinsley a bit.

Instead, she sighed, disappointment etching her expression lines. She didn't answer. I ran my finger over her cheek and asked again.

"Too much. No one wants it. They want ice cream, no truck. Scared about it melting away. The truck isn't worth anything without ice cream."

Anger clenched my jaw. Who the bloody hell had given her the impression she was only good for sex, like all she had to offer was her body? Sure, I'd lusted like mad over this body myself, hit on her repeatedly, but no bloody way I'd allow her to think her body was all she was good for. She was everything!

"I want all of it. How much, my sweet?"

I kissed her temple and smoothed her hair, more to comfort me than her with my temper flaring.

"You don't want it. You said value is dinimished."

My lips tightened at her slurred mispronunciation and what a prick I'd been.

"I'll forever regret the empty words I said during a jealous moment. I'm willing to pay for my mistake in addition to buying your truck, woman. How much?"

"I've given ice cream that belongs to my husband to others. They are his, Klive. He won't want me. Calls me whore even though he made me share." Tears wet her cheeks. Her voice was raw and throatier than usual.

I thought I'd delivered a death blow that day at the track, but I now found Jase had ripped a damn hole in her heart. However cohesive they seemed last night at the restaurant didn't matter.

How awful she thought Jase was the buyer when *I'd* gone through hell to prove myself to her! How unfair if that's how she viewed their relationship.

"Kinsley, Jase wants to buy the truck, but I don't think he knows how to drive it properly."

Lord, please!

"He's good. Good driver, Klive," she mumbled.

I rolled my eyes. I needed to get her past my stupid flirtation and keep her focused.

"I'm a better driver, Kinsley."

"You're scary driver, Klive."

My mouth twisted into an automatic smile. Last night, yes, I'd scared the bloody hell out of her. And ... I suppose on the bike too ... so, yes, I was a scary driver, both physically and metaphorically speaking.

"I might be a scary driver; however, your truck is scary to drive. It needs power steering, new brakes, it's missing a few ice cream sandwiches." I snickered. She smiled. "It's *my* bloody truck and I love it. *I'm* the only one who knows how to drive it properly, how to fix the mechanical issues. I'm not mad about a few missing popsicles or sandwiches."

"You have pretty cars," she sighed.

"Your ice cream truck, it's the prettiest I've ever seen. I'd trade my pretty cars in a heartbeat for your truck. Hell, I'll trade them and throw down a hell of a lot of money to buy yours. Now, may I buy your bloody truck, woman?"

"Do I get to drive the black one again?" She smiled brightly. I chuckled.

"I just told you it's yours, but is that all you want me for? My pretty black car?" I teased. She hummed like she wasn't sure. I prodded her again, but she shook her head like a defiant child. The little witch! "Kinsley, answer the question."

"No. I don't want to."

I laughed and cupped my mouth when she stirred, frozen for moments until she turned and nestled against me.

"Klive, make me mad, but you are so ...."

"So what?" I asked. Did I want to know? Was she going to answer?

"Everything." She sighed in frustration. I exhaled and ran a hand over my mouth. My exact description of her when I haven't anything valid to describe how much she is to me. "Klive, if I sell you my truck, will you be sweet when you drive?"

"I swear, I'll drive it better than anyone else ever could. I will always make sure that the ice cream is properly refrigerated, that she is running smoothly. I will make reparations when they come and handle her as best I can," I told her in earnest. My chest swelled with a deep breath. This was a form of spouting vows! I pressed on. "I'll even remove any dents or dings those others may have carelessly left in her in their manhandling."

"Really, Klive? You would do that?"

"Only a fool wouldn't, my sweet." For the life of me, I'd never understand what Kinsley had in her makeup that seemed tailor made to bring me to my knees to make her happy. I grinned. "Do I have to buy it outright, or may I taste the ice cream after I throw down a deposit?" My tongue danced over my teeth. I couldn't help being a bit of a bad boy.

"Hmm ... only if you are a man of your word, sir."

Bloody hell. I groaned in renewed pain-filled lust.

"Kinsley, I never break my promises, and I promise not to taste any ice cream until I've made my down payment."

I propped myself on my elbow and leaned over to kiss her long enough to make her beg me with her body to sample her flavors, then I rolled out of bed. After tucking pillows around her so she didn't feel lonely, I took a desperately needed cold shower, then quietly dressed, wrote her a note, left the necessities and managed to get out of the house before the sun rose.

There were a great many pressing matters to attend to in honor of my sweet love. First, off to the station to cash in yet another favor for her. Good thing I was taking Eric up on his advice of going public with Kinsley being my girl, because everyone at the station was sure to know by now. Word would've spread since I'd already kept her from being arrested at the club, now her naughty driving? My, she was bad for being so good. I rubbed my palms together in thought of getting my hands on last night's dash cam footage.

Second, I'd be stopping in to see a man about a down payment, because I wasn't too sure how much longer I'd last without some ice cream from Kinsley Hayes' truck. For the first time in my life, I was excited about the prospect of brain freeze.

18 | ♀

I woke up to a bright room and stretched like a contented kitty in the smooth satin of Klive's sheets. Talk about damn good sleep! Hmm … Klive wasn't in bed. Or the room. I sat up, rubbing my eyes, then looked around and listened. The library passage was closed. Maybe he was in the kitchen, but I couldn't hear him.

I got out of bed and walked to the bathroom, the thick carpet squishing between my toes as I padded across the room. After taking care of my business, I walked into my closet.

Wow. My closet. I have a closet at a hitman's house. I chewed my cheek as I rifled through the clothing. A plush robe wrapped my body before I twisted the Shisha dog and walked through the passage into the kitchen.

No Klive. Bummer. The two times we'd shared a room, he'd either left before I'd gotten up, or he'd been awake and dressed before me. I wanted to see bedhead, sleepy, bleary-eyed, imperfect, morning Klive. What were his rituals and habits? When did the cologne come out and what was the name of the fragrance? We must've cuddled at some point because I caught the faint scent somewhere on my skin or hair. Heavenly bliss. No showers for me today.

A fancy espresso machine sat on one of the counters, but the hell if I was brave enough to test the machine without a lesson first. Did he use that and drink coffee at home or did he prefer grabbing coffee at work? Both?

A slip of paper on the refrigerator caught my eye as the only item of clutter.

Kins, good morning gorgeous.

Went to take care of the matter with the cops. You may thank me properly later, wink wink. Afterword, I have pressing matters to take care of, so I will be gone all day. Jase told me you had a day to yourself planned. I've left my credit card on the counter along with the keys. Have fun, treat her as if she were yours, and no more tickets. Don't make me use all my favors in such short timing.

X - Klive

P.S. Sky's the limit.

"Holy shit," I whispered, holding the keys to the Ferrari. "I didn't even sleep with him! Hell yeah!" I pumped my fist. Behind the note was a card with the code for the alarm, the gate and instructions for how to get back into the neighborhood. On the keyring next to the Ferrari fob was a key to his house.

The items collected in my hand felt heavier than moments ago as I realized how much trust Klive was putting in me. Add in that he never shared his room or bed with anyone, and the restraint he'd shown last night, I was really starting to suspect he was interested beyond a roll in the sheets. Figures, the damn criminal would be the deepest of all of them; the one I couldn't have even if I decided I did. Those thoughts were for another day and time. "I will say no moor on the mattah, love," I said in Klive's accent.

Should I drive the car and chance being seen in public with his things, the attention? Or should I explore his house and the grounds and use this place as my palatial haven for my day alone? As much as I wanted to explore Klive's kingdom, I also loved him opening up to me on his own. If I gave him something else to show me about himself, he may give extended glimpses into his life, and I had a built-in excuse to ask more about him without coming off too nosy.

I ran back to the closet to shop for today's clothing options. No way I wasn't going to the beach and showing the car off to Jase in the light of day. The Ferrari was an excellent symbol of my progress with Klive. He should be proud, though after our fight, I wasn't so sure what to think of Jase's reasons. Finding a little polka dotted bikini, I shrugged at my birthmark showing in the mirror with Rustin's comments about the mark replaying in my mind.

Everyone had something they didn't like about themselves. If I didn't mind other people's flaws, I should extend the mercy to myself. Easier said than done, but I'd call today practice. I threw on a short tank top and a pair of track shorts but could only resist temptation to a certain extent.

I walked into Klive's closet. Ah, ha! So, this was how he got into the bathroom last night! He had a door from the bedroom into his closet that also connected to the bathroom. My palm fumbled for a light switch and flipped the lights on to reveal Klive had his own boutique filled to the max with designer suits, pressed dress shirts, jeans of all different styles and washes, tee shirts, ball caps, newsboy hats, fedoras, belts, scarves, was that an ascot? Damn, the man loved clothing and accessories!

He had the same built-in dresser and safe combo as mine. Let's see ... behind drawer number one ... a large grid with a vast variety of rolled ties of all different patterns, organized in the order of the color wheel. The drawer beneath revealed another color wheel of ties. His jewelry drawer held a lot of cufflinks; some obviously expensive and sophisticated, others made me giggle as they must've been gag gifts.

Who is in your life that gives you gifts, Klive? Will I meet them soon? Will they like me?

I cringed when I saw a pair that were nude women. Did he ever wear those?

Several rings caught my attention, two jumped out. Nightshade. Plain as day, the thick band with the *fleur de lis* carving and amethyst on top.

"Holy shit," I whispered as I took in the platinum band with a single amethyst stone and one onyx right beside the Nightshade ring. *I'd seen this before!* My hand trembled a little as I lifted the piece. Last year, on a flight home from Tennessee, I'd been gifted a seat in business class beside a man who'd labeled me his wife to sell his kindness to those around us. When I'd inquired about his real wife due this ring on his wedded ring finger, he'd told me he was unmarried, but wore this ring as a symbol to a woman he loved. I'd picked his brain all about her.

The other rings in Klive's jewelry stash were spread apart in even inches. These two were tucked side-by-side against each other. Was this a *leadership* ring? If so, had a member of Nightshade's leadership bought me an upgraded airline ticket somehow knowing my connection to Klive? Even before I'd truly known Klive beyond the elevator? No way that guy wore this exact style ring by coincidence.

I snapped a photo with my phone. Unease filled the pit of my empty stomach. This ring may indicate the higher ranks Jase was looking for if he didn't know what a leadership ring looked like. Assuming I was correct, did this mean Nightshade had eyes on me all this time? Was that good or bad? Maybe Klive had a reason for hiding our developing relationship for so long?

Our public display last night may have been more significant than I'd realized.

If I brought this up to Klive, he'd know I'd snooped. I could create a way for him to show me his closet on his own ....

On a hook on the back of the closet door leading to the bathroom, I saw Klive's jacket he'd worn last night inside a plastic dry-cleaning bag with his pinstriped shirt. I pulled the plastic away for a closer look at the jacket and saw blood spatter; a good enough amount that I'd have given him shit had I seen. Did this mean Klive had a dry cleaner in his pocket as well? A housekeeper to clean his messes, too? Why not? Obviously, cops could be purchased like nothing.

Whoa, girl. If he didn't have those cops, you'd have a world of trouble on your hands, a flushed scholarship, a ruined reputation.

I exhaled and looked around, afraid he may change his mind and come home. What would Klive do if he caught me snooping? Chewing my cheek, I pulled his jacket lapel open and reached into an inner pocket. I saw the designer label, smelled his cologne, felt guilt when my fingers wrapped around the folded paper the guy at the bar had given him. Did I want to know? Did Klive forget this was in here? What if this were damning information that could be used against him if the cleaner found the note? I was about to pull the slip from his pocket when acute warning bells told me to keep my nose out of particular affairs. Plausible deniability.

The lapel fell back in place as I removed my hand. Jase could dig up dirt on his own. I wasn't sure what kept me from pressing forward, maybe the flickers of true kindness in Klive, or the helpless desperation in his eyes when he held me last night; the weariness I saw after I'd insulted him at the faire. He'd been so deflated. There was something to this man that made me question the case against him, who Klive really was, whether Constance had me pegged all along on my loyalty to him.

I sighed, ready to cry for prying. Klive trusted me. Or, whatever he thought I'd find, he didn't mind my knowing? That was a scary proposition. Was he daring me to make a fatal mistake so he wouldn't have to feel guilty about killing me? Ugh! I hated my own mind sometimes.

The plastic fell back over the jacket and shirt. Rather than collecting clues, I opted to borrow a pair of Ray Bans from his sunglasses section. Er, make that *glasses* section since he had non-prescriptive frames as another accessory in his metro-sexual collection.

Hmm ... so had the guy wearing the ring on my flight ... whoa!

No effing way in hell! No. Effing. Way! My breathing shallowed. He'd told me he'd fallen ass over tit for a woman he'd talked to once. A British expression. He then confessed to thinking with a British accent though he hadn't used one.

When I lifted a set of black-rimmed frames, my stomach did a tiny flip-flop at the implication, everything this could mean about my interactions with Klive before knowing who he was. How to digest this possibility?

I replaced them and slipped on aviator style sunglasses, my reflection morphing into a different character so easily with the change of clothing, glasses, hair. I swallowed. Carmen had praised my chameleon ability to pull off so many different looks.

Was the possibility of Klive being an expert in disguise so foreign? Sure, as a man, changing his appearance seemed a steeper challenge, but if he'd managed to fool me into thinking he was a stranger on a plane when I'd been a smitten goner for the pirate, how long had I been played? Was he pretending to be others to get near me? What a scary, thrilling, nauseating idea! I was both flattered and floored, but without proof or his confirmation, I may be reaching too far.

However, as far as I reached, I liked the idea of him in disguise far more than some Nightshade superior getting too close to me, especially since I'd kissed the stranger on the plane at the end of our evening. That certainly upped the fear-factor. If I'd kissed Klive without knowing, how taboo sexy! If I'd kissed one of his bosses or another member, *terrifying*!

I pulled the aviators down my nose, eying my reflection. "Do yourself a favor, love. Quit bloody thinking so much. You're headed to the beach in a *Ferrari*! If Moonlight is a master of disguise, does it change how you feel about him? Or how amazing this is?"

Actually ... I waved my head in a more or less gesture, nodded. It kind of does because that would take our history to a level I'd never anticipated. My eyes met the reflection in the mirror again.

"Bring it up to him when you can. Until then, live for the moment."

I grabbed my effects and made my way out of the passage, cautious to make sure the shelving unit closed behind me. Last night, Klive hadn't come inside the house the same way as before. I closed my eyes to remember the feeling of him carrying me inside last night. We'd been outside for part of the walk. Hmm ... I walked down the long hallway toward the garage I knew, entered the code for the alarm and saw another door to the back yard from his main garage. My guess paid off. A private path to a single garage was right outside the door. Klive's house was like a schematic of the maze I traversed trying to figure out his brain and how he planned things. He'd obviously put a lot of thought into the layout of this property and house.

In the light of day, the grounds were gorgeous. His stucco had a bright cheery glow in the sunshine. Tropical flowers lined all the pathways. Hummingbirds raced between bright yellow hibiscus blooms while I figured out the lock on the door. I relocked when I stepped inside the Ferrari's guest house. That's what I'd call this garage because he'd clearly built this just to house this car. The walls held care items for grooming and polishing the beautiful black paint and upholstery. The windows were still down from last night, but the car's anti-theft system was armed.

I disarmed the other woman and got inside the car. My little bag rested in the passenger seat. I sat for several moments appreciating the reality, tracing my fingers over the emblem in the center of the steering wheel. The days wouldn't all be good. No day was promised, especially when the stakes of my life were like a trapeze act. For today, these minutes, I could say this was fun. However long this lasted with Klive, I'd enjoy for the times I may not ever get back.

Would being with Klive really be such a crime? I touched my lips in remembrance of the way he'd kissed me last night, his flesh against mine, his scent and, damn, he was a good kisser!

The stranger from the plane had been a great kisser, too ... dammit, Klive! You smooth asshole!

Why couldn't he be normal, God? Why do things have to be this impossible? Why are we prone to love the ones we cannot have?

"Kins," I whispered, "quit being so melancholy. You have no idea what the future holds. Why he may have had to disguise himself to speak to you. Hope. Faith. Love this day. This is the day the Lord has made. Rejoice. Be glad. Start the damn car."

I placed the shiny key in the ignition, then pressed the button to start her up. Kitty growl! I was so glad Klive wasn't here when the car roared to life or else, I may have jumped his bones! The engine inside the car with me intensified the heat that filled my body every time Jase started his car. This was worse. I hit the *auto* button so I wouldn't have to worry about shifting gears. After last night I wasn't planning to blow my luck to smithereens. Plus, I wanted to respect Klive's request of me to behave. However, as I opened the garage door and gingerly backed out like my life depended on every millimeter, I called Rustin to ask if there were any cops on the highway between here and the beach.

He snorted. "Why? You afraid of being pulled over for speeding?"

"Rustin, just answer the question please?"

"No, I don't know of anyone from our precinct who's running patrols. Watch for state troopers, though."

"Thanks, bye," I sang and hung up before he could say anything else or pry into how my night with Klive went. I scooped my hair into a bun and pulled a hair tie from between my teeth while watching the garage door close to be sure before I left the property that everything was as Klive preferred. When I tapped Klive's touch screen, I noticed GPS was programmed for his house so I could find my way back through the neighborhood. I took a screenshot on my phone for my own personal use should I need to drive to Klive's house on my own in my Civic one day. Would he want to be casual like that? I mean, if he gave me his card, didn't that say something about our dynamic shift?

After Klive's main gate to his property closed behind me, I eased the car through the neighborhood, then out to the main streets, getting more comfortable as I went. My smile permanently plastered to my lips when I gunned the gas onto the highway, which was far more crowded than last night. I had to really focus to keep Klive's true love safe, but the car's maneuverability was so seamless and smooth, I understood how he likened this experience to a vacation. Since I decided he was right, the wind blowing in at the perfect temperature, the morning sun shining down, the tension lost in the drive, I looked forward to not only rubbing this car in Jase's face, but a pampering my mother swore by. The stress of last night, the discoveries this morning, were a crescendo that would likely make me cry during my massage today; Sara dying, Ray and Pat threatening me, type-A asshole Will interrogating me, Jase coming clean as a type of undercover cop, Rustin worming his way into bed with us during a weak moment of mine, meeting Nate and his wife and little daughter, Jase almost killing us on the bridge when he'd raced, being drugged by a jerk at a party, fighting Angela and getting bruised and bloody while getting grounded from running, Jase trashing the shit out of me, Klive's dangerous games, yeah, to name a few high points over the past, what, month or so?

Damn. No wonder I was wound way too tight. I had to find a better option than sex to ease my anxiety. I'd known when I was sleeping with Jase that the coping mechanism was unhealthy, but sometimes unhealthy tasted so much better than the alternative. As much as I enjoyed having sex, the emotional toll afterward made the pleasure less worth having.

How were people so able to sleep around without feeling tied forever to those they gave their bodies to? Was I defective for feeling like I'd committed adultery on the man I was supposed to marry?

I shoved that away, too. As I cruised closer to the beach, I wished I had a button like the car where I could turn my mind on and off with the touch of a finger and silence the chronic analysis. The worst? The closest thing to having one of those buttons was being around Klive, because I found around Klive that voice wasn't so thunderous. When I was away from him, the voice wouldn't shut up! Case in point! *Enough! Silencio, por favor! Calme, s'il vous plait!*

Driving along the main drag beside the beach, the speed limit slowed to thirty-five.

Someone shouted, "Let's go, Mi-Cro! Woot! Woot! Woot, woot, woot!"

"Where'd you get the ride?!" her friend shouted.

Great. Guess since the viral video of my fight, sightings would be a regular occurrence. I was certain my parents would be notified about this by nightfall. Shit! I'd forgotten to call my mom to tell her I was alive and well!

"So, she lives another day," Mom said when she answered.

"I'm alive and very well, thank you."

"What's that noise?"

"I'm at the beach visiting Jase. You know how loud the cars are."

"Visiting Jase after you went on a date with Mr. King? Did it not go well?"

"I had a great time. I'm here to wish him condolences," I joked. She chuckled. "For real, though. I'm taking a cue from my mother and hitting the spa for a much-needed time-out from love. Jase just happens to be working across the street from the one I like."

"Uh, huh. Well, I'm proud of you, but the neighbors said you didn't come home last night."

"Mom, that old lady isn't up when I come home from work, so I doubt she saw me come in."

"Point fairly taken. I'm glad you called. Enjoy yourself, though I wish you would come with me next time I have a girl day. I'm going to need a week at a spa to recover from your father's idea of a vacation."

"Deal. I love you. Give him my love too."

"Hold on, honey. Should I call a doctor? Are you saying you called just to talk to me and not to get through me to speak to him?"

"Don't make a deal of it. I have to go. Love you. Bye."

I hung up the phone before she went gushy on me. My palm beeped the horn behind Jase's stand as I drove into the parking lot, cautious to park the Ferrari away from other vehicles. I rolled the window up and shimmied out of my shorts and tank to give Jase something to think about while he may be thinking of dating other women. Never said I wasn't vindictive.

After I rolled the windows up, I swung my legs out of the car, pushing off the leather seat to stand in my bikini. Getting out of a Ferrari. In front of gawkers galore. A mischievous grin spread across my lips. Thank goodness no one could see my eyes beyond these shiny lenses otherwise they'd know I was all show and nerves. If I tripped after this, I swear I was gonna give up and leave without the spa. I reached for my bag, then chirped the car alarm over my shoulder as I made my way across the street, eyes on me the whole time. To remove any snobby bitch assumptions, I smiled and waved like a casual passerby. Like one of them, because that's who I was. No car could change my insides.

Jase cast a huge grin and an appreciative whistle when I sauntered up to his stand. I pulled my hair down and shook out the crazy tangles, the waves softly slapping my back in the breeze. Klive's' glasses went onto my head so he could see my eyes, though I had to squint against the sun.

"Baby, baby, baby. What did you have to do to earn that?" he asked with a naughty lilt.

"Well, let's see. I kicked him in the balls and put him in his place, then kneed him in the balls again for getting out of his place. Then, I made him listen to girly soft music and sit in a bubble bath to chill out." Yeah, I took a bit of creative license on the latter, but I wasn't lying. I gave him a winning smile and enjoyed his hearty laughter. No damn way I was confessing the make-out session.

Jase peered over the waves, keeping an eye on the crowds at the beach. I looked back at Klive's amazing car. Jase did, too.

"No sex?" he asked.

I shook my head.

"And you abused him?"

I nodded.

"If I was down there, I'd kiss you!" He gave me the proudest smile. "See some ligature marks on your wrists. Heard you almost got arrested last night ...." Jase's grin morphed to a shit-eating buffet of a beam. "Gotta watch that speed, sweet Kins."

I immediately checked my wrists and saw the fine red lines I'd somehow ignored in all my suspicious bullshit over Klive.

"How did you hear about last night?! No one was supposed to know!" Ooh, Klive was so gonna hear from me ... *he* was in *so* much trouble!

Jase chuckled. "C'mon, Kins. That video went viral around the station. Rustin was sweet enough to send it to me on my way to work this morning. Don't worry, the original was put away."

My tongue traced the inside of my cheek while my arms crossed under my boobs.

"That was super-hot the way your dress came up high when Jerry made you bend over the car. A refined woman like that bent over a damn Ferrari. Being cuffed, no less? Sorry, but that one's not getting destroyed. You're lucky Klive's one scary sonuvabitch, or else I'm sure Jerry would've leaked the footage online." Fear flew through every vein. Jase opened his palm as if to say, *down girl*. "Don't worry, Klive wouldn't let that happen. Hell, Klive probably took the footage for himself. I especially liked when Jerry handed you over to him so he could finish cuffing you after you said it was consensual." He rubbed his chin before tilting his head. "No sex? Really? After that?"

I gaped in offended shock. I mean what the hell did he think I was? One of his skanky ass groupies? I was so calling Klive. If he had the footage, I was going to find the video and destroy the evidence. How many others had recorded the taboo scene on their phones the way Rustin had? What if someone sent the scandal to my parents? My every other stressor took a backseat to this one.

"No effing sex, Jase Taylor. Why do you think I put him in his place? He made me ride home in those cuffs because stupid ass Jerry didn't give him the key before he left! Maybe *that* is why he left me the keys to the Ferrari and his credit card with no limit."

I needed to cool my jets because the last thing Jase and I needed was another fight.

Jase's jaw dropped. "Tell me you're about to burn a hole in it, baby."

"After that news, I'm thinking about it." I shook my head. "As much as I like the idea, I won't be able to do that. A) I'm not that kind of girl. B) he's being too nice. I may just have to ream his ass when I get back later, though. Whatever he's doing today, he's going to be gone all day. Thought you should know. Full disclosure? I feel very uncomfortable sharing info. It makes me nervous, Jase." *And I feel like a betraying traitor to someone I have no business feeling that way with* ... the fact that I didn't mention the rings ... yeah.

"Don't worry about that, Kins. I've got everything under control. I don't need info. I only need you for distraction, remember? So have fun doing your part because you're a natural. Ask me how I know," he teased and waggled his brows. I rolled my eyes. "He's going to be gone all day because we have plans to have drinks together later. Bribery, remember?" I frowned in recollection. "Guess where we are all going?" He lifted his shades and winked down at me, drawing a surprised smile.

"You're coming to visit me at work?" I guessed, uncertain. "I thought you said you guys were going to a strip club tonight for Rustin's birthday?"

"We were, but Klive is so into you, Kins." He looked at the shore and water through his binoculars. "Do you think he wants to piss you off now with that? Hell, after what you just old me, he's probably afraid you'll hand him his balls again!" We both laughed. I watched his smile fade as the binoculars came down.

"You okay, Jase? This getting to you?" Damn right, or else why did we fight so bad last weekend? If he was this dedicated to his task, our fight, and his willingness to let me get in so close with Klive told me volumes about the progress he must be making since he pushed me to continue. I couldn't help wondering what went on behind my back because of all the progress I was making. Hard not to resent his mission.

"Baby, as long as you come back to me when it's all said and done, I'll be fine. In the meantime, I'm going to enjoy the ride along with you. Hopefully, sometimes *within* you." He winked down at me again, then the shades went back over his eyes.

"Jase Taylor, I'm gonna pretend you didn't just say that to sweet Kins and that you're still just my best friend's big brother who's a flirty pervert. Deal?"

He chuckled and nodded. "I'll take it. Is that what I always was to you?"

"Not perverted to me. Toward everyone else maybe." I pursed my grin. "Now, if you'll excuse me, I need to get a massage, then burn a hole in my favorite drug lord/crime boss's credit card." I blew him a kiss. I jumped away a second later when he landed in front of me like a vampire before tilting my neck to plant a salacious kiss to my open lips. He pulled up to scan the shore, then smothered my reprimand of his name with a follow-up kiss hotter than the first. Grrr. Did this mean he missed me or just missed being inside me?

"Baby, I can't wait much longer for you. Please, come over soon. We need to make up for lost time."

Guess I had my answer. "I'll let you know," I told him rather than getting upset in public. Some pining on both our parts like Klive told me about would be nice. I wasn't sure Jase knew the definition of pining. The only definition he probably cared about was the tone in his muscles so he could keep looking so sexy in his lifeguard uniform. He was sexy with that whistle between his pecs and his hair all messy in the breeze.

"Hey, where is Rustin?" I asked. "Tell me Ansley gave him some reprieve for his birthday."

Jase scoffed and climbed his tower again. "Nope. He's on a bicycle reading meters. He sent me some nice photos when you drove up and got out of the car. Natural born detective getting that evidence."

"Right. Well, wherever he is, tell him happy birthday for me."

"Tell him yourself when you see him later. Have fun, Kins."

I nodded and waved before heading across the street toward the spa. Were Rustin's the eyes I'd felt watching me earlier?

19 | ♀

When I walked through the door, my massage therapist took me immediately back to her room. Oh, the soothing sounds of a babbling water wall, Oriental music and — *record skip* — Angela effing Ansley's southern drawl instructing her masseuse to give her a facial afterward.

"I can't," I said and waved my hand. "I just can't."

"Miss? Did I do something wrong?" my masseuse asked, alarm over her face.

I sighed, a little defeated. "You did nothing wrong. God is mad at me and he's choosing to smite me for my evil deeds at every turn. Just know that you have some knots to work out of my poor muscles."

"So, you're okay? You're staying?"

I nodded and she clapped her hands, then instructed me to disrobe and she'd be back in five minutes. Since I wasn't wearing much, disrobing took about one minute which left me with four too many to listen to Angela's awful voice through the thin walls. Two other smaller voices sounded further toward the front of the building, but Angela's was prevalent.

Dear, Lord, I'm sorry for everything I've done to deserve this drama I've brought upon my head like heaping coals. Please forgive my foolery at every turn. I'm bad at life.

My massage therapist knocked on the door and I cleared her to come inside.

"Is there any way we can turn the music up?"

"Oh, I'm sorry, but it's on a main system for the whole spa. I'm gonna tuck this in around your legs." She pulled the sheet off my back and tucked the remainder around my thighs. Warm stones lined my spinal column while she went to work on my calves and feet first. "I'll be careful with your legs. I worked for a sports medicine facility when I graduated college. Just the community college, not anything like you've done at a real university."

"Please don't demean yourself like I'm somehow better than you. A degree is a degree whether you earned it online, at community or some Ivy league school. The work was put in. I'm surprised you know who I am."

"We all do. The girl you got into the fight with is in the other room. I'll be sure to go easy around your obliques. She kicked you pretty hard there, but you didn't even go down, you kicked her right back."

I sighed. "Now you know why God is mad at me."

She chortled and rubbed in ways that made me wince, then melt. When I heard my name from Angela's drawl, my whole body tensed.

"Try to relax," the masseuse said in a soothing tone like a mental health therapist.

"Shh, listen." I lifted my head, inclining my ear toward the grating voice. "Crack the door."

She hustled to do as I said.

"... yeah. I took that bitch down as soon as I saw a chance. About time I got my hands on her for all the shit she's done to me since we were kids."

Oh, hell naw! Constance's voice ran through my mind.

Angela's massage therapist asked a question about Klive. My name and Klive's in one tiny conversation? I asked my masseuse to remove the stones from my back. She swallowed, a little nervous and excited at once.

"Yeah, he gave her his shirt and she probably gave him head after. If you think that was bad, you should've seen the video captured last night. Hold on, I'm gonna have one of the guys send it to me."

My blood went cold and hot at the same time. Sonuvabitch, Angela worked at the station! Duh! Jase said the video went viral at the station! Of course, she'd have seen! I wanted to throw one of these hot stones at her face!

"She already has two guys in knots and now Klive King of all guys? It's like she sees me with a guy and can't stand them paying attention to me. One of them works at the station with me and he's so defensive of her he made me and everyone else delete the video from our phones. Then Klive came in and took the original before we could record it again, he also went one-by-one checking our phones with his sidekick tech guru to make sure we didn't have it. Whatever. I know Jerry probably made a copy on his phone before he turned it in. He'll do anything I ask him. He even offered to divorce his wife to be with me, but I'm not ready for all that, plus I ain't interested in being a stepmother to anyone's brats."

I sat up and gathered the sheet around my body as I said silent prayers. Me stealing her guys? Me making her life hell? The nerve! That bitch never knew to keep her damn hands to herself even in high school when I was with Jack Carter! I wasn't the only one suffering from this issue. Jerry's wife and others had this problem. What a sick bitch. I felt gross remembering how Jerry checked me out when I'd gotten out of the car. Where were all the good men? Had they gone extinct?

If I sat here counting back from ten much longer, I'd run out of sand in the hourglass of patience and snap her arm over my knee!

"Oh, look!" Angela gushed. "He had it. Look at her bent over like a whore in heat begging Klive to cuff her. I bet he opened that slit in her dress when Jerry left and got his fill."

I clenched my jaw. "Please pass me my phone from on top of that little bag?" I asked my masseuse. Her eyes were round with alarm. She'd been listening with me.

The phone barely hit my palm before my thumbs glanced the keyboard as the rage rained through my mass text to Jase, Klive and Rustin.

Get 2 spa on boardwalk n next 5 or I'm getting arrested 4 beating Angela's ass n this fine establishment!!! She's sharing vid from last night & telling them I'm a whore in heat!!! Get here NOW!!! Claws at ready! Room 4. Hurry!"

As hard as holding myself in check was, I laid back down to give the guys, whichever could make the deadline, time to arrive and hold me back from adding a mistake.

"Please do my shoulders for as long as I can handle sitting still."

The masseuse nodded. Her thin fingers went to work on the rock-solid tension hardening my heart to all repercussions. Angela's voice grated my nerves like a cat's claws scouring a car's paint right off the hood. Her damn masseuse was getting a blistering review from me when I was done for her part in this slanderous gossip. If I could hear them, so could everyone else. My massage therapist switched to rubbing soothing circles into my temples.

"No one likes her. She's two-faced," she whispered near my ear.

"If she keeps talking, you're gonna need to strap me down."

Klive tapped his knuckle on my door first, Rustin just behind him in his uniform, which was perfect for when he'd have to arrest me. Jase couldn't get away from work. My masseuse backed away to give Klive her spot beside me. I sat up and wrapped the sheet around myself again.

"Klive, I swear, you need to do something about this. She has a thing for you. Put her in her damn place before I do once and for all," I said, low and calm, though trembling with rage.

Klive evaluated me while I guess he was deciding how to proceed. He looked over at Rustin.

His palms rose. "Don't look at me. I'm down for letting Kinsley loose on her. I'm this close to identifying as a woman so I can slap her and call it a cat fight."

Okay, though he was dead serious, I fought a tiny grin. Rustin pulled his phone from his pocket and placed the device on video, ready to record another fight rather than lifting a single law-enforcing finger to stop me this time.

"I made her delete the copies of the video. Everyone else too. I'm not sure where she got it," Rustin told Klive.

"I did, too," Klive said, his brows drawing in confusion.

Time to tattle on Jerry the Jerkoff. When I finished, Klive nodded, his eyes narrowed like his wheels were turning on something terrible. Ruh, ro. Had I'd gone too far?

Klive ordered me to stay put unless he changed his mind. He walked out of the room with Rustin on his heels. They left my door wide open, and we heard Angela gasp a moment later. The masseuse and I trotted up to the door to listen.

"Miss Ansley, fancy running into you here. What an *awful* coincidence ..." Klive purred, all charm.

"Klive! Uh — um, how long have you been here?" she asked, her voice nowhere near the previous strength. My massage therapist and I smiled together.

"Long *enough* ...." I could almost see him in my mind: hands in pockets like this was the most casual thing in the world, smug, threatening smiles throwing one off their axis, a little twisted seduction as he held eye contact and stepped closer before lowering his tone like sharing an intimate secret.

Angela cleared her throat but didn't speak.

Klive continued. "If I didn't know any better, I'd say you're still a mite sore from my repeated refusals to sleep with you. Dare I say, even a bit jealous I've become quite taken with your little nemesis."

"No, Klive. It's personal with her. She's always been out to steal the men I'm into. The reason she's into you is probably to screw me the way she screwed Officer Keane when she found out I was into him."

Oh, bitch wanted to die! The masseuse grabbed me by the sheet and yanked me and my near wardrobe malfunction back into the room.

Klive chuckled. "Angela, how long have you known me?"

"Uh —"

"Allow me to save you from doing basic addition. You've known me long enough to realize what's good for you. Long enough to know I do not tolerate a liar or suffer fools gladly. Long enough to know that if what you say about Kinsley is true, then she should have come across my radar years ago when you began sleeping your way through the ranks. Shouldn't she have wanted to steal at least one of those Johns from you?"

Johns?

She stammered in defense, but Klive spoke over her.

"Silence!" His tone dropped from charming warmth to frigid dick. "You have single-handedly just confirmed with your attempted denial that you are both of that which I do not tolerate. You see, Angela, had Kinsley Hayes come into the picture sooner, I'd have remembered her, because Kinsley Hayes commanded my attention the first time I set eyes on her. Never for the same reasons you've garnered attention from men, mind you.

"There's a difference between desire and respect. A desire is born of selfishness. Respect is born of integrity. Ms. Hayes not only holds my selfish desire to have her, but her integrity earned my respect to the degree of walking on glass to earn a single date. Of course, when I saw her, I didn't know she loathed you, but now that I do, her hatred of you is another thread I've found in common and only makes her more appealing in my eyes."

Boom! Death blow! I'd love to see him lean closer and watch her back away!

"When I saw her, do you know what captured me?" Klive asked elegantly.

I swallowed and gripped my sheet at my chest with both fists, nervous about what he'd say next because his words had already stunned me to my spot.

"I saw a humble heart in pain, mistreated, but strong and beautiful. She was mean to me, and now, I know why. Because before I knew her, a spoiled little bitch who rides her father's privilege for everything tormented those around her to make herself seem superior when really, she was completely insignificant, and the spoiled little bitch tormented the beautiful girl."

My masseuse's mouth fell open. She cooed like Klive had just said the sweetest words.

"I'm tired of your antics. I cannot imagine a lifetime dealing with you," Klive told Angela. "If I so much as catch wind that you shared that video with another person, even mentioned Kinsley Hayes again, tried to further defame her good name, I'm cashing in a favor with your name on it. Is that clear or shall I be more specific?" he asked in that white or wheat way. I couldn't believe the things he'd said about me. Even if I hated Angela, I knew what a Klive vanquishing felt like, and I did hate that part.

"Yes, sir," she said like a sullen teen where I'd have been spitting tears for less.

Klive must've observed the same, because he said, "You know what? You've been put in your place before, made promises to behave, only to renege. I don't *believe* you. I'm going to make a phone call now —"

"No! Please, Klive, don't. I understand. Look."

My masseuse and I tiptoed to the edge of their doorway to watch what we could. I couldn't see Klive or Rustin from this angle, but I did see Angela showing him her phone with the video paused. I blushed when I caught a glimpse of myself bent over the Ferrari with Jerry at my side.

"I'm deleting it now. I promise." She deleted the video with the phone facing Klive so he could see the whole time. Klive ordered her to open her email accounts. She blushed a deeper red than I had. My tongue traced my teeth. All sympathy I'd had for her vanished. Klive grunted and I saw his phone in his hand tapping a contact. Angela opened her archives in her email, but her hand shook so hard I rushed into her room, capturing her phone before the device shattered on the floor. She sucked a gasp like I'd stung her, but I indicated with my eyes that she get busy deleting the videos. Klive seemed unfazed by my presence.

"Remember that matter we discussed?" Klive asked into his phone. A sob escaped Angela's throat. She looked at me and shook her head over and over, her other hand cupping mine helping her hold the phone.

"Klive?" I said, eyes darting between him and Angela.

"Just a second." He pulled his phone over his chest. "What is it, love?"

"They're gone. All of them." I helped Angela raise her phone again.

"I don't believe it. Not that I don't trust you, Kinsley. I do. It's her. For all I know she's got accounts we don't know of." He pulled his phone back to his ear.

"No!" Angela begged. "No, I don't! I swear! Kinsley, please! Make him believe me!"

Klive gaped at her. "Are you daft? You've the audacity to ask her to do anything for you when you sought to destroy her? To destroy *me*? You've not even apologized. Deputy Keane, has she ever apologized to you for making your life miserable at the station? She's the reason you've been punished by her father. She requested it because you like her enemy instead of her."

Rustin glared at her while I gasped.

"She's never apologized," Rustin said.

"Remain on standby. If you get a text, do it." Klive disconnected his phone call.

Angela dropped her phone and gripped my hands. I watched the glass crack as the device hit the floor, but when I looked at her, she stared at me, chin trembling, eyes full of tears.

"I'm — I'm —" Her voice broke. "I'm so sorry," she barely whispered. Her fingers squeezed mine. "Deputy Keane." She peered at Rustin. "Kinsley. Both of you. Please, forgive me? I'm sorry I've been so mean. I won't do it again. I p — pro — promise." She looked at me again. "Please, Kinsley. Please."

She knew more about Klive than I did. I knew by the genuine plea in her eyes she was deathly afraid of this man and to whoever he had spoken. I was afraid for her. Klive moved to my side and removed Angela's grip on my hands as if he didn't want her touching me anymore. He pressed my palms together and cupped my hands between his palms. He planted a soft kiss to my forehead.

"Kinsley, my love, it's come to my attention this woman has made your life a living hell for far too long. In fact, I suspect she saw you at the party and used the excuse to touch me against my will. Pretty mental she has the nerve to claim we must be fucking when you have yet to allow me more than kissing, yet she propositions me at every opportunity and somehow *you're* the slut?" he enunciated the *T*.

Rustin whistled, a smug satisfaction lighting his eyes on her. Wow. Here, I'd thought he'd liked her.

Klive tucked my hair behind my ear. "Since I'm so fond of you, I'm especially disgusted with her disrespect of you, love. Do you accept her apology or would you like me to text my contact in your honor?"

Whoa! Gulp! His eyes held warm affection rather than hard stone. Amazing how they shifted from fire to ice when transferring between Angela and me.

"Anything you want," Klive said. Holy shit! He glared at Angela again. "Does it look like I treat this woman like a *whore in heat*?" Tears spilled onto Angela's cheeks as she shook her head. "Does it appear Deputy Keane treats her like she's a whore? Or Jase Taylor, who's been openly sweet on her for years?"

"No," she whispered, her neck muscles tensing.

"Is it any of your business if this woman has the affections of multiple men because she's an irresistible person? I should think not," Klive said. "This is it, Angela, because she's the one calling the shots now. I am at her disposal whenever she needs me, whatever she needs me for. I am the head, Angela, but *Kinsley* is the *neck*."

My knees turned to rubber and my body sagged against Klive's side. I couldn't breathe! Was he serious?! No way Tyndall's foolish prayers were happening! He had to be scaring her ... he was scaring me ....

"Kinsley," Angela broke my inner monologue. I blinked a couple dumbfounded times until she came into focus. She held my eyes with the sincerest expression I never knew she was capable of. "You used to ask what you'd done to make me mad. You've never done anything to deserve my hatred and jealousy of you. I put you through pain and torment and fed off it for years. I'm a sick person. I need help. Professional help to fix this sickness inside me. Someone said you were going to college to be a counselor. I hope you can look past my attacks and see the truth because my attacks were always to keep you and everyone else from seeing my sickness."

Her chin fell to her chest like her spirit surrendered. There was something awful like watching a dragon lose the wings that enabled the beast to harm a town. Even though others would be better off, watching a creature defeated gripped my heart. I couldn't stand seeing someone in pain. As I wrapped my arms around her, felt her body shudder, heard heavy sobs and hiccups pour from her shame, I knew this might be what my professor was trying to imply about me. This fatal flaw that even Klive appeared frustrated with, though he allowed a flicker of soft understanding to bleed into his disappointment. I surmised this may be how Klive kept from killing sweet Kinsleys. He had others willing to do dirtier work than he was at his disposal, and those resources now extended to me.

Was I as green as Angela yet? I stroked her hair like my mom stroked mine after every crying spell this bitch caused me, but was I trying to soothe her or myself more? In this experience, I'd at least gleaned my capacity for hatred was no match for Angela's, which was a lucky thing for her. I couldn't say if the shoes were on her feet that she'd do the same for me.

"I forgive you," I said at her ear. "I forgive you." She didn't deserve forgiveness, but that was the point. I didn't deserve forgiveness, but if I wanted to be forgiven, I'd be forgiven to the degree I forgave others. I exhaled, squeezed her shoulders one last time, then surrendered my own anger and hatred, the sickness she'd created inside me.

"No favors, Klive." I sought his eyes over my shoulder.

He nodded. "Very well. As you wish, love."

"Angela, none of us has to remain the things we've become," I said to her, but prayed Klive would hear my words as well. I thought of the faire, the possibility she was mixed up with drugs or someone in Nightshade.

She nodded, her lower lip shaking. "Thank you."

Klive offered tissues I took and helped clean Angela's face with. He cleared his throat, commanding her attention. Her eyes jumped over my shoulder toward his.

"She may have forgiven you, but I do not forgive easily. Daddy will understand if I deploy forces beyond his control to contain you."

My eyes bugged. Hers held his, unblinking, wide with fear. She nodded.

"Yes, sir. I understand."

"Very well. Make sure she gets the rest of that massage. She needs it. I'll pay," Klive told Angela's massage therapist who was rooted to her spot, unmoving, silent. Klive bypassed her expression and tugged me gently before him. His hand smoothed my hair, his face lit with the softest affection that sent both butterflies and nausea through my belly. Numb heat flooded my limbs like the fear paralyzing me last night. "Make sure this one gets anything she wants." When he smiled, my eyes cast down to my bare toes near his Italian loafers.

Klive reached into his blazer for his wallet. He handed each masseuse three hundred dollars. "For your discretion. I am a private person. Obviously, I'm not keen on my or my friends' dirty laundry being aired. Do we have an understanding?" I looked up at him again. His authoritative expression. The one that said no one fucks with Klive King.

They took his offering, swearing oaths of silence. Klive thanked them, then said, "All right, Angela, enjoy your reprieve. Kinsley, love, let's get you back to your room and taken care of. I must get back to business. Buy yourself something pretty. I'll take care of Marcus. Take the night off and meet me at the bar later just for fun." He kissed my lips in front of everyone. In fact, he kissed me until I kissed him back. "Let me know if you have any more problems or need anything else." His icy eyes shined on Angela to send the point home. No way she'd enjoy anything for the rest of this day.

"Deputy Keane, I trust we will see you tonight. She's got a fondness for you."

Rustin smiled like a fool. Whether because of what happened here, or from some claim of me being fond, I couldn't know. He nodded and said, "With bells on."

Klive grinned. "Good. Tonight's on me. Happy birthday." The sweet one was back. The scary crime boss gone like a passing thunderstorm, after which the sun came back out and caused a beautiful rainbow across the clearing sky.

Klive kissed my hand as he led us out of Angela's room, then whistled while he walked toward the front door, leaving us in his wake. Before he opened the front door, he placed his finger to his lips, kissed the tip and held the offering up to me. I beamed in surprise as I placed my own finger to my lips and returned the action, earning a beautiful smile as he placed his finger back to his lips, then vanished outside.

20 | ♀

As soon as Klive left, Rustin rushed me back into my room and eased the door closed.

"Jase is gonna flip his shit!"

"What? Rusty, did you record that?"

"No! That's not what I'm talking about. *You!* And *Klive!* I won't give you a hard time about whatever happened at the party, but that last thing was deep, Kins! You'd better be damn careful, hear me?"

"What kissing our fingertips? I blow kisses to my father all the time," I said, hoping to dispel his astonishment.

"Uh, huh. Last I checked, your father wasn't kissing the tip of a finger he uses to pull triggers for pay, is he?"

Yikes! I chewed my cheek, trying like hell not to go into petulant teen mode after such an amazing and terrifying interlude.

Rustin lowered his voice to a whisper. "Do we need to pull you? When Jase told you he wanted you to distract Klive, we never imagined you'd freakin' enslave the man. Did you hear all that shit, Kins? You're the *neck* to his head? Jase told me Ray issued you a dare to prove who his boss was, but we figured after what happened at the club when Klive let Ray disrespect you that he'd changed his mind. Whatever you're doing that's made him go public, slow down! This is bad."

Rustin ran his hand through his hair and dragged his palm down to his jaw. He was right. Klive was openly attached to me, and we hadn't even had sex, so not like I'd wooed him in bed the way I'd told Tyndall the miracle would take. The closer I got to Klive, the more he jogged laps through my thoughts. I couldn't help the sappy happiness I derived from him saying and doing so much without sex being my golden ticket to his affection. I held these cards close to my chest and played like I was chill.

"Rustin, relax. Do your jobs. I'm doing mine. That's all."

He scoffed and shook his head. Rustin pulled his badge forward from his uniform. "Kins, remember who you're talking to? I can read your ass like the journal you thought you buried beneath the mattress."

My head bucked like he'd slapped me. "What the hell, Rustin?!"

His palm smothered my outrage. "I didn't read your damn journal. I didn't even know you had one until now. Way to be transparent and predictable. At least hide it in a bag inside the toilet tank. Something clever. I'm almost disappointed. You pull this awesome shit with our perp, then turn out like every other girl?"

"I am *not* like every other girl." I narrowed my eyes as I heard myself saying such an annoying line, but I wasn't who he compared me to. "Rematch on the beach," I dared, proving why I wasn't like every other girl.

"As much as I'd love to take your ass in the sand for my birthday, quit trying to distract law enforcement, Mizz Hayes. You already did a number on the men at the station. Now, admit it, you like him. *Genuinely* like him."

I nodded. No use lying. I'd already confessed the same to Jase, including being attracted to Klive. What could I say? The man was surprisingly likable when he wasn't threatening to kill me or give me to rapist Ray. When he'd cut that shit out, I found a kinder side I wanted to draw forth. That side was a sweet reward for my effort in this case and I'd enjoy that side for as long as I was able.

I whispered, too. "Rustin, don't pretend you didn't admit to liking him yourself. I heard you and Jase talking. Both of you confessed to enjoying his company. Neither of you were complaining last night. If you don't feel comfortable letting me get close, then one of you should try harder to get closer yourself. Do you feel me? I'm doing my part, now both of you get the hell on yours! I already told Jase this morning I was uncomfortable sharing information, and this is mundane stuff. If you two want to do the heavy lifting, do it! I'll continue doing what I'm doing because it's working. I enjoy his company, and frankly, I have an opportunity to do good. I'm taking it whether you two like it or not. I'll tell you just like I told Jase. If you two want to date me, ask me, otherwise I'll be getting to know Klive better. The two of you set me up for this. Don't be pissed when it bites Jase and me in the ass."

Too bad that bite didn't sting as bad anymore.

Rustin's palms rested on either side of my hips where I sat on the massage table.

"You make a valid argument, Kins. I'll give you that much. Just be extra cautious. You're important to Jase. To me, too. After today, the danger climbed to the HNL."

"HNL?"

He arched an eyebrow, then his hand climbed with each letter he repeated. "Come on. You never watched *Mad TV*? Hole Notha Level?"

"That's pretty special, Rusty." I smirked. "Add it to your disappointments in me."

"I will." His smile dimmed. "You can count on us. Do your good. See if you're truly the neck. Could've been great words for the moment, but maybe they weren't empty." He sighed. "Enough of this heavy shit. Can I commend you on your amazing knot-tying skills?"

He earned a bright smile from me.

"Kins, you never cease to amaze me. Such a big woman in a cute, tiny package. So easily underestimated and I'm the first to admit I'm guilty."

I patted him on the head like a good dog. He wiggled his hips like he had a tail and let his tongue hang out the side of his mouth like an idiot.

"Can I kiss you for my birthday?"

"Ha! How about you ask Klive later and if he says yes, I'll consider your offer."

His hips wagged harder, and I laughed. "Deal. I gotta go back to meter-reading so I'll be off work in time to go play later."

"Bye, sir. Thanks for coming."

"That's what I like to hear," he mocked Klive, accent included.

"Rustin, get out of my bloody room so I can get my massage. I'll let you know if I want to press charges later."

Rustin snickered at my fake threat to Angela if she could still hear me. My masseuse entered the room with the brightest eyes and smile.

"That was *amazing*!" she gushed, though she kept her voice low. "Miss Ansley left the building, by the way."

I nodded and situated myself on the table the way she instructed. What was I supposed to do with the attention or with Angela leaving like I deserved to get a massage and she didn't?

Rather than elaborate on any of the points the massage therapist brought up during the massage, I complimented her technique and killed the gossip. She was disappointed but disguised her curiosity behind pleasantry and did her job. Three hours later, I was pampered and relaxed with almost every service they offered. No facials for me, thanks. Didn't want to look like a pizza face when I had to be out in public today.

I left a generous tip for her on Klive's card, knowing he would want me to, then strolled along the boardwalk, staring at the beach until I caught Rock-N-Awe's bassist, Dan, and Jase walking around Klive's car once I neared the parking lot. To be an ass, I hit the panic button and watched them leap back. Both men looked around themselves to see if anyone saw their reactions. I snickered and hit the button to unlock the car. The alarm silenced, but I laughed at the guys.

"Whoa, Kinsley, who gave you the keys?" Dan asked me when I opened the driver's side.

Jase's brows rose. "That would be Klive King, my friend."

"Hold up!" Dan whirred around toward Jase. "Do you have some sort of death wish screwing Klive's girl?!"

"Excuse me?" I paused, my fists on my hips so I didn't pop Dan in the face. Clearly, Dan knew the unsavory side of Klive's affairs, but he also knew too much about Jase's and my relationship. More locker talk? Jase didn't flinch at my offense.

"On the contrary. Klive King is screwing with my girl."

I pursed my lips but couldn't keep them closed. "Technically, she's not *anyone's* girl right now."

Jase grinned. "True. What can I say, Dan? She's a bad, bad girlfriend."

I rolled my eyes while Dan chuckled at the reference to one of their favorite songs to perform. Dan refocused on me, then the car and back.

"Is it the cars?" he asked. "'Cuz I gotta tricked out Miata, just sayin'."

That got a giggle from me. "I'll keep that in mind but dating guys in a band is so five days ago." I cheesed and batted my lashes at Jase when he gave a smart-ass expression. "Dan, don't worry about me. I'm no idiot."

He nodded, but the concern remained, which was a nice surprise since we didn't know each other very well.

"Hey," Dan said, "No matter what kind of break you're on or whether you've moved on, I'm glad to see you two getting along and that you made up. I'll see ya on Monday, Jase."

A blush consumed my cheeks. I'd forgotten he'd been there the night of our fight. Hey, speaking of people who'd been there for our fight. Where was Quentin? Was he staying in Constance's apartment still? Maybe he'd heard from her?

"Thanks, man." Jase waved as Dan walked toward the boardwalk. "He works at the surf shop when he's not playing bass for me and three other bands."

"Ah." I asked about Quentin. Jase made duck lips and looked away.

"He bowed out of his audition for Rock-N-Awe after our showdown. Said it was too toxic for a happily married man. Gave me some advice on treating you better that I flushed in his face. I'm contemplating sobriety," he finished sheepishly. I blushed, hating the bad impression we'd made on Constance's company.

"That sucks ass," I said. "I'm sorry."

"Me too."

"Thank you." Things became a little quiet. "Where's your truck?"

"At home. I rode with Rustin since we were gonna hang for his birthday. This way I'm the designated driver."

"I see. Since you're not at your post, does this mean you're off and just waiting on him?"

"It does. I was gonna catch some waves in my off-time till he's finished, maybe see a man about a boat, whatever."

The corner of my mouth tilted. "In other words, you have nowhere to be and no way to get there till your sidekick is off work?"

"Affirmative, baby."

"I have some shopping to do since Klive practically commanded me to buy something pretty and meet him at the bar. If you can behave yourself and respect him and me, would you like to come with me?"

He winced. "After the bomb-ass shit Rustin told me happened, you might want to ask Klive if that's cool with him first. I mean you know how picky I am about who sits in my car. I can't imagine Klive allowing just anyone in his Italia."

He had a very valid point. I grabbed my phone. *Klive ... may I ask a favor?* I texted.

K: *Anything, love. Clearly ;)*

I chuckled to myself, his voice in my head.

Me: *May I bring Jase shopping with me in your car? He's waiting on Rustin to finish reading meters.*

K: *Sure. If you want another adrenaline rush, feel free to let him drive =D*

Me: *Very funny, sir. For real, though.*

K: *Yes, for real. Remember, I know he can drive. I pay him to do so. Besides, what kind of man would I be to trust him with your heart, but not an inanimate object?*

A few seconds later, I heard Jase's phone chime. He snorted to himself. "Klive texted me. He told me to be sweet to you and that when we're done shopping, he'd better not find his Italia in the same condition as the last thing he entrusted me with. Whatever that means? I have no idea what else he's entrusted me with that I didn't guard with my life."

I swallowed. "Me, Jase. *I'm* what he entrusted you with." Before Jase could argue or defend his actions, I threw my palm between us and relayed what Klive said about Jase driving his car. Jase's jaw hit the pavement. I almost laughed at his ridiculous expression. My latter words worked like an eraser for the first, because he didn't broach the subject again. He walked around the car with new reverence. When I pulled the door open for him, Jase yanked me into his arms and landed a super sexy kiss on my lips, hot groan included.

"Jase Taylor!" I slapped his chest. "You can't do that in public when Klive has marked me in his car."

"That the only way he's marked his territory?" His Adam's apple bobbed with boisterous laughter when I punched his bicep. "I'm playing, Kins. Get in." He sat in the Ferrari like eggs would crack under his bottom if he went too fast. I walked around to the passenger. Jase's hands stroked the steering wheel, the emblem, the paddle shifters a lot like I'd done last night and this morning.

"Damn, Kinsley, my black beauty would be so angry at me if she knew my little white mistress tempted me with this sexy siren. I'm a dirty cheater."

"You're also a total dork." I produced the key. "Foot on the brake, please."

Jase shook his head. "I shouldn't drive. I can't drive. Klive will own me for the rest of my life because I'll sign it over."

"Shall I draw up the Devil's paperwork for you, sir?"

Jase chuckled at my secretary voice, then moaned when I pressed the start button and the car growled to life.

"I'm gonna blow my wad here and now!" Jase's head tilted back against the headrest; his eyes closed in ecstasy. No wonder Klive had thrown himself on top of me the moment we'd stopped at the light last night. My cheeks heated at the sight of Jase turned on, but also in remembrance of Klive's roaming hands and the feel of him cuffing my other wrist, his firm body pressed to my legs and bottom. His hands gripping my waist and lifting me onto the back. Air puffed from my lips while I tried forgetting his on my neck, on mine in the bathtub, both of us nude.

"Good thing Klive gave me permission to buy you some clothes, too," I joked, fighting the way my body pulsed in naughty places. "Let's roll the windows down." *Fresh oxygen, please.*

Klive texted to ask if Jase was ever getting his ass in gear or gonna sit there all day. I clucked my tongue after throwing those words to Jase. "Guess he has tracking on his car."

Jase nodded. "Or your phone."

I narrowed my eyes. "Do you know something I don't?"

Jase shook his head, refocused on the steering wheel and gave himself a pep-talk. "I can do this. No pressure. Just like the races. Except with pavement and an exotic art piece that holds people. With the owner's girlfriend in the passenger. A girl I accidentally kissed. Fuck! Next time slap the shit out of me, Kins. On my face, not my bicep or abs. A real slap like cold water. I don't want to piss him off. K?"

"Remember you told me to do it," I teased to lighten the intensity he eyed me with. "I promise. Come on before we run out of time."

When Jase backed out of the spot, paranoid and timid, shoulders tight, knuckles white, Klive pinged with an atta boy.

K: *Have fun, my sweet. Let this be a time to heal the pain you inflicted on each other, but do save your love for me?*

Ooh la la!

Me: *Trying to get me into that plush bed?*

K: *In my bed, out of my head, love O_ o*

I chuckled at Klive's emoji.

K: *Technically, I had you right where I wanted you last night ... shame to have been grounded for bad behavior.*

Me: *You've earned reprieve. The spa was epic! Thank you Klive!*

♥

K: *You're welcome. Is that heart for Asshole Dick throwing his weight around? Or was your masseuse that good?*

Me: *Funny. She was good, but yes that's for AD*

K: *That's what I like to hear*

21 | ♀

When Jase got more comfortable, he pulled one hand off the steering wheel, wiped his palm on his lifeguard shorts, then reached for my hand. This I did allow.

"You want boutiques or mall?" he asked.

He shook his head and said in unison with me, "Not the mall. Too many cars." I laughed while he grinned.

I added, "If we do boutique, we can park right in front of the shops and see the car the whole time."

"Agreed. Damn, Kins, this is insane, right?" He checked his mirrors and those surrounding us. Rather than flying around the way I'd done last night and this morning, Jase almost cruised at a pace to make this last longer. Not what I'd expected. Then again, if you had a muscle car and racing to get that adrenaline need out of your system, I supposed the rush wouldn't be a dire need the way mine had seemed to call from my very bones the moment I first saw this car … the way I felt about a lane on a track … would Coach Walton allow me to run tomorrow, or was I still grounded? He hadn't ungrounded me, but letting me practice had to mean something, right?

I must've stayed in my head the next fifteen minutes because Jase's voice startled me from my thoughts when he asked if a certain shop was good. "It's got an open space front and center, baby."

"Yeah, this is perfect. Bobbie works here!" I clapped my hands. "Should we ask her how things went with Rustin last night?"

Jase chuckled. "We rode together, remember? He didn't even make second base. Even if they'd ridden together, I'm pretty sure she'd have left him with only a kiss."

"Good. He needs strength training in the waiting department. Plus, I love the idea of him in pain."

"Who named you *Sweet Kins* again?"

He chuckled when I slapped his thigh, then said, "Hands off for this. I need to be hella careful." He waited for traffic to pass on his right, then cut the wheel and eased the Ferrari into the perfect space. "Stay, girl." Jase cheesed before getting out.

"Oh, shit," I whispered when he walked around toward my door. Brayden and one of his friends walked along the sidewalk, but Shay and Lucy were with them. "Come on, Jase, wait till they pass. Recognize Lucy and wait," I prayed and watched Jase through the window. Was the tint on this car dark enough not to see who was inside if we waited? I had the best damn luck.

Brayden not only stopped, but asked Jase how he knew him, that he looked familiar, then when he'd bought a Ferrari, what he did to afford an exotic car. Jase exacerbated Brayden's bull by opening my door and saying, "I'm not the owner, I'm the chauffeur."

I peeked up in the small crack he'd made. "Let them pass," I hissed through gritted teeth.

"Haters gonna hate, Miss Hayes," he said back, then opened the door further. His hand extended like he was my damn escort or something. I gripped his fingers too hard. Jase's tongue traveled across his teeth, but he couldn't hide that shit-eating snicker. Bastard didn't know the significance of standing before this group.

"Thank you," I said like I hadn't been giving him crap. Their gasps pumped a nervous tingle from my heart to my toes and back. Chin up. Smile. Gracious not growl. I waved at them, unsuspecting smile and eyes cast their way. After Klive vanquishing Angela, could I really allow these frenemies to kill my happiness? My drug lord, crime boss, hitman gave me his unlimited credit card and time off work, let me drive this exotic car and extended the blessing to my ex. This was a day to be glad. I'd think of the heavy later.

"Kinsley, is this Mr. King's car?" Lucy gushed and clapped her hands, huge smile.

"Yes, it is. He sent the two of us on an errand for him. One of our friends is celebrating his birthday, and while Klive plans the party at the bar, we are shopping for gifts."

"Damn," Brayden drooled over the car. He looked up at me when I stepped onto the sidewalk in front of Bobbie's shop. "Klive King? Are y'all together?" He swallowed like he was out of his depth. I hated that instant fear when he'd been so kind to me all this time.

"Oh, Frat Toy," I teased, hoping he'd lighten up, "don't you know it'd be impolite to confirm or deny in front of my ex?" I cast a saccharine smile over my shoulder at Jase.

My chauffeur twirled Klive's keyring on one finger and grabbed his heart through his white tank. I formed a gun with my hand, aimed at Jase, fired, then blew the tip of my finger, winked at Brayden when I grinned back at him. The strain in his answering smile said he knew exactly who Klive was outside the pretty high-rise, as did his friend.

I shifted my attention to Shay and Lucy. "Good luck at tomorrow's meet, Shay."

Jase opened the door to the boutique for me. Shay wasn't sure what to do with me since I didn't aim any bitch factor her way for once. I realized right now I wasn't jealous or envious of anyone.

"Thanks," she said after an uncertain silence.

"Y'all do me a favor?" I asked from beneath Jase's arm, halfway over the threshold. Shay and Lucy waited. "Whip their asses tomorrow, but also, when the races are done and you relay this encounter in the bathroom, know that I'm not a lesbian, don't want any hidden touches to the T&A and I'm not sleeping with anyone. P.S. I couldn't fit my Bible in this small clutch. Better to get the feed straight from the horse's mouth than speculate. Makes the difference between disinformation and honesty."

Jase whistled and tapped his temple, then walked inside behind me, the heavy door closing behind us.

"Omigosh! Omigosh! Omigosh! Kinsley, I'm so happy you came in!" Bobbie bubbled from behind her check-out counter. She ran around and her arms flew around my neck like we hadn't seen each other last night. I giggled while she pulled back.

"I'm glad to see you, too, girl. What's got such a bright smile on your face? Is it the cowboy?"

She giggled and waved my words away, but the cutest blush filled her cheeks. "He was so much fun. But I have something perfect that came in yesterday. After last night, I pulled your size. I was gonna see you later at the bar to give it to you. It's just fate you came in. Oh, hey, Jase. You can't get mad at me for what I give her."

"Why would I get mad?" he asked. She ignored him and left us, disappearing into a back room. The rest of the boutique was empty. Jase asked what that stuff I'd said to Lucy and Shay was all about. I filled him in while we rifled through racks of clothing.

"I wasn't trying to be rude, but we both know they're gonna go gossip. This way I'm in charge of my own narrative. Shouldn't that be the way things are for everyone?" I lifted a rugged pair of blue jeans. "You have to try these on, Jase."

"In charge of your own narrative?" Jase mulled my words and took the jeans. "Yeah, I'll try them on. This King's effect?"

"Huh?"

"Look, Kins! Isn't it perfect?" Bobbie rushed toward me holding a hanger she shoved in my personal space.

"Pft!" Jase rolled his eyes and asked where the fitting room was. She gave him the brightest smile and pointed toward the back.

"You need to go put this on so I can see if it will fit as well as I have in my head," Bobbie ordered. I couldn't wipe my own bright grin from my face enough to have any sensitivity toward Jase. When I walked out of my dressing room beside Jase's, he was posed shirtless in the jeans I picked. I cackled and clapped my hands.

"Revenge," he said, chin raised, smug smirk, but his eyes lit with a smile as they traveled my figure clad in a short British flag tee shirt dress.

"You look hot, sir." I bit my lip and trailed my fingertips along his hip bone beneath his cut muscles.

"You look hot, too. Between this and the car, my balls are as blue as your dress. Rustin's right to call you bitch," he said under his breath, then lifted those lips into that panty-dropping grin he uses like a weapon to weaken women around him to his rugged charm.

I tsked and ripped the tags from his pants. He flinched in fear. My head tossed back with a villainous laugh. "I need the tags if I'm gonna pay for these, duh, what were you thinking?"

"Gimme those tags. Keep it on!" Bobbie nearly had spirit fingers when she cheered at her own talent for style.

"You have a great sense of humor, Bobbie." I handed her the tags to Jase's jeans while he picked through shirts on the other side of the store.

"I know right? When y'all get married," she whispered, "you should let me be your personal shopper, Kins."

I scoffed. "Me and Jase?"

She snorted and rolled her eyes. "No. Girl, I just put you in my team colors. Figured a sports analogy might help you there."

"Nice."

She patted a stack of her picks on the counter. "These are for your future husband. If I got the sizes wrong, just come and exchange, but I'm rarely wrong and I think he'd look sexy AF in these. For you, of course." She scrunched her nose, cutesy and excited. Her hand balled and her other took mine, held my fingers open. She looked around the shop, then wrapped my hand around something soft. "Go put these on under that dress." When I tried to look at what she'd given me, she clamped my fingers closed. "No, no. You go back there and do the deed. Here's a little baggie."

I took the plastic and placed my bikini inside, then shimmied the gauzy thong up my thighs. Hell, no I wasn't gonna survive in butt floss, especially in a short dress. I hated thongs. And no bra was for emergency burned breasts only. Jase would be thrilled, but I wasn't going into public like this. Bobbie loved the look when I came out. Jase asked if we'd had a sudden cool front. I popped his belly and handed Bobbie Klive's credit card.

She peeked at the name, pursed her smiling lips and told me she was putting Mr. King's things on her employee discount since she was the one who suggested them. "Receipt in the bag?" she asked. I nodded. When we walked out of the shop, three people lined for a selfie in front of Klive's car. I shot Jase a look he shot back. He ushered them away, then closed me inside the passenger side.

When he backed out of the spot, that group gawked like excited spectators and took more photos. I sighed.

"You gotta be fair," he reasoned. "They probably stared at you more than the car when you were getting in. You win. I'm officially feeling the pain of mistreating what Klive trusted me with. Hats off to both of you."

I only half-smiled. He gripped my fingers.

"I was kidding, Kins. You okay?"

"Yeah. Don't get on the highway. Keep going under the overpass toward the base."

"MacDill? Why?"

"Not all the way. Just close by. I need a trim."

"It's not a good area to bring King's car, Kins."

"Keep it safe for me. I need to see Sweetness, Constance's cousin. I haven't heard from her and I'm worried. He does hair."

"Sweetness?"

"His real name is Antoine."

Jase didn't say anything else but nodded.

22 | ♀

Twenty minutes later, Mr. Taylor stood guard over Klive's car, looking very much like he had when he'd beaten the shit out of Pat Connor. He wasn't pleased with me coming here, that much was clear, but Antoine greeted me with pleasant surprise. I sat in his chair, requested the fastest mini makeover possible, then cut to the chase of Constance.

"Oh, *cher*, she's okay. She reached out through an internet cafe two days ago. They made it safely to their first destination a few days late. Flight delays led to rental car problems. Delia forgot they couldn't charge their phones without adapters, forgot to get an international phone plan. Constance told me to pass word to you but neglected to give me your phone number or email address. Typical." He rolled his eyes. "She's lucky to have someone looking out for her."

He filled the time with the things Constance's family said to her and him about me, how he put them in their places, told Constance to hop a flight so her mama couldn't come to Florida and force her home. "See, you have allies, too. Now, let me do that, don't wipe, dab." He ran a cotton pad beneath my eyes where tears spilled over.

"I'm so sorry, Antoine."

"Sweetness to you, *cher*. Don't apologize. You have nothing to be sorry for. Constance is standing up for herself and her friends for the first time. She's too big to go back to that small parish." His face neared mine in the mirror. "Even if she gave you a hard time about your fight, she joked that she'd picked the right white girl from the wrong side of the tracks to have her back if she needed to lose weave."

I did cackle at that. His brilliant white smile lit my inner turmoil on fire and vanquished all the tension I realized I'd carried since that day in Pensacola when Constance went off on me for things I couldn't help or undo.

He dabbed the remaining wetness while I thanked him, now with a smile through my blurry eyes.

"You're welcome. I'm glad you love her enough to investigate. Now, with that car you've got outside, this dress, combined with the things Constance has confided about a certain beautiful Brit, can I assume this mini makeover is for him and not for the bodyguard you left outside? He's bangin' ...." Sweetness leaned back checking Jase out through the glass doors. "Shame he's straight."

"It is for the Brit, yes." I gave him a few delicious deets on our date last night. Antoine groaned, made little comments, or asked questions as he used a straightener to make organized waves in my hair. He teased certain areas, formed them, sprayed texturizer, then went to work on my makeup. A customer walked inside and made a comment about white girls invading everything.

"Ignore him," Sweetness whispered. "He asked me out, but I told him I was taken. Not two nights later, he comes into the Dallas Bull and catches me dancing with a white girl who happens to be the sister of my boyfriend. They're not technically white. They're mixed Koreans."

Sweetness pulled his phone to show me pics of himself with who appeared the type to wear mismatching patterns and create a new trend rather than a faux pas. His laugh expanded through the space when I told him so.

"I can't wait to tell him your thoughts because he likes you. He thinks you're beautiful with that tone you got and red hair. Me too. I love the challenge you bring me to enhance rather than mask all this. Ta-da! Now, let's see what your bodyguard thinks as our litmus?"

"Can I pay first?"

He chuckled. "That, I will never have a problem with." He took Klive's card and when we finished with the transaction, I grinned at Jase when he animatedly grabbed his heart and pretended to fall like he had after I'd taken body shots with Angela.

"*Magnifique!*" Sweetness gushed. "Nice to see you, man."

"You too, Sweets." They pulled each other into a guy hug. "You're better at this shit than I ever knew. Not just good at shining that dome of yours." Jase rubbed Sweetness's bald head. They both laughed. "She's beautiful."

"Thanks. Y'all get out of here while I take out the trash."

Jase peered beyond Sweetness toward the inside of the shop. "Need any help? Looks heavy."

Hmm ….

"Nah. Once I throw in some names, you know this one's gonna shit blood without me using a boot." Sweetness and Jase laughed. Amazing how improper Sweetness sounded around Jase when he was so strong in his creole with me. He resumed that tone of voice with me when he cupped both my hands inside his, bowed his head until his forehead touched the back of one of his hands over mine. When he stood upright, he said, "This has been my sincere pleasure, and I pray I've earned your business beyond Constance's connections."

He released my hands to give me a card from his shirt pocket. I nodded at him, complimented his work and him as a person all in fluent French to appease him till he smiled again in that way that eased my sudden trepidation about the exchange between him and Jase.

Jase opened the passenger door for me, but I told him to get in on that side. When I was back behind the wheel, I tried not asking or nosing around in their business but couldn't resist.

"I get that y'all probably served together, and I'm not asking about that because you'd have to kill me if you divulged, but that last bit about the guy in his shop ... the way he said bye to me this time was nothing like last time." I had white knuckles as I navigated the heavy street traffic. I hated how close every car was to this one. I didn't want to disappoint Klive.

"You mean the names comment and the reverence? Nightshade employs his brother, remember? Seems you're the last to realize that neck description Klive gave in the spa."

"Let's not talk. I need quiet. And shoes for this dress. I don't want to go to anymore shops or burn a huge hole in Klive's card. I'm not a pretentious princess to any King. And new undies! This butt floss is gonna carve a deeper crack in my ass!"

Jase laughed but pursed his lips and looked out the window. He remained silent while I used the GPS to get back home. Ugh! Klive's house.

"I'm just running inside to add proper undergarments and pick shoes, then we will head to the bar. Good?" I peered into the Ferrari after exiting.

Jase got out of the car and shook his head. "May I at least stand in the foyer, Miss Hayes? It's awful hot and I could use a cool glass of iced tea iff'n you have one."

"I'm gonna kill you. Quit being an asshole." I strode toward the front door rather than using the back entry. Should I have called Klive to ask him if I could bring Jase back to the house with me so I could change? The bad side about being in my own head too long, I neglected the obvious things until they stared me in the face. I swallowed as I entered the key and code into Klive's door. The mechanical lock slid, and the door beeped our permission to enter. This was my first time crossing the threshold into the open, three-story spire of Klive's lighthouse-reminiscent foyer. A staircase hugged the walls of the tall cylinder just like a lighthouse, too. As much as I wanted to stand and marvel at the beauty of Klive's architectural talent, I left Jase beside a round console table in the center of the space and rushed inside, through the living room, up the small steps into the kitchen and down the hallway to the library. The stone Shisha dog twisted under my palm for the passage.

"Coolest house ever," I whispered to myself, then rifled through the drawers in the Closet of Kinsley for the perfect bra and undies. I shucked the dress over my head, snaked into the bra, then tossed the thong into a hamper in the corner rather than the trash can where I wanted to throw them. As I pulled a pair of seamless panties up my thighs, eyeing the shoe selection, the door to my closet pressed open. I shrieked and jerked my dress off the floor, clutching the flag to my chest.

"Kiss. My. Grits." Jase filled the doorway, his mouth agape, head turning slowly as he took in the mini boutique.

"You shouldn't be in here, Jase!"

"Well, your phone was buzzing with a call from Constance. I figured you'd want to take it. I went upstairs where the bedrooms are, where I thought Klive's master bedroom was, but you were nowhere to be found, so I looked around." He looked around now. Into the bathroom, at the tub and the stone wall with the fireplace, the huge shower, peeked in Klive's closet, then stopped in the bedroom before the foot of the massive bed, still messy from where we'd slept.

Hot dread filled my belly and traveled up my neck into my cheeks.

"Upstairs is a decoy," Jase said so quietly I almost didn't hear him. "Very impressive, King. I've underestimated you." He turned around and came back into the closet where I felt suspended in animation. This was so bad. Jase bypassed my evident fear and tension. Though I stared at the stone wall, through the fireplace into the room at the bed, I saw nothing but the terrible outcomes of each scenario I imagined were Klive to come home now and find another man in his inner sanctum or find out that Jase even knew this existed. A decoy room? I heard Jase whistle behind me.

"Baby, baby, baby ... Klive's got big plans for you."

I twisted. Jase held a strappy leather corset and super slutty panties in each hand.

"No sex?" he asked, skeptical.

Can a sister get some water to wash the cotton down, please? Constance's voice sounded in my head.

I thought about the fear I'd had of Klive last night. How rather than run, I'd faced him, made myself clear. I'd have to be clear with him later about this mishap if he didn't already know since he'd somehow known about the car's location. In a way, I was pissed at Jase, too. This space Klive shared with me was hallowed ground. Other than those who'd help build this, I was the only other person invited inside and now Jase had walked right into Klive's space.

"Jase, would you like if I brought Klive back to your house after allowing him to drive your black beauty and him going into your private bedroom, through my drawers at your house, if I'd had any?"

He dropped the articles from his hands back into the drawer and slowly looked at me with a different understanding. "No. No I wouldn't. Not at all. Fuck! This is so much worse than when I'd kissed you! I'll be in the living room waiting."

Jase jetted from the area. All the tension the massage therapist rubbed from my back, shoulders and neck was back worse than before. Last night I hadn't deserved Klive's temper, right now, I did. I wasn't afraid of him hurting me. He'd trusted me and I'd ruined that. Ugh. Was this why Klive's men were so loyal? Were they driven less through fear and more the fear of displeasing their leader?

I didn't want to think about any of this anymore. In the full-length mirror in the closet, I shifted the British flag back over my curves and stepped into a pair of shimmery royal blue heels. If I looked cute enough when I poured my confessions to Klive, would he be less upset?

Hell, he wouldn't be as mad at me as he would Jase. My heels clicked on the hard floor as I walked confidently into the kitchen with Klive's secret lair tucked back behind the safety of the library. Jase whipped around from the art on the wall and watched me descend the small steps into the living area. His expression grave, I saw his Adam's apple bob.

"I'm so sorry, Kins. For everything. I feel green, not only from my mistakes, but with envy for how he handles you while I'm so fucked-up I screw the pooch at every opportunity. I don't know what I'm doing. I mean, shit, look at this place! That closet. The bed —"

"Hey, shh, come here." I opened my arms. He tucked his head on my shoulder. "Jase, you know me. Am I a high-maintenance girl? Is this house my style?"

"Not exactly, but who's to say you won't get used to this? You spent the day shopping, at the spa, getting made up, all while cruising in a damn Ferrari to get it done. Now, you don't have to work tonight because he doesn't want you to, while the bar is short-handed during the busy season." He pulled away and gripped his hair. He closed his eyes for several seconds and when they opened, he looked at me differently. "This suits you. You're beautiful. You're not slouching or blushing. Your chin is high and your makeup and hair aren't weird on you anymore —"

"My makeup and hair were weird —"

"That came out wrong, dammit. I can't think straight. Do you know when someone hardly ever wears makeup and keeps that big bun on their head? Then they do something with their appearance and it's like jarring? Beautiful to anyone else, but jarring to someone who sees them every day? That's how it was when you wore those red heels to work and had your hair and makeup done. Like a damn Hooters girl in the wrong uniform or something. Too sexy. You're like a secret you kept from the patrons, until you let the world know what you were holding back. Not like I haven't seen you prettied up before, Kins, but you — ah — shit." He rubbed the back of his head, down his neck, then suddenly dropped to his knees and wrapped his arms around my waist.

"Last night suited you. This, here, the makeup, hair, dress, posture, all of it suits you. You stand next to him, and I can fucking see it!" His forehead rested against my belly while I wasn't sure what to do with my hands or how to soothe him. His head tilted back. Jase's honey eyes held the worst plea. "Baby, tell me I'm not losing you. Tell me this is all temporary. That he isn't sweeping you off your feet while you sweep him off-balance. Tell me that urging you to get involved with him wasn't a colossal mistake on my part. Tell me I'm the *only* one you're mad about."

He had legitimate reason to worry. Inside I'd be honest about that. I cleared my throat and held his face in my palms, his eyes with my eyes.

"Jase, you need to be real. Do you know anyone who wouldn't love driving, let alone riding in, a Ferrari? How about a great pampering? You had a stupid grin the whole trip all the way back home. *Here*, dammit. You know what I meant. Remember me. I'm just me, the girl you liked in high school, your sister's bestie. My mother makes me dress like that, like this, well, ish, every time I am expected at one of her frilly events, so what you see isn't new. You were right. I kept it secret because I didn't want exactly what you're doing now to happen.

"Don't get sloppy because of emotions. All of this, it's for you, not because of you. I was on Klive's radar no matter what. You've helped me manipulate the situation to be human to him. Now, he sees what you see. Do you blame him for caring about me the way you do? Do you blame him for caring the way you care? If someone feels what you feel, is that so wrong?"

Jase sighed. "During my emotional tirade, I forgot to mention how great you've become at chewing ass."

I rolled my eyes. "Did I not tell you on our first date that you might not like me so much after you spend time with me? Why do you think that is? The talent is all mine, no drug lord, crime boss, hitmen necessary."

Jase snorted. "Is that what you call him?"

"If the shoe fits." I gripped his cheeks a little harder and felt my mother's look come through in my body language. "Jase Taylor, you listen to me. On a serious note, if I can help someone like that grow a heart and change things from within while I'm here, I'm going to. I cannot be in any friendship or relationship without feelings. I'm not a robot. I'm sorry in that regard, but I don't think you'd love me as much as you say if I were able to be robotic and unfeeling. Now, get your head back in the game and quit throwing me off mine with your jealousy. There's no place for that in all this.

"In the meantime, I'll get as deep as we need until we are free to be together. Then you can get down on your knee, marry me and make me a pretty baby without fearing that some killer wants to steal it all away. Got it?"

Referring to Klive that way helped put this mission back in perspective for me, too. How quickly I'd forgotten my resolve to enjoy this ride for as long as I could before I helped throw the brakes on the roller coaster. Klive was wonderfully charming when he chose to be, but charm was a deceptive trait. As much as I wanted Klive to be normal, he wasn't. He wasn't some hot guy that had a crush the way Tyndall said or loved me the way Constance overplayed that card while downplaying the Nightshade part. Constance was biased because of her cousin and likely she wouldn't want Nightshade going anywhere because Gustav might go down with the ship. Had Jase considered this?

"You want to marry me?"

"Jase, stand up. I need to lock the door and we have an appointment at the bar where you will put all this bullshit behind you. The subject of marriage will not come up again until we are free. Your weakness is endangering both of us. Now, are we going to do this shit or not?"

"We're gonna do this shit, yes ma'am." He saluted me from his knees, then jumped to his feet and headed for the door. As I double-checked the lights were off, that the lock slid back into place, I mentally reasoned that there was no way I could compete with Nightshade, so why bother with the foolish notions and mental mindset of a girly crush when I needed to man the hell up, too?

23 | ♀

I WALKED ALONG THE **flagstones** toward the circle drive where Jase waited on the passenger side of the Ferrari.

"Here. You can drive, sir. These heels and those pedals don't mix. Not to mention, it might be the last time you ever get to if Klive confronts me about taking you back to his place without permission." I thanked him when he opened the door for me, then passed him the fob.

We took Klive's driveway nice and slow, waited for the large gates to close behind us, then Jase proceeded to work through the maze of streets in Klive's neighborhood like he lived here, too. When he saw my curious expression, he shrugged.

"I've been to his house about five or six times. Spent the night in his guest room once. How do you think I knew about the rooms upstairs?"

"Wow, so he's not gonna be pissed about you going into his house?"

"Not that I know of unless he doesn't trust us to be alone together with so many extra beds."

I shook my head. "Tell me about —" I cut my question about this decoy master bedroom and made a slicing motion with my hand at my throat that we cut this chat. I tapped my ear. His eyebrows lifted and he nodded. "Tell me about why you got to spend the night in His Majesty's palace?"

That was a natural question I'd ask and Klive would expect if he could in fact hear us when we were in the car.

"Nightshade, baby. How can he get to know me better if we never spend time outside the bar or clubs?"

"Ah."

"Do me a solid, Kins. Have fun. Be young. Be naïve. It's safer. Act like a twenty-four-year-old co-ed who cares more about the environment and college causes. These things are heavy. Those things are distractions from the darkness I never want you knowing too much about. Let me, Klive, Rustin, hell, even our parents worry about the negatives of life. You're still pure and sweet. You haven't seen horror yet. It always gets you at some point, but why make it sooner than it needs to be?"

I sighed. "Jase, that's just wishful thinking. Do you know what naïveté has gotten me? Disrespected, looked down upon like I'm weak or too excited when you or any other guy shows interest. It landed me in bed with two men at once. It left me with this impression that the worst things in the world were the curse words I couldn't quit saying at work when really the world and the humans inside it have the potential to be the best or worst parts of life. In this way, you're right to be upset at the possibility you're losing me, because you are. I can't go back after Inferno hurt Sara and me, after someone murdered her, and pretend that's some random situation when it's all around us, everywhere. It's not like innocence is some cloak you can slip off and on when you wish. Sometimes I wish to pull it on and hide but hiding is for cowards and I can't long to be around courage and not abide in the same.

"I'm sorry if that came off bitchy. It's just hard when everyone is asking so many favors of me like they want to preserve me. You can't hide me away. Life is gonna happen and the last thing I want to do is wilt when shit gets hard. I might cry or throw a fit sometimes, but by the grace of God I'm still gonna do what I need to do."

Jase cleared his throat. "To quote my father, 'and God saw that no helper was fit for Adam, so he made him fall into a deep sleep where he took one of Adam's ribs and created the woman who would be his helper and she used the rib to beat Adam over the head when he was an idiot or bossing her around.'"

I laughed and he seemed happy to make me.

On the way to the bar, Jase filled the space between us with his voice and my laughter when he serenaded me in sync with the stereo. When he requested *Kickstart My Heart*, I glared but couldn't hold true anger.

"C'mon, baby. I know you've got this. Rock out. No drinks around to risk pouring on yourself in the finale."

I cackled and backhanded his chest. He grabbed my hand, folded my fingers in, then placed my fist beneath my mouth.

"It's no wooden spoon but works just as well. I'd take the guitar, but gotta keep this between the stripes. Check-check-one-two," he said into my fist as the opening chords came through the speakers. He turned the volume up so loud our real voices wouldn't be heard, so I did release myself to the moment. Even if I felt like an idiot, Jase needed some silly after giving me a peek at his burdens. At least now I knew he wasn't some numb jerk who could turn off his emotions.

By the time we reached the lot, Jase had professed his undying love and loyalty for me through songs both serendipitous and serious. I relished them as much as the public serenade he'd given me before the whole bar; eh, more since I wasn't under obligation to appease patrons.

Gus stood on the sidewalk beside the street rather than the door, directing parking. When he saw the Ferrari, he held a palm flat, backed up from the far end to the VIP spot right beside the bar and forced a clearing in the line that extended beyond our lot. Damn, this was a lucrative sign for the servers! Gus walked into the street to stop traffic in both directions. Jase turned into the oncoming lane then backed over the itsy-bitsy curb I realized was more like a little ramp across the front of the lot for this very reason. Made so much sense now. None of the exotics were driving in the gravel.

"This is so bizarre! What universe have we stumbled into?" I asked, taking in the groups Jarrell and Gustav stood in front of to keep the clearing for Jase to back the car into the space.

"Don't you know the little queen has arrived, baby?" He winked when the car came to a complete stop. Jase huffed a breath like he'd been tensed. "That was fun, but I've had my fill for a while. Thanks to both you and Klive." He threw a hand to silence my correction. "Don't bother. That breakdown at his house won't happen again. Do the shit." He pumped his fist, Kinsley style. "I'd kiss your grin if I wouldn't have a number on my head."

"Wait, Jase." I grabbed his shoulder. "People here don't know that realm, who Klive is, like the Nightshade stuff, do they? Like they won't look at me that way, will they?"

Jase chuckled. "The tourists don't." He held his hands at two different levels. "Think of the underground like a parallel universe of sorts. There's the surface-level where consumers consume and enjoy their distractions, then there's the other level known only to those who've peered beyond the curtain. Like Oz, remember? I'm not saying King is the ultimate wizard, but in *this* region, those in the underground think of him as their ultimate wizard. When that wizard takes a special interest in someone, that's gonna spark curiosity, jealousy, anger, or veneration depending upon the view of the wizard himself. Some of this might be for me, not you, because of Klive's interest in me joining Nightshade beyond the beginner levels, but you are absolutely an intrigue. Keep it up, Kins. You may be the shiny lure who distracts those foes while he swims up behind them and devours them before they devour you."

Whoa. I swallowed. "Yay. I'm handy in all sorts of ways. Can I just go back to being a boring bartender?" I popped my lower lip.

Jase snorted. "You're the one who said you'd handle your shit, even if you cried or threw a fit about it. Time to smile, love."

Jase got out while Gustav opened my door for me. I took his hand, and his low timbre vibrated his chest as he took me in.

"Nice dress. Lookin' mighty fine tonight, Little Red."

"Thanks, Gus." I pulled him down for a kiss to his cheek. "Thank you for *everything*," I whispered in case he was doing more than met the eye. He stood taller and the brightest smile I'd never seen branded his face. What a feeling! My bright smile lined my lips.

"Let's get you inside." Gus walked beside me with his big palm at my back while Jase walked in front of us. Okay, this was a bit weird, like I was some sort of celebrity rather than one of the bartenders. I'd walked to the front of the line for years using my power as an employee. This was a far different vibe and those in line noticed, their heads whipping toward me whether they knew me or not. Their phones came up in their hands in case I was someone they'd need to note later. I hated that shit, especially where school mixed into the picture.

Gustav took the door Jase opened for me. Jase assumed the position behind/beside me with his hand at my back as we walked inside the bumping bar.

"Chad's here?" I shouted over the loud, early two-thousand's era rap he was known to love.

"He's your favorite damn deejay, ain't he?" Jase asked at my ear. "Look at all the extra servers."

More men in uniforms mixed with the bitch server and Bayleigh than I'd ever seen here.

Rustin snagged my hand and led me to the dance floor. "Helluva birthday bash, huh?" he asked.

"Yeah! It almost looks like a company was hired to fill in the blanks! This is great!" I gushed.

"I think you're right!" he shouted over the music. "Don't let that go to your head along with all that power you have behind you now, Mizz Hayes. I love your smart-ass choice in dress! You're pretty with these colors."

"Thanks, Rusty. You look deceptively pure in a white Polo, sir!" I had a hard time accepting a real compliment from him without edging a joke in there. "Where's Klive?" I asked.

"Ha! That's exactly what I was goin' for. Bobbie's coming in soon. Gotta keep a good rep for as long as I can!" Rustin weaved between groups and couples grinding to the song, then pointed to a table near the dance floor. An unexpected thrill rushed through my belly, automatic smile included, when I saw Klive who saw me first. Our eyes met. I spun on my heel and fanned my fingers over my shoulder to make him smile. He rewarded my effort with that dazzling grin he rarely showed. *Be still my heart and nerves!*

Rather than trotting over like a desperate fool, Rustin and I fell into the rhythm of the heavy bass and crowds around us. I didn't have to tell him not to grind against me. He'd already taken in Klive's company at the table. A table Jase joined, fresh brew in his hand. Several guys from the football game we'd played at Jase's house gathered with their group, including Devon the Douche. However, I noticed multiple men dressed to the caliber Klive deployed when he worked in the high-rise; though they appeared relaxed and confidently casual, as if that level of style and wealth were natural. Hmm ... they didn't look like Nightshade, though.

Chad was in a dirty happy mood tonight and he wasn't shy about pulling his fedora from his head to fan himself when he caught my eye. I laughed and waved my hands toward myself so he'd keep the music coming. I was feelin' the vibe like I had permission to for the first time. Jase's talk in the car really helped release me from our feelings for each other for now. Sucked to hurt him in the process, but at the end of the day he decided his direction and mine. If I held back, I'd seem fake or stiff with Klive. After what Klive had done for me earlier, I relaxed the tension with the music like another massage, this time for my senses. I was free! No more Angela Ansley! Ding dong the witch is dead! But not *dead* dead ... I almost cringed but caught myself.

Rustin spun me beneath his arm and grabbed my hips a second later.

"You thinkin' the birthday card is gonna save your ass?" I joked over my shoulder as we kept working our bodies to the music.

"Maybe I'm testing my limits."

"Or mine," I said.

"Damn, I love when you're mean. I'm helping you. See how Klive, Jase and even Devon are watching? Isn't it just a little thrilling to torture them? Be honest."

"Meh, I guess."

Rustin tickled my waist.

"Okay, okay, yes!" I giggled and slapped his hands.

"Sure, slap my hands when I touch you here but not lower."

"Rustin Keane, you wanna play that game?"

"Finally, she gets it!"

I grabbed Rustin's hands and kept them at my waist. Jase was back in full flirt mode because he was working with the women who trickled into their space, though he tugged a couple who seemed aimed at Klive like he ran interference for both Klive and me. Life was odd to say the least. Devon leaned toward Jase to say something, but neither of them quit watching me with Rustin. Okay, Rustin was right. This was kind of fun. I waved at Devon with a sweet smile, then made duck lips and waved my palm in front of my face like he couldn't see or touch this. Jase busted out laughing. Klive did, too.

When two songs passed, Rustin took my hand, insisting I needed to hydrate. Why argue if we were finally heading to the table?

Electricity surged through my palm when Klive took my hand from Rustin's and tugged me close. Even in my heels, I was barely taller than a sitting Klive. He released my hand to wrap his hand around my waist. His fingers tip-toed down my spine and stopped at the top of my bottom. His hot breath warmed my ear.

"This dress is doing very naughty things to me."

Oh. Shit. Klive sexual harassment? Guess if sexual advancement wasn't offensive, I couldn't say harassment because this was sensual as hell!

"I love it with those heels. Your legs look like stems I need to pluck from the ground." He blew slightly against my ear. My knees softened when everything inside flamed and melted. "Like a dandelion, if I blow against the petals, can I make as many wishes as I'd like?"

My face turned, my cheek to his subtle stubble rubbing my skin, making this weakness worse.

"Klive …." My teeth dragged over my lower lip.

"I know. You don't have to tell me to behave, because I'd have to clear everyone out of here to behave the way I want to."

I pulled back and smiled at him. "Is that all that's holding you back?"

He chuckled. His hand remained very low on my back. I noted his green shirt, the cuffs rolled up his forearms, the veins and muscles leading to his long fingers.

"Sir, did you wear this color on purpose after I got onto you for buying the green Polo?"

"I like the bloody color, so I'll wear the bloody color unless you'd like to divest me of my misbehavior?"

My fingers reached into the back of his hair and tugged enough for him to spread his palm over my back and press me fully against him.

"Have you all met Kinsley?" Klive asked the group. I swallowed and plastered a smile, making eye contact with the other table-members I'd forgotten the existence of during that sexual tension. Klive introduced me to several men from the office. Was that a code for peeps higher up in Nightshade or were these men from the high-rise? If so, I prayed they wouldn't tell my father about this.

They all seemed very pleased to meet me but chatting amid heavy bass and volume wasn't the easiest.

"If you'll excuse us," Klive told them when the pleasantries finished. He stood, my hand in his, and walked me to the bar.

Bayleigh squealed when she saw us together. "Look who the hell rolled in! Love the dress! Come here!" She leaned over the bar and wrapped an arm around my neck. "If you weren't with him, I'd be mad at you for calling in. I wish I could keep the help. These servers look like Chippendales. You want the pickle pop?"

"Is that what you've named it?"

"For now. But it might make your breath too sour for later." She cast a winky smile at Klive over my head. "Unless you like sour," she said to him.

"Or perhaps we should both have one so we match," Klive offered. "Problem solved."

"Ooh, I like his style!" Bayleigh gushed. "Coming right up. If you don't like it, you can always give your pickle to Kins."

"Bayleigh Blue!" I chastised her naughty mouth while Klive ate her comment like an appetizer. She went about making our drinks without caring about my tone.

A stool opened in our area. Klive steered me toward the leather I scooted onto. Rather than face the bar, I faced him. His eyes held something too hypnotically erotic to stifle. I struggled to keep my hands on my thighs. He placed his over them like he knew. I didn't look at his hands. I held his eyes, wishing I were free to grab the back of his head and force his hot mouth on mine. *Dammit, Bay, hurry with the drinks! I'm so thirsty!*

"You look good in the color, Klive." I grabbed his belt buckle and tugged him beyond my personal space into intimate territory.

He wet his lips. "Thank you." He leaned close. "In honor of you surrendering your weapon, I'll lay my own down at your feet. The night I made you cry at this very bar; I lied my ass off. Kinsley, you're the hardest target I've ever acquired. You're not easy. You've never looked like a ho. You were never a stranger because I knew I needed you from the moment we met. Please, forgive me."

Bloody hell. How did a few words sew a beautiful thread of affection into the lust between us? "Damn, Klive. You're forgiven. You shouldn't say such things, because I'll want so much more," I confessed and tilted my head. Our mouths drew closer.

"Ditto." His lips lifted. I giggled.

Bayleigh set two small mason jars on the lacquered slab of wood. "Don't let me intrude. But if you're gonna kiss before consuming vinegar, do it now so I can watch. Y'all are heating the bar to the point we'll have to lower the AC."

My chin swiveled toward her, one eye bugged, the other squinting. She showed every tooth in smart-ass answer to dashing my moment. Klive snagged his pickle and bit into the crunchy flesh, chewing through a grin at her. His brows quirked as he lifted his mason jar to silently toast her timing.

"You should thank her for keeping me from telling you more secrets." He winked at me, downed some of the pickle juice and vodka. I followed and bit into my pickle a second later. Beyond Klive, I caught Chad's eyes watching us from his post onstage like no one else existed. Interesting. Was Jase right about Chad having a thing for me or was Chad interested in Klive? Not in a gay way, but he seemed deeply intrigued. He caught me watching him and blew me a kiss. I fanned my fingers in wave, then snagged Klive's empty hand. He held his jar in the other while I draped his arm over my shoulder and led him back to his table, subtly dancing the whole way.

Mel and Dan stood near Jase with Devon.

"I didn't realize you guys were coming!" I greeted them. Mel shook Klive's hand while Dan side-eyed Jase. Jase ignored his look like he couldn't see. "Dan," I said, "tell Bayleigh to make your bourbon and Coke."

Dan nodded and left us. Jase's smiling eyes met mine. I didn't like that hyper-awareness of Dan's conviction. Klive's hand at my back drew circles that ran all the way down over my bottom. Was he doing that to tease me or to make a point to those like Dan and Chad?

I leaned back against him so he could hear me. "Behave, sir." His hand holding the jar came around my waist, his forearm pinning my back to his chest.

"What? No ice cream for me, love?"

I twisted in his grasp, my chest pressing to his now. "No. You drink your sour pickle pop, but you may have a taste of mine to compare." I held my drink up but wrapped my other hand behind his head and urged his mouth to mine. Klive's lips opened enough to pull my lower lips between his teeth. Damn, he was delish! Did pheromones have flavor because I'd swear he tasted better than ever before.

"Who knew pickle pops were so good?" he asked when I disconnected so we didn't get gross in public the way my hormones wanted to.

"I did," I teased.

Bobbie bubbled up to me and apologized for interrupting.

"Nothing to apologize for, dear. Good to see you again," Klive told her. She thanked him, then asked his opinion on the dress she'd picked for me. "I couldn't have asked for better," he said. "It's perfect."

Bobbie clapped her hands cheerleader style, then begged me to dance with her and our friends. When I nodded, she took my hand and herded us into the group who graded the physicality of those around us. Bayleigh wasn't the only one enjoying tonight's hired help.

"What do you think?" Bobbie's friend asked me. She'd never spoken to me before. At first, I couldn't help feeling a set-up, then I hushed my insecurities.

"Meh, they aren't my type," I joked.

"Oh, crap! I'm so sorry. Women, right?"

Bobbie shook her head. "No!" she shouted over the music while disappointment riddled the atmosphere around me. "Her type is Alpha male."

"Is that one of the fraternities?" another asked, clearly having hearing issues in our environment.

I looked toward the ceiling and caught Chad's eye. He crooked a finger. Hell, yes, please!

"Bobbie, Chad needs me. I'm usually in charge of his drinks so maybe he's having trouble getting a refill while stuck onstage."

"Yeah, I think I'm gonna head to the bar for a bit myself," she said, then mouthed an apology. I waved the sentiment away.

"Nothing to apologize for, babes. I'll see you in a bit," I said, then made my way to the stairs beside the stage. When I walked across toward Chad, several on the floor turned like they thought I was part of some entertainment. From up here I marveled at the number of bodies crammed inside. Was fire marshal Ray no longer an issue?

24 | ♀

Behind the deejay booth, Chad wrapped a brewski-bearing arm around my waist as he danced with the tracks he mixed.

"Not empty then?" I asked. He shook his head and handed me the extra beer sweating beside his sound board.

"Nah, Kins, I wanted an excuse to chat. You look great tonight!"

"Thanks, Chaddy Cake. When you going on break so you can swing me around this floor?"

"I'd love to on my break. Do you still want to come to that swing club I asked you about? Did you ever ask if you could?"

My tongue traced my cheek at the permission in the statement. Granted, I'd been with Jase-ish when he'd asked me at the club before my fight, but I hated the idea of asking permission to go out with a friend if I wanted.

"No permission necessary," I told him. "I'm unattached."

He leaned back with a pointed look at my dress, eyebrow arched like who was I foolin'.

"What? This ol' thing?" I waved and arm down my torso. "Bobbie bought it for me. I couldn't say no."

He rolled his eyes. "You know, I left Oz so I didn't have to honor the Queen anymore. Now you force my hand." He winked while my mouth dried. Did Chad know too much about Klive as well?

"What's that supposed to mean?" I acted truly confused.

"You think I didn't see you kiss King? Just a play on words like you're his little queen is all. I wasn't meaning to compare you to the bloody Queen of England. You're hotter than she is. If you were who we had to honor, I'm sure there'd be more loyalty to the crown."

My head tossed back when I cackled.

"He give you any roses?"

My brows knit with genuine confusion, though I nodded.

"Sorry to pry, Kins, but you have no idea how long I've followed him for the society pages. No dates. *Ever.*"

Society pages?! Was this why my mom knew about Klive's eligibility? I wanted to ask more and what he'd meant about the roses, but he interrupted my thoughts.

"He's okay with you seeing other people?" He removed his arm from my waist, took a long draw from his bottle and set the glass on the booth like he'd sobered. I didn't like that look at all.

"Chad, just because I kissed him doesn't mean we are anything exclusive. He's a tasty flirt."

"Bullshit. Sell it elsewhere, darl."

"Chad, I'm my own woman. If I want to go to a club with you, I will, and he won't have anything to say. Don't worry about him, please." I bit my lip. "If you are uncomfortable taking me out, I understand." Was my disappointment showing?

"Aw, Kins, those eyes ... we'll go, okay? I respect you as your own person but do me a solid and make sure he knows so he doesn't get mad. I'm not keen on landing on his bad side." Again, did Chad know more than the society pages stuff? Ugh. I couldn't think of this shit!

"I promise," I said with an encouraging smile, praying to lift us both from this depth. "Now, play me something I love."

His expression shifted to relief. "Make a request." I watched him adjust the sliding button things every so often during our chat and he slid one up now. He handed me a dangling earbud, the other tucked into his ear. "Want to help? Put that in so you hear what your audience hears. As you can tell the sound is different up here than down there."

"No way!" My face lit.

"I don't play when it comes to my equipment and I don't share my equipment with just any woman," he teased. I smacked his belly, enjoying his laugh and our dynamic picking up where we normally stayed. Jase might not have loved our friendship, but I really was my own person and Chad was my friend, dammit. He grabbed a microphone, slid some more toggles till the sound muted. My excitement morphed to anxiety.

"As we say in the south, how y'all doin' tonight?"

I burst out laughing at Chad's accent with the lingo. He held the mic toward the audience who shouted their happiness. He nodded his approval.

"Give it up for my girl, Kinsley. She's helping mix your tracks. Give her some love and she might be really sweet." He held the mic toward them again. I rolled my eyes at him but couldn't fight an enormous grin at the audience' response. I pumped my hands over my head and thanked them. He encouraged their requests while I told him mine at his ear. Chad chuckled and nodded, replaced the mic, then thumbed his phone's screen. I took the mic and walked out to the middle of the stage, officially greeting the rowdy groups. Marcus leaned against the mouth of the hallway in his normal spot. I saw his huge grin and took that as approval, though I suspected he loved my nod to Klive's heritage.

"Good evening, everyone. I'm so glad you're here because tonight is a celebration. Please, Rustin, will you please come to the stage?"

Rustin, the ham he is, ran onstage and waved for their cheering to get louder. Chad began 50 Cent's *In Da Club* after we sang *Happy Birthday* to our off-duty deputy. Still no Inferno that I could see from my overhead view. Rustin seemed truly relaxed rather than on-watch like he really wanted to chill and celebrate. After he left the stage, I encouraged the patrons to buy Rustin's drinks and give him a good time. Chad and I cringed when three women groped Rustin in various places. I threw my hand out, laughing away from the mic before coming back.

"That's not what I meant, ladies. Hold it down till later," I teased. Rustin pouted but changed tune when we threw the music back to the disco era. Rustin could dance. Dude pulled moves like he was in a reproduction of Saturday Night Fever.

Chad let me stay behind the booth and taught me what the sound board did, well, he tried, but I was far too enamored in watching the talent in the crowds.

"Here, you'll like this more." Chad passed a small camera. "I use photos for promo on social media. They'll tag themselves after we post."

"Don't you need their permission?" I took the camera.

"I got unanimous consent when I set up and asked over the mic checks." He quirked his brows. I shook my head in disapproval I didn't really feel. "Go on."

I did what he said for about three songs, then Chad came over the mic. "I'm bringing it forward a few decades with a track that's a favorite of my favorite local track star."

Chad gave me my beer, ordered me to chug until the crowds chanted with him and I raced the booze raining down my throat.

"It's not karaoke night, and this girl cannot sing, but you give her alcohol and a mic, she becomes a rap goddess with a certain song." He muted the mic and leaned toward my ear.

I wiped my mouth and slapped the empty bottle down beside the sound board. "You've lost your damn mind —"

"You got into a brutal fight and stirred shit, Kinsley. You love this when the bar is closed and you're cleaning. They'll love if you share that silly side. I'm doing this for you. Use it. Change their minds. Give good publicity to play with, dammit."

The opening beats to Eminem's *'Till I Collapse* came on. The crowds cheered so loud they drowned the music. My mouth dried. I stole the rest of Chad's beer while Eminem's opening lyrics played under their rambunctious revelry. This was bullshit, even if he had a point.

"Chad! I can't —"

He shoved the mic into my hand, then pushed me away from the booth toward the open space onstage. The audience roared so loud; I couldn't help the shocked smile I cast back at Chad. Jase and Rock-N-Awe might be jealous if this continued. I watched the audience members a bit older than me start singing like they had representation and wanted to join my impromptu karaoke session.

As the group sang the first chorus, I spoke into the mic. "This goes out to the deejay whose ass I'll be kicking when this is over."

Chad cracked up while the audience laughed and sang in an intoxicating mixture, blending into the alcohol that hit my brain.

"This also goes out to everyone who wishes I'd lose a race."

Marcus whistled between his fingers. I shook my head at the last person I'd have expected to cheer any of my antics.

I picked up with Marshall Mathers' voice and giggled through the first few words at their encouraging cheers. Soon, I walked the stage in these amazing heels singing to them with the words like I really meant every one of them because in a way I did. On the next chorus, I pretended like Bayleigh and the bartenders were my only company and threw my hands and attitude, dance moves and full energy into having fun like I'd never do this again, because I never wanted to do this again.

Chad was right about good publicity over bad, but without Constance, I was like an invitation for white girl poser comments. Something about being buzzed and throwing myself into the moment made me care less, though. Hell, Jase was likely recording this to send to Constance. For her, I did rip into this song, though I avoided their whole table and any looks from people I knew until I held the mic toward the audience and my hand cupped my ear for them to sing the rest of the song through the end. My laughter echoed over the speakers when the song ended, and I'd survived one of my biggest public fears.

"Someone's in big trouble," I said into the cheering when I walked back to Chad. He gave the audience a panicked face I couldn't help cackling at. "I think my time as helper is done, but it's been my pleasure," I told the audience. "I have one more." I leaned toward Chad and pulled the mic down to my thigh. When the signature curses at the beginning of Fergie's *London Bridge* began, I lifted the mic to my lips again. "This goes out to the fittest Brit in the place," I said in a British accent. Chad busted out laughing while Klive's hand wrapped around his smirk like I couldn't see him smiling. "I know y'all didn't think I was talking about this guy." I waved my thumb toward Chad. "He's from Down Under. Mine's over there. Klive, please wave your hand so I won't make any more viral fight videos?"

Klive's hand lifted from his mouth. He stood and waved to minimize confusion. I set the mic into the stand at the sound board and grabbed Chad's fedora from his head, placed the hat on my head, then grabbed Chad's skinny tie like a leash and towed him behind me toward the middle of the stage. I whirled around and jerked his tie. The audience went wild.

"You want me to die?" he asked at my ear.

"Turnabout's fair play, right?" I ruffled his hair, ran my fingers smoothly across the brim of his hat on my head, then grabbed my own hips before rolling them with the music.

"I'm heading back to the safety of my booth, darl. Heads up, your Brit is aimed your way."

I cursed in time with the song like a playful idiot so Chad would see I wasn't afraid. When I turned around and kept working my body to the music from the stage, a wild thrill rushed belly. Klive weaved through the dancers and shook his head at a couple of women who touched him. He pointed at me. I grinned; the best triumph rubbed in their faces without my having to say another word. My sexy Brit stood at the base of the stage. I playfully bent forward lip-syncing the lyrics to him before I walked into the hands he held toward me.

25 | ♀

HIS FINGERS GRIPPED MY hips as I grabbed his shoulders for support when he lifted me from the stage. He pulled me down against him so my dress lifted to my waist. I squealed and yanked at the material.

"Klive King!" I looked around us to be sure no one had seen my undies. Thank God I'd changed from what Bobbie wanted me to wear earlier! Klive only laughed. Chad watched us again, so I dropped the words I'd planned to unleash and tugged him through the crowds toward the bar for another drink.

He followed very close with the hand I wasn't holding glued to my hip "You are an unexpected surprise, love. I'd much rather take you home right now and find out how far down your London Bridge falls."

I clapped my hands with a wicked laugh. "Provocation confirmed." I tossed a flirty smile over my shoulder, then sent Bayleigh big eyes like I was outta my league at Klive's answering sex appeal. She peered at him over my shoulder then cast gleaming eyes my way.

"Mind if I steal her behind the bar for some drink instructions?" Bayleigh asked, chin in hand, eyes banging him in her mind. "I'm still training and Kinsley's my favorite instructor." I shook my head at her innuendo, not to mention the fact that Bayleigh had worked here for over a year.

"Aren't you lucky? I've not yet had the pleasure, but I'll not get in the way of you getting yours," Klive tossed back to punish her and increase her turmoil. She licked her lower lip and sent her naughty thoughts my direction. Klive's head dipped to my ear. "Take your time. I'll be out back for a few. Come find me if you'd like to take the pants off and let someone else be in charge for a breather." He planted a wet kiss to my neck beneath my earlobe.

"You're killing me, sir." I swallowed.

"Nope. I promised not to, remember?" He winked and left me at the mouth of the hallway. Klive fanned his fingers over his shoulder then pressed through the back door. Marcus watched then met my eyes, that toothpick turning circles between his smiling lips.

"Bar's all yours, Little Red." He gestured I was welcome to step behind the bar without clocking in unless I wanted to help.

"Wow." I waited for him to give me any shit, but none came. I joined Bayleigh, asking what she needed me to teach her.

"Ha! I didn't need your help with drinks, but I'd love you to teach me how you seduce Complicated Moonlight," she said. "Will you please make drinks with me for a few minutes to keep these fine assholes from coming behind the bar? I miss Garrett. He doesn't make my body heat, but have you seen the guy with the cuffs on his arms?"

I shook my head, oblivious to everyone but Klive.

"He knows how to do tricks with bottles, has awards for mixology, talking to me all night like I'm slow. Works in like three big hotels and talks like he's got a ten-inch peen or something. I need a break from him. I mean yours is big, but at least you're not always telling me."

I cackled and passed shots to a big group. "Thanks, but where is he now?"

"Bathroom break. Probably needs to adjust that plastic in his pants like models wear to make them look equipped."

I snorted. "You like him."

"Ugh! No damn way." She shriveled her nose. "Oh, here he comes."

I hid my amusement when he walked back behind the bar. "Now this is what I call a British invasion." He extended a hand with a name that came and went. I shook his hand and introduced myself. "Nice rapping up there."

"Thanks." I smiled at Bayleigh.

"Did she tell you she needs help?" he asked me. Oh, snap! I bit my lip to keep my smile from spreading in front of Bayleigh's glare beyond me. "What?" he asked like he wasn't sure what her issue was. "I told her I'd help but she doesn't want my help. Told her I'm more than qualified, listed my quals, she refused."

"How about you show me some of that flair I've heard about?"

Bayleigh's glare fell on my face for spilling her beans. Hotshot nodded at her. I worked between their tension for about thirty minutes, watching him prove why he won awards. He, like Garrett, tried to teach us how to spin bottles, but I joked that the only spin the bottle needing played was between them. Bayleigh spanked me and sent me to the timeout hallway after that.

"You should bribe that one to come help out when he has free time," I told Marcus. He chuckled, clearly aware of Hotshot perturbing Bayleigh.

"She is a lot faster in his company. The owner is gonna be very pleased with tonight's cash flow," Marcus said. "King's out back still. Never seen him let loose and partake as he has tonight. Shots, shots, shots at their table for Rustin's birthday, but I think I'll have Jarrell or Gus take him home."

"There are a lot of things I could, maybe should, say right now, but I'm just not."

"Well, there's a first," he teased.

"Nice. Don't worry about them driving. I'll drive Klive home. Any danger I should know about?"

"Nope. Coast is clear. Taylor took his keys. Be safe, Little Red. Don't bust his chops too much. He doesn't relax. He's having fun."

I nodded. Even if he said the coast was clear, I almost asked if I should pack a pistol with Klive's guard down, but I waved and walked through the back door. Not that I didn't want Klive to have fun, but tension coiled between my drawn back shoulder blades as I strode along the sidewalk toward a group of about fifteen in search of Klive. If he let his guard down, who might lurk to hurt him, outside of Jase, that is …? Was Henley somewhere watching?

The more I thought about this, the more I wanted to leave so bad I fought trotting toward them. Klive leaned against the stucco wall near where Jase had smeared Pat Connor's face. Yes, we needed to leave. Constance had implied if Klive or Nightshade was watching our backs we could sleep easy, but tipsy Klive? I'd never seen him drink much at all. If he were drunk and something happened, would he be able to handle shit that came his way?

At the sound of my heels, the guys, including Jase and Rustin, parted for me. Jase and Rustin released the waists they held like they'd been caught in the wrong. I rolled my eyes and shook my head. I could care less right now. Klive was all that mattered.

Rustin wrapped an arm over my shoulders. "Hey, honey, you ready to go home and make my birthday the happiest one I've ever had?"

I arched an eyebrow at him, seeing he was tanked as well, and peeled his arm from my shoulders. "No thanks. Your birthday is on track to be a very happy one if you don't ruin it by hitting on someone else." I cleared my throat to get him to see the obvious, then I focused on Klive who focused on the hem of my dress. "I'm going home with Klive."

Klive's hand snaked out to pull me to him, obviously heated as he ran his hands along my hips. My eyes darted to the group watching Klive's grip like they wanted to steal his place. Not good. Jase was so inebriated he didn't look jealous, he seemed ready to ask Klive if Klive might share. My eye twitched. Though concerned with his recent alcohol consumption, I let his lust slide because of how much alcohol he'd consumed.

"Klive, can this wait, sir? This doesn't appear to be the best time." I chewed my lower lip, studying each gaze, trying not to be afraid. Klive was scarier than their hunger, though, without even trying, which supported Constance's ability to sleep. He pulled up from the wall and placed me where he'd been, turning to face me and cage me with an arm against the wall by my head. His other hand traced circles on my belly in a contrasting softness to the harsh order he barked for them to vaporize.

The group dispersed on command. Hot damn!

Rustin grabbed Jase. He winked at me while reading my awe of Klive's authority. Like a fool who wanted to die, Rustin leaned in the small space between Klive and me. I was so shocked when Rustin seized my open mouth for a kiss, I robotically allowed him because I had told him he could have a kiss for his birthday. He pulled away with a huge grin and told Klive of my birthday promise. Klive's eyes grabbed my fearful ones. I pursed a guilty smile that came unbidden in the tension.

"Bye, Klive. Thanks for the party. Enjoy Kinsley. She is so *sweet*." Rustin licked his finger and drew a tally behind Klive's back. I narrowed my eyes then looked back at Klive's, catching him scanning my body now.

"Kins!" Jase called over his shoulder, a woman holding him for stability. I swallowed any bullshit jealousy and caught the keys he tossed. "Thanks!"

He loosely saluted me and walked back inside the bar. Klive's fingers walked down my belly till I captured them before they charted naughty territory. He cursed and whined. I couldn't help laughing.

"Alright, naughty boy. You okay with me driving your car still?"

"You follow. I lead."

I tsked and shook my head. "No, sir. You're riding with me. I'm driving."

He hummed as his fingers dug into my hips. "I need a ride so bloody bad, and I'd trust no one else to drive."

Oh, boy. Desire permeated the air between us.

"I will let you lead me to the car, though," I urged, hoping he'd take the bait.

"Gladly." He walked me toward the Ferrari in front of the still-long line.

"Day-um! That fine-ass woman is driving that fine-ass car?!" Some fool in line held the crotch of his pants like he needed to keep them from falling since they rode around his ass. "Say, man, how you make your money? How do I get what you got?"

Klive opened the driver's door for me and smiled at him. "I kill people."

I gasped and clapped a hand over Klive's triumphant smile at the guy's open mouth.

"Hey, man, I'm sorry for what I said about your girl. She's pretty. Ima move on now." The guy scampered like Klive had threatened him. I tilted my head at Klive's misbehavior, eyebrow arched.

"What? He asked? I was perfectly kind."

Dammit. I didn't want to smile. "I think I should be opening the door for you first. Let's get you inside so you don't tell the world all your secrets, shall we?"

I urged him by the small of his back for once toward the passenger side. Though the one guy was gone, the groups in the line watched us instead of the phones in their palms. Klive ignored the door I opened for him and patted his chest with both palms, resting his hands there. Oh, hell.

"That's right, you nesh wankers!" his accent slurred. I rushed to cover his mouth again, but he chuckled and grabbed my hands. "This fine-ass woman is driving this fine-ass car and taking *me* home where we are going to get totally dirty! Don't you wish you were me!"

The line cheered while I wrestled my hands from Klive's and face-palmed. "Klive, you need to be quiet and get in the car, please."

"Aw, why, love? I didn't mean to upset you. You heard that bloke. They think you're pretty. I think you're prettier than my car," he offered like he was proud of that compliment. Okay, the puppy face was adorable.

I placed my hands on his shoulders, pushing him to get in the seat. He sat down like a good boy but argued he didn't want to buckle his seatbelt. I sighed and bent over him to buckle the belt for him. He pulled my mouth to his and held me there to worship my lips with dewy kisses that sent a fog through my brain. He released my left cheek and ran his right hand up my leg, under my dress. I jumped and swatted his scandalous hand away. He laughed while I cursed at the cat calls and hollers he'd brought out of the line.

Damn Klive. I shut his door and endured their comments before dipping down into the seat I had to readjust from Jase's settings.

Without asking, somehow Gus stopped traffic again; Jarrell clearing the line for me to drive through. I cringed and inched out of the lot, nervous I'd scrape the front end on the pavement. Klive shrugged and told me to angle the car to prevent that from happening. In the silence, I caught Klive humming low and slow music that sounded like what we'd danced to last night. Damn that was only one night ago. Felt like a week. I got on the highway headed home — ugh! To Klive's — cautioning myself not to earn another traffic stop to destroy everything that was awesome today. I only knew I wanted to get there and shower, relax in bed and watch something.

Klive's humming gave way to mumbling about how pretty he thought I was, how shiny my hair looked, how good I smelled, how hot my legs are, how hot I looked onstage, in his flag, behind the bar, in his car, *bent over* his car, in his bed, in his bath — that was his favorite — in my closet ... the list went on and on.

"I'd love some ice cream," he said. Okay, cute. I indulged him.

"What kind of ice cream do you want? Do you already have some in the freezer, Klive?" I grinned and looked over my shoulder to exit the highway.

He tilted his head against the headrest, looked up through his lashes and grinned. "What kind may I have?" he asked excitedly.

"What kind is your favorite?"

"My favorite ...?" He peered at me with his brows drawn, seeming confused and a bit unfocused. I snickered. "I don't know what my favorite flavor is because I have never had it, Kins."

My chin snapped his way. "Never had it? Okay, we'll revisit this conversation when you're sober."

The adoration I had for that chat faded when Klive took to complimenting me on every street we turned down. "Kinsley, you look so pretty on such and such street ...." Every time. Eventually, I tuned him out and quit indulging him. The front gate rose when I drove toward the guard house to Klive's neighborhood. Klive waved to the man on-duty.

"He couldn't see you, sir. These windows are too dark."

His mouth twisted to a pout. I caved to a giggle and meandered through the neighborhood streets with a now quiet Klive. Thank goodness for GPS. I'd have never found this place on my own. The heavy gates parted for Klive's car. I waited for them to close behind us, then drove toward the single-car garage he kept the Ferrari in. Klive stared up at me when I opened his door for him. His fingers brushed my thighs at the hemline. I stared down at him the way he does me, then bent to unbuckle his seatbelt.

"Who's the kid now?" I joked. "Sorry I forgot the booster seat in my other car. You could've used it."

"You are definitely not a kid. I watched you transform from a whiny girl into a strong woman. You're all woman." He touched my breasts.

I gasped, stunned how unreserved he was tonight when he'd been so stingy. "No, sir. I don't think so. Not tonight," I told him and hoisted him out of the car. Not easy, especially in these heels. Thank goodness he could walk. He watched me enter the code for the alarm. Before I grabbed the doorknob, Klive spun me and pressed my back to the door. He lifted my thighs from the ground while I grabbed for his neck to keep from falling. Stunning he was able to so swiftly maneuver in this capacity.

"Why not tonight? Are you punishing me for making you wait so long? Reciprocating now that I want you so damn bad, I can barely keep myself in check?"

Hot damn! Klive's tongue dragged across my throat as he kissed my sensitive skin. For a moment I stopped resisting and indulged in the sinful sensations swimming through my body as visions of him losing control threatened to absorb all rationality.

"Cinnamon. That's what you look like. That's the flavor I want," he said, tasting my flesh.

"K — Klive, let's go inside so you can tell me in there, okay?" I beeped the car's alarm to distract him. He turned to look, and I wriggled from his hold. Barely.

"Ah, Kins, pretty baby, come back ... please?" he begged in the sweetest, most pathetic way. I grabbed his hand to guide him inside the dark hallway. I had a feeling if he couldn't resist that area sober, I was in for a battle. I stayed behind him and shoved him ahead of me.

"You like to lead. Lead me to your room, Klive."

I was able to get him through the kitchen, the library, into his bedroom with only a few sexually laced come-ons. While he shuffled toward the bathroom, I went back to the garage door and entered the code to re-arm his alarm, then closed the library passage behind myself to rid the worry that plagued me from my mind. When I closed his bedroom door behind me, locking that, too, I rested my back against the wood. Great. I didn't see him anywhere. He'd probably pounce on me from some crazy hidey-hole.

I looked around myself, walking toward the bathroom. Klive was lying in my closet the way I had Monday night when I'd been the drunk one. My shoulder perched against the door frame as I smiled down at him. I crossed my arms and admired him while he peered at all the pretty things.

"Whatcha doin', Klive?"

"Your closet is amazing. Much more fun than mine. I've only bland colors, neutrals. Yours is so prismatic and sexy. Like *you*." He grinned like he was clever. I chuckled and walked across to play with him. How could I leave him alone when he was so adorable? I paused beside where his head rested on the floor. He looked up at me, his eyes running the length of my legs, then he scooted his head to the side and looked up my dress like a grade-schooler. I smirked and shifted so he couldn't see. He groaned a protest. "C'mon, love, just a peek? I'm so tied up, here, I hurt." His lip popped in pout as he grabbed himself.

Wow. This was happening. I grinned at this intimidating man reduced to putty in my hands. Would he hate himself in the morning? I was going to make sure I had a story to tell him. He could brush me off in the sober light of day, play by the high road he wanted to keep me on, but right now he was mine for the taking and openly wanting me. If he forgot tonight because he was drunk, he deserved the torment tomorrow.

26 | ♀

THE SEXY BLACK LINGERIE Jase pulled from the drawer earlier laid on a shelf. I took the corset and panties while Klive was too distracted pointing out the shoes he'd picked and why.

"You mean *these* would look too naughty to wear outside the bedroom?" I lifted the pair the spoke of. He nodded like a pretty pervert with plans he had no idea I was about to put into motion. "I agree with you. Presumptuous as always, Mr. King."

"I prefer *hopeful*, Miss Hayes. They say a failure to plan is a plan to fail. They also say you should visualize your goals. Goals are born of dreams, and dreams come true only through planning and hard work. I've worked *so* hard."

A soft smile curled my lips. "Are you tired of working?"

"For you? Never. Working for you has been tremendous fun, except for the part where you hated me."

"And after you achieve your goal? What are your plans?"

"Conquer the world because anything will become possible."

"Great answer, sir." I held another pair of shoes to distract him, and he was off chattering about what inspired him to buy those. I loved his answer and I loved hearing his inner thoughts and confessions. I also loved the idea of him being in disguise on the plane telling me about loving me, assuming that may have been him. If so, he'd worked very, very hard.

Klive whined when I walked out of the closet into the room to figure out how to put on the lingerie. I set the naughty outfit on the bed and walked into the kitchen, rifling through cupboards until I found some bread. I walked back into the room carrying a cup of water and the food I hoped would absorb some of the alcohol. After all the dreams I'd had of him over the past two years, the dreams that consumed what felt like every single night since he'd come into the bar, I'd like if he sobered some so we'd both enjoy this.

He cheered when I re-entered the closet. I knelt beside him and helped him sit.

"Here, Klive. Be a good boy and eat. Drink the water. I won't come back until both are gone, understand?"

"Bread and water? What am I? A bloody prisoner?"

Yeesh. If Klive was destined for prison, I was going to seize the moments I was given for the time I had them. Screw waiting any longer when I didn't know how much time we had left to wait for one another. *Can't help who you ... who you ....*

I gulped and put the glass to his lips with another small order to drink.

"Kinsley, love, I am not so besotted. I did walk in here without your assistance, did I not?" I had to smile at how elegant Klive managed to stay in such a state.

"Klive, my sweet, must you be so trifling?" I asked in his accent. "Until you are able to speak without slurring, I say you *are* that besotted."

He smirked and kissed my lips. "I'd be less trifling if you bribed me."

"Your stalling is stalling my bribery. Just drink the water, please."

"You should remove the words *just*, *maybe* and *kind of* from your vocabulary and be direct."

"Do you never tire from being the boss of everything? I'm the bloody neck, and I say drink the damn water or else I'm giving you an attitude adjustment."

He threatened to keep misbehaving, so I walked out of the closet. "I'm drinking!"

"Not if you're talking!" I chuckled to myself and picked the naughty costume up from the bed. A thrill coursed my belly. I'd never worn lingerie for the purpose of seduction, only for the lack of lines beneath a dress, and that was not very sexy but more something Grandma might approve of. This was something Grandma would disown me for wearing and was like putting on a whole different personality. Unlike the Gasparilla costume and my Ren faire corset, this black corset tied in the front. No help necessary. Let me tell you, I felt like one bad-ass woman! Sara came unbidden to my mind; the confession of riding a pole and whoring herself to make money. This was for the spotlight stripper or dominatrix. The costume commanded attention and submission.

Had she felt this power surge in the beginning or was it all negative from the start? How had she gotten into stripping and had Patrick Scott rescued her from the life or played a part in her demise of character and eventual life? Was I still in danger now that they were both gone?

"I'm talking with my mouth full so you'll hear I'm eating!" Klive's silly voice pulled my mind from darker thoughts. He did sound like a chipmunk. I snorted and toyed with the leather strips and eyelets after I'd finished lacing myself with the black ribbons. My boobs plumped as big as the peacock costume at the Renaissance! Like then, they swelled with every breath. Klive was going to love this!

"That's what I like to hear!" I called back while pulling the scrap of panties up my legs. At last, I stepped into the killer platform high heels and tested walking in them, changed levels, squatted, bent, knelt, twirled to be sure I learned my balance. The best part of doing this while Klive was inebriated was if I failed, he might forget or move past my moment. In fact, had he been sober, I doubted very much my capacity to do something so audacious. I'd never done anything like this before. I couldn't wait to see myself in the mirror!

"Kins! Oh, Kins! I drank my water!"

I walked through the bathroom, inside his closet to look for the sound system controls. Unable to find them, I put my phone on Bluetooth and found the link. Cheers to improvisation and spying an accessory I wouldn't have thought to use before. The handcuffs gleamed from a shelf near his tie drawer. Intent on blowing his damn mind, I grabbed them and hooked them to one of the leather strips on my corset. I rolled one of his ties and stuffed the silk deep in my cleavage, along with the key to the cuffs. I considered a belt but decided to use the one he was wearing. Finally, I tapped the music app on my phone and picked a song I reserved only for being my secret self in the apartment. After all, Jase and Rustin had gotten a show without asking. Klive deserved a show for all his patience and waiting. I'd prove myself worth his pain. I tapped Nickelback's *Burn It to the Ground* and looped before turning the volume up on my phone to hear the heavy rock spring to life over his system.

The music rushed my heartbeat. *You can do this! Pretend you're at home in your apartment, cleaning, playing dress-up.* I blew my breath at my bangs and watched them flutter before I gathered the no-turning-back courage to walk into my closet. In the reflection of the full-length mirror, I ruffled my mane and turned my back to the glass to peer at my ass over my shoulder. My hands ran over my bottom. When I braved a look down at Klive, his expression stopped my heart. His jaw had fallen open, his breathing visibly increased, remarkably like the very first time the elevator doors had opened on the autocratic pirate whose evident attraction had alarmed the hell out of me. Now, I walked to where he laid and placed my foot on his chest, granting him a very good view of the barely there panties. He swallowed as he struggled to focus like a man seeing a mirage. I reached down to my foot, pulling my hand slowly up my leg. Klive released a heavy enough rush of air, his chest fell. *Oh, yes ....*

I removed my foot to straddle his head and sat down on his chest, smiling down at him as I bent and licked his cheek. My fingers ran through his hair, where I pulled, then delivered a sweet smack like retaliation for the time he'd smacked me. Klive snatched my wrist, but I jerked his hand from mine and sucked one of his fingers into my mouth, relishing his long moan. His eyes closed as his head tilted back.

"Nuh, uh, Klive. Don't close your eyes. You look right here!" I shifted to my knees on his chest, knowing my one-hundred-and-seventeen-pound frame was nothing to him. My hands clasped his to run them up my body as I threw my head back, my hair brushing against him. I lifted and ran my fingers up his throat. His eyes glued to mine flared with electricity when I squeezed a fraction. *Another delish moan. Yum!*

I let go and rolled off him to stand up and spin the cuffs on one of my fingers, an evil smile cast down at him as I backed out of the closet ever so slowly, bending forward to give him a sumptuous view of my bulging breasts. *Here boy ....* I crooked my finger, then reached for my phone on the vanity, turning the volume to a roar. Not worrying about noise was amazing! When I glanced back at Klive, he was on his knees rubbing his chin like he wondered whether this was real. I walked in and grabbed his hair, forced his head back and indulged in a deep kiss before parting our connection to prance out of the closet, twisting my hips with the music. As I turned back to him, I flipped my hair, threw the mane out of my face, ran my hands through my tresses, down over my body like they were his. Klive sat slack-faced shocked for a hypnotic moment, then crawled toward me, so I dropped to my knees and crawled toward him, too. I bit my lip when we met right outside the closet. Good. Progress.

Klive pulled up against me, wrapping his arms tightly around my waist. I used them to do a back bend until my head touched the floor between my heels — *a wonder my breasts didn't pop out!* I pulled myself up and grabbed his chin while his hands came to my hair. He jerked me to him for an urgent, demanding, desperately hungry kiss, intoxicated in a whole new way like he was less drunk on liquor and now drunk on lust. The taste of his desire amplified my own need to have Klive at least once, but I sensed I'd never get enough of being kissed like tomorrow may never come. As we changed angles and gripped each other tighter, I wondered if that was how Klive felt all the time.

I broke our kiss and forced his hands down my hips to the floor where I crawled backward. He crawled toward me like a lion about to pounce. *Yes!* He was coming to life now! My tongue danced across my lower lip as I scrunched my nose in play with his predator. He crawled faster. When I reached the threshold for the bedroom, I backed through the passage until he was through the doorway with me, then I jumped to my feet. I smiled at him like an innocent sweetie-pie as I walked away and watched him growing to look the polar opposite. He poised to take me down, but in his inebriation, I was too quick for him. The cuffs twirled once more on my finger while I dared him with my eyes to come at me again. He lurched to his feet and grabbed me for another starving kiss, his hand digging into my hair, the other skimming across my cleavage. I reached up and cuffed that wrist, then turned him to catch the other behind his back, clamping the metal closed before he had a fighting chance.

He whirred around with the attitude problem I loved, but I placed my palms on his chest and ran my fingers down his abdominal muscles through his shirt, lowering my body with my hands as I went until I was on my knees level with his favorite appendage, daring a look into eyes that sent shivers to my core. Klive leered like a vampire contemplating how to devour his meal. My eyes sent an evil glee of mutual desire as his belt unbuckled between my fingers. His hips bucked when I ripped the leather free.

Adventure and wonder lifted his lust-laden eyelids as he relished me rising before him. I stretched the belt behind my shoulders, arching my cleavage toward his parted lips, but before he snagged a sample, I threw the belt around him, forcing his flesh against me while I rolled my body to the music as I went low then dragged my chest up his legs, against that sword straining to be unsheathed. Klive wriggled closer, his hands trapped while his shoulders and hips tried to do what he needed. I grinned and dropped the belt to unbutton his pants. He nodded like I needed instructions.

I tilted my head in mock confusion, loving the little fit he threw before I chuckled and pulled his pants to his ankles.

Damn, Klive pitched an impressive tent! Lord Rion hadn't exaggerated about that sword. I dared to do what I'd never done before and ran my palm over him. The music was so loud, but I didn't need a mute button to see Klive's knees nearly buckle or his head fall back. He squirmed harder for me to do more.

When I removed my hand, his head lifted, eyes desperate and dark. I turned around, reached my hand behind his neck and danced like a very naughty woman against his erection. Klive's lips latched onto my neck, his smooth tongue glancing across my sensitive flesh. My head fell back, eyes fell shut, till he sucked. Hard! Like he wanted me marked!

Shame on him!

I whirled and popped his cheek for such behavior. His mischievous grin lit bright and ready for more punishment. Ha! I barely kept a straight face to sell my annoyance. I hated hickeys but loved seeing Klive light up in ways I'd never seen before. To distract us both, I tugged the tie from between my breasts, unrolling the red silk inch-by-slow-inch, careful not to lose the key to the cuffs that was in there, too. Klive's tongue darted across his lower lips as his hungry eyes ravaged my cleavage. The ends of the tie wound around my palms. I yanked the silk tight, snapping his attention before I stole his sight and tied the accessory over his eyes. Klive's lips sipped at mine when I rewarded a kiss for his suffering. Seemed the more I took away from him, the more aware and sober he became. *Fun, fun, fun!*

Now that he couldn't see me, I sucked a breath and rolled my shoulders. Nervous tension, fear, lust, and too much emotion had my neck popping like a bazillion times. Klive King stood before me a blind, helpless, sexy fool ensnared in the web of my dreams come true, mine for the taking. I thought of Rustin's words again about thinking versus doing. I knew what I wanted to do — I wanted to touch him everywhere and watch him squirm to the point of losing his cool.

The beast coiled beneath that pretty skin knew how to strike a target to kill, but I sensed I might run fingers over his flesh and teach him a whole new form of consumption, the same form engulfing me. I forged ahead, my hands groping and skimming his body, lips brushing skin I was certain had never been kissed if the trembling in his thighs said what his open mouth didn't. His knee, the inside of his right thigh, my nose over his shaft as I breathed the true scent of arousal, of Klive, like the ultimate aphrodisiac. My palms caressed down the outside of his legs, drawing up the inside until I boldly gripped him through his boxer briefs. Klive panted, groaned my name loud enough to be heard over the music, begging me to heal the ache he'd had for two years. His words.

Two years. Had he told the truth about waiting for me? Did he love the pain of longing?

I hated waiting anymore! Klive's waistband in my fingers, I slipped his undies down to his ankles, unable to avoid the freedom spring that almost slapped me in the face. Ha! He'd have loved that! Since he couldn't see me, I wrapped his warm, hard flesh in my hand and studied the way he looked in my grasp. My mouth dried at the pace his chest rose and fell. Heavy breaths rushed through his parted lips. My mother had always taught me that women were never the inferior sex, that they were the ones who had the ability to make men great or cause them to stumble when desire captivated their brains and erased all rationality; the choice was mine to decide which type of woman I'd become: the helper or the hindrance. In my palm, I held the power to control Klive. Jase wanted Klive to stumble, but did I have the power to make Klive great?

An intimate rush of emotion heated my cheeks. I *hated* my stupid, bashful reaction when I was in costume as the vixen I wished to be for him! He couldn't have known my thoughts, but I was angry at myself and the innocence everyone handled me with, the power I possessed and the idea of relinquishing such into hands that would hurt this man!

I released Klive and knelt for the belt before walking behind him. My fingers tip-toed up his spine until my hand wrapped his throat the way his had wrapped mine on Monday when *I'd* been vulnerable in *his* hands. His groan vibrated my palm before I trailed my touch down his chest, down to his erection, around to his fine ass. I rubbed then backed away, folding the belt before landing a line across that pretty, pale flesh of his.

Oh, boy, did he *love* this! His cry of pleasure drove me to give him more.

His body jolted forward as another cry of pleasure sounded with the hard music. I palmed his pained flesh, squeezed, rubbed, caressed to soothe the sting he loved, then ran my hand around the erection to rub and soothe what I knew only caused more painful build-up. Just as he was finding a rhythm in my hand, I released him and spanked him again like I could punish him for this wretched predicament he'd put me in with Jase.

What if Klive had made his move rather than giving Jase a chance with me the way he'd insisted? Would Jase have gotten closer in the case? Taken Klive down with faster fervor to get him out of the way if he wanted me? I knew if Klive had taken the shot and asked me not to see Jase, I'd have dropped everything else to go out with the pretty pirate. Jase wouldn't have seduced me and Klive's hands would've been the first and *only* to touch me after *years* of waiting, hoping, praying for this man to come back into my life! To cross my path! To take the place beside me he'd held within me from day one!

The belt landed harder while I fought longing of a different sort. When he shouted my name, I pulled his hair, forcing his head back to kiss him, parting his pliant lips, stroking my tongue against his as I dropped the belt and held his face. *I love you! I love you! I LOVE YOU! I want to keep you!*

When I broke our kiss, he begged and pleaded more desperately than before. Thank goodness I'd blindfolded him so I could hide my conviction and the forbidden truth. I slinked around to his front, ran my hands up his torso, gripped the open collar of his shirt and ripped the linen wide open, scattering the buttons to the floor. The shirt shoved off his shoulders beneath my hungry hands. Tormenting him tormented me, too. My lips traced his collar bone as I trailed kisses across his skin up to his ear.

"Klive, are you ready for me now or will you force me to wait?"

He nodded a lot. I grinned.

"What, Klive? What are you nodding about? You want me to wait?"

He shook his head, then tilted for me when I put my ear near his lips. "Kinsley, I've never been more ready to nail you to the floor. Please! Un-cuff me so I can grip your ass and fuck you the way you were made to be."

Hot damn! I nearly clapped my hands and did a happy dance. He grinned, though his eyes were still covered. I loved his evident enjoyment mixing with the pained torment.

I shoved him to sit on the bench at the foot of his bed and yanked the tie from his eyes. He blinked and focused as I backed up a few paces, bowed my arms above my head like a ballerina, twirled my back to him and pulled the panties down my legs very sensually as I bent over, praying I wouldn't topple in the midst of this awesome. When I risked a peek around my legs, his grin took on an evil glint, eyes sober and bright. I quirked my brows as I twirled and kicked the cloth toward his face, unable to help giggling when he dove for them with his teeth. Poor guy missed but looked back at me like I was the ultimate prize. I bit my lip with a bashful naughty smirk, silently asking if he was ready for this. The corner of his lips lifted like I'd better bring the shit.

As you wish, Your Majesty.

What a fun fantasy. The concubine of the king, though I'd rather be the queen who'd kill any concubine that dared a glance at the sexy physique before me ripe for the pleasing. I ran my hand down my body the way I had my reflection at my apartment. He licked his lips when I dropped my emotional baggage and released myself to dance like a trashy whore just for him, the bad girl dance skills put to use for the first time outside my apartment. If I couldn't be the queen because he'd never have a chance to marry, then I'd be sure to be the concubine he could never forget for the rest of his life, or mine. I wanted my image seared into his brain, for him to be so consumed the way he consumed me. I rolled my body, feeling my curves for him since he was cuffed and helpless.

Klive's knee bounced, jaw muscle flinched, cords in his arms tightened like he battled the cuffs behind his back. I pulled the key from my cleavage and put the metal in my mouth, then walked toward him until I pressed against his chest, forcing him to scoot back where I straddled him. His erection in my hand again, I rubbed him against me to prep us both and watched him tilt his head while my eyes went heavy.

"Pay attention," I said in a tone I barely recognized. His hair fisted in my grip while I made him look in my eyes as I guided him inside me, slowly sinking inch-by-burning-inch all the way down onto him as pain and pleasure collided through my everything. We moaned in unison. My cheeks felt on fire when he leaned forward to steal my breath and open lips for several hot, dewy kisses that seemed too sweet to belong with the sin we were tangled up in.

"You're. So. Beautiful," Klive breathed between tugs of my lips. He shifted his hips and twitched inside me. My brain went blank under the spell of his magic wand, even as I sat still adjusting to the intense pressure-pleasure. This right here was probably a huge source of confidence and contributor to the air he carried himself with.

My mouth sought to erase his brief sweetness as pure lust consumed me to have as much of him joined to me as physically possible. I wrapped my arms around his head and legs around his back when he subtly shifted again. Our moans mingled, tongues tangled, and I passed the key from my mouth to his, then sat back. As I sucked wind, he narrowed his eyes and smiled with the key between his teeth. I grinned back and wiggled in his lap. Klive's grin dropped, and he clenched his teeth around the key as he writhed with me, trying his best to help. Against my body's will, I stopped our pace.

"Don't bloody stop! Not now, dammit! I *need* you!"

"I need you, too, but I need to unlock the cuffs! Pass the key!" Our mouths rushed together so fast we hit heads. We each winced then bypassed the pain while he passed the key. I unwrapped my legs and we moaned again, ground together a few more hard times before I regained enough will to get on my knees and reach behind him. Klive's hot breath brandished the tops of my breasts in his face, making my fingers jitter along the keyhole when his tongue tasted my body. "Klive, I don't know if I can unlock you if you keep doing that!"

"I don't know how long I can keep from bucking you on your back and taking you on the floor with my tongue!"

"You—" I moaned as his mouth drank my throat. "You. Shouldn't. Say. Such. Things," I panted. At last, the damn key fit into the hole! My fingers twisted. The metal opened. The song looped for the umpteenth time.

Klive's whole face lit like the Grinch about to rob Christmas from any other man who dared take another present from me. The muscles of his shoulders shifted beneath my fingers as I held on while he ripped the sleeves of his shirt down his arms. The cuffs flew from his freed his hands. He wrapped my back to brace my landing when he threw us to the carpet. We landed with a hard thud I barely felt as overwhelming pleasure wrecked all rationality and blurred everything but the sight of Klive King over me, his hair hanging, fingers clutching my waist as he hammered the hell out of me like he could tenderize the last remaining shell over the hardened heart I'd formed against him in our battles. Klive grabbed my wrists and slammed my hands over my head as if taking retaliation. I arched, shouted, begged, whined, panted, pleaded.

Klive King is having sex with me! Me! A man with the power of the town under his trigger finger who gets whatever the hell he wants has my *body at his mercy because* I *am what he wants! Me! Me! Me!*

My eyes closed while my head lolled to the side during the wildest ride I'd ever experienced. A light smack jerked my eyes open, and thrills leapt through my belly.

"Don't close your eyes, love. Right here." His gruff tone accompanied rough thrusts inching us along the soft carpet fibers burning my back, contrasting ecstasy ripping through my body. I peered up at his eyes like a lifeline. *Surely this singing surge would kill me!* I managed a nod, but pleaded for more, for less, for who the hell could know?

I wanted the climbing to continue but I didn't know what was happening inside me! The backs of my hands rubbed the carpet as inches turned to feet under Klive's delicious force. My muscles tensed, hips jerked up and I felt like a demon was exorcising from my body in how pleasure of the most acute type I'd ever experience contorted me. I shouted. Tears burned my eyes. My face numbed at the start of the most intense climax I'd never known existed. Klive released my hands and hooked his arms beneath my thighs so I couldn't squirm away as I struggled to handle the ferocity of my body's response to his. Klive refused me rest. He pounded himself and all these swimming sensations into my memory, heart, mind, and nerves as if cursing me to crave him for the rest of my life!

My limbs went limp. All tension lifted and Klive leaned over me, his nose nuzzling, lips tugging like CPR for my noodle body. His pace slowed to a smooth, climbing ache inside me, massaging ripened nerve endings to liquid life.

Each pull from his lips lifted my eyelids a millimeter from the lazy haze. Klive sat up on his knees, a self-satisfied smile in his heavy eyes, pleased with his prey.

He tilted toward a small end table I'd not noticed near the foyer of his room. *Damn! We'd traveled!* I blinked and looked around as he popped the underside of the wood.

"Someone call for a psycho with a knife?"

I gasped and swiveled my attention to him again. My eyes rounded as he brought a knife before his grin.

"What the fu —" His free hand covered my curse. He leaned down for another kiss, the knife on the carpet in his right fist beside my head.

"Be very still," he said at my ear before his tongue teased the lobe. My breath rushed in heavy pants as cold fear crashed into hot desire. My limbs tensed, thighs clenched tight against his hips like I might keep him pinned from doing something crazy as he sat up, all the while he remained inside me. *Still*, he mouthed, and brought the tip of the blade to the ribbons lacing the corset. With the whisper of the stainless steel, each black lace sliced apart. I stopped breathing as my eyes watched his slow cuts, my breasts losing pressure, the firm bodice around my ribs falling free. Klive licked his lips, then blew the scraps of ribbon from my skin like extinguishing flames from birthday candles. The knife pushed across the room and Klive ran his strong hands over my bare torso, cupped and kneaded my breasts, then trailed his fingertips back down until I bucked when he toyed with the most sensitive flesh where we connected. He rubbed and I squirmed with fresh desire, drunk on his scary side now delivering a new high.

"To whom does this belong?"

"You, Klive, yours!" I shouted and arched, then Klive hooked my thighs again and angled himself to slam that bundle of nerves inside me over and over. "I can't! I can't! I can't!" was all I cried even as I clawed for his shoulders, tightened my legs around his hips so he couldn't stop. "Klive, keep going! Keep going! I can't! Keep going!"

"I can't!" Klive shoved my thighs down his legs like rushing pants off before an emergency. He ripped himself out of my body then came all over my torso. I didn't notice the spurts slapping my skin as much as I relished the sound and sight of Klive in climax. *I did that! I caused that look, that cry from this man! What a feeling!*

Klive's shoulders sagged as heavy as his eyelids. The corner of his mouth tilted, then his fingers smeared his semen all over my belly and breasts. I gaped at the audacity, and Klive was so dirty he shoved two of his fingers into my mouth and ripped them away before I could slap or bite him.

"Gross, asshole!"

"But you loved my dick, so I guess he's not part of the insult anymore." Klive's hearty laughter bounced off the walls as he lifted himself off the carpet. He peered down at me, formed the gun with his nasty hand, aimed, fired, then left me a limp mess on his floor while he turned the shower on to clean the crime scene from his body.

Holy shit, that just happened!

27 | ♀

My muscles clenched, desire rekindling from sparks of reliving what just transpired, far better than the dreams Klive inspired. I groaned, already missing him within me. Never in my entire being had I experienced a buzz in my brain and body like I had now. The closest I'd ever come was a runner's high and exertion with Jase, but where Jase hit my places of pleasure, Klive yanked the reins on every emotion and steered them into the mix of ecstasy.

"I have found the one my soul longs for," I whispered into my hands as I covered my face. Was that what waiting for marriage was supposed to be like? Oh, to have waited for Klive ... truly waited.

I rolled to my side as the music changed and the shower door closed.

Damn Klive, marking his territory all over me like an animal. Who'd have known such a refined man refusing me so long, restrained, and resilient, was such a rake when the cuffs came off? I snickered to myself recalling his entrapment. If I weren't caked and gross, I'd have crawled across the carpet to the bed and drizzled my fluid limbs over the comforter to sleep.

As I rolled to my hands and knees, I noted the knife near the wall and shook my head. The psycho with the knife certainly delivered fear, adrenaline and chased me across the floor in the yummiest fashion. My lips tilted at the redness over the backs of my hands. If rug burn were the price for lovin' that left me resplendent with relaxation, mark me down for as many sessions as my skin could handle before rubbing off. I groaned at the memory of that evil grin; those eyes closed in climax ... so freaking sexy!

How much could the body handle? Because if this was what the honeymoon experience was supposed to be like, I knew the appeal of a week in a hotel room and wanted to yank Klive from the shower for more.

I kicked the heels near the knife and stood, the corset and remaining ribbon shards falling to the floor. Did they sell corset ribbons the way you'd buy shoestrings?

Listen to your happy, silly heart and head, love! I twirled on my toes, arms out, eyes closed, head back in bliss of this afterglow.

I slinked lazily into the bathroom for a peek of the naked *Million Dollar Man* humming with Lana Del Rey's sultry voice. His muscles lathered in body wash. The glass fogged with steam, masking the sharp details. He was beautiful and I wanted to climb into his cloud and float in the weightlessness he exuded.

"Jeez, Klive, thanks for the invite, sir," I popped like a playful smart ass. I threw the scraps of my corset in the closet then tapped my toes with my hands on my hips in front of the shower, waiting for him to notice. He wiped the glass and smiled, nearly robbing my breath with his radiance. Definitely sober, he was practically glowing! What a feeling! Fist pump!

"May I help you, love?"

I raised my eyebrows and gestured to the nasty mess he'd made of me. He nodded with a proud smile, then turned his back to continue washing himself. Oh, damn this sexy man.

"Klive King!" I yelled over the music. He turned back to me with that shit-eating grin.

"Yes, love, what is it? I am trying to get cleaned up, here! Some of us don't care for marinating in bodily fluids." His eyes roved over my body again, nothing but satisfaction swimming in those gray pools. "Oh, wait, surely you don't want to wash me off of you?" His mock confusion melted me more than his playful side. I groaned and leaned on the glass as I turned away from him. So much for torturing him; he was torturing me! Lana Del Rey sang about being ready for her man, and I screamed the lyrics in my head with her.

The shower door opened beside me, and Klive snagged my hand. He tugged me lightly, and I gazed at him, my weakness on display.

He pulled me into the shower and kissed me hard. The water poured over our faces and intensified fresh desire. He fingers speared through my hair, wetting my mane beneath the stream. He released my hair and drew soft scratches down my spine, gripping my bottom, groaning into my mouth while I hummed into his. That pulse of lust became a snare pounding through the sexual places on my body. Klive released my bottom to hit a button, then water rained down from the ceiling, too! I reached up into the torrent and twirled around slowly, loving the playful feel, the sweet music playing, the man I opened my eyes to and watched through the deluge. *Sigh*....

"Omigosh, Klive! This is so neat!" I gushed. "Can this be real? Tell me we're really playing in the rain! That this isn't some amazing dream I'll wake from." I smiled up at him, wiping the water from my eyes. His answering smile was soft, fuzzy. The water rushed over his face, down his glorious body and I wanted to touch him to confirm this was real.

"I'd say this is real, but I fear I'm the one dreaming. You are so sweet, innocent. How am I so lucky?" he asked. A glimpse of the sweet one. I grinned. How he could say that after the experience I just gave him, I wasn't sure. The song looped.

The sensuous rhythm combined with the fact that I'd just been a scene straight from a naughty movie made me brave. I shook my head at him and raised my arms over my head once more, fanning my fingers in the water. His hands gripped my hips, ran gently over my ribs and back down, testing the minutes of my hourglass. I took advantage of his grip and folded my arms over my head and bent back, letting the water cascade down between my breasts before slowly pulling myself back up. My hips swayed to the music, my hands glancing across the skin of my belly, over my breasts, up into my hair as I watched his expression. Klive's eyes locked on my hands. While I swayed, I kissed a fingertip and pressed my print to his soft lips. He bit softly. Now my gaze glued to his mouth.

My fingers traveled into his hair as I pressed my flesh to his, urging him to move with me. I turned around and placed my palm behind his neck the way I had earlier, only this time was slow and sensuous to match the music. My other hand scrolled past his ribs, his hips, down his thigh as I lowered myself, rubbing my shoulders against his erection before bringing my hand and body back up against him as he pressed along the length of my back. I twisted back around to take in his unfathomable expression. My fingertips caressed his thigh and pranced along the unavoidable growth hardened between our bodies. I gripped him and stayed true to the sultry, slow rhythm of the song, my grasp danced gradually down, up and back. Klive's lips parted as his eyes closed. His forehead tilted against mine. His hands traversed my back down to my bottom. He kneaded my flesh with hungry fingers as I continued to stroke him with the song. I let go of him to pull his cheek to mine as I sang along with the song about how it really wasn't that hard to be into him. I kissed his ear, his jaw, his throat, finally his lips.

Klive's arms wrapped around my waist where he leaned down on top of me as he bent me back so deeply my hair dragged on the floor. I closed my eyes as he raised me with the grace of a ballroom dancer, but his elegance vanished when I had firm balance. His hands cupped my face, mouth descended on my gasp at his sudden shift. The water poured down onto our faces as I wrapped my arms around his neck to keep from slipping. Our kisses were open-mouthed and sloppy to sip oxygen between unrestrained angle-changing and all-consuming need. I swallowed water as his warm tongue brushed eagerly against mine. He walked me back against the tile wall, and I winced into his mouth with the freezing temperature contrast. He lifted me and gingerly guided himself inside me, filling and stretching me to the point of pain, but bliss killed all aches as he worked me into a weakened, lust-drunken frenzy with his talented hips.

The song looped again. Klive paused and I protested. He grinned and lifted his brows at my attitude problem.

"Please! Klive, don't stop!"

"Shall we call this revenge for earlier?" he chuckled. "Patience, love. You'll get more." Holding me in place, he tapped the touchscreen and a whole music library displayed! Insane! He grinned as he pressed play on The Sundays' *Wild Horses*.

I smiled up at him. "Will you never tire of calling my sappy shit?"

"I call your sappy shit to keep you from seeing mine, but here and now, I'm not hiding it." His hips stayed still though he dipped to my lips for affectionate kisses instead of the erotic sort we'd started with. "You worried about me killing you, but it's you who'll be the death of me ... You, Kinsley Hayes, are the one who is unbelievable. I'd never have killed you. Had I done so, I'd have extinguished the brightest light in my life." Before I could coo, he gripped my hips and thrust again, making me cry against his shoulder. I swallowed more water as I moaned and digested the beautiful, haunting words he'd gifted. Klive pulled and pushed harder again, moving me against the tile. My arm tightened around his neck. My other hand touched his throat sweetly, not dominatrix. I squeezed slightly, testing his response. If he'd done this to me, maybe he did what he wanted done to him ...?

He gasped against my mouth as I brought mine back to his and drank the water with his open lips. His tongue met mine. He shoved harder and faster, held tightly to my thighs, supported me and groaned into my mouth. I squeezed harder. My other hand fisted his soaked hair, pulling automatically as I held onto him while he moved me against the shower wall. He pulled back and looked down at our bodies pressed together.

"Oh, Kins, look at you," he said breathlessly while he kept working. He watched my body with his, naughty X-rated observations and hidden desires pouring from his elegant accent into the chemistry permeating the thick steam.

"More, Klive! Who knew you were such a bad, bad boy inside your mind?" My head tilted back against the tile as I got off on this other side unveiling itself when he was weak with pleasure.

He released one of my thighs. I wrapped my leg around him to hold myself up. He reached between our connection to rub, soothe, torture, and effectively cause my muscles to full-out gridlock him inside me while I moaned wildly against his shoulder. Without realizing, I squeezed his throat harder, pulled the hell out of his hair, till he cried out in pain. Rather than making me stop, he rocked harder, my head thumping the tiles without a care for anything other than the blinding lights behind my eyelids. His rough growls and need were so hot, so contrasting to the serene song.

Klive kissed me one last time while I held fast to him. "Bloody woman! You are so worth the wait!" He squeezed my thighs again to pin me to the wall while he pulled quickly out of me to let himself release on my tummy again. His forehead rested against the tile next to my face while he twitched and huffed like he'd come off a sprint. His clouded eyes refocused on me. I smiled like the triumphant fool this time as I watched him in this unguarded moment.

"Yikes. Guess I held too tight." He grimaced and lowered me to the floor. Small fingerprints made red dots on my legs.

I chortled. "If I forgive you for those, you have to forgive me for your throat." I cringed like an idiot. Klive mirrored my silly expression and laughed.

"A scarf in the springtime? Challenge accepted. You'll have to wear one too, so no one sees the hickey I gave you."

I slapped my neck, now remembering, and gaped at him, the back of my hand smacking his belly. Klive's hearty laugh and brilliant toothy smile tempted me to let him leave more marks if they made him this happy.

He squeezed body wash onto a loofah and scrubbed me from neck to toe, cautious not to graze the coarse material on my sensitive areas. I loved that I smelled like Klive now.

Klive wrapped his arms around me and slid my soapy body against his as he kept me out of the water to enjoy the suds all over me. I laughed and chided him when he blatantly dipped his face down to rub all over my slick breasts.

"I have to wash my face and my hands are too busy washing you, love."

My laughter rang over the song. "What should I do with my hands? Wash your hair? Make shapes?"

"I'd much rather you wash other areas. Not sure what you put in my water and bread, but if you want to run straight for track, use less next time."

He pulled us back under the raining water and watched all the soap rinse away after he rinsed his face.

Again, he touched the screen and selected another song. He pressed play and looked over at me, watching, waiting as if he was testing my responses. Deftones. *Change*. Interesting. Unexpected.

My eyes locked on his.

Before coherent thought, chemistry engulfed me, and I yanked him against me, kissing him furiously. After all the waiting, I couldn't get enough of him! His hands roamed everywhere as though he felt the same. He pinned me with his body against the wall once more and lifted me a little higher, sliding me up the tiles. He sucked my nipples into his mouth one at a time. My head smacked the tile when I arched. I used his hair like reins urging his mouth harder, prodding him on. Warm heat licked up my cheeks when he pushed two fingers inside of me. I relished every surge he sent, every stroke of his tongue, every thrust of his fingers massaging inside me. Suddenly, he ripped his fingers away from me, and without warning he flipped me, so my breasts pressed against the tile like cold compresses to my aching nipples. If his mouth wasn't delivering delicious torment, this was a nice second for sure!

He parted my thighs and guided himself up into me again. Tears prickled the corners of my eyes at the new pain of so much sex in such a concentrated time. My body didn't care, nor did my brain when he proceeded to pound into me hard and rough. Rougher than in the room. I held myself against the wall and pushed back against his thrusts, moaning with my eyes closed. He spanked me, causing me to cry out at the watery sting mixed with the pleasure pain of his force. His palm smacked my butt again. Seemed the more it stung, the better the release of angst and emotion trapped inside for too long.

"More!" I pleaded for depletion of my constant stress.

He sent another stinging slap to my ass with a pleasured curse on his lips joining the moans I let loose. He ran his left hand up to my throat and pressed me harder against the wall as his chest met my back. His fingers splayed and squeezed against me the way I had done to him. When Klive did this, those hands capable of death, he sent fear pumping through my veins to mingle with the incredible pleasure he delivered. The combination was unmatched. He leaned forward and kissed behind my ear.

"Say my fucking name, Kinsley!"

I moaned as climax stole rationale.

"Klive!! Oh, Klive!! *Ooohhh, Kkkllliiivveeee!!!*"

He squeezed harder, stealing more of my precious oxygen, sending more adrenaline spiking through my veins. His mouth met my ear again. "Just like that, baby," he said with zero accent, more fear lancing my orgasm. Holy shit! Klive was the man on the plane without an accent! He sounded like someone else, too, though, but who? "That's how I envisioned killing your sweet ass, making you yell my name, your sweet cunt squeezing me, your helpless cries the last thing you uttered before I stole the beautiful life you so foolishly trusted me with," he growled against my ear.

I couldn't take anymore! So much fear, adrenaline, ecstasy, mixed with his crude words! I begged his name again and felt like I was shattering both against him and this wall he kept thrusting me against. He squeezed when he came again, too. *Inside* of me this time! *Shit!!* I was so overcome, I didn't care. I got mad, though.

"Your turn, Klive!" I choked. "Say *my* name! The damn woman you can't kill because she is too much for you to go without! Say it!" I commanded him, gasping through his grip, him still coming inside of me.

"Oh, fucking, sweet, Kinsley!" He moaned. "You're so much sweeter than I imagined. No wonder you have so many begging to get inside you!" He thrust once more and shuddered at my back as he emptied himself into my body. He froze inside of me for a moment and laid his head on my shoulders as he caught his breath, releasing my throat so I could breathe normally again.

"Shit!" I knew he realized his mistake, too. He turned off the music and let the silence wash over us.

When he pulled out of me, I felt empty. I slid down the wall to my feet again as he lowered me gently. I leaned against the cold tile, sobering. Afraid. My period was done. There was a fat chance I was fertile right now! *Dear God!! What would I do? What would he do?*

"Hey, turn around. Are you on birth control?" he demanded. I sagged against the wall and turned my back against the tile. Concerned sobriety colored his previously glowing irises as he searched my face. I didn't answer, just stood in shock before finally shaking my head. He closed his eyes to the potentially devastating enormity of his mistake and released a heavy sigh. When he opened them, they were much softer. He sighed again as he cupped one of my cheeks and urged me against him. His arm wrapped around my waist while his free hand tipped my chin. Klive forced me to face him in all my new fear. "Love, whatever happens, I will not leave you. I own up to my responsibilities. That's if you decide to keep it should it turn into that."

I gasped. "Of course, I would keep it, Klive!" I told him, unable to hide my disappointment, though I knew I was shell-shocked right now. I shouldn't be. I mean I'm in the arms of a man who had my name at the top of his hit list last week. What would he care if I terminated a pregnancy? His expression hardened, became authoritative once again.

"Did I just ask you to get one, or did I tell you I own up to my responsibilities? I wasn't sure if you were the kind of girl that would operate that way or not, especially given that you know who I truly am," he reasoned. He was right. He talked of taking care of a baby first but gave me the option as though he had no say in the matter. Imagine that. A heartless killer having a heart for an unborn child ... the ultimate change ... oh, Tyndall!

I pushed that out of my head. I had to. If I were pregnant with Klive King's child, I wouldn't be Mrs. Jase Taylor or have his pretty babies ....

I pushed this out of my mind, too. Would Klive still leave money for a baby if he were locked up? Ugh! The idea repulsed me, though which part repulsed me the most, I didn't really want to ponder, or else I might have another nauseous moment where my feelings for this man were concerned. All of this was just too much to think of. I tried to force the thoughts out of my head. I looked up at him and nodded.

"You're right, I misjudged you. It's not in my code of ethics, though why should you take that code seriously when everything we've done tonight, what I've done up to this point, isn't in my code either. I'm sorry," I said genuinely. "Thank you. Please, forgive me."

28 | ♀

KLIVE KISSED MY FOREHEAD and trailed his hand down my wet hair.

"What did I tell you about talking down on yourself?" He continued forcing me to look into his gray eyes when I really wanted to hide from them.

"I'm sorry. There's just so much ... so much I ... now this ..." I blinked back involuntary tears at the depth of pain in his face.

"Oh, Kinsley, I know it's not what you probably ever wanted, that *I* am not what you want, or *who* you want, but I am here if you decide you do. I apologize for my clumsy mistake."

"I've hurt you, disappointed you, caused you to stumble into something you don't need or want."

"Hush now. You're no mind reader. Nor am I. You've not pained me. I'm pained seeing you in anguish after I just *finally* made love to you."

My heart softened at his face, his words, his offer. How could I betray a man willing to raise a child with me without a second thought otherwise, even being involved in the shit he was? I felt guilty because as I looked into his eyes, I absolutely loved this man — bad side and all. Numb fear rendered my limbs useless. How fickle I am. What I'd told Jase earlier was true enough when I'd told him, but in the span of what? Twelve hours at the most, everything changed. He'd be shattered, and so would I. Sweet Jase would probably stay by my side and watch me live my life with

Klive just to stay near me. Ha! That's if he allowed me to have a life with Klive since he was seeking to put his ass away. Nausea gripped my guts. Klive turned the water to a cooler temperature, which thankfully helped keep my last meal down.

"Klive, I ..." I didn't know what to say. My voice trailed into silence.

"How about this? Put it out of your mind, and if you miss your next period, we will worry then. For now, there is nothing you can do."

Not true. If Bayleigh knew, she'd escort me to the drugstore for the morning after pill.

"Worrying will get you nowhere," Klive's voice continued. "Or me. We will take it as it comes, all right, love?" He was right again.

Worrying would serve me no good and I wasn't breathing a word of this to anyone, not even Tyndall. The only advice I wanted was from the parties involved. If I were going to have to break Jase's heart, I'd worry about that when the time came. For now, I was a twenty-five-year-old woman, well almost, who was an amazing runner about to graduate college. A young woman with an unwritten life ahead of her full of promise with three options if she wanted to take the commitment route. Although the one on the top of the list right now, given the circumstances, was a scary crime boss who would probably be in prison soon....

Ugh! I threw my hands up in exasperation, glared at him.

"Damn it, Klive! *Why?* Why did you have to be in that stupid elevator? To come along and quit being so scary? Draw me into you? Why couldn't you have kept me a target on your radar and let me outsmart you to keep my life intact? Now, I am potentially making a life with a damned drug lord, crime boss, hitman, whatever the hell you are! How the hell will I raise a baby with *you*? How will *I* get out of this unscathed? Where is there a peaceful resolution?" My frustration melted into sorrow. "Why do you have to be so charming and sweet to me? To protect me and come to my aide when I need you? Why can't you let me down so I can walk away and not look back?" I beat my fists on his chest in angry emphasis.

He smiled softly, chuckled, then outright laughed as he mulled over everything I said. A charming smile crossed his features, warming his whole face, that dimple creasing in his cheek.

"Drug lord, crime boss, hitman, eh? That is quite a title, if I do say so myself." He looked up like he was thinking before looking back down at me in adoration. "Outsmart *me* to keep your life, huh?" He smoothed his hand over my hair again and studied my face. "You? I think it may have just been possible if I could have gotten you out of my bloody head long enough to let you skitter off my radar. No such luck there, my sweet. The first time I saw your pretty face, I couldn't get you out of my damned mind. That was before you presented a problem for me. Perhaps had you only been a pretty face, I could have moved on. Then your charm and that vicious little attitude of yours had to challenge my own."

"Klive, you really are so very inappropriate for being such a gentleman. Though we've had our interludes, you hardly know me, yet allow yourself to be smitten with me. I'd label you a fool if I weren't so happy about your impropriety."

"And your shamelessness matches my own. I know you've done your homework, but how is it that you play into my hands *so* easily? Too easily. Maybe you are being deceptive?" he asked me with a little bite to his tone and backed me up against the wall again, making me wince against the cold.

"Too easily? Klive, do I need to kick you in the balls again? There's been nothing easy about anything to do with you and I swear if you label me easy ever again, I'll rob you of the appendage I love so much. Have you known me to put on a front? To hold my emotions back? To pretend?" I demanded, hoping to God he'd put his suspicion out of his mind. Sure, I'd been deceptive when I slathered the charm on thick, but the only one I was deceiving was myself if I thought I wouldn't fall more in love with this man if he kept inviting me closer.

"Klive King, for claiming you're complicated, I think *you've* been too easy." *Too easy to desire, to laugh with, to have butterflies around, to kiss, now to sleep with ... to love.*

He *was* so complicated, so complex for my mind to ponder, so much of everything that I thought of him too much in trying to figure him out. I crossed my arms under my boobs and turned my chin.

He chuckled. "The only easy thing about me is defending you. You make a valid point. Could you contain yourself, I'd not have needed to come to your aide and jeopardize relations. Oh, Kinsley. What the hell will I do about you? Jase was right. You're dangerous."

Jase! Sweet Jase.

"I know you love him. Remember, no attachments unless you are ready to commit. You did a fantastic job last night." Evident pride flashed on his face. Oh, what a look! Was he being manipulative purposefully, or was I just that easy to play? The latter, or both, really. "This water is getting hard to bear, my sweet. You ready to get out?"

I nodded. He shut the amazing shower down and got out. I trembled instantly with the cold, but he coaxed me from the shower. A thick towel draped around his waist. He opened another and wrapped me snugly so that my arms were trapped, then hugged me to his chest. I laid my head against his heart and listened to the beat, suspecting his blood wasn't as cold as Jase told me. Or was this man's heart changing because of me? Was this side always there, but hidden? Tyndall's words rang like an alarm bell I kept snoozing. *Time to wake and ask yourself the hard questions, Kins. You have the opportunity to do good. Do good.*

I craned my head back to peer into his eyes. His soft lips caressed mine. I returned his languid sweetness the way he gave.

He released me to step into my closet and came back with a red satin nightie he set on the vanity. He unwrapped me the way I unwrap gifts so I can save the paper, openly relishing in my naked body. I noticed him trying to contain himself all over again! Wow! I wasn't the only one with an insatiable appetite, was I? He held the nightie out for me, but I held my arms up over my head, so he'd have to dress me, that, and adore me just a little more. He chuckled again as he drizzled the satin over my head and guided the hem just past my hips.

"Thank you, sir."

He nodded and watched me in the mirror while I brushed my hair. Yes, Klive had a brush for me. And a toothbrush. Presumptuous was an understatement.

We brushed our teeth and cleaned our mess together. Klive scooped the scraps of black ribbon into the waste basket. I walked into his closet to replace his tie. I smiled as I hid the cuffs in my naughty lingerie drawer instead of his closet. When I walked back through the bathroom the lights were out, and the fireplace flickered.

As I padded out into his bedroom, I enjoyed the tranquil light of the fire casting pretty shadows about. Klive donned drawstring pajama pants, no shirt. He looked so *human*. So inviting. He sat on the bench at the foot of his bed texting on his phone. *At this time of night?* I looked up at the clock. *Oops, I mean morning. Jeez, it was 4:45!* We had gone at it for a while! Well, so much for an early workout at the beach.

I sauntered across the thick carpet and pulled his chin. Oh, no, he looked upset! I pushed his hand holding the phone to the side, and I crawled onto his lap to wrap my legs around him as I held onto his neck. "What's wrong, love?" I asked him in his accent with a warm smile, hoping to cheer him.

"Repercussions. Nothing I can't take care of in a few hours. Just frustrating." Yikes! His tone was surprisingly harsh.

"From me?" I chewed my cheek. He stayed quiet. I swallowed, disturbed that I'd done something to make him look like this. His fingers drew circles on my back. "Klive, I'm sorry for whatever I've done."

"No. Please, do not apologize for this," he said, changing to his sweet mode. He cupped my face, sending relief all through me. He mumbled against my mouth through loose kisses, "If you want to apologize for anything, apologize for allowing yourself to get wrapped up with me. For making me crazy with longing for you." He smiled through pulls of my lips. I sighed against his mouth. What woman wouldn't love being told such things?

"Well, sir, in that case, I apologize for being so damn unforgettable." I winked and kissed him some more.

"Yeah, you'd better," he teased through kisses like talking with his mouth full. His phone chimed. His arm rose, eyes glancing over my shoulder. "Son of a bitch!" His voice exploded. I yelped and wrapped my arms around his neck as he surged to his feet. "I am going to fucking kill him right now!" He shook loose and hurled me onto the bed in one swift motion. Klive stormed from the room, the passage left open. I heard the bread box slam from all the way in here.

"Oh, shit," I whispered, stunned to my place. "What the hell do I do?" I gulped, trying to push the fear and anxiety like a rock down my throat as I heard him load a fresh clip into his gun. *Oh, God! He really meant it! He was going to kill someone!*

29 | ♀

I DASHED OFF THE bed and rushed into the kitchen where Klive furiously cursed into his phone. He arranged to meet someone. *In twenty minutes!* I don't know what happened. Autopilot? I jerked the gun from his hand to the counter, tossed the phone to the living room, then gripped his face in my palms. "Klive, baby, look at me. Look at me, Klive," I said in a way steadier voice than I felt. How was I calm right now?

His icy glare froze my breathing. "Have a death wish, do you?! What kind of daft fool grabs a loaded gun without knowing whether the safety was on?! Whether my finger teased the trigger?!" He pushed me out of his path and moved toward his phone still on an active call. I grabbed his hand and jerked, forcing him to face me. He turned on me quickly, but I wasn't taking any shit.

"Kinsley Hayes, I'm warning you, you're in way, *way* over your head right now. Let. Me. Go." He ripped his hand from mine.

"Klive King." I snapped my fingers. "Don't talk to me that way," I said showing no fear. "You promised, remember?" His jaw muscle clenched and unclenched, back and forth as he stared. "You *promised*." I forced his word, his honor as a dishonorable man, to the forefront. He growled under his breath like an attack dog ordered to heel. He strode to the couch and yanked his phone from the floor to resume yelling, undaunted.

While he lost himself in his anger, I stole his gun and went to the room, tucked the pistol as far as I could reach beneath the mattress, and sat, waiting for him to finish barking his evil orders. Remembering the buttons from the other night, I turned on the projection TV and resumed the episode of *Too Cute* I'd watched Monday night. Fluffy kittens hopped after each other, pouncing and playing before my eyes as I tried my best to ignore the insanity that was this damn criminal in the kitchen yelling on the phone in a rage I'd never known. Another facet to my dear Mr. King. Perhaps he wasn't good father material after all.

"Blast, Kinsley!" He marched into the room with wide strides a couple of moments later, pissed off. He stopped next to me and looked down in that way he had. He no longer shouted. His voice dropped to a low threat, just like his expression. "What the fuck did you do with my gun?" I shrugged my shoulders and ignored his scowl. Kittens meowed for their mother as their father was introduced for the first time. I snorted in bitterness and tossed my hand to the show.

Klive threw his face into the comforter and screamed into the down feathers all the fury he had for me right now. I chewed the inside of my cheek so bad I'd have open sores in my mouth for a week. A lump of fear swallowed to my stomach before I found my voice.

"When you're ready to calm down, I'll give it back," I said simply, somehow not conveying the fact that I quaked on the inside. My freaking survival instincts screamed at me to quit being a total moron.

"It's my bloody job, woman!" he exclaimed as he pushed off the bed and grabbed me, tossing me to the other side. He rifled through the pillows, under the blanket, the sheets. He tossed me back to my side and rifled through his. Coming up empty, he punched his fist into a pillow so hard, feathers came flying out in a flurried cloud of softness that was almost amusing by contrast. At the worst of times, the giggle loop tickled my tummy and twitched my lips. The immaturity of this grown ass man who'd told *me* to grow up ...?

He narrowed his eyes like my thoughts projected on my forehead. *Don't laugh! Don't laugh!*

Klive rolled off the bed and dusted feathers from his chest. He disappeared into the bathroom. When he came out, he'd dressed in jeans and an A-frame tank with a linen button-up hanging open. An even bigger gun now weighted his right hand. Holy shit! A .50 caliber pistol. I recognized that gun from my daddy's hunting magazines at the house. *Not good!*

Klive displayed the Desert Eagle and unscrewed what must have been a silencer from the end that he tucked into his pocket with a pat afterward to indicate he'd be using this tool. I watched him and he watched me as he shoved a fresh clip into the gun and tucked the shiny weapon into a shoulder holster. His eyes never wavered from mine as his fingers buttoned the linen over the concealed weapon, then rolled the cuffs up his forearms.

Though I wanted to look away, my stubborn pride refused.

Klive pulled on a pair of boots before he walked over to my side of the bed again. I squealed when he pulled me against him. I swallowed hard. My damn heart hammered my ribs when he gripped the back of my neck. I had no choice but to look up at him. His thumb and fingers massaged my tension as he glared down at me. His gaze roved over my breasts as they heaved against his chest in this tiny nightie with my erratic breathing in all the mayhem. His eyes drifted up to my mouth before resting on my eyes again. His expression resolute, he cupped the back of my head, bent his face to mine and gave me the softest, sweetest, most contradicting kiss to his everything. I understood. He was proving he was well within control of himself, that what he was doing was of his own volition.

He lifted away from my mouth and looked down at me with hard affection in his eyes.

"You are so foolishly brave, love." He nipped at my lips a few more times. "I will be back in an hour max."

He released my neck and twisted the Shisha dog on his way out of the room. The passage closed behind him.

Wow! Had that shit just happened?

I leaped off the bed and twisted the Shisha dog, grateful I wasn't somehow locked in Klive's castle as the bookcase opened.

I never heard the Ferrari, so I walked out into the living room and looked. He backed a Range Rover out of the driveway. How ...? Where had *that* vehicle come from? I pushed off the windowsill and sighed. Klive was right, again. I was in way over my head. Perhaps I'd been a daft fool in thinking I was capable of this task for Jase. *Should I call him?*

When I recalled how drunk Jase had been only a few short hours ago, I shook my head. In only a few short hours, I'd put on a costume and played a part I'd never, ever known I could be, then had sweet love made to me by my murderous companion in the shower, finally rounding off with some fantastically rough sex that could have altered my life. I put my hands on my abdomen as I thoughtfully looked down. *Dear Lord, if this happens, please ... I don't know ....*

I had no idea how to finish that prayer. This hypothetical baby's father was going to kill someone right now in the criminal nature of his job that was going to be the very reason for his not being available to that potential life-to-be.

30 | ♀

IN THE CLOSET OF Kinsley, I dressed in workout gear, wide awake with energy I needed to expel the best way I knew how. When I went inside the garage, Klive's Tesla parked in the same place he'd parked Monday night, plugged into a wall charger. What in the world? If he'd driven his car to the bar last night, had someone driven back home for him? They would have had to, right? Which meant this someone also had the garage door opener and the code for Klive's gate. Eric, maybe?

I found a key fob inside the same breadbox he kept his gun. Should I replace the gun in here or leave the weapon beneath the mattress and let Klive seek the pistol on his own? He deserved to look for his gun for a long time. But, when someone was vindictive toward me, I grew angrier rather than coming to repentance. If Klive was like me, replacing his gun without a word was a show of respect and surrendering my weapon of an attitude so he'd lay his down too.

My arm strained to reach the heavy forty-caliber, conscious this time of the seriousness I'd neglected when taking the gun from him earlier. As my fingers wrapped the pistol grip, I gingerly eased the heavy metal from under the mattress and checked the safety with the muzzle pointed firmly away from me. As I released the magazine and checked the chamber, I wondered how Klive handled the weight of this in his hand every day? Not the weapon so much as the power of life and death? That's the part I struggled to overcome anytime I held a gun. The whole way back to the kitchen I imagined the pain in my shoulder from the kickback of firing this heavy thing. I was more than happy to pass the pistol and the parts into the breadbox.

My fingers wrapped the Tesla fob. I fought a tinge of guilt at taking Klive's personal car without permission. Bizarre, but he'd handed me the keys to the Ferrari with the all-clear. The Tesla was his everyday personal car, and there was something that felt more intimate at taking her from the garage without asking. As if I should even give a flying F about getting permission from that man, especially after our fight, but I did.

After unplugging his vehicle and figuring out how to handle the electric car— thank goodness no one was here to watch my clumsy idiocy in touching the wrong buttons! —I drove straight to the obstacle course. Screw leaving Klive a note. Let him call wondering where I had gone with his car! Maybe he would think he'd pissed me off for good, and I just up and left because of that damn attitude problem of his. *Damn, that man could switch gears like I had never seen!*

Like ... *me.*

Ugh.

I got out and made my way onto the sand. My jog was not aggressive as much as necessary for sanity this morning. The stitch built in my side fast, but I also had new muscle pain I'd never expected having nothing to do with my fight injuries and everything to do with the ways I'd twisted, bowed, arched and flexed when tangling limbs and private parts with Klive. Of all days to put me back in a meet! Maybe second or third wouldn't be so bad ...?

With every footfall, I thought of Klive, mulled his whole existence in my life from pirate to present. I knew the words of my journal from the day we'd met by heart.

Nathan Knox, the man I'd pledged to marry, stood me up instead of showing up to Gasparilla. He'd hinted at marriage for months, toyed with the L-word like a man in fear, urged me closer to fooling around behind closed doors even though I wanted to wait. I see now, Nate was a stupid boy unwilling to commit. Guess it's better he didn't show up and sleep with me before making his cowardice known.

If Nate had shown up, those frat boys wouldn't have attacked me. I think I'm still reeling from the reality of how close I was to being raped in the middle of a festival. If I call the cops, I inconvenience the school again after my drama with the atheists. They both graduate with Nate. I'm supposed to graduate with Nathan, too, but I don't think I'm ready to yet.

They say when God closes one door, he opens another. In my case, I was praying at Amy's empty reception desk, having a pity party after puking from getting emotional when TWO doors opened. Elevator doors. No joke, right after I'd told God I was so done with relationships, that maybe marriage was for older people, or from a more traditional time, I said aloud, "I hate guessing games and I want to fall in love with someone who won't leave me! Can't you just show me my husband?"

The bell to the elevator pinged like a microwave on a TV dinner. The doors opened and there stood the sexiest pirate checking me out like he'd prayed the same prayer and approved of God's selection. I didn't know what to do so I ran because God must've gotten it wrong. The pirate chased me, grabbed me, reprimanded me like one of those scenes from an old black and white movie. When I wanted him to kiss me, I realized there was something different about this total stranger.

Of course, I don't know how to tell Daddy that the man God might have for me is in his building. How would I describe him beyond being tall and having the prettiest gray eyes? I heard an accent, but on Gasparilla sometimes thespians use accents when in costume to sell their role. If I found his cologne, I could spray it in Daddy's face and tell him to hunt like a bloodhound, heehee.

Anyway, this is all fun and games like whiskey for the pain of Nathan's wound to my heart, but I doubt I'll ever see him again. Both them actually. Nathan by choice. But I suppose if God wasn't playing a joke on me, I'll see the pirate again. Hopefully, I'll know who he is, and he won't hate me. I left my hat with him since I stole his coat. I'm cuddled in it now like a security blanket. At least God gave me a hint of him to hold for the rest of my lonely life if I never see him again, but I pray God is kind to me, that if I wait, the one whom my soul desires will desire me the same. Who knows, maybe he's trying to figure if he will ever see me again too? One can hope.

I weighed my remembrance while replaying Klive's charming flirtation, the pining, the scary moments, the erotic ones. How was I expected not to think about being pregnant as well? This wasn't the same as when Jase and I played with the idea and didn't protect against the possibility. I knew a lot about the mechanics of the feminine form from the medical courses I'd taken. Jase and I hadn't had sex during ovulation. Klive and I just did. The possibility carried heavy weight for my future! I wanted kids; this I knew for sure. Taking care of a sweet little human of my own warmed my heart and the fuzzy places of my dreamy brain, but how was I to reconcile falling into bed with a known killer? Not to mention two other damned men. Oh, the madness! The shame!

Once again, I imagined reaching Constance and Delia, hopping a flight to join them. When and if they wanted to go home, I could figure a way to stay. I mean, how could I face my father with this? The idea of leaving his presence for any considerable length of time pained me, but this? What if he was disappointed in me? I'd rather escape, just leave all of this behind and simplify by only loving one sweet little person rather than loving ... never mind. I am not completing that bullshit thought.

Funny to think that Klive's coming to my rescue with Angela had changed my life now that I faced this.

Another thought that chilled me to my core. What if ...?

I stopped running and grabbed my knees to stave off nausea.

What if Angela tattled to her father and they found *another* hitman as revenge? Klive had torn her up one side and down the other, doused her in gasoline, and lit her on fire, officially vanquishing her in public. I pictured Angela's sincere eyes begging *me* for her life. *What if?* Surely Klive wasn't the only one who was a known killer? I shivered despite sweating in the humidity.

Klive! Klive! Klive! Where are you?

I wanted his arms protecting me. Were Ray and Inferno distracting Klive into tunnel vision while Sheriff Ansley worked on a bigger plan in the background? He had an angle against me, no matter what he'd said in the cruiser. Why punish Rustin for weeks if this wasn't personal? I wanted someone every bit as lethal as any potential threat that may be headed my way, for Klive to kick Ray to the side and tell me he had an eye on the big picture. Sure, I could call Jase or Rustin, but I didn't want their chivalrous, above-board protection. Even Rustin expressed frustration with not being able to defend people against harm because of bureaucracy.

No, I wanted *Klive's* dangerous protection. The one who could beat someone like him at his own game! Didn't one of the guys make a comment about Klive dropping bodies like rungs on a ladder he climbed to the top? Klive himself said he was the most dangerous person I should cross in my apartment. I didn't want to go to my apartment in the face of this fear. The hidden room behind the bookcase with the man who'd brandished the biggest pistol I'd seen in real life sounded great right now.

Looking around myself, I saw how easy a target I was. The cover of darkness, the desertion, an open invitation without telling Klive where I was. What a stupid idea!

I turned back the way I'd come, forcing myself not to glance over my shoulder or at rooftops, see shifting shadows in the empty lifeguard stands as I ran. When I passed the post before the obstacle course, I sprinted, convinced someone followed me. Was Henley somewhere watching when he shouldn't be? Maybe that's who I sensed? Would the Sheriff make an alliance with Henley?

Quit being ridiculous! The Sheriff and Klive have ties. Klive called him to keep me free. He'd probably called Ansley as soon as he finished reaming Angela to smooth over potential damage. But Klive bitched about repercussions to do with me. If he wasn't talking about Angela and the Sheriff, was Henley an issue along with Ray, Inferno, everyone?

I stopped before the obstacle course unable to concentrate on exercise. The powdery sand carried my feet over the hard-packed portion close to the waves crashing ashore. I wilted ready to sit and weep in the silence of the sunrise. Rather than the normal radiance, distant thunderheads and thick gray cloud cover smothered the golden warmth in the eerie calm. No seagulls laughing or diving for fish. No plover seeking ghost crabs. No little old couple with a metal detector.

The breeze tugged at my still damp hair, tossing tresses over my face, twisting wisps into my view of the ocean. Was rain in today's forecast? Obviously, I'd lost touch with the outside world since involving myself with three men no one had business being in a relationship with. Nope. Not going to keep tormenting myself with further slut-shaming.

If you weren't being a slut, you'd have nothing to be ashamed of. Shut the hell up, Kinsley brain! Please!

I texted Klive where I was, defeated instead of defensive. A soft sob escaped my thick throat. My forehead fell onto my bent knees, and I watched through blurred eyes the first of many tears drip off my face onto my legs, down to the sand.

Not even five minutes later, Klive's arm crossed my shoulders and pulled me against him. I clutched his fresh tee-shirt as weary relief swept the tension from my back.

"You're here."

"I am." He kissed the top of my head.

I love you. "Don't leave me."

"Shh, I'm here, love." His presence somehow hit *stop* on the madness of my scattered, cluttered, mess of a brain. *Oh, Klive.* I nestled into the crook of his neck and searched his pants for blood evidence. He must go through a lot of clothes.

"Kinsley, *mon amour, je vous n'importe quoi ne permets pas de n'arrive pas. Comprend ? Vous êtes sûr pourvu que vous êtes avec moi. Je promets.*" He told me I was safe, that he wouldn't let anything happen to me as long as I was with him. What I wanted to know was, how he knew that was on my mind in the first place when what *should've* been on his mind was the fact that he had been so damn angry before we'd parted. Whatever. I closed my tired eyes and nodded against him. "I'm sorry I scared you, love."

"*Merci*, Klive," I said softly. "But I don't want to be the girl always accepting apologies."

"Understood." He hooked my chin and brought my lips to his for one of those amazing movie kisses like I'd longed for in my journal. Was there any better therapy than his soft lips and firm arms? He lingered till I sighed, then helped me to my feet. Klive kept my hand as we walked the silent distance back to the cars. I loved that Klive didn't give me any crap or seem to care that I had taken his Tesla. In fact, he paid no mind to his car and all attention to me.

"I have to run an errand. I'll be about thirty minutes behind you."

My face fell into disappointment.

"Kinsley, don't look at me that way. This is nothing business related. Please relax." He planted another kiss to my forehead. I looked up fearfully but nodded. He shook his head. "I am not a liar, Kins. Trust me. Go back to my place and re-shower, get cuddled up in my plush bed." A soft affection smoothed the hard expression on his face. "I'll probably be there before you fall asleep, love."

31 | ♂

MY HANDS SPLAYED ON the steering wheel of my Range Rover. No evidence. Why would there be? Jase had done well. I wanted more of everything I'd had this week with Kinsley and none of what I'd just come from at the shipyard. Pitting both thugs against each other with guns we'd supplied them, the men in charge of bringing Kinsley to Juan Perez turned on each other under pressure and confessed everything.

"What do I have to do to prove I'm telling the truth?" one asked Jase after an informative monologue.

Jase nodded at the guy's buddy. "Kill him before he kills you. Whoever wins is who we keep for our team."

The thug had lifted his weapon but the other stole the Desert Eagle I'd worn openly within his reach and fired on his friend at the exact time he was fired upon. As the men bled out, Jase and I stared at one another in a state of disbelief. Neither of us expected them to listen or to do so without hesitation.

Jase cursed and side-eyed me, backing away from a spreading pool on the concrete. "I can't believe that shit just went down." He looked around us to see if anyone heard the shots. "I thought one of them would come out alive. Collect the weapons or leave them?"

"Leave them. The gun shot residue will prove what happened. We were never here. Hurry."

Jase nodded. We walked outside of camera angles and motion lights to the crappy Toyota Tercel I used for dirty work. We got in and I drove to an area I knew the car would be stolen before sunrise. Jase wiped the car for prints and removed the booties I'd supplied us for the scene. He placed them in his glove compartment after we walked to our vehicles two blocks away.

He held his hand to me. "Want me to burn yours at my place, too?"

I shook my head. "Thanks. I've somewhere to be and a fireplace of my own."

"Two more assholes bite the dust and Kins is safer. My job here is done. See ya, King."

"A Nightshade ring is in your future very soon." I'd waved and gotten into the Rover, glad to see he was happy at the prospect of a Nightshade ring when he'd been so hesitant.

My phone now pinged as I drove. "Text from My Sweet Love," the automated voice told me. I thumbed the display. Kinsley sent her location with GPS coordinates. Though I both hated and worried that she'd left the sanctity of my home, I was in no position to lecture her on what was wise or foolish after how I'd cocked-up yet again.

I placed my left ring finger into my mouth and removed the Nightshade leadership ring with my teeth, then spat the metal into a napkin and wiped my hand on my jeans.

Five minutes later, I walked across the empty sand, loathing the way Kinsley's forehead planted on her knees. I'd caused that sorrow, dammit.

Lightning flickered through distant thunderheads. Time to get her off the open beach before the storm arrived.

"You're here," she said, much like the first night I'd come into her room during her sleepwalking. The peace after fear, like then, was present in her tone now.

"I am," I said against her hair and kissed the top of her head.

"Don't leave me." Was she afraid of losing me?

"Shh, I'm here, love." I swiped the damp hair from her forehead as she nuzzled my neck. Her fingers gripped my waist as if afraid I'd push her away. My jaw tensed at the insecurity I may have implanted inside her with my temper tantrum. As I surveyed our surroundings, I calmed her fears in soft French, hoping to soothe her. "I'm sorry I scared you, love," I finished in English.

"*Merci*, Klive," she whispered. "But I don't want to be the girl always accepting apologies."

I nodded. I didn't want her to become that girl either. Can't desire a spirited woman, kill the spirit you wanted, then wonder where the chemistry went, now can you?

"Understood." I hooked her chin and kissed her lips like I might convey my passion for her beyond words. Helping her to feet when I'd rather press her to the sand proved difficult when my body couldn't get enough of our new connection. I feared I'd have an auto-erotic reaction to her walking into a room for years after coming so hard so many times only short hours ago.

I'd officially fallen ass over tit for this woman and I now knew what pussy-whipped felt like ... and why.

I smirked to myself in new understanding and zero shame in the concept. No wonder my brothers were eager to please their wives no matter the shit I'd given them. *I* was the ignorant fool *they* pitied.

She studied me as we walked together to my vehicles.

"I have to run an errand," I told her as we stood behind the Tesla. If I asked her for round four in the back seat, would she slap me or shove me inside before the question finished tumbling from my lips? She bit her lip. Her eyes tired and puffy from crying met mine. *Behave yourself! Heed the Kinsley compass!* "I'll be about thirty minutes behind you." I'd like to be behind her for thirty minutes!

Her eyes rounded into that painstaking plea I buckled beneath.

"Kinsley, don't look at me that way. This is nothing business related. Please relax." I kissed her forehead, avoiding the fear in her eyes. "I am not a liar, Kins. Trust me. Go back to my place and re-shower, get cuddled up in my plush bed." *Where you belong, where you're safe, where I will do my best to soothe your sorrow.* "I'll probably be there before you fall asleep, love."

She surrendered, defeated, exhausted, a little disappointed in what her imagination conjured for my errands. One way or another, I hoped she'd find trust in my assurances. I watched her drive away in my car wearing clothes I'd supplied toward a home I'd built with her in mind. This was real. Goals manifested before my very eyes that lived too long in my mind. If we'd created life amid our death-defying endeavor, I prayed the heart would be allowed to beat and grow with me there to watch and participate.

First, I needed to earn my way back into her good graces.

When I honked the locks on my Rover, Joey opened his door with a less than welcoming frown on his puffy face. His nose glowed red, and his eyes swelled with glistening tears.

"Who died?" I joked.

"Hopefully those two pricks I warned you about. Taylor come through?" he asked, sniffled, sneezed into his sleeve.

"He did. They're dead."

"Good, 'cuz there's no way I could've aimed through eyes I can barely hold open. I'm never doing this again, just so we're clear. You should've asked Adrian instead. He's not allergic."

"Where would the fun be in that?" I chuckled.

Joey's head tilted. "You're usually uptight after wet work. You're *smiling*, King. *Really* smiling. Like a moron."

"You're just jealous I can open my eyes, mate."

Joey snorted. "Is that what I'm jealous of? I'm no fool. Makes sense why you sent me to my parents' house for this instead of keeping me on-duty overnight." He walked through his beach house to the laundry room, several sneezes echoing off the windows and throwing him off-balance along the way. I noted the darkening sky tossing white caps into the waves.

"I hope I got the one you said you wanted because I'm not going back to the vineyard for a while. Mom always puts me to work." Joey opened the door. I grinned.

"That's the one I picked." I knelt.

"Christophe know about this?"

"Nope and you're not to say a bloody word. I'll tell him when I'm ready."

"As long as you get that thing out of my house, my lips are sealed, but there's no hiding that you've gotten laid, my friend. Was she worth the suffering?"

"For last night, I'd have suffered two more celibate years, Joe."

"*That* hot, huh?"

I nodded, unable to keep from gloating with my grin alone.

"Hope she likes this damn thing because I hate it."

"Joe, she'll love it. Get to bed. I'll let myself out."

"Send her friend, Tyndall, to nurse me back to health while you're at it," Joe called down the hall.

My laughter echoed off the walls. "Taylor's about to become Nightshade. I don't want my trainee fighting with my bodyguard for shagging his sister. Conflict of interest."

"Whoa!" Joey snapped his fingers. I twisted. "You're giving him a ring?"

"He's not the only one. What can I say, Joe? Commitment is in the air."

Joey cursed. "Dangerous words, Klive."

"Joe, tell me when the last time I lived a safe life was."

"I don't trust him yet." Joey bypassed the part Kinsley might play in that statement. "Something's wrong with how he handles her, Klive. I know you don't want to imagine this, but he might have her working with him against you."

"I know." I waved over my shoulder, locked his door and headed home.

32 | ♀

After Klive sent me home, well, to *his* home, I did just what he said. I showered and tried not to worry that he was doing more bad things. I got out and selected a soothing cotton nightgown with simple bikini briefs. Normal me instead of sex appeal. My fingers absently traded damp tresses as I braided my hair over my shoulder and made my way into the bedroom.

"Ooh! Oh, my goodness! Oh, my goodness!" I ran to the bed and scooped a sweet, tiny, white fur baby to my chest. The kitten's fuzzy fur tickled my lips when I kissed her head and massaged her into purring. When I paused, she looked up at me with pretty blue eyes and meowed for more. I lifted her to my cheek, rubbing her fleecy softness against my face. She wore a pink, diamond-studded collar. Klive came behind me, wrapped my waist and kissed my temple.

"Oh, Klive, I *love* her!" I exclaimed. Sure, I was a huge sucker right now, but I didn't care. She was adorable and my frazzled emotions needed this!

He reached out to pet the kitten, too, and she arched against his palm.

When I set her back on the bed, a little feather fluttered, capturing her attention. I giggled as she pounced and rolled over, clawing the feather with her back paws. The bed was still an awful mess, giving the kitten plenty to play with. She wasn't shy or fearful. She was content and comfortable as though she belonged here. I relaxed. Her sixth sense wasn't nervous in the least.

"This way you don't have to watch kittens on the telly now. When I upset you, although I will work my ass off not to, you can cuddle her to soothe yourself while I'm under construction."

"Under construction, eh?"

"Did you expect me to be an expert when I've never shared my life with anyone?" He turned me in his arms.

Shared his life!

I felt fuzzy, like I had when Etta James sang her beautiful ballad as Klive danced with me on our date.

"No, Klive. I can't expect that, but I do expect better of someone who told me to grow up. Fair?"

He nodded. Extreme exhaustion, his raw honesty, the gift of the sweet kitten, my heart surrendered every defense against him. I playfully placed my ear to his chest again.

"Klive, your Grinch heart must've grown three sizes!" I jostled his arm while he chuckled at my ear as I snuggled close. A large peal of thunder slammed the house like God's fist upon us. The kitten scurried into the pillows while I jolted in Klive's arms. Klive squeezed me tightly against him as another rumble cracked the quiet like a dislodged boulder rolling across the roof. "Klive! I hate storms!"

I'd once hidden in a basement in Tennessee when visiting my grandparents. I'd never forget that tornado warning as long as I lived.

Klive pried out of my grasp as bright light lashed through the room. He yanked heavy drapes over his windows and blocked out the lightning before the next thunderbolt rocked the walls.

"Come on, love, get in bed. I'll clean the mess I made and be right back. Do you still have a meet tonight if there's bad weather?"

Good question. I checked my phone, and sure enough, I had a text from Coach Walton apologizing to me, that he knew tonight was my first time back, but the invitational was canceled due to severe weather that was supposed to last through tomorrow evening. He also warned me not to get complacent, that he'd train me extra hard if I slacked up and missed anymore meets. I smiled and texted him a quick promise to behave. When I glanced up at Klive with a shake of my head, his lips split into the warmest grin, melting my sucker's heart while he finished stuffing feathers into the pillowcase of the pillow he'd ruined. I noticed he'd already straightened the bed, too.

"Good boy!"

He snickered and ruffled the kitten's head. I answered another quick text and noticed Klive pull three feathers from the case and lay them down for the kitten to play with. He waved one as he coaxed her out of hiding with the cutest baby tone I'd never heard from him before. Ah, hell. I was a goner for that bad boy being sweet thing. This sweet bad boy rested his head on the comforter. The kitten shimmied her way into the same crook between his neck and chin that I loved.

He leaned into her fur as she arched against his chin and meowed at him. His eyes closed while she rubbed back and forth along his cheek and jawline. I scrolled to the camera on my phone and silently snapped several photos while appearing to text in case he glanced my way, but he'd opened his eyes and busied waving a feather she batted from his fingers. I laid my phone on the nightstand.

Was Klive doing a better job of getting under my skin than I was his? Was he doing so on purpose? Was the rug to be ripped from beneath my feet once I was in too deep to walk away? I loathed the idea, which made me resent Jase's orders even more. If Klive was playing me, would a pregnancy change the game? My hip sagged against the nightstand. Watching this man with this animal, I saw he could become a very attentive father if I were pregnant.

To experiment, I picked the kitten up and walked her over to the foyer where I set her down and shut the door on her. I smiled to myself when he gasped.

"Come now, love," he pleaded like a child. "You can't be serious. The poor thing will be scared," he whined — actually whined!

I beamed in amazement at watching something so little twist him so instantly around her finger. My smile turned to an O when thunder pummeled the house and vibrated the walls and vases on the night tables. I tensed and the kitten furiously meowed. Aw, poor thing!

Klive rushed to the door, opening and scooping her into his arms before walking through the library passage. I hustled on his heels. The kitchen was scary since all the curtains in the recessed den were wide open and the lightning flashed in bright strobes, silent and foreboding before the rolling thunder shook the house.

Unfazed, Klive dug through a bunch of bags on the counter. He pulled out a little bed and stuffed animal. Klive walked back toward the library like I wasn't suctioned to the wall frozen in fear. He stopped short and dipped back for a quick peck on my lips.

"Don't want that jealous streak coming out, now do we?" he teased.

I laughed while I trailed him back to the room. He set the bed down beneath the bench at the foot of the bed and put the kitten down, the stuffed cat nestled next to her. He coaxed her into lying down. Soon she curled beside the stuffed animal and fell asleep, her purr vibrating the brief seconds of silence between the storm's wrath. Klive straightened and smiled in triumph, then went to his nightstand for a tablet he lifted and tapped. The familiar piano chords of *Stay* turned up to nearly cover the thunder. Guess he could see I was wound tight.

Klive sauntered up to me and placed a hand to the small of my back while holding my hand in his other, tucking our entwined fingers between our chests. My mouth fell into a sappy smile. He was dancing with me! Klive's cheek rested upon my hair rather than my temple since I was much shorter without high heels. He swayed us softly, and I heard him humming along. Hot tears stung my eyes. I struggled to keep them from spilling. They fell anyway. Heavily. He hooked my chin and tilted my face to his intense assessment. Gone was the boyish happiness, in his place, a grown man. Older. Lawyer-like authority. His brows knit slightly like my flowing tears confused him. He didn't wipe them away. He kept swaying us, holding me tightly to him. I watched him swallow, that muscle in his jaw flinching. I think we shared the same feeling. The 'what the hell am I going to do' feeling. Fine by me. We could panic together.

He tucked my cheek to his chest and began moving us in proper steps around his room. How surreal. I giggled when he dipped me deeply and wrapped my arms around his neck when he brought himself down over me. Klive kissed my throat. His hands ran up my back as he slowly pulled me up again. His lips met mine and our mouths opened. All the while he weaved us in soft circles around the room. He smiled against my lips, then pushed me away to twirl me under his arm, surprising me. I laughed as he tugged me back to him.

Heartache took over then and I was awash with emotion at the impossibility of this situation. One-hundred-percent failure rate, right here. I traditionally held hope in most situations, and there weren't too many that made me feel quite as hopeless as I did in this hopelessly romantic moment with an unattainable man.

How I wished no one else was in the picture. That he was the lawyer he looked like. That maybe I was pregnant with that imaginary Klive's baby. That he would be an excited father, and everything could be this way. To have nights like this after putting that sweet baby to bed. To be held in arms that weren't making money shedding blood, pushing drugs and illegal firearms. *He* was so amazing.

If looking at me wasn't enough, I knew he felt me tense again. He pushed me back out to play some more, twirling me multiple times until he coaxed a grin from me. I squealed with delight when he scooped me into his arms and spun us until he dizzied and walked like a clumsy drunkard toward the bed.

"You're gonna crash! Don't drop me!" I cried through laughter. Klive stumbled sideways.

"No bloody idea what you mean. I've not been drinking, I swear. I can drive just fine." His lips split into the radiant toothy grin I loved. He dropped me onto my side of his bed. Otis Redding began *A Change is Gonna Come*. The playful air grew thick with heavy sorrow.

Gosh, how I wish! Was he trying to tell me something? First with Stay, *now with* A Change?

Kinsley Hayes how stupid are you, you damn fool? For once in your life, quit trying to analyze everything, and take it for what it is. Just some pretty music in a romantic moment.

He hopped onto his side of the bed and turned out the light. The room drenched in darkness. Thunder rumbled the bed through the floor. Klive stood upon the mattress and went to each corner, loosening the lush taffeta fabric tied back like drapes. He tugged them closed and proceeded to envelop us in a cozy cocoon.

"Damn it, Klive. Are you trying to keep me forever?" I teased, trying to lighten some.

"If that were possible, absolutely," he told me without playing. *Ouch!* A good and sad answer in one.

He crawled under the covers and pulled me against him, covering me, too. He spooned me, and his hand went to my abdomen. "There is no easy way out of my life, Kins. But you may have everything I am free to give, for as long as you like."

Oh, God! How long would he be free to give me everything I wanted? How long until he may screw up because of me distracting him? Shit! What was I doing here?

Fresh tears spilled down my cheeks, sliding from the sides of my face as I stared at the canopy. I sighed too loud. Frustrated. *What the hell is it about wanting something you can't truly have? Is that why I was feeling this way right now?*

"Kinsley, do you think that I haven't questioned my life from the moment you captured my attention?" he said at my ear. Nice. "Love, any way out puts you in so much danger that it wouldn't be worth the risk. I am under contract, sure not legally-binding, however they are kept intact by blood oath, and even fulfilled as agreed upon, they aren't easily resolved. I promised to keep you safe. That means doing the awful job you resent me for. If I don't do my job, I don't get to keep you. If I do my job, I still risk losing you. Any day could be the day that someone is sloppy, and I may not cover our asses in time. The day that someone could take me down for good.

"If there was a way, I would take it if it meant that I would have days of your beautiful smiles and nights causing your sweet moans."

I gasped on an involuntary sob. "Damn it, Klive, what has it been? Like a month or two?! What a damn fool I am! Are you seriously rethinking all your choices for a woman you met two years ago, yet only got to know weeks ago? A woman who has told you that she loves another man? A woman you can't truly have?" I wiped furiously at my cheeks as my eyes rained.

"Am I really crying over a man who reappeared after years of silence only weeks ago even though I love another? Why, because he was so taken with me that he decided I should get to live? How damn demented is that, Klive? How sick is it that I might be pregnant with that man's child now? Son of a bitch, I am good at getting myself into impossible situations lately!" I sobbed. "Did you just want to hook me, too, so that I couldn't function without you? Tease me? Enslave me?" I shut my mouth, getting a little hysterical.

I pushed away from Klive and shoved through the thick curtain and marched around the bed to tap his tablet, silencing the sound system. Thunder crashed into the room while I went and sat on the floor. I scooped the kitten to my chest, resting my head over her purring form. How blessed she was to be held and loved, no issues, no worries, just resting. I wanted that, too, but rest would not come. There was no peaceful resolution with any of the men in my life.

Klive sat next to me, a heavy sigh. "Love, you are over-emotional. Replete with exhaustion. Come to bed. Sleep. When you wake, you will be clear-headed, able to rationalize."

I nodded. He was right. I'd been awake for over twenty-four hours now. He pulled me up and put the sweet kitten back down after kissing her head. He grabbed my hand but led me to the kitchen instead of the bed and opened the fridge to pull eggs and bacon. He took me down into the soothing living room, piled pillows at one end of a cushy couch and told me to lie down as he drew the curtains. He snagged a soft blanket from an ottoman. The warm fleece draped over me and Klive turned on more music. I watched him stride up into the kitchen and mill around like he cooked every day. *Hmm ... so much for that whole, 'never having to lift a finger,' eh? What's that they say about assumptions ...?*

I nodded off to the sound of frying bacon. He roused me some time later and helped me to sit so he could set a plate of breakfast tacos on my lap. Yum! My stomach growled. I was so hungry. He extended a mug of coffee and dropped cream and sugar packets onto a tray he placed on the ottoman beside me. Two glasses of ice water sat near his cup of coffee and food.

"It's decaf. Eat, drink some water, then go back to sleep."

"Thank you, Klive. This smells and looks so delicious."

"Ditto, my sweet." He winked. I gave into a grin.

Klive grabbed his own plate from the tray and settled into the couch adjacent to mine. The music was off, and he watched TV.

"What is this? *World's Dumbest?*" I asked with a huge smile.

He returned my beam and nodded. "I am especially fond of the dumbest criminal episodes. I'm sure I needn't explain why." He took a huge bite of his taco. No manners, there!

"Where are your manners, Mr. King?" I asked in his accent. "To think, I thought I was working with a gentleman." I tsked. He laughed and took an even bigger bite, chipmunking his cheeks. I noticed the kitten curled upon a pillow beside him, leading me to speculate as to exactly whom he'd really bought this fur baby for in the first place. Someone had told me they didn't keep pets and was merciless. Perhaps someone had been lacking?

I smiled to myself as I focused on the TV. We both busted out laughing at some pathetic schmuck while Mike Trainor made fun of him.

33 | ♀

I STIRRED AT DUSK. My eyes fluttered open. A serene peace took rest seeing Klive asleep on the adjacent couch. He'd pulled a throw blanket to his chin. The kitten curled on his chest rose and fell with his quiet breaths. His left arm tucked behind his head. The other dangled off the cushion. The remote laid upside down on the floor beneath his hand. His plate sat beside mine on the large ottoman, half my burrito peeled apart, eggs and potato spilled over the ceramic dish.

Wow, did I fall asleep in the middle of eating somehow? Now, that's what I'd call exhausted!

I slid off the couch, emotions in check enough to view this adorable sight and not become bleary-eyed again. This time I simply smiled and patted the kitten as I grabbed the plates. Klive got me a kitten. Let that sink in!

However long this lasts, Lord, thank you. I'm sorry for sinning with Klive, please forgive me, but last night, well, this morning, in my heart I made love to the one whom my soul desires. I love him so much. I'd totally marry him and have his kids if he were a good man. Oh, Father, why intersect our paths if there's nothing I can do to keep him? All I can do is ask for a miracle, until then I'll do my best with what I'm given and as it comes my way. I love you, so much, too. Please hear me ...

I busied praying in my heart and mind while running hot soapy water and scrubbing the dishes. Since I wasn't sure where everything went, and I didn't want to wake Klive, I left them drying on a hand towel. I wiped his counter tops and cleaned the little messes he'd made when cooking us breakfast. The white counters gleamed under the single light over the sink as I ran my washcloth in circles and eyed the newest, extra most bestest Keurig available seated between the espresso machine and the refrigerator. This wasn't here yesterday. Did Klive buy this for me?

Hmm, did Klive use cream? Sugar? What flavors of coffee did he have, or would I find an assortment of tea instead? He was a Brit after all ....

I chugged water to earn a caffeinated cup of the coffee assortment I found among the teas in a drawer beneath the machine. Flavored creamers littered a small bin beside stir sticks and teaspoons. In his refrigerator, however, I found a white porcelain tea pot of heavy cream. A container of square sugar cubes sat between the fridge and Keurig. Coach wouldn't want me having any of those or the flavored creamer. I could have the heavy cream as a nice alternative with a dash of cinnamon and vanilla in a pumpkin spice cup of coffee. These matched the pumpkin spice K-cup Klive had attached to the three dozen lavender roses he'd sent for Valentine's Day. Something about having coffee from his house made the roses more special.

I thought of our impromptu coffee date at the beach bar and his comment about having an idea of how hard these were to get outside autumn. How long did he know exactly?

The machine hummed to life, then suctioned and spewed the water through the K-cup inside. I cringed and looked over my shoulder. *Hello! This will wake him!* The kitten's head popped into view, her little nose sniffing the air. *Crap.*

Meh, the rain poured like a waterfall over the house. Maybe Klive wouldn't wake from this? What would he want to do tonight? Ha!

You're sleeping together, Kins, what do you think he's gonna want to do?

I lifted the coffee mug and poured the heavy cream unable to help thinking of Lucy and how she was able to make such pretty designs with the cream in her customer's cups. *How did she do that? Speaking of customers, I should go to work since I missed last night.*

I sprinkled cinnamon and vanilla and gave up on the idea of a pretty design with the cream. Klive reached around me and snatched the mug. I shrieked and bumped the lower cabinets. Klive tilted a sip to his lips with a wicked gleam lighting his eyes.

"Hey! That was mine!"

He reached over my head for another mug and placed the ceramic in my hand. His coffee-warm lips kissed my cheek.

"Good evening, love. This is delicious, thank you." He walked back into the living room, settling into the soft cushions.

No shame, that one. I turned back around and made myself another cup of coffee, then walked into the living room, too. This time, I swiped the kitten from him and put her on my lap to pet her while the coffee brought me to life.

"Did you buy me a Keurig for your place?"

He smiled over the rim of his cup. "While I'd love to flatter you, I keep it put away. I switch between coffee, tea and espresso depending upon my various moods. Since you're here, I thought you might want to use it."

"That's sweet. Thank you." I loved these tiny insights into his personality.

He nodded, sipped, then a devilish glint colored his irises. "What would you like to do tonight, love?" Jolts of heat fired through my core at the dark tone of voice. "You feel like playing more dress-up? You were so good at it last time."

Yes, I sure as hell did! Instead, I opted for behaving so I didn't seem too much of a trashy slut. I battled for some semblance of myself that didn't pertain to sex.

"Actually, Klive, I think you need to take me home."

"Whaaaaat?" He immediately pouted as pathetic as he possible, which was pretty damn adorable. He cracked a smile at my razzing him and proceeded to beg me to stay longer.

"Klive, I need to go to work. I *want* to. I need some normalcy. Plus, Saturday nights are my best for tips."

"Tips? Really, love? You're going to leave the sanctity of my lair to shamelessly flirt and make that money over making me please you, eh?"

"Ha! Behave. And, it worked with you, didn't it?" I winked with a wry smile. "Come on, no arguments, I am going. I need you to take me home."

"All right, I guess I'd better go get dressed down to buy some ladies some drinks since this one doesn't want me anymore," he said in mock sadness.

"Sounds good to me," I sang and hopped off the couch, making my way into his room. I walked into the closet and grabbed some panties and a bra, but he slapped them from my hands.

"This is my field of expertise. If you're keen to torture me tonight, I may as well know what you're working with beneath that skimpy uniform."

My hands found my hips when he pulled a pair of sexy black panties and an even sexier black Bombshell from the drawer.

"Klive! Have you lost your mind? I can't wear this under that skin-tight shirt! Do you know how many drunks will be pawing all over me?!"

He nodded and told me to put them on, no arguments.

"So, if I am going to work, you are going to punish me the whole time, is that what this is?" I asked, unable to hide an incredulous smile.

"Unless you'd rather stay here and wear it for me before I peel it off with my teeth," he told me salaciously, eyes darkening while I took a deep breath. *Restrain yourself, woman! Your body will do what the mind tells it! Tell it no!*

I firmly shook my head against his sexy invitation.

"Such a shame. Suit yourself. Your boyfriends have likely missed you, and I'll have a blast watching them fall all over you, too."

By eight, I punched the time clock buttons on the register behind the bar. Marcus marched around the corner from his office. "Damn, Kins, I thought that was you on the monitor. What's gotten into you? The bold shit from last night? Coming to work just to be nice?"

I grinned and stood on tippy toes to kiss his cheek.

"Being affectionate. Look at your rack, for goodness sakes!" he exclaimed. "This King's affect?"

"Marcus! He may be magic in some ways, but he can't make boobs grow overnight." I snickered to myself. "Behave, you are my manager." I reminded him about that sexual harassment in the workplace seminar he'd forced us to snooze through last year.

"I'll take that as confirmation on King."

I smiled to myself as I rolled my eyes, though he was right.

The place was jammed tonight. Bayleigh hustled through orders and glanced over to thank me, then her eyes nearly popped out of her head. When I turned to pour drafts, she walked up behind me and grabbed a boob!

"Bayleigh! What the hell?!" I gaped.

"Sorry, Kins, I had to know! Is that one of those bras that adds cup sizes?" I nodded and continued to work.

"Two to be precise." Yup, punishment sucked. Right now, I rocked DD bazookas on a tiny frame.

"Looks like the little teapot about to tip over," she joked. "Do you have insecurities about your rack? I mean your boobs are stacked for an athlete already!" she told me, trying to boost a self-esteem issue I didn't have.

"Bayleigh, I am being punished for leaving a certain gentleman's bed," I admitted.

"Kinsley Hayes, shut the front freakin' door! No way!" She beamed.

I passed the ordered drafts across the bar while men stared and threw extra money down for me to keep. I pretended not to notice they hardly saw my face, even though I'd done my makeup extra pretty tonight. Pathetic what boobs will do, huh?

"Have you seen The Punisher yet?" I asked.

"Who? Jase? He and Mel were talking to some guy that's starting a label or something. He's around here somewhere."

"Uh, no, not Jase." Though I looked all around myself to watch my mouth before clarifying. "Moonlight. As in Complicated."

"Oh, damn." She halted to drape herself against the liquor counter. "Are you serious? I'd love to be punished by him. Why would you ever leave *his* bed? You'd better fess to how you landed there, too!"

I poured shots and pulled tops off beers. Garrett came in from break and took a double take. Bayleigh snorted and booty bumped my hip.

"Dude, he knows there's no way that these are mine!" I said at her ear.

"Well, if I wasn't sure and had to touch them, how do you think your assistant manager is feeling?" She winked and called drinks he helped with. "I haven't seen Complicated Moonlight yet!" she yelled over the music. "How did you get here?"

"He brought me but had to park. Guess he's having guy time out in the parking lot."

"Or someone's getting a handy because you left him."

I popped her ass with a rolled towel. She winced but growled like I turned her on.

"What about your uniform?"

"Locker."

"Figures the prude is the only one brave enough to change in a public locker room."

Over the next hour, I subconsciously pulled my shirt up over my ridiculous cleavage and replayed how fun whipping Klive's ass with his own belt had been. Klive was absolutely begging for another ass whippin' with this stupid stunt.

"Kamikaze, baby!" Unexpected butterflies fluttered through my belly at Jase being so much like before we'd ever crossed the romantic line beyond friendship. I beamed before I turned around with the Kamikaze ingredients in the shaker. Jase had the *te-he* dumbstruck jaw drop. "Kiss my grits, woman. What have you done to the tatas?"

Marcus called a warning that Jase behave, but Jase gestured toward my breasts and gaped. Marcus and I both puzzled for the same reason. Jase seemed affronted rather than attracted.

"I'm waiting on an answer," Jase said, eyebrow up.

"Oh, really? If a woman wants to exercise her need to feel sexy, should she be judged for it?" I tossed his words from the beach in his face while trying to keep mine from cracking a huge smile.

"Did King make you feel you weren't sexy the way God made you? I figured he was such a sick puppy he'd settle for a handful and his hand in the shower if you let him cop a feel."

"Jase Michael Taylor! You kiss your mama with that mouth?"

"I kissed you with this mouth and you weren't complainin' too long ago. As it happens, I've been working on my mouth since Sunday now that I know what my mouth can do, thank you very much."

"You sound like you've spent a lot of time around Hickleberry. You're adopting his country."

Jase grinned and rolled his eyes. "Hickleberry instead of Huckleberry? Cute. Ya gonna tell me why your boobs are up to your chin tonight and way too big for your body? I hope you're not throwing your self-esteem away on Klive with this."

"Nah, I thew it away on you."

"Ooh." He winced. "Wouldn't sting so bad if I didn't deserve it."

"Amen on that," Rustin chimed in and took the stool beside Jase. He swirled whiskey in a plastic cup and nodded at my package. "There's much to be said, but now I seem at a loss for words, Mizz Hayes. I'll settle for sayin' you're looking pretty tonight. Tips pouring in?"

I cackled and made him another round without him asking and slid Jase's drink across with Rustin's. Jase told me I did look very pretty, but that he'd always been a sucker for my natural state. I was so happy to feel normal around Jase again, I overlooked him implying my *au natural* state soon after and settled for laughing with Rustin. The insecurity and nagging jealousy plaguing me where he was concerned was nowhere to be found! I had no idea how to fathom this.

"To answer your question, no I don't have a self-esteem issue, and Klive is only good at boosting my ego, thank you. He felt you and Rustin would have something nice to look at while I worked if I wore this. You are playing right into his hands, love!" I finished in my British accent. I traded between making drinks and coming back to talk to them. "I think since he didn't take you guys to the strip club last night, he's dressing me up to drive you mad!" I yelled over the music.

"Well, I applaud his strategy, though I'd rather watch *you* strip," Jase said.

"Jase! Behave. Look at all these liquored up horn-balls around you staring at my rack! You are going to make things ten times worse for me if you keep openly talking like that! They will think it's an invitation!" I yelled. "What did y'all do last night, boys?" I waggled my brows. In truth, somehow, I wasn't feeling jealous at the thought of Jase hooking-up with someone. This must've been what Klive had talked about. Dating as a version of foreplay. The heavy felt gone for the moment.

Rustin copped to having a kinky *ménage* for his birthday, sans Jase, so no worries. I raised my eyebrows, asking if that was true. Jase nodded.

"Don't worry, Jase only watched," Rustin said wickedly. "No touching at all."

"Rustin! Are you serious?!" I asked. Again, somehow, I wasn't bothered. I was more impressed Rustin could handle having his hands so full, though I'd never admit to such.

I turned to Jase and raised my eyebrows expectantly, a smirk playing on my face. He looked pleasantly surprised. "No touching! Not sure there were really two women with him or if that was my blurred vision. Could've sworn he had another guy in there, but he insists it was only him. Likely story, doesn't want me thinking he was unfaithful to me in any way."

I busted out laughing and tugged Jase's chin to plant a sweet kiss of gratitude to his cheek. He gave me a fond smile of understanding.

"Hey, now. I thought *he* would be the one pawing all over *you*, my sweet, not the other way around." Klive grinned when he made his way over to us. Rather than remain the gentleman as was his custom in public, Klive cupped my cheek and leaned across the bar to kiss the hell out of me. So long propriety, hello PDA! Should I feel guilty for enjoying this with Jase right here? I mean, *he* was the one who wanted me to be involved with Klive, wasn't he?

Marcus didn't utter a single word. Jase quipped, "Marcus! Come on, man! That's not fair!"

Klive's laugh hummed through my lips that spread with delight. Affection behind closed doors was one thing. Klive claiming me in public after what we'd shared, what we'd done, this was like a wax seal on written promises folded between sheets of paper never to be broken.

"Marcus is going to label me a bad influence on you," Klive said, nipped my lips again.

"I agree with him." I sighed like a smitten fool and nudged his nose for another kiss.

"Told you we should've stayed home, love."

I waved my finger in mock disapproval and turned to serve several patrons. The guys goofed with one another like good friends. Bayleigh shot me a scandalous smile and craved to know every dirty detail where TDH was concerned. I quietly spilled brief secrets to her as we danced while we made drinks. I caught a patron settling upon a free stool sending Klive a flirty smile as I delivered a Hole-in-One for a regular. She chatted with two of her friends and asked Jase about his next performance, whether Rustin was gonna sing or play guitar, but asked about their new friend with eyes hungry for fresh meat. Jase and Rustin shared a worried side-eye.

"He's gay," I said and placed a Hurricane in front of her, pointing down the way like the guy on the end had bought her a drink.

She pouted at me. "The hottest ones always are. So hard to find straight men who dress well."

I cupped my chin in my hand, rested my elbow on the bar and nodded at her. "I know. Such a shame."

Jase and Rustin almost made me break character in the background. Klive smirked and shook his head, but leaned between us to ask her on the down low, "Is Jase straight or gay? And do you know if he's with anyone right now?"

Jase pursed his lips and averted his eyes to the stage area like he hadn't heard. Rustin busied with his best silent laughter behind her back. Klive had an excellent hold on his role play. Mmm ... role play with Klive ....

"Well, Jase is straight, but his guitar player might swing your way," she told Klive. Jase's fist covered his grin as he fought laughter. "Jase is with someone. A bartender. One of them might know her," she finished telling Klive.

"Thank you. I'll be sure to ask." Klive gave her a polite smile when she walked toward the dance floor with her friends. His sexy narrowed eyes landed on me. "You are in so much trouble."

"But I'm already being punished," I flirted.

Klive tsked. "Well, I've places to be. Here are the keys to my Tesla if you'd like them." He dangled the key from his middle finger. "Or Jarrell can offer you a ride to your place when you get off work."

"You're leaving? What place do you have to be?" I slowly took his key, examining his expression.

"I am taking your boyfriends for their rain check." My jaw fell as I gaped, angry, claws out. "Relax, love. You're free to join if you'd like. Who knows, maybe you can learn some new moves to add to that stellar repertoire of yours." He hooked my chin and tipped my jaw shut, playing his thumb over my bottom lip as he teased me. "Bayleigh, my dear, please get Kinsley a shot of rum?"

Rum drove straight to my southern border. Was that normal for everyone? How did he know?

She set the glass down in front of me. He thanked her and kissed her hand, giving her the smile he reserved for thigh-clenching torment. Klive threw a hefty tip onto the bar. Her jaw dropped as she gaped at him in stunned shock. He tipped her chin the way he did mine. I inhaled sharply right along with her, but for different reason. She was ready to take him right on the bar! For good reason, that asshole!

I narrowed my eyes at him as I fisted my hands on my hips.

"Easy, love, 'tis only you." He kissed my lips then stood at his full height to look down at me in that domineering way I hated loving. He arched an authoritative eyebrow. "Now, I am going to stoke appetites. Although —" He paused and ran his fingertip down over the tops of my breasts. "— *I* am already starving." I couldn't breathe, I was so angry and jealous ... and ... and ... *grrr*!!!

A slew of French expletives flew from my mouth to his face. He cracked up.

"Such a foul mouth, my sweet. Ready, boys?" Jase and Rustin stood behind him. Rustin's eyes loaded with mischief. Jase shoved his hands in his pockets and shifted from one foot to the other. I cursed them in French, too, and they both lit up and thanked Klive. "Don't mention it. Now let's go." He turned back to my spitting mad expression, smiling smugly. "I will text you the name of the club if you decide to join us. I so hope you will." He brushed his finger across my jaw. "To think, this would've been avoided had I someone at home to keep me in line."

He yanked his hand away from my face, pretending I might bite, then winked at Bayleigh.

"Holy hell, Kinsley. I bet if Garrett comes over here, he'll notice the scent of bitches in heat!"

I shook my head in disapproval. We giggled when Garrett came near to grab some vodka. He arched an eyebrow in question as we both stared to see if she was right. When he turned with a confused shake of his head, we gave each other knuckles. I sighed and looked at her. "Bayleigh, what the hell do I wear to a skanky strip club that won't be outdone by a bunch of whores dancing naked in front of my men?" I asked bitterly.

34 | ♀

BAYLEIGH'S TIPS AND IDEAS wafted through one ear and out the other while I chewed my lower lip in calculation. How to handle this? Quite frankly, Klive seemed to be in boundary-testing mode. My biggest mistake with Jase was making those too flexible. What good was a barbed fence if you stepped on the rusted wire so someone could climb over? I glanced at Marcus. His toothpick churned circles as he studied me. His eyebrows rose while his head tipped the direction of the back employee door.

Thirty minutes later, I waved bye to the group of women who'd left the bar at the same time as I'd needed a ride home. Marcus could give Klive his keys. I wasn't playing with men who relished the bodies of others before coming home to me. Tell me I'm beautiful, valuable, worthy whatever bullshit, then look at women who were what? Less somehow?

The whole idea of Klive defiling himself that way after the high standards he'd trained me to expect repulsed me. So did thinking of Sara inside one of those clubs dancing for Inferno and their ilk. Dancing for Klive, one man whom I had a deep-rooted, heart-felt connection with was emotionally charged and fun; an activity for us to enjoy like a game. How could that be fun without the heart and soul behind the act?

Ah, and therein sat the crux of men and women. I ought to know better. Men equaled visual. Women, emotional, cerebral. But Klive was cerebral too, dammit! Right?

"Screw this shit!" I bitched at my full-length reflection as I trudged down the hallway toward my room. "Screw this stupid bra, these dumb panties, the moronic love games!"

Like a bulb in the dark, my thoughts glowed above my head. *Chad!* He hadn't been tonight's deejay. Maybe this was a day off?

Me: Hey, u busy? I texted.

C: Just finished adjusting my tie. Why? I grinned at the photo he sent.

Me: How very Pitbull you look tonight.

C: I was going for Dick Tracy, but I'll take it.

Me: Who?

C: You have the world in your palm. So disappointed. Themed night at my favorite speakeasy. Care to join?

Me: Speakeasy? I don't think I've heard that word outside of a book. I'd love to join. Addy? Time?

Chad texted the address and info while I did an internet search for *Dick Tracy*. My own closet didn't have the clothing for this, but I knew of one dress in particular my mother had in hers, petticoat and all, and I didn't think she'd mind me borrowing the frock for this. As I dressed, I wondered how did so many of my friends have such cool hobbies and know of these special interests while I had no clue? Even Klive clearly had a thing for *Gasparilla* and any festival he might wear his pirate costume at. The closest thing I'd ever come to cosplay outside the Renaissance Festival we'd attended was a murder mystery dinner Julie begged me to attend for theater points last year. Wonder if she knew Chad ... might be a good match ....

One red vintage dress and head-full of classic curls later, I locked my parents' house and clicked my shiny black pumps across the sidewalk to my own car.

Before I left the driveway, I sent the guys a group text. *I won't be needing directions or the name for your skanky club. I have a date at a speakeasy with my favorite deejay! Too bad I don't have a boyfriend to keep me from going out with other men, isn't it? =D have fun boys! I know I will! ;P*

There. Let them have fun. I wasn't serving dinner to go with any of their appetizers, that's for damn sure.

Lightning flashed in the distance. The storms would intensify later, but for now the sky over me was clear.

Tonight, I'd clink glasses with a sexy Aussie and pray dancing was allowed at this party, because Chad knew how to dance without any dirty and all flirty.

· · · · • · • · · ·

I arrived sharply at the time we'd agreed upon. Chad waited outside with a cigar, of all things, in his hand. He whistled as he held his arms open at my appearance. I smiled, though admitted to feeling very fish out of water, poser-ish.

"You did your research. I'm impressed and dare I say flattered that you'd choose to come as Tess Trueheart."

"Ha! Don't let that go to your head. Since when do you smoke cigars?"

"I'm a social cigar smoker, but most of the time, I like having an unlit one in my mouth or between my fingers for effect." He winked and waved the unlit cigar. "You are stunningly beautiful, *Kinsley*."

"Aw, Chad, thank you. You're pretty stunning yourself, sir."

"Well, thank you, darl." He held his arm open for me to hold. I accepted his offering and how he appreciated this dress. "What do you say we get you in there and make those pretty skirts fly?"

"Buy me a drink first? To loosen my nerves. I'm so out of my element. If anything, I will be content watching you make other dancers' skirts fly so you won't miss out."

"Nonsense! I've observed the dance floors you've graced with the Latins. You've advanced ballroom. You're good at the fast Salsa steps. I have no doubt you'll catch on, but I'll go easy on you at first." He opened the door smack during the chorus of *Jailhouse Rock*. The upbeat music accompanied several dancers twisting and swirling skirts on a glossy checkered floor.

Chad held my hand behind him as we shifted between bodies and groups like the ones I worked through on busy nights at the bar, but these patrons looked like the cast of *Grease* ran right off the stage and joined those from *The Great Gatsby*. I saw more super short skirts with little ruffles than long ones like my June Cleaver dress. Their hair curled high and tight on their heads or in long wavy ponytails while mine hung long and loose with one side pinned behind my temple. At least most of us had red lips and high heels. I noted some tap shoes and Mary Janes while watching the floor to avoid toes.

Chad greeted everyone we passed. I blushed when he was complimented on his Tess.

"Should I call you Dick?" I joked at Chad's shoulder. He wrapped my arm around his belly so I had to follow against his back. I giggled when he smiled over his shoulder.

"What's your pleasure?" the bartender donning a black bowler on his head asked.

"Shirley Temple?" I asked Chad and lifted my shoulder. He ignored my cutesy shrug, though his lips twitched.

"Seven and Seven for both of us, please." He turned to me. "No guff about whiskey. You can handle it."

When he passed me my glass, I used the stir stick as a sippy straw. He twisted me on my stool and stood against my back, head over my shoulder, cheek next to mine. "See what she's doing?" He pointed at a woman wearing a short dress with cute bloomers flashing every time she turned on her toes. Her partner wore cuffed jeans and a white pocket tee. Hmm, Jase might look sexy sitting here in his blue's performance gear, cigarette tucked behind his ear, small bit of hair fallen loose from the slicked-back strands.

"See her footwork? If you can dance with that redneck at the bar, you can do these cradles and turns."

"Rustin?"

"Meh. There were a lot of rednecks on Valentine's Day."

When I said, "Country nights," he said the same over my own voice, little nod.

"I know."

"Chad, if you say swing is similar to country, how do you hate country dancing so much?" He shrugged. I glanced at his eyes; our faces too close for friends. "If I do this, you have to come to the bar on a Country night and pull these East Coast Swing moves there."

"We talking off-time, or will you be working?" he asked.

We watched the couples leave the floor who didn't want to slow dance when the music changed. People parted for their tables and groups, yanking drinks to their lips. The male with the cuffed jeans aimed our way. I figured he headed for the stool behind us or something.

He stopped in front of me, offered his hand. "Tired of watching?"

"Oh, no thanks. I am trying to memorize the steps."

"I teach outside this establishment if you're interested." He produced a business card from his shirt pocket. I took his card. Bernard.

"Thanks for the card, Bernard. No rhyme intended," I joked. He laughed. "Do you dance to country as well?" I asked.

Chad's fingers pinched my waist. "Beat it, Bernie. She's here with me. Poach customers somewhere else."

"I love country dancing," Bernard said. "Where do you go?"

I told him the name of the bar. "I work there, but I'm off Wednesdays. Country night. I invited Chad, but he hates country dancing."

"I might see you there sometime!" Bernard called after us when Chad yanked me from my stool toward the dance floor. I chuckled the whole way. He twirled me under his arm and cradled me in a surprise dip. My brightest smile glowed with unconcealed mischief seeing Chad's feathers ruffled.

"You win," Chad said, "but I don't want to be left dancing with a bunch of backwoods bumpkins while you serve shots. Deal?"

"Chaddy Cake! What a snob you are!" I teased. He pulled me from the dip and took the same form as we'd slow-danced to at the club before my fight.

Like he thought of the same, he asked, "How is your recovery? Does it hurt if I bend you certain ways after your fight?"

"I'm good. Even if it hurts, I welcome the challenge."

Thank goodness he shifted to lighter topics and settled for playing with me rather than giving me a hard time. Three Seven and Sevens, nine songs, four partners, one stitch in my side, a blister forming on the back of one of my ankles and a very smiley Chad later, we clinked glasses and I laughed with his friends and flexed freely in his arms with the ways he'd turn, dip, twist or even toss me to the fun music. He faltered in his footwork and caught me when I slipped. Thank goodness he appeared to perform another swing move so we weren't embarrassed.

"What happened? Chad, is everything all right?" I asked, confused. He spun me three fast times beneath his arms and faced me away to hoist me in the air. I gasped with the momentary overhead view. *Rustin!*

"Did you see?" Chad asked when he turned me toward him again. Our feet trotted to the fast music, but our faces shared the same shock.

"Yeah! I swear I didn't tell anyone where I was going. No way this is coincidence!"

He nodded his agreement. "Guess you were right about redneck dancing and swing," he grumbled near my ear. "He's good at this. The girl is Bernard's business partner. She's an instructor and he's forcing her advanced work." He sighed.

"Chad, will you please stay my date?"

He smiled at the people next to us and looked back at me. "If I barely let Bernard teach you new moves, you think I'd relinquish you to the redneck? Hell, I want to come on Country night to torment him all over again."

"Gimme a break. He's real torn up," I joked.

"He's having fun, but he's shifting closer to cut in. I promise you."

"So, let's sip some more Seven."

"I'll drink to that." Chad danced us toward the edge of the floor. Rustin nodded like we shared no connection. I almost glared but bumped into Chad's back when he stopped short. "He's brought an entourage."

Jase and Klive. Fabulous. Klive snickered at something Jase said. Indeed, Mr. Player Taylor looked the part I'd imagined. Klive appeared the mobster in a pinstripe suit and matching fedora. The spies had gathered enough intelligence to dress the part.

"Well, Kinsley, this is where we part. I can't compete with that."

"Can't? Or won't?"

"Do you want me to? Isn't he kinda your guy?"

"I'm sorry," I said to him. "I shouldn't have put it that way. No, don't compete. We're just friends."

"You two or us?"

"Us, Chad." I tilted my head. "Even if I were here with Bayleigh, I'd be annoyed at the party crashers."

"Good to know."

"Are you mad at me?" I gazed up into his face.

Chad's tension melted into an endearing softness. "I swear. Is there anyone who can hold their own under that expression? No wonder King is afraid of losing you. The irony of the whole story is unbelievable. I'd have never seen this coming."

"Story? Are you writing about me?"

"No, Kinsley. Never mind. Care to get out of here or would you rather we head to the bar and sit with them?"

Chad's friends gathered to the side at a different area than the guys. I pointed at them. Chad nodded. I squeezed between the group and hid as best I could my inspection of Klive and Jase. Klive sat with the air of a mobster, too. A woman approached. Jase shook his head. Klive did nothing because I realized he didn't have to when he had someone else doing the dirty work. Interesting. As if he sensed me watching, his head swiveled my way. His eyes held mine and I couldn't help wearing the sad plea for him not to be some pervert watching naked women on a pole. I jumped out of my skin when Rustin's voice at my back asked Chad if he could have a dance with his date.

"Best behavior?" Chad asked.

"I promise."

I rounded and found Rustin's kind eyes asking my permission. After I snagged permission from Chad out of respect, I took Rustin's invitation to the floor.

"Mizz Hayes, you look very *Mad Men*! You're gorgeous this way. Flushed cheeks, hair a bit wispy and stuck to your face." I didn't want to smile when I was upset with them. "This come from that infamous closet I've heard so much about?"

One eye bugged, the other narrowed. "Does Jase keep nothing between us?" I muttered not thinking of how even *I* was shared with Rustin.

"Easy now. Be nice."

"Really, Rustin? You crash my date and tell me to be nice? No, this came from my mother's closet. I didn't take Klive's car. I hitched a ride with regulars. Women — don't worry since y'all can't handle me hanging with other men, apparently. What happened to the strip club?"

He laughed like I wasn't ready to rip his ass a new one. "I think your deejay is playing with the tracks again."

Dion sang about *Donna the Prima Donna.*

"Maybe you read too much into coincidences. Glad to know what you think of me, though."

"Does it really bother you having the love and loyalty of those around you? Offended, are you?"

"Love and loyalty? Is that what y'all call going to the strip club to stoke your appetites like I'm not enough?" I followed Rustin's lead without a second thought.

"We put Klive up to pranking you after his pathetic ass kept whining about some bloody female choosing work over his company." Smug satisfaction lit his radiant face while dawning dropped my jaw. "No harm to the messenger. You have that man in so many knots. As much as Jase hates to allow it, he is both entertained and sympathetic. Pretty sure he is starting his own support group, happy to have members to recruit. Klive could be the VP. Looks like the deejay should have an invitation."

"Rustin, I'm not playing jealous games. Chad is my friend."

"So am I."

"I swear, if anyone should be in knots, it's your balls before I castrate you."

"Mmm ... hurts so good. Klive's tangled hard with the rest of us in your intricate yet simple web. Whose blood are you going to drain first, honey?"

"I beg to differ. You all toss me like a ball on the beach, so I don't want to hear it. Back to the matter at hand. You were all screwing with me? No strip club?"

"You walked right into it. Did you really not know?" he asked me. "We were planning to hang at Jase's until you sent that text."

"Really?"

"True story. Don't you remember Jase telling you Klive didn't want to ruin things with you?" He spun me twice. "I like the way this dress looks when you turn," he said. "Fans nearly in a perfect circle if I get you going fast enough." I smiled as he twirled me once more for fun. "Yeah, well, don't say anything, but I haven't seen pigs in a greased contest slip and slide as fast in panic. One mention of *Moves Like Jagger* over there, they raced to change. Can you believe Klive's vain enough to keep a spare suit in his Rover?" Oh, Rustin, thank you for this info! He shifted us with ease around the floor, but I couldn't help noting he held and watched me the same as he held his precious guitar. "Did you think he wanted to piss you off for some reason? Trouble in paradise?" Rustin interrupted my observation.

"Not at all. Quite the contrary." I melted like a Klive-crazy fool on purpose. "Klive surprised me with a kitten." Okay, I wasn't as vindictive as I'd have wished to be.

"A *kitten*? Smooth." He pushed and pulled me, swiveled with the song. I matched his silly play. "Come to Country night with me on Wednesday," he said.

"Sorry, you'll have to bring the dance instructor you were with. I promised her partner a country night first."

Rustin chuffed.

"Oh!" I tapped my lips while my heels jumped all over the place. "Chad's in line ahead of him, so that makes you third in line. Need a pager?"

He tugged me into his arms and dipped us side to side till I giggled. "What am I gonna do with you?"

"Not what you've done in the past, that's for damn sure." I shimmied my shoulders forward and back then we clapped like the others around us with parts of the song that played.

"You were so good at it, though." Rustin cruised for a bruise.

"The threesome? Real or fake?" I asked, our palms pressing like we washed a window between us. Before we pushed off each other to turn in a circle, he looked nervous I might claw his eyes out. "Real, then," I observed, raised my eyebrows, scooped the opposite direction as Rustin. Our hands joined again. He turned under my arms, then me under his like a figure eight. "You're a very dirty man, Rustin. I never stood a chance against you and Jase. He really didn't participate?" I prodded into dangerous territory.

Rustin shook his head. "Nah, they offered for him to lie back and relax, but he really was way too drunk. Now, had he not been, I can't say if he would have or not, though I'd like to think he learned a lesson since your fight. Had to spell it out for him that you were still in pain. Don't deny that's why you've hooked your nails into Klive's back." I spun away from Rustin. He didn't touch me while we performed the same dance steps in unison with the rest around us. Rustin bent forward. "You finally gave him a chance to be sweet to you because your douche bag asshole of a boyfriend hurt you. He refused all favors."

I hated spinning back to face him, joining hands for the double overhead when I'd rather he cuddle me to the side or something to avoid eye-contact with such vulnerable conversation.

"He's sorry, Kinsley. Those women were smokin' and so willing, but it was like I was babysitting or something. We got a room.

Another reason he had to watch. He had no choice because I was his designated driver." Rustin waggled his eyebrows and resumed a jitterbug. I rolled my eyes and caught Klive and Jase talking to Chad. My eyes flared at Chad. He tipped his hat, smoothed his tie and sent the devilish gaze reserved for pissing in Jase's Cheerios as he strode right up to me. He stole me out of a spin from Rustin's hands. I squealed and kicked a leg high as Chad wrapped his arms around my waist and made my hair touch the floor.

"All finished with your business? I have a surprise for you."

"I'm so finished, yes. What's the surprise?" I asked and grabbed his shoulders for stability as my head swam for a second when he lifted me.

"The next song. After that, let's get something in your stomach. Good?"

"Yes. I'd love that. Without our spies, please?"

"Agreed."

Christina Aguilera's *Candyman* began, and I beamed up at Chad. "I requested this one just for you, darl," he bragged. Yes, Chad knew what I liked after all the years of doing the gig at the bar. "You ready for this, Kins? We're gonna put Rustin's basic Jitterbug to shame. Stay flexible and relaxed for me."

"Psh! Work me over in front of the date crashers like you won't have another chance, Chaddy Cake!"

"Hell yes!" He backed up and made room by moon walking, out of genre, his shoulders rolling before he cleared a circle through break dancing, pulling the Polly Pocket, then yanking my clapping hands and forcing us all over the floor. Thank God I was in shape, or else I would have been gasping for air. The more I flexed with him, the more daring he became in the way he lifted or tossed me. All I knew was my belly tickled and dipped and I giggled until snorting like a little girl, I was having such a blast. "This is how you should always smile!" He caught me and swung me beneath his parted legs, so I slid on my dress across the slick floor. He straddled his feet over my waist, twisted his hands and plucked me off the floor.

"No more! I need water and oxygen!" I wrapped my arms around his neck and squeezed my eyes closed when he spun us in too many circles. The tighter I held, the more I thought of Klive playing with me this morning in his room. Chad patted my back as he slowed, then held me still as my head swam.

"Don't throw up. That's an order," Chad said.

"Don't talk about throwing up or make me dizzy and I won't."

"You did a great job. You're so much fun to toss." Chad hugged me to his shoulder and thanked someone for their cold glass. A second later I winced when he touched the icy glass to my cheek.

Klive's eyes. I sensed them through the crowd, felt my gravitational pull to his sun, even if his eyes were the color of the scariest storms.

"Ready for a change of scenery, darl?"

"You bet."

35 | ♀

Chad, who'd used a ride-share to get to the speakeasy, buckled himself into the passenger seat of my car and suggested we eat at one of the bazillion Waffle Houses in the area. No need to worry about libation, propriety, or pretty bites, yes please! We slid into a booth opposite each other. He ordered an All-Star Special with grits.

"Ooh, that sounds yummy, but hash-browns with mine, please," I told the server.

Chad waited for her to busy behind the counter, then raised his eyebrows at me. "That's a lot of food for such a petite woman."

"Runners have to eat. Coach Walton's been training me again. Today was supposed to be my first time back on the track for races, but the weather had other plans."

"Back on the track again, eh? I hate the rumors about how you're still on the team, but I know Walton's a good man. Neither of you deserve the stupidity."

My brows creased. Chad sighed and scrubbed his face with the palms of his hands. I pulled his hands from his face. "Let me guess. Am I sleeping with him now even though last month I was a lesbian?"

"Bi-sexual Bible thumper, remember?"

I snorted bitterly. Sad that even Chad knew what was said behind my back.

"Those things are contradictory from what I know of Christianity."

"Yeah, well, so is beating your enemy's ass over loving them. Along with my bad mouth and other recent deeds. If I'm such a hypocrite, why not label me a contradiction or speculate that I'm bangin' my trainer?"

"Don't worry, you're not sleeping with him, you're on your knees for Walton because the track manager can't contain her jealousy over your apparent affiliation with a certain gentleman."

"Fabulous." I paused my sarcasm for a genuine smile at the server when she delivered our food with super speed. "Guess this is the great part about being the only ones here."

She smiled, nodded and asked if there was anything more she could bring. Chad asked for extra napkins and lemon for his tea. After she accommodated him, I asked, "Lucy?"

"Who else? I can't figure if she's in love with you or with King, though I'm not certain how she knows him outside of articles I've written. Have you ever read my work?"

"She works in the building my father does. Barista at the coffee shop. Coincidentally, Mr. King works there too. Not with my father, but in the building, and no, I've never read. I stay away from all online content as well as newspapers. My father's always muttering about the miserable news and politics. Bad flavor in my mouth."

"Ah, the ol' head in the sand approach to life."

"Chad, you should eat, so you'll stop talking." I cut into my waffle after using all my butter.

He cut into his as well, chewed through his chuckle. "No syrup?"

"Nope." I nipped the food from my fork.

"No sugar. Is this how you eat like a fat man and look like a fitness model?"

"That and an average of twenty long-distance miles per week, plus weight training and sprints. Amazing I have time for fellatio, though I've heard swallowing helps block fat."

Chad chortled through chewing, then outright laughed when he'd downed his food. "Such vulgarity from your sweet mouth. I'm impressed."

"With my vulgarity?"

Again, he laughed. "With your athleticism. I'd be miserable running one-hundred meters, let alone kilometers to stay in shape."

"Coach hates when I run long-distance. He'd rather I condition only certain muscles, but I need the long jogs for sanity."

"Runner's high?"

I nodded through another bite. "Enough about me. I want to know about you."

He filled me in on his being born in India, their move to Australia when he was small, his parents sending him to America for his education. "They're doctors. I was to become one as well, initially up North, but I hate blood. I'm a disappointment to them."

"How'd you end up down here in Florida?"

"Ever hear of amateur sleuths?"

I tilted my head and grinned.

He nodded. "I was a big gamer, then stumbled upon one of those groups who looks into cold cases, and I became addicted to the real-life game. I followed the clues down here and helped police solve a thirty-four-year-old missing persons case. The lead detective asked if I was an investigative journalist. When I said no, he suggested I had the makings of a great one. I stayed because of the climate, changed my major, transferred credits and now I'm on the cusp of graduating with an advanced degree in Journalism. Who knows? Maybe I'll be on TV one day and show my parents I made it to the big time."

"Chad, that's amazing! What was it like bringing resolution to that case?"

I listened over the course of our meal and found myself with few bites left on my plate and my chin in my palm as I held to the extended story of a kidnapped girl from Iowa ending up in Tampa.

"Bittersweet, because part of you prays you'll find them with a new identity, a couple kids and a husband, happy life. Then you uncover she was murdered at the age of ten and realize life is truly ugly outside the walls we've built around ourselves."

"That's so sad. Did she have family looking for her still?"

He nodded. "Her mother was in her sixties when I showed up at her door beside the detective. Can you believe he was only going to call her on the phone?" Chad shook his head, disgusted. "I paid for us both to get on the plane with part of my grant money for school."

"Oh, Chad, you're a good person." I placed my hand over his. He peeled at the corner of a napkin and stared at the table.

"So are you." He met my eyes with a deeper expression than I'd ever seen. "So, Klive King ...."

My cheeks heated like Chad could read Klive's signature on my heart.

He whistled. "You two meet in the coffee shop?"

"Coffee shop?"

"Your father's building. Lucy the barista ...?"

"Oh!" I laughed nervously, shook my head. "No." Alarm bells warned me not to give Chad the real story. "He came into the bar, shamelessly flirted with me, bought me a drink. Nothing different from anyone else."

"Shamelessly flirted? That's uncharacteristic. I think there's more. If he's no different, how come you are so ... pink? Is it his status?" My eyes shot to his in a bit of confusion and offended surprise.

"Status? I'm not sure what you mean, Chad. Klive is sweet, he's come to my defense on different occasions."

"Like your fight with the beauty queen?"

I swallowed. "Yes, but he's friends with Jase. Since I've been hanging out with Jase so much, our paths couldn't help but to keep crossing," I told him and tried not to overreact.

"Jase has friends in high places. That guy, he's particular about the company he keeps." Was there a double meaning to that? Or was I too sensitive about Nightshade? I shrugged as though I didn't know either way, which I really didn't know much about Klive's company. "Jase is cool with his girlfriend adding another man to the group?"

"The *group*?!"

"A blind man could see Rustin Keane's attraction to you. He couldn't wait to get you out of my arms on the dance floor tonight. Jase allows this and now King, too? The three of them together like they all belong to you, like you belong to them, it makes no sense."

"Chad! I — I ... am so dumbfounded, so stunned, I don't know what to even say to this."

"You know, as long as I've written about Klive King, he's never dated, nor has he given the impression of sharing with others. As long as I've covered your career, you're the same. Seems a good match on paper, and I salivate at publishing the prospect, but, Kinsley, do you know how *dangerous* that man is? If he's playing a game to get them out of the way to get to y —"

I chopped my hand through the space between us. "Give me a break, Chad! That's ridiculous." I worried my napkin in my lap with my other hand.

"Dammit, Kinsley, you are one of my favorite people. I can't sit idly by watching you do this without informing you of the danger." He peered out the window for a moment. When he looked back at me once more, I saw a different air about him. "Did you know they recovered two bodies at the shipyard this morning?" He paused, waiting, watching. I shook my head, a crease in my brows.

"I told you I don't read the news. Why should I know?"

He spoke over my last word. "Unconfirmed report is they were here shopping for the Colombians."

"Shopping?" My mouth twisted.

"Kidnapping someone special as revenge for a botched coke drop and hit on their failed leader two years ago. Now they're also creatively dead? You know anything about that?"

"What the fuck? Why would *I* know anything about that?"

"I've never heard you use words like that."

"Well, why would you ask me something like that when I've never done drugs. Hell, I don't even go to parties. You're making no sense asking me shit like this."

"I've never seen anything like it. Both Colombians had GSR on their hands. Shot each other. My source in the department says wit reports speak of tension between the two for days prior to the shooting. Investigators closed the case as a double-homicidal suicide. Ever heard of anything so ridiculous in your life? Does that even sound like a legitimate charge? One or the other. Homicide or suicide, not both. Can't be both. What I want to know is where is the guy who made them so afraid that they drew on each other, and how does a low-level grunt get his hands on a fifty-caliber Desert Eagle? Neither of these dope dealers were kingpins. Another tasty morsel, criminals file serial numbers from weapons. This one's number was clear as day, but when entered into the database, it didn't *exist*...."

He studied my face. I shook my head, still baffled in ways, disgusted in others. "I'm not sure what you are searching for or what you want me to say. Do you share this like another disclosure of your personal work?"

He shook his head very slowly, never losing eye-contact. My eyes narrowed.

"You'll have to excuse me, please."

I threw the lock on the restroom, then threw up in the toilet. Holy shit, shit, *shit*!

Shopping? Kidnapping? Revenge for a bad drug deal? A hit? The Desert Eagle? Dammit, why did I have to know guns? If only I'd been ignorant! How do I navigate this?

Klive *had* gotten to the beach really fast after my text this morning. Was Klive scary enough to talk a couple of drug dealers into shooting each other? How did that make any sense? Chad was right, though. People didn't just shoot each other like the Wild West anymore. I didn't see Klive come home with the gun, but then again, I was in the shower. He could have gone into his closet through his room instead of the bathroom just like he had when he'd sneaked into my bath.

But he'd gone shopping for the kitten's bed and collar, the stuffed animal. Ugh. I couldn't create a sensible timeline and I *could* officially be used as a witness against him if anyone found out. I held my reflection in the mirror after rinsing my mouth. These eyes were too wide, skin too pale. Get a grip! Oh, Chad, why can't you leave things alone …?

I pinched my cheeks to coax some color back into them, released a heavy breath and shook my hands and shoulders to loosen the tension in my frame.

When I sat back in the booth, I replaced my napkin on my lap and chugged water. I stared into Chad's eyes for a long, silent while. He stared back reminiscent of the type A asshole Rustin was partners with at the station. Was Chad more than a journalism student? My head tilted; eyes narrowed but never wavered. Holy shit, if Jase were undercover, why couldn't others be too? Was Chad part of Jase's team while they pretended to hate each other for the case? Was anyone real in my life?

Klive. He was real. Our time in the elevator was real and had nothing to do with anyone but the two of us.

The longer Chad and I stared, the more intense our silent battle and the worse my heart ached at my friend maybe not being my friend at all.

Finally, resentfully, I spoke.

"Chad, while I have no idea what the hell you're talking about concerning the shipyard, I can say Klive and I spent all night together." When he arched a skeptical eyebrow, my patience and propriety snapped. "We fucked for *hours*," I purred like a bitch. "Lots of dirty, kinky sex. Then, we slept until this evening. Take your weird implications elsewhere. You are also one of my favorite people, so this is particularly rich coming from you. Where the hell do you get off?"

He held his napkin like a white flag of surrender, the prick. He had the class to at least pretend to appear stung, but at this time, I had no idea what I really didn't know about Chad. What a fool to allow people so close to me and never dive deeper into their lives to protect my own! Sure, I'd been overly icy, but I was freaking out on the inside! Please, nobody ever put me on a stand! I'd crack under pressure!

What was Klive doing with me if he didn't want to get caught?!

As I freaked, Chad gulped the remainder of his tea before leaning forward on his arms.

"Well, since you were busy *fucking* him when the murder happened, it must have been someone else. I am not a detective, but I am not obtuse, either. Don't insult my intelligence. You were just sick. Look at you! If you fucked him all night, he must have left this morning, then, huh? Maybe while you were asleep?" he pushed. "At least now I know the two who held out on relationships hold nothing back from each other."

"Nope. I'm done with this shit." I tossed my napkin on the table with enough cash to cover our bill before I walked right out of the restaurant. He could call another ride share!

I drove home scrubbing the blur of tears from my eyes. In my room, I shed my clothing and bundled in Klive's pirate coat, then hid under the covers as though this would disappear as easily as the fake monsters my father had always scared out of my imagination. I tossed and turned through terrorizing thunderstorms. I wanted Klive to chase this all away. For Nightshade to be a nightmare rather than real.

I woke from several night terrors with the most recent one being Jerry arresting me, then forcing me to look at Klive and tell him I'd lied while he held his Desert Eagle to my head. Chad stood in the corner with a smug smile telling me he'd told me so.

Though Klive's coat was my security blanket, I realized the crushed velvet made me sweat, which could've caused my bad dreams. You know, instead of the blinding fear of everyone closing in on the man I loved. When I finally fell asleep, the sweetest dream stole the nightmares. Klive was there. Klive carried me somewhere safe. No more lightning and the thunder became a distant rumble for fear in other places outside this realm. He laid me onto a sweet cloud where he curled himself around me, cocooning me, enveloping me in cologne and tranquility.

Oh, Klive. My bodyguard, my protector, my lover, my husband in my heart of hearts.

"Klive," I whispered.

"Yes, love?"

"Don't let anyone hurt me. I'm so scared."

"Shh, I'm scarier than any nightmare. Tell me your bad dreams, love, and I promise I'll take them all away."

"I think I love you."

"I know I love you." His mouth brushed my temple, my neck, my shoulder. "Say no more. Rest now, my sweet." I did, sinking into the softness of the puffy, white heavenly cloud with the most celestial body warming me. I said a silent prayer of thanks to the

Lord who must be nearby in this divine place, asking him to forgive and protect my sweet Klive and teach him how to separate himself from the bad.

36 | ♀

I SIGHED SOFTLY AS I rolled to my back, nestling into the feather pillows, running my legs against the satin, the kitten rubbing her soft fur against my cheek. I smiled and rolled over to my other side. Fingers brushed my cheek.

"Oh!" I screamed as I scrambled away.

"Kins! Kinsley, it's me! It's Klive! Calm down, love! You're safe! It's only me!" Klive caught me before I fell off the bed.

"Klive?" I struggled to gain my bearings, looking around myself. Klive's room. "How? I don't ...." I shook my head, seeking my memory, coming up blank.

"Last night I came to your place to check on you. I heard you scream. I came in after you, afraid someone was hurting you. You were in a fit, a nightmare. I soothed you to sleep only to watch you go into another fit. When I roused you from your panic, I asked if you wanted to come home with me. You nodded, so I brought you here. You walked to the bed. I thought you were awake," he told me. "You really don't remember?" He leaned upon one elbow, his chest bare, hair messy, face unshaven, gray eyes worried.

"Oh, gosh, Klive." My face fell into my palms. "I don't remember. I should have said something, but I hoped it wouldn't happen with you. I sleepwalk when I'm stressed." Tears rushed to my eyes, spilling onto my cheeks. I did recall the nightmares. "Klive," I choked his name. "This is so embarrassing. Humiliating. I'm so sorry."

"Hey. Come now." He pulled me against him. "Shh ... Kins, you've nothing to apologize for. I'm here. Nothing's gonna hurt you as long as I'm here, all right?" He seemed so sweetly disturbed by my pain. I gazed up at him with last night weighing heavily on my heart. "Tell that head of yours to quiet down, Kins. It's interfering with what I'm telling you." He brushed hair from my face, then dipped down for a chaste kiss, but I put my hands into his hair, desperate for his Novocain.

"I need you, Klive. Silence my mind! I'm so tired of thinking about all this."

He leaned away for a better look.

"What's wrong, love? Did I do something? I was only jesting last night." His pretty gray eyes searched my face before he kissed my eyelids, my cheeks, my forehead, ran his nose along mine, then leaned back again.

"Rustin told me you were just screwing with me. It's nothing to do with any of that. I'm just exhausted from everything."

"Nightshade." An observation. Not a question. He nodded. "Put it out of your mind, Kinsley. It is not for you to concern yourself with. The burden is mine to bear for however long. There is nothing you can do about it, so why waste the energy? If someone threatens you, I'll take care of it. Concerning Nightshade and the underground, consider my authority your umbrella. You're safe."

I nodded. "Klive —"

"Shh ... what did I tell you, woman? Quiet down." His lips curled.

"How are you so sweet and mean and impossible?" I smiled up at him leaning over me. He chuckled and ran a hand through his hair, over his neck. His eyebrows raised while his eyes searched unseeingly around the room until he sighed. "Klive, you make no sense to me, and I, well, I love it." I bit my lip, heat stealing through my cheeks.

"Mmm ... you know what *I* love?" he asked with that wicked undercurrent, a smirk unfurling.

"I've no bloody idea!" I exclaimed in his accent. "Considering you are cruel, keeping no pets and such, what the hell could you be referring to, my dear, mean ass, Mr. King?" I asked in mock seriousness. His lips twitched as his eyes narrowed. Klive's mouth descended to my neck where he growled and made me cackle like crazy while I tried to push him off me. "Klive, you merciless ass! Cut it out before I sic your sweet pet on you, you bloody liar!" I squealed as he added hands that found every ticklish spot I never knew I had! He rolled me to my stomach and landed his hand on my bottom in a sound spanking.

"Woman, you need to behave your damn self! I imagine this is payback for the naughty shit I've done to drive my mum insane."

I puffed a breath against the pillows, my hands tucked beneath my torso.

"Now, Miss Hayes, whatever shall we do with your naughty ass?" He trailed his fingers over my spine. I inhaled sharply when his hand stole under the comforter, then the cotton nightgown he must have put me in.

"You dressed me, Klive?" I asked, my voice muffled against the covers.

"I did. Couldn't have you provoking me to take you against your will in your sleep now, could I?" he asked playfully dark. "I much prefer you put up a good fight while you are coherent enough to use some of those self-defense skills to try and outsmart me ..." I exhaled as desire of the dirtiest kind consumed me. His hand slipped beneath the cotton panties. I moaned softly. "Aw ... no fight, eh?" Suddenly, I was on my back, him between my legs while my hands were pinned over my head against the pillows by one of his strong hands. He ground himself against me. "I should have known you would go down easily, in fact, perhaps we should see exactly how easy it is to make you go down." His pupils dilated, eyes hooded, voice taunted to piss me off. I remained calm, awaiting anything else he'd throw to provoke me. His free hand caressed my breast then pinched the shit out of my nipple the way he'd done at Jase's. I cried out and slapped the shit out of his hand. He chuckled. "I believe it's been a week since the last time I did that. Who knew that you would have shagged my brains out in the dirtiest fashion, been willingly lying beneath me in my plush bed, spreading these beautiful legs of yours for the villain of the story … the killer. You love fucking him, don't you, my sweet?"

Twisted, raw desire unfurled inside me at that dark statement. I did love a lot more than that about him very much.

His head tilted to study me in that threatening way that had earned him a knee to the nuts last time.

"You are a glutton for punishment, aren't you, sir?"

"Ever the submissive even as I threaten you," he shot back.

"For the killer, perhaps I am playing a part to keep my life." A smirk crossed my lips, my expression mirroring his.

"And how desperately do you want that life of yours, my sweet?" he asked, enunciating the T at the end. His jaw muscle flinched. How long I'd dreamed of devouring him. Of him consuming me with unrestrained type of passion when he'd restrained himself around me. Now, here he truly was, beautifully bare of products and everything but basic attire, open and hungry for me to play with every side of his personality. Who says dreams don't come true?

"What would you like me to do to prove that I want to keep it, sir?" I blinked up at him. My smirk changed into an angelic smile. Thunder rumbled through the room, but I wasn't afraid this morning. The sound enhanced the sexy dangerous game we played.

"I'd love to watch you go down on me, that is, if you think you can handle this ..." he trailed, half-teasing, half-serious. I knew why. My fingertips barely met when I'd stroked him. The concept of going down did scare me. I may not be a virgin in his bed, but parts of me were still brand new in this department.

Though nervous, I said, "I am all yours, do what you will."

What would he do?

His hand released mine as he sat back onto his heels. I got to my knees before him and intertwined my fingers behind his neck, arching like the kitten against his chest with mine. He inhaled deeply, and the next thing I knew, I was on my back, my panties being pulled roughly down my legs. He stood to shuck his undies. I kicked his feet out from under him and rolled off the bed while *he* went down. I bolted out of the bedroom.

"I lied, you sucker!" I shouted.

His bare feet slapped the tile behind me when I rushed through the kitchen toward the small steps down into the den. Klive caught me around my belly, pulled me back against him and rolled us over the back of one of the couches, landing us on the thick cushions. My elbow thrust into his ribs, and I nailed the pressure point in his thigh. He cursed and lost his hold and balance. I scrambled away on my hands and knees until gaining enough traction to stand and sprint back into the bedroom, into my closet where I grabbed the cuffs and grasped the first hook in preparation.

Just as he darted toward my closet, I slipped past his open closet door, intending on running out of the other into his room again, but he suddenly blocked the passage. When I jerked the other direction, he met me in the bathroom. Oh, was this ever fun! Klive was *so* fast! Faster than I ever hoped to be!

We deadlocked. I juked like I was gonna run to the other door again, doubled-back and escaped out of the bathroom, but Klive tackled me down to the floor beside his bed and pulled the cuffs from my hand, snaring my wrist in a metal bracelet while the other locked around the leg of the bed beneath the bed skirt. I lay trapped, catching my breath on the thick carpeting, glad for the softness as he looked down at me in Nightshade boss mode. Sexy!

"Oh, Kinsley, my love." He flipped me onto my stomach and pulled my hips off the floor, positioning me on my forearms and knees. "You have been so disobedient." He sent a stinging slap to the right side of my bottom. "Here I order you to put Nightshade out of your head, and you draw it to you instead." He popped my left side. "Now you are in so much trouble, you must face their leader. You stay like that, and he will be back to deal with you." His tone was not so sweet. Yum!

I rolled to my back on purpose so that when he came back his mouth lifted in a lazy, evil grin. "How did I know that my little novice would be curious with the ways I may want to torture or punish her?" He set some things down on the bed before telling me to get onto my knees. I stayed put. He laughed and came to the floor, pulling my nightgown up to taste and tease so many yummy places. I wrapped my hand in his hair.

"Oh! Klive, you're so good at this." Not that I knew what much of 'this' was like. Klive was a scandalous SOB! His chuckle vibrated against my flesh.

"Good. Maybe I will haunt your mind the way you haunt my own."

I practically squirmed against the carpet like a cat in heat when he ceased his talented tongue to instead loom over me. His soft hair fell forward. His thick, black eyelashes stood out in striking contrast to the gray of his bright eyes in the dim room.

"But you got onto me for how Nightshade haunts my mind, sir."

"Nightshade or me?"

"Without you, there'd be no Nightshade."

"Is that so?" He spoke with a mouthful of kisses down between my breasts, along the bottoms of their swells. "Either you give me far too much credit, or perhaps you know too much ...." Pain hissed through my lips when he circled a bud and pulled with his teeth like a warning. Fear filled my belly along with the quickening in my nether region. "I like your birthmark." He planted a soft kiss to that ugly skin while I scoffed and rolled my eyes. "A unique identifier." Rather than scare me, he smiled over the bubble of my left breast. "You are so beautiful, Kinsley." He sighed and crawled over my body, his hands traveling to the cuff to release his prisoner. Did I look as stunned as I felt? He captured my newly freed fingers in his hand and brought my wrist to his mouth to kiss the line of tender flesh. "Spend the day with me, love?"

Aw! I melted. "I can't, Klive. I am headed to see my parents for vacation."

"I thought you had track soon."

"I do, but not till next weekend. I already had this planned and told Walton. Not my fault he hit play after pausing my action for so long. I'm not foregoing plans with my parents for a maybe moment on the track. You'd better not follow me, either, stalker."

He snickered, then his face fell into an adorable pout that had me clawing his hair to draw that beautiful mouth to mine. I rolled him over, and without thinking, I kissed my way down his glorious torso until I reached Rion's sword.

"Let's see if I am in the category of women with freakishly large mouths that get paid the big bucks to please the King, shall we?" I teased. He chuckled and waved me on.

"How do you know I've paid for that?" he asked in a charming lilt, though I sensed his dog hunted for what I truly knew about him.

"Are there women voluntarily willing to take this thing in their mouths?" I asked in mock surprise. He laughed, filling the room with a happy sound. Here goes nothin'.

His head tilted back. Laughter morphed into a long moan. When his hand went to my hair, his hips flexed beneath me, and a burst of encouragement made me joyous rather than grossed out or intimidated.

Two-hundred-and-eighteen super silent seconds later, inadequacy feasted on my insecurities till he finally sucked a huge gulp of air.

"Feels so good ... Kins...." Oh, weakness in Klive King!

"So, I have a freakishly big mouth, then?" I asked as I rose with the same smile of victory I can't hide after my races.

He huffed, a little breathless. "How the hell else would you have such a brilliant smile?"

"Were you holding your breath?"

"I've been without for so long; it was hard to breathe through the rush."

And there went all reluctance in the act.

Rather than pressing for more as I expected, he rolled out from under me and stood.

"Where are you going?" I asked, confused. I watched as he absently held himself in his hand. My body begged for his. My mind craved his wisdom. My heart hoped the strings on his would tangle too tightly with mine to untie. My spirit prayed for a way to keep him.

I laid on my side, my head in my hand while my other drew invisible shapes into the carpet as I studied him.

"I'm hungry, love. Are you not?" he asked as he opened a box and tore a foil packet with his teeth.

"I'm starving, Klive." My gaze roamed him sheathing himself. I squealed with delight when he plucked me from the floor. My legs wrapped around his waist while he sank into me. A wispy moan stole my breath. Heat hit my cheeks, eyes closed, head tilted back. His lips tasted the column of my throat, but he never moved inside me. Instead, he carried me this way into the kitchen. He powered on his Keurig. A second later, the sound of the heating coffee maker bounced off the cabinets while he opened the fridge. I shrank into him as the cold air smacked my back.

"What would you like for breakfast, Kins?" He flexed his hips and moved inside me.

"Oh, I want you!" I dug my nails into his shoulders, greedy for more. He closed the fridge.

"I dunno ..." He clucked his tongue. "I'm not a very healthy option ... sure, this might taste good now, but what happens when you crash later from lack of nourishment?" He shifted again. My back met cold stainless steel. I whined, and he took my mouth with his. I understood he didn't think he was good for me, and I knew he wasn't, but, dammit, *I wanted him!*

I scraped my nails down his back like punishment. He arched and winced against my mouth.

"Maybe I don't want healthy!" I ground out before sucking his tongue. His mouth crushed against mine then, lust consuming him as he growled in warning. I disconnected our kiss with a hard, daring glare of pure resentment. "Bring the shit, Klive. Do your worst."

His eyes flared, and he began thrusting hard, fast, angry with fingertips digging into my thighs.

"Damn you! Why the fuck must you consume me?" He unleashed restrained resentment. "I don't want to want you! I want to be mean, bad, do my bloody job without your fucking conscience beating through my brain! Why can't I kill you and get on with life, you blasted witch?"

He rushed us down to the couch and took us over the back like before. I landed on my back. He came down on top of me without disconnecting, then slammed into me harder and rougher than he'd previously dared. His hand landed across my cheek, and I moaned in triumphant ecstasy, because as hard as he pummeled me, this smack was more a sound effect, meaning he *couldn't* hurt me! He wanted me as badly as I wanted him! He hated hurting me as much as I hated hurting him! My misery, the sickness inside of me, loved the pain, the fear, the anger he carried because we matched. I wasn't alone! I knew if the things that made us enemies vanished, nothing but pure unadulterated love for each other existed.

"Give him to me, Klive! Let me have him! I want him, you nasty son of a bitch! Holding back what belongs to me! Only me!"

"Nasty?! I'll fucking show you nasty, I don't think you can handle the shit I like to dole out, Kinsley." He pulled out and all but threw me to the floor and rolled me to my stomach. He shoved inside me from behind with a hard spanking. He pinned my legs together with his, then pressed me flat to the floor with his weight as he laid on top of me. Klive's hands traveled beneath my arms, palms wrapping around my shoulders to keep me pinned as he thrust.

I shouted, moaned, groaned, pleaded, whined, whimpered, all in a mixture of pleasure, desire, anger and elation. I loved the all-consuming attention in this position, the heaviness of him, the softness of his hold on my shoulders contrasting with the ferocity of his thrusts.

"Yes, Klive, more!" I shouted. His chest kept in constant friction with my back. His breathing, growls, grunts turned me on to no end. He was raw, unchecked, primal and oh, *so* good!

"I love fucking you, Klive!" *I fucking love you!*

"Ohhh!" he moaned as though involuntary, a weak sound. Holy crap! Had I accidentally said that aloud? His open lips brushed my shoulder. "More!" he commanded as though I were able to do anything in the position he trapped me in.

"More? More what?"

"Tell me more. Who do you want?!" he demanded.

"I want you, you impossible prick! Shame on you for not making yourself available to me in every way!" I griped at him in a husky tone I didn't recognize. Hot damn! I cried out when he pulled his torso off me and shifted our legs so that I spread on my knees for him once more. "Don't stop!"

He chuckled without humor. "I can make myself available in ways you might be afraid of, love." His arm wrapped my waist to hold me still. His other held himself and flirted with a very forbidden idea. I felt the rubber condom tap my bottom.

Rather than squirm in fear like he wanted to provoke, I laughed the throatiest wicked plan laugh I'd ever heard outside of a movie, like someone else. His hold loosened.

"What the hell?" he breathed.

"You won't do that," I told him, looking over my shoulder at his naughty position.

"Ha! You said you wanted him."

"I *own* him and if he wants to keep me, he'd never hurt me. He's far too afraid of losing me. I'm not a whore and he'd never feel right treating me as such. Need I say more on the matter?" I used his tone of finality and watched his jaw muscle tense while gray eyes held true fear for the first time in my recollection.

Klive King taught me that with a trusted partner, I loved adrenaline with sex the same as I enjoyed the adrenaline rush of the most intense conditioning and training sessions for sports. Klive King also taught me that he had everything I wanted.

I wanted everything, including the killer.

The killer understood his vulnerability to me.

I saw the truth in my power over him.

That was the scariest part of all.

37 | ♀

Klive got up and walked into the kitchen to trash the condom and wash his hands, cleaning himself without bothering to redress. He remained nude, which I found endearing in a twisted way. He was comfortable with me. He studied me while I studied him from his floor. I needed to get the hell out of here, but when Klive was cooking naked, how the could I?

"Up you go! In the plush bed. That's an order." When I realized I could barely move from satiation, he shook his head and walked down to scoop me into his arms. "You trying to burn my bacon, woman?"

I giggled as he cradled me. He chuckled, too, as he carried me past the kitchen. "Klive, I want to watch you." I pouted with my lip out, mustering my biggest innocent doe eyes. His head tilted back, Adam's apple bobbing with laughter. He sat me on a barstool instead. I pointed to an apron printed with cupcakes, hem lined with ruffles hanging from a hook on the wall. "Housekeeper, or am I a dirty affair after all?" I narrowed my eyes. He snickered.

"A dirty affair. I damn sure don't want to admit to having a housekeeper since I was forced into slave labor the last time I wasn't planning on getting my hands dirty."

His tongue darted over his lower lip as he walked over to his fridge. Impossible not to check his ass out. Pretty and muscular, not tan like the rest of his torso. My nails itched to mar that skin, so he'd have to think of me while I was gone all week. The red lines over his back would have to do. I yanked my eyes and mind out of the gutter when he spun around with juice in his hand.

"You think I couldn't feel that?"

"Ha!" I scoffed. "I wouldn't give you the satisfaction."

He scoffed at the absurdity. Yes.

"Klive, will you wear your wife's apron for me while you're cooking, sir?" I batted my lashes like a fool. "Please, because you love me and not her?" My chin found my palm, elbow rested on the white counter as I looked up at the corner with innocent play.

"Oh, Kinsley Hayes, what the hell will we do with you?" He walked around the island to plant his mouth to my neck and tickle my skin with a silly growl, then he vanished into his library.

When I hopped off the stool, he called for me to stay put. When he came back, something dangled off his fingertip. "If I am to wear my wife's apron for my mistress, then my mistress better damn well wear whatever I want her to." He caught my lips in a dirty kiss, his renewed lust back in full force. I hummed against his mouth. What a fun game!

I snatched the outfit off his finger and walked into the guest bathroom off the den, smiling over my shoulder before I shut the door. When I finished shrugging into the tiniest French maid lingerie, I was excited for him to peel the black and white satin and lace back off of me! The itsy skirt fanned away from my hips, not even long enough to fully cover my bottom in trashy panties. The sides laced up my ribs while my breasts oozed from the top, frilly white ruffles adorning them. Guess we matched in the ruffle department, hee-hee.

I opened the bathroom door and posed in the frame while he whistled his approval and removed a pancake from a griddle. He turned around to place the hotcake on a plate. I grinned with a little kitty growl. Klive's fine ass had tied the ruffled apron on like a good boy. *"S'il vous plaît ... "* I continued praising his sexy appearance in French to sell my part for him. My nails trailed over the island when I rounded behind the bar where he cooked. He barely looked at the batter he poured onto his griddle.

"Madam, do you wish to be fired? How will it look when my wife demands breakfast, but finds I've burned her pancakes because the naughty maid distracted me?" he reasoned with a graceful gesture of his free hand. I tossed my head back on a laugh.

"Oh, so now she's in the house, eh? That's really damn dangerous, sir." I waved my finger with a charming smile. "Especially given my uniform and the fact that everything seems *awful* clean around here to merit needing a maid ..." I trailed. "Making your infidelities a little obvious now, aren't we?" I teased with a French accent instead of playing with his British one.

"Maybe you aren't my eye candy or lover, perhaps you are *hers* ..." His gray eyes gleamed with the naughtiest smolder as they narrowed. "I mean, this is *my* fantasy marriage, is it not?"

My mouth dropped, amused, as I gaped at him. He tipped my chin with the end of his spatula.

"What does your wife look like, though I am a bit uncomfortable with other women being into me," I admitted.

The tip of his spatula tapped his lip as he looked up in thought. "Since this is my fantasy, she is your naughty twin."

"Klive King! You are getting off on my shock and awe, sir!"

"Not yet, I'm sure we can work something out as soon as I am done here," he said as a matter of fact. I stood on the rungs of my stool and leaned across the bar to snatch his chin for a kiss. His fingers slithered over my breasts. Klive popped my butt with his spatula to disconnect us, then flipped his pancakes.

"That is a recipe for cross-contamination, *monsieur.*" I hopped off the stool.

"Thanks for stating the obvious since it's not like I've had my mouth all over your body or anything."

"Touché. Where shall I clean first?" I asked.

"The refrigerator needs cleaning," he told me as though I were nothing of desire for him. Like I could have been walking around in a tent, plain Jane, nothing to him. I arched an eyebrow and opened the fridge to find stark white spotlessness. "I meant the freezer, forgive me."

His pancakes scooped onto the plate. He turned off the burner as I pulled the large drawer to look in the equally clean freezer. I scoffed and bumped the drawer shut as I turned to face him. He stood right in front of me, looking down at my breasts against his cupcake-covered chest. He lifted his chin and smirked, amusement dancing in his eyes.

"Your nipples are really hard now, and I love the way your breasts feel against me when you're breathing this way."

"So, am I to understand I am not only some treat you got for your wife?" My hands traveled around to his naked ass. I skimmed my nails over his skin while he smiled.

"Did I get you for her?" he asked. "Or did you merely take the job to get to me, love?"

"Considering how submissive I am to you, I took the job because you told me to," I answered.

"On your knees," he ordered, his face hardening at my words. I complied.

"I may be here under the impression that I am for this naughty wife of yours, but I only please her to keep her sidetracked from the fact that I serve you as soon as she is asleep." He groaned. I ran my hands up his legs and disappeared beneath the apron to take him into my mouth once more.

"This. Has to be. The most. Interesting head. I have. Ever. Had. In my. Life." His hand caressed my hair through the fabric as though urging me on, but afraid to scare me away. His praise drove me harder. I wanted to be the only head *he wanted* ever again! *My* mouth! *My* body! *Me* in his head! In his heart! In his dreams!

When the tip became too large, I pulled off him and got to my feet once more.

"What are you doing?" he asked as though I were disobedient, which was so damn hot. I walked past him toward his room as I looked over my shoulder with a crook of my finger. He smiled and trailed slowly behind me, staying about ten feet back. I ran my hands over my bottom as I walked, enjoying the guttural sound that came from his throat.

"What if I don't want to be the naughty maid, Klive?" I asked, my bad girl taking over. He swallowed as I paused in the room outside the bathroom and placed my hands against his chest when he drew close.

"What do you want to be instead, love?"

"The wife who is pissed off that she found you in bed with her maid."

His bad side walked me back toward the bed until my legs touched the mattress. The intoxicating authority emanating from him practically dilated my pupils.

"First, I have to sleep with the maid in order to be caught."

Klive made divesting me of my costume a work of pure artistic debauchery. I loved every single second. Once upon the mattress beneath him, he touched me like I was truly forbidden, looked at the door to his room like he feared being caught and spun suspenseful what-ifs with his accent about how he couldn't stand watching me a second longer without giving into temptation.

"May I ask you something?" I panted.

"If you can talk through what I'm about to do, be my guest."

I sucked my teeth, arched off the mattress and fisted the comforter in my fingers. The only thing I could say was his name through incoherent pants and mewls. By the time he crawled over me again, I was as useless as a container of slime and just as fluid.

He collapsed beside me onto my pillow, his arm behind his head, satisfied arrogance in his eyes. "Found my new favorite food."

"You. What will I do with you?" My head lolled to the side so I could see him better. "For someone who hasn't finished once today, you're awful relaxed."

"How kind of you to keep track. Orgasm isn't my sole source of pleasure, Kinsley. I derive the most from pleasing and playing with you, learning you, earning your favor."

My face must've done the girly melting thing because he laughed and stared at his canopy. I swear he looked years younger.

"What did you want to ask?"

"How you waited. I mean, how did you refuse when we were at Delia's, and I asked you to be with me? Why if you'd waited so long?"

He cleared his throat. A shadow crossed over his sunshine. I hated that.

Klive rolled to his side to face me. His fingertips caressed my belly. I noticed he stared at my birthmark when speaking.

"I know the sting of regret. In my life, I've seen firsthand too many times to count people throw their lives, goals, happiness away for a moment of pleasure. I've seen people used. People do things in an altered state of mind that they'd never do when coherent."

"I wasn't under the sedative anymore. My feelings haven't changed. They've only grown stronger. I meant it then and I mean it now. I still want you."

He met my eyes. Happy light brightened his again. "Kins, you know that now, but I didn't know that then. I waited for so long to prove you wrong about me as a man, no way I was cashing that in when you might not have given your true consent or when Jase was the star in your show. You say you want me, but you love him."

"Do you love her?" I pushed him to his back and climbed on top of him.

"What?" He watched me push the apron aside. His hands gripped my hips as I adjusted myself to take him in.

"Your mistress? What does she have that I don't?" I created a slow pace to match the slow burn inside myself. Klive had depleted me from the inside out, now he deserved the same. I leaned close to his lips, offering a taste. He cupped my back to force my breasts closer.

"Nothing," he breathed between suckling samples. I almost enjoyed this as much as what he'd done down under.

"I ask again, sir," I panted, "what does *she* have that has caused your eye to roam?"

"You really want to know?" He cupped the back of my head and rolled me onto the mattress. He inhaled before dipping to kiss my lips, then matched the pace I'd started. I bit his shoulder through quiet moans. "She smells like cinnamon, melts like sugar on my tongue, has the fittest fucking body."

"Is that all?"

"She makes me stand taller, dares me to be exactly who I am. Forgives my faults and tickles my fantasies. There will never be anyone else who does to me what she does. Should I kill her for what she does to me, wife?" He enunciated the *F* and shoved hard, punishing. My fingernails scoured his skin, head thrashed on the bed beneath him. He rose to his knees and stole my hands to slam them over my head like when I'd first released him from the handcuffs. "Or will you let me keep her?" He growled through gritted teeth then grunted his exertion.

"I'll let you keep her if you never stop loving me!"

"Dangerous words, my sweet. I'll let you keep him if you never stop loving me either."

"I don't want him anymore!"

"Don't. Lie. To. Me!" He pinned me, pummeled me with the most fantastic pain and pleasure that had me digging my heels into his bottom, grinding my teeth while I whined his name in a plea for mercy he refused. "You're so satisfying! What if I decide to keep you all week while everyone thinks you left to visit your parents? I can chain you to my bed and shag you whenever I want to, however I want to, as long as I want to." My body arched again. Sensation spiraled out of control. My thighs gripped his hips as tight as possible.

I looked up at his sweaty face, his lip beneath his teeth as his gray gaze bored into my memory. His pelvis weighed heavy against mine. No telling where our bodies weren't joined in all the sweaty madness. His hands released their hold as his lips dipped to pull very loose kisses through heavy breaths. I ran my fingers through his damp hair, forcing his mouth harder so his tongue delved against mine seeking more of him. Klive's weight pressed me deeper into the comforter and I loved the reality. He was real! His taste on my tongue. His breathy moans in my mouth.

"Klive, I *need* you," I said against him as I changed angles. "I need *you*," I admitted. "All of you."

All of you was like mouthing *olive juice* in place of *I love you*. *Olive juice* looked like *I love you*. *All of you* could be *I love you* in his accent.

His arm wound beneath me. My chest mashed against his in the apron. Soon, his mouth was everywhere, my face, my neck, my ear, my lips once more, his tongue making me prisoner to whatever he wished.

"Kinsley ..." He huffed away from my lips a moment. "I would *never* be unfaithful to you if you were mine," he confessed. I moaned and closed my eyes as that delicious burn stole my rationality and exploded like a kaleidoscope of twisted colors and pieces. He bucked one hard, last time, moaning my name as his eyes closed. His lip pinched under his teeth while his body went still, save for the damn pulsating inside me, which he quickly pulled out to finish doing on my tummy. "What the hell is the matter with me?!" he shouted angrily before rolling off me for a wet washcloth to clean me with.

He avoided eye-contact, which sucked ass, especially since my throat was thick with the fact that I wasn't sure what was going on here. *Did he want me pregnant?*

"I'm sorry, Kins, I, uh, I ... well, I ..." he trailed at a loss for words when he so obviously never lacked the right ones at the right time.

In a numb stupor, I crawled off the bed and changed into a little yellow sun dress and sandals; bright and cheery in the midst of a dismal turn of events. Klive never came to the closet, never messed with me, never said anything. When I came out to the room he was no longer there. I found him in the kitchen. He was fully dressed. The pancakes he'd made sat on the counter untouched. He was disturbed. I *hated* that look. I was too busy twisting in the wind to offer him comfort.

What could I say? *Don't worry, Klive. It's okay if you knocked me up, just please make sure the checks come in on time every month so I can afford to take care of our illegitimate child while you're in prison. By the way, sorry about that whole throwing you off your game bit that I'd agreed to help Jase with. No hard feelings, cool?*

Tears pricked my eyes when I saw him grab his keys and walk to the garage as though he were done with me or something. His silence gnawed and gnashed at my gut the entire way back to my apartment. Anytime I offered mundane conversation, his answers were clipped responses, nothing that said he was in any way paying attention. When we pulled into my neighborhood, he spoke.

"I fucked up, Kinsley. I'm sorry for everything." The F-bomb he rarely used. His eyes had such a look of finality, I unbuckled my seatbelt and nodded without a word. I didn't look over my shoulder when I left his car. My apartment door slammed behind me. I twisted the deadbolt then slid the chain before going into my bedroom and locking that door, too. I blared music attempting to drown everything as I walked into my bathroom and locked the door behind me. Thirty Seconds to Mars accompanied my reflection in the large vanity mirror I strode past toward the closet. I slammed that door, too, then slid to the floor and sobbed into my hands as *The Kill* seemed so damn apt for how I felt right now.

If Klive knocked, I had no way of knowing. If he called, I wouldn't hear my phone over Jared Leto's lyrics. Now, if only I could shove Klive the hell out of my head, out of my heart, out of my body that could be growing a part of him that would be joined with me forever.

After the crying spell tamed to shuddering breaths and sandpaper eyeballs, I stood under the hottest shower spray unable to shake the chill of the ugliest truth I refused to tell myself just yet. When I pushed the glass open, thick steam clouded the whole bathroom. I wrapped the towel around my body and twisted my hair into a turban. I wiped a round spot on the mirror. My reflection stared back with new resolve. *Courage. Strength. You took down a killer. You did your job. Now put him out!*

My gramma's rhyme danced in my head: *Put all of this away for another day, get out of the way so the chips will fall where they may!*

No more sad, angry music. I tapped my phone, ignoring any notifications. Youngblood Hawke's *We Come Running* lifted my spirits and reminded me that beyond this bad there was a girl with another life that had zero to do with men and everything to do with personal pressure, grace, and endurance. I was taking that open door all right. Normal me would've already crashed my parents' vacation after they'd gotten their alone time outta the way. I put my packed suitcase in my trunk, prepped a motivating play list for the long drive and programmed my GPS.

HOSTILE TAKEOVER

I drove away from my apartment, from Jase, Rustin, friggin' Chad, my ailing Klive who was probably kicking himself for making the biggest mistake of potentially creating a child he didn't want with a woman he only wanted to 'shag' to get out of his system. I was sick of being something that these men felt they'd get over once they'd worked through their desires like wanting me was akin to an illness or fever they'd be cured of once they'd hooked-up and had their fill. I wanted to be special! Like the kind of woman a man couldn't live without because he loved me so much. Not because he loved the way his penis felt inside my vagina. I was a conquered conquest for Jase. I was a pair of legs Rustin wanted wrapped around his waist for a night. A fantasy Klive enjoyed dressing up in kinky lingerie and pretty dresses.

Klive's playtime had taken a very different turn than he'd likely planned.

No matter what the asshole pirate said about running to Daddy for coddling, I needed a man who loved me unconditionally for what *God* had created me to be instead of the walking sin they'd crafted for me to deal with inside my now haunted spirit.

About eight hours into the ten-hour drive, Bluetooth's automated voice broke the music with "new text from Asshole Dick". My heart somersaulted, even if all Klive sent was a heart emoji beside a broken heart emoji. Confirmation we shared the same helpless ache. Distance was good. He'd told me his girl didn't wilt. *His girl was courageous, spirited and didn't run from pain.* She sounded as strong as he'd indicated; strong enough to endure the suffering and allow him the space to sort his emotions without my cloud of perfume distorting his rationality so he'd keep from getting caught or arrested.

Yup. Let's not go there anymore! My mind is shutting off, dammit!

Once I turned into the driveway of the cabin hidden in the Tennessee Smoky Mountains, I turned off my phone, content to be simple Kinsley if only for a borrowed moment.

1 | ♀ - Target Acquired

I SPENT THE NEXT five days with my phone turned off, blissfully unaware. The guys were probably irritated, but, hey, I didn't really belong to anyone, now did I? If I wanted to be an individual female without having to answer to anyone once again, that was my damn prerogative.

If my parents were told about Klive's Ferrari in our driveway, they hadn't said anything. I think they were afraid I'd go rebellious teenager on them if they did. Pretty sure they knew, though, since they'd both watch me with that speculative concern before side-eying each other in that silent couple's speak thing. I pretended not to notice and read books on the balcony surrounded by tall, thick evergreens while listening to the birds native to this scenery. A couple times I joined my parents on hikes through the mountainous terrain. We drove into the scenic town to eat. Daddy introduced me to the friends they'd made, but when they offered me to come with them for drinks, I bowed out.

"I'm on a break from booze since I serve it every other day," I'd joked. Their friends understood and offered something about touring an abandoned town with a cool cemetery. In one ear out the other. I couldn't concentrate even on the fiction between my fingers when I was alone again. Sometimes, I found myself flipping the book and resting the open pages face-down on my lap before gazing into the woods.

"Bigfoot could come barreling through and you'd just stare him down," Daddy said five nights in. "He'd probably tuck tail and haul his hairy butt back into the pines."

I snorted. "Do I look mean?"

What little smile he had faded. "You look lost. Frustrated. Like when I gave you the Rubik's cube." We snickered at his smart-ass humor.

"I miss you."

"I'm right here," he said, but he knew what I meant. We had the same silent speaking ability he and Mom did, with different dialect.

"Just stay here. For a little while," I told him.

He nodded and shifted a camp chair beside mine. His feet propped on the wooden railing in front of us, crossed at the ankles like mine. We sat in the silent solitude of nature through the sunset until the stars salted the sky. Mars shined bright. Daddy quizzed me on constellations, taught me some I couldn't see from our Florida home that were visible here.

"Did Gramma and Grandpa come to visit?"

"Yeah. They were sad to have missed you."

"Your twang comes out when you're back here," I observed, loved.

"Can't take the country outta the boy, Kins. Mom and Dad mentioned the idea of Claire and me maybe moving here to help in their old age."

I gasped and tucked my feet back to the decking as I sat forward, hands gripping the camp chair. "Have you been thinking about this for a while?"

He nodded once. "I thought your mom would turn me down flat, but when I brought it up to her, she pointed out that you're grown now."

I arched an eyebrow, disbelieving my ears. "What about her friends? Social gatherings? Tea parties? Political events? Do you really think she'd just up and leave all that behind?"

"She loves those things but doesn't want to be stuck in Florida caring for her own mother in the years to come. If she helps care for mine instead, she's absolved."

"Meh." I tilted my head but nodded with a cringe. "Mom's mother is kind of a bitch." I threw my hand when his brows raised. "You said it, I'm grown now."

Daddy chuckled. "Lord love her, she sure is, and I'd love to see Claire live without trying to please her. Your mother has spent the last twenty-five years walking a tight rope to be what *her* mother wants over who she really is. My parents loved her when I brought her home and they still do. I'd love to see her relaxed."

The view of my mother shifted under a new scope. Twenty-five years? I wanted to ask what he meant and the correlation between my birth and Mom living to please grandmother. Yeah. Grandmother. Not gram. Not granny. Not grandma or gramma. She hated those. Grandmother. To be rebellious, I'd always called her Grandmama with an accent like Klive's to play with her decorum.

I sighed. "Guess life can't stay the same forever. I don't know why it seemed nothing would change."

"Because your mother and I built a stable, predictable life around you."

"Cliché, in other words? Boring? Borderline worshipful."

Dad didn't even laugh like I'd thought he would. My heart clenched at the way *he* now stared into the dark trees. "Yes. Kinsley, when you worship humanity, you'll always end up with a broken heart."

"Whoa! Daddy! What is this?"

His eyes held a sheen of unshed tears when he looked at me. "What happened with Jase?" he asked.

I faltered for words, then managed, "We got into a bad fight. We're taking a time-out as friends for a bit. Are you trying to change the subject? If something is bothering you, I'd rather you talk to me about it. You're always there for me, let me be here for you, too, Daddy."

"I laid something on your bed. When you turn-in, take a break from fiction to read real life."

"You know I hate the news."

"Believe me, so do I, but part of 'adulting' is knowing the world around you and the people in it to make the best decisions and alignments for your life." His camp chair scooted along the planks as he stood. Daddy kissed my hair and left me alone. I craned my head when the sliding door closed. Through the floor-to-ceiling glass, my mother's hand rested on her chest, an anxious expression following my father's ascent up the cabin stairs to the second floor. She chewed her lip. Did my mother do those events and social parties to somehow appear like a better mother to *her* mother? She looked worried I'd be upset. I pushed my chair across the planks of the deck, too, and slid the glass door open.

"I love you, Mom. *You.* Not your social constructs or affiliations. You. Whatever you decide, I'll support you." I kissed her cheek and said, "Dad assigned me homework."

"I know." She clutched her robe at her chest still, eyes nervous and troubled. "I love you, too, Kinsley. Whatever *you* decide, I'll support you, too." My brow dipped in confusion. She swallowed and turned the lights out before trotting upstairs. Rather than going to bed, I walked into the downstairs bedroom I slept in. Where I'd expected a newspaper, a stapled packet laid on my pillow. I lifted the papers and went back into the cozy kitchen. I set the packet on the little round table, flipped the light on over the sink and made myself a pot of coffee.

What real life story would my father want me to know about to the point of printing out at what I guessed was the public library? The Wi-Fi and cell signals here were non-existent, part of the allure, but that made me uneasy about what I was about to read. I settled at the table with a hot mug between my fingers and read the cover page, recognizing a well-known newspaper from Tampa. The mug met my lips while my fingers flipped to the next page. Coffee clogged my windpipe as I read the headline. I jerked back from spilling on myself and beat my chest. Best the mug stay on the table. Both hands lifted the article.

FINALLY A QUEEN FOR KING?
PHILANTHROPIST BACHELOR CHASES TRACK STAR

Abstinent pair finds love inside the walls they've built around themselves, entrapping each other for cozy forays about town, igniting speculation with their hot run-ins. Coincidence? I safely dismissed the first reports of Klive King and Kinsley Hayes in the same places as happenstance, but with the advent of cameras in hands everywhere, so are the eyes who know what they see and snap confirmation of rumors and gossip as fact.

Philanthropist? Abstinent? Hot run-ins? Ugh. A silent whistle whipped between my puckered lips as my eyes darted upstairs to see if Daddy secretly watched my shock and awe. No wonder my father was pissed! This immediately implied we were sleeping together!

Kinsley Hayes, better known as Micro Machine on the University track team, has an unbeatable record, but has slowed her pace for Klive King's pursuit, all too glad to lose time on the track since he's captured her fancy. Will she leave the sport paying her scholarship before the final season is over?

"I know she got into that fight, and I think it was over him. She got hurt and has to recover, but how long does she need? It's been weeks. Where is she and what is the school paying for?" one student said when asked to comment. "I have to pay

for my classes. My loans are huge and it's hard not to resent her not even going to practice."

"Oh, hell no!" I almost shouted, fury flavoring my lips. Did no one convey to the writer that I wasn't *allowed* to practice or run after my fight? WTF?! You'd think my punishment would've been nice and juicy for this article. This came off like I neglected my track career and took my scholarship for granted. Everything opposite of who I was!

Though I contemplated tossing this garbage into the can fit for this bull, I forced myself to keep reading for my father's sake.

A nice overview on Klive King followed for anyone unfamiliar with *Bachelor of the Year* winner three years running.

"Wow," I whispered. No wonder people watched us! Here I was so worried about Nightshade, I'd never known anything beyond that world concerning Klive. He was into charity, helping the community, known to donate his money generously, spend spare time making visits to the children's ward at the hospital and give supplies to the Children's Cancer Center's art program, even participate when available.

My tongue traced the inside of my cheek. Klive looked amazing on the back of a horse playing Polo at the annual charity tournament. In another photo, he was pictured talking with two balding children at the Cancer Center from his knees in front of them, holding their hand while they smiled brightly at him. Klive hosted one of the largest charity events that helped fund the rebuilding of half the houses in our area hit by the last devastating hurricane. There was even the sexiest picture of Klive at a home site helping with the physical rebuilding! Another of him smiling with the family whose house he had been working on.

Whiplash! As if I wasn't already attracted enough! How did he reconcile his bad life with these good deeds? Was this all an elaborate cover he'd created for himself to keep those around him fooled while he walked in darkness? I forced myself to focus back on the article.

Architectural Engineer and Real Estate Attorney, Klive developed a reputation as a stellar negotiator for the East Coast chapter of an international architectural and development firm. He'd broken several records for his local office before earning the privilege of representing the entire eastern region of the United States. Dual citizenship enabled him to assist the company in the United Kingdom as well.

Klive's best advice for tricks of the trade: "Listen to the client. Respect their wishes. Entertain *their* vision first, then intertwine your plans to marry both concepts. Happy clients bring further business and refer others."

I played my finger on the lower corner of the page, preparing to turn to the next, intimidated by Klive's normal life before realizing I'd partially gotten the lawyer part correct. Though I'd imagined him being a cut-throat defense attorney for that vibe he gives, Klive did have a very normal side! One to be proud of! The writer seemed almost biased in painting Klive's positive coverage versus my defamatory irresponsibility.

My head shook as I thought of what Jase and Rustin had told me about Klive. They'd subtracted a substantial amount from their report. No wonder Klive was so frustrated with me sometimes! Then again, I wouldn't have feared this man at all. Now, I saw what others were enamored with or why people looked at Klive with reverent respect. He wasn't only famous for dropping bodies. How did he manage to juggle the huge tasks of this very professional career with Nightshade's underworld at once? How had he made any time in his busy schedule to get to know me? Flirt and follow me?

This must've been what my mother was referring to when we'd had girl talk on the beach. No wonder she was annoyed with my ignorance. What could I say? I never read the papers or local news except to look at the glamorous pictures of the charity ball hosted in Miami every year. Mom used to study them for pageant dress and hair ideas, then my proms, and now we kept up annually out of habit to gawk at local and national celebrities and their attire. Had Klive ever gone to those if he was so charitable? Was he important enough to merit an invitation?

I turned the page to read of how Klive had managed to stay unattached, despite his evident desirability. His love life was rumored to be nonexistent until sightings of the elusive bachelor with me. I was again described as popular and controversial for the scandal of my recent fight with Sheriff's daughter, Angela Ansley.

The author went into my track career, referenced past articles written on my career as well as podcasts and newspaper interviews I'd given. Those also came with a hint of speculation like the writer knew of my non-disclosure agreement with the university where I agreed to stop kissing my fingertip and pointing to God in the sky to appease the atheists on campus who brought friction against me for subjecting them to my prayers before I took to the blocks on the track. Had one of them broken their NDA rules by talking to this writer? Wow, Klive was really slumming with me, I guess. My knee bounced like crazy, lip chewed under my teeth.

The story shifted toward my GPA, charitable works through church events, school rallies and fundraisers, my professional goals to counsel diabetic children. Each of these attributes came with an accompanying photo concluding with the one of me smiling with my track team, medals around my neck, grin at Julie. How nice. Klive had like three paragraphs of awesome while I had one dedicated to obligatory redemption. Could I sue for defamation?

Next page:
Klive's and Kinsley's Hottest Exchanges
Together or coincidence?

Klive King (34) and Kinsley Hayes (24) appear in stage performance at Renaissance Festival (Photo 1)

Kinsley receives three-dozen roses from secret admirer on Valentine's Day. Klive made purchase from floral shop two blocks from his firm that morning. (Photo 2)

Kinsley seen wearing Klive's hat while sharing a drink (Photo 3)

Pair have brunch in Clearwater Beach before leaving on Klive's motorcycle (Photo 4, 5)

Pair canoodling at private party where they purportedly spent the night together (Photo 6)

Pair have drinks with Kinsley's track team (Photo 7)

Pair eat brunch at hotel after spending night in St. Augustine (Photo 8)

Skating couple's skate at local rink (Photo 9)

Share kiss (Photo 10)

Reservations for dinner and dancing at exclusive rooftop bar (Photo 11)

Kinsley driving Klive's Ferrari during shopping spree with Klive's credit card (Photo 12, 13)

Klive and Kinsley kissing at bar (Photo 14)

I rubbed my forehead and looked at the photo collage on the next page. The prominent picture, photo number one, was a large close-up of that *Gone With the Wind* moment onstage at the ren faire. Klive had me pulled tightly against him. He looked down at me while I smiled up at him. Amazing how I appeared more happy than afraid or shocked since that's what I was.

The surrounding photos depicted the previous captions well enough, but some had chills breaking over my skin. Photos four through eight matched photos the police had pulled from the phone found at Sara Scott's murder scene. Klive and me were pictured at the surfboard table together at the beach bar, coffee cups in both our hands while we grinned at each other. Klive on his blue Ducati while I had just climbed on behind him and snuggled as close as possible. The two of us at Delia's party on her balcony. Klive's nose to my throat as my head had fallen back. We'd thought we were alone. No photos were allowed. Someone had broken the rules to capture our scandal and knew about us staying in the room together ... *how?*

I shuddered and skimmed the photo of me wearing Klive's fedora while he held my hand over his glass at the bar. That picture rested beside the one of us toasting my team with shot glasses at the bar in St. Augustine before we'd bailed on my friends to run together from two thugs chasing us. There was no photo of us at the St. George Inn, but someone knew we'd spent part of the night together there *and* that we'd done so before leaving in the middle of the night and heading to the hotel in Tampa where we'd had brunch the next morning. *Again, how?* Who knew, but we sat at a table across from each other. Klive played on his phone appearing to ignore me while I'd stared pissed off at him denying us in public. Klive had told me in that moment that people were watching and scrutinizing our every move. Did he somehow know we were being photographed? Stalked? Hunted?

For the second time, I wished I weren't away from Klive. I wanted to be as close to him as possible to protect myself from whoever was doing this.

I strode to my bedroom and powered on my phone for the first time in days. As I walked back to the kitchen, I thumbed Rustin's number, but cursed when I got the *emergency calls only* notification. I huffed and sat in the chair when I really needed to do the opposite and run my ass off to dispel nervous tension. This felt like an emergency. Someone was following us and either the police leaked evidence, or the original photographer had connections to Inferno. If Rustin didn't have answers, he could certainly track the leak at the station. My palms slapped my forehead before pulling down my face. Duh! The video of my traffic stop leaked through the station like a burst pipe. Did Angela or her father also leak these as a passive threat?

Focus!

I had to read this to see what my father saw so I didn't add any worries to his plate with what *I* saw in this article.

If I weren't nauseous, I'd love these photos. The normal female without a care apart from relationships needed to see that side, too, to defend myself when I faced my father with my own point of view of the evidence he'd thrown on my bed.

I smiled at the photo of Klive and me dancing at the rooftop bar. He was so dapper in his pin-striped shirt. My finger pressed to his lips, his eyes full of adoration, a pretty smile on my face as I looked up at him like no one else existed. Who the hell had snapped that? Staff? A super chill skittered down my spine, causing me to sit straight up. *Henley! He'd been in the restaurant! He'd warned me about Klive!*

My eyes closed as cold fear chased away the warmth of the coffee. Yes, I wanted Klive *now*! If I asked him about this, would we be on the same wavelength concerning his former Nightshade secret weapon?

Oh, Klive .... The photo of us at the skating rink was sweet. We held hands while looking at each other during the couple's skate. Hearts dotted the floor and our clothing. A photo of me in Mr. Miller's Color Theory class smelling the huge lavender rose bouquet added the same sort of sweetness, like the purple on the flowers matched the purple hearts at the rink.

Just as fast, the pendulum swung. I cringed at the picture of us kissing at the end of the Renaissance Festival. That one was a tad inappropriate to be in a regular feature. Out of context, we confirmed rich chemistry with our lip lock, closed eyes, peek at our tongues brushing during an angle change.

Welp, that one was probably what put tears in my father's eyes. Er ... never mind. The Ferrari. I stood outside the car in my little bikini, ready to close the door. Well, hell, that was a risqué picture! Had I known I was being stalked by paparazzi, I may have kept the shorts and tank. Another showed me all done up in my British T-shirt dress, sans bra, getting into the Ferrari with shopping bags. How they had managed to keep Jase out of the picture, I wasn't sure, but seeing the direction this article had taken to make me appear Klive's young piece of ass using him as a sugar daddy, I was glad. The last photo showed us at the bar that night, me holding the back of Klive's head for a kiss while his hand skimmed my bottom in my short dress.

My cheeks puffed before I released a heavy sigh. Yeah, Daddy had a right to be pissed and disappointed. I turned the page, afraid to keep going.

Are they or aren't they? Locals weigh in:

"She never dates. He never dates. What if they've been together for years and now they're letting the rest of us in on their secret? Sounds crazy but makes sense." - Tyra Lindley

Wow, never thought of us appearing that way. Interesting.

"It's been my recent experience that Miss Hayes drives a hard bargain. (From) what I know of Klive, he doesn't back away from a challenge. Let's hope he comes out winning. Though I'm sure there are many gentlemen who hope he loses so they may swipe the pretty peacock for themselves." - Mayor David White

Whoa! The mayor! My eyes scanned upstairs again for any signs of my parents spying on me. What a disconcerting comment. The mayor was a good-looking guy and quite the social media whore, but something about him had always made me ... uncomfortable.

Maybe because my classmates loved to vote for him because of his photo without knowing anything of his platform. He pandered to popular ideas but didn't seem to get much done. The idea of him trying to swipe me from Klive I found bizarre; as bizarre as him hitting on me at the Renaissance party.

Join the conversation. Cast your vote and share your supporting photos online.*

Shit! This writer was *encouraging* photos of us! Ugh! I rubbed my temples and prayed about this addition to the stalkers I already felt every day.

I sighed heavily and flipped back through the pages to find the author's name. My heart came to a stuttering halt.

Chad Patel!

Sonuvabitch! He was so lucky I hadn't gotten this paper before I'd left, or else I'd have driven right to his place and told him off so publicly that the newspaper would have to report on the altercation the next week!

He must've been up all night to get some of that shit in on time to have published the next day! I felt so betrayed and disgusted, not to mention suspicious about where Chad stood in the grand scheme if he had access to those photos! Had he taken some of those? Who was his source? Henley? Angela? Inferno? All the above?

Had Klive read this? Did Chad write this article with a positive view on Klive to keep Klive's scary side off his ass?

I chuffed to myself. Good luck. Chad was in danger.

According to Klive he was the head, but *I* was his neck and right now I was trained on a good friend turned enemy.

Acknowledgments

As always, this book wouldn't be as polished or as true to character without my second set of editing eyes, Dr. TK Cassidy, and technical advisor, LCDR AJ Alford. Thank you both for your hard work and dedication to helping my dream paint these pages.

To my readers who have (im)patiently waited for this installment of the series. Thank you for your emails and messages of encouragement and continuous query as to when this volume would be ready.

I broke my wrist and halted the original release date as well as all progress with my inability to write at even half my normal pace. Your words kept my spirits up through that unexpected set-back.

About Lynessa Layne

Lynessa Layne is a native Texan from the small town of Plantersville. She's a fan of exploration, history, the beach (though she's photosensitive), Jesus, and America too (RIP Tom). Besides being an avid reader, she's obsessed with music of all types (hence her reference to Tom Petty). As a child, she created music videos in her mind and played Barbies perhaps a little longer than most with her little sister, not yet realizing she was writing and enacting stories all along.

Though she's put away the dolls, she now uses her novels as an updated, grown-up version of the same play.

Lynessa is also a certified copy editor and a member of Mystery Writers of America, with work featured by Writer's Digest and Mystery and Suspense Magazine. She has also graced the cover of GEMS (Godly Entrepreneurs & Marketers) Magazine and was a finalist for Killer Nashville's 2022 Silver Falchion Awards for Best Suspense and Reader's Choice.

For more visit lynessalayne.com and sign up for her newsletter, Lit with Lynnie and follow on social media:

https://www.facebook.com/authorlynessalayne

https://www.instagram.com/lynessalayne/

https://twitter.com/LynessaLayne

> Writers like me depend on readers like you.
> Please leave a positive review.
> Thanks
> ♡ - *Lynessa*

Made in the USA
Middletown, DE
27 July 2024

57908637R00260